CHEAT THE HANGMAN

So Eileen:
Hope you
enjoy this tale!
Gloria

GLORIA FERRIS

CHEAT THE HANGMAN

http://www.gloriaferrismysteries.blogspot.com

FIRST EDITION

Imajin Books

October 2011

ISBN: 978-1-926997-23-0

Cover designed by Sapphire Designs: http://www.designs.sapphiredreams.org

Praise for Gloria Ferris

"Gloria Ferris is a storyteller of the highest caliber. Sometimes witty, sometimes dark, Ferris hits all the right buttons in *Cheat the Hangman*, a refreshing and chilling paranormal mystery you won't want to miss. Ten out of ten!" —Jeff Bennington, author of *Reunion*

"Some families really do have skeletons in the closet. In *Cheat the Hangman*, Gloria Ferris offers Southern Ontario Gothic at its spine-chilling, provocative, hilarious best...In a dazzling blend of the bizarre and the domestic, horror and humour, nostalgia and intrigue, Ferris enthralls her readers in the most frightening and delightful ways." — John Moss, author of *Reluctant Dead*

"Lyris Pembrooke has an ironic, hilarious way of looking at life, even in the direst circumstances. Her witty personality instantly captivates and endears the reader... satisfying and romantic. Cheat the Hangman is an excellent, enjoyable read!" —Catherine Astolfo, author of the *Emily Taylor Mysteries*

"Ferris weaves an exciting story demonstrating her work is worth keeping an eye on. *Cheat the Hangman* is a non-stop guessing game...An intriguing and immensely entertaining read that blends paranormal with mystery and a touch of romance." —*Midwest Book Review*

"Sometimes you just want to sink into a really good mystery. Ferris has managed to blend the past with the present in this Ontario-grown who-dun-it, heading her cast of characters with heroine Lyris Pembrooke, amateur sleuth, armed with latent psychic abilities and a twisted sense of humour. Entertaining and well written, *Cheat the Hangman*, is a great first book. No wonder it was shortlisted for Canada's Unhanged Arthur Ellis Award." —N.A.T. Grant, author of *Race Without Rules*

"Women's intuition, spirit guides, our ancestors crying out to us—call it what you will, *Cheat The Hangman* says so much about both what we owe our ancestors and the burdens they pass down to us. A mysterious family death long ago sends Lyris on a search for the truth about those who came before her. A powerful, layered story told with clarity, pizzazz, and humour." —Eileen Schuh, author of *Schrödinger's Cat*

For my special loves: Olyvia, Talia, Dante, Aimee, and Rowyn.
You have enriched my life beyond measure.

Acknowledgements

Thank you to my sister/editor, Donna Warner, who not only read and edited this manuscript a dozen times, but encouraged me (sometimes quite loudly) when I faltered. She also came up with the perfect title for the book over a couple of coolers at the cottage.

Thanks also to my first readers: Lara, Alyssa, Pam, Desneiges, Frances, Cheryl, Vicki, Barb, Marlene, John, and Marilyn. Their suggestions and comments were constructive and thoughtful, and many were incorporated into Cheat the Hangman.

Special thanks to Cheryl Tardif of Imajin Books for making my dream a reality and for good-naturedly steering me through the unfamiliar waters leading to publication.

I must also express my appreciation to the judges of the 2009 Crime Writers of Canada Unhanged Arthur Award contest. It was truly an honour for Cheat the Hangman to be short-listed and I thank you all.

PROLOGUE

Hammersleigh House, Blackshore, Ontario
Saturday, July 24, 1943

A faint glow from campfires dotting the field beyond the house barely penetrated the windows of the tower room, but it was more than enough light for the task at hand—one that would condemn a soul to dwell in eternal fire.

With laboured breathing, the thin figure hurried across the floor, the wrapped bundle almost slipping through fingers numb with shock. A storage door set low in the wall opened to expose three wooden boxes. The figure selected the sturdiest one and the jumble of mouldy books inside was upended onto a nearby demilune table.

There is room now.

A voice outside the windows generated a cry of alarm from the figure.

They are already searching.

No, it was just a reveller's radio—Vera Lynn was singing about nightingales.

Despair welled up, overcoming the fear of discovery. For a moment, a low keening sound echoed through the room. With hasty care, the figure set the bundle in the bottom of the box. A soft object was tucked inside and newspapers were placed on top. The box was returned to the darkest recess behind the door. The other two boxes followed.

Sobbing, the figure pulled a hammer and nails from a pocket and drove four long nails into the casing, one at each corner of the door. Table legs scraped along the wood planks until the half-moon-shaped table came to rest against the closet door. Several books fell to the floor and were kicked aside.

May God forgive me.

The tower room door closed with a soft click. Music drifted up through the windows, the notes filling the dark spaces in the tower room.

Then silence returned. The nightingales no longer sang in Berkeley Square.

CHAPTER 1

Hammersleigh House, Blackshore, Ontario
Saturday, July 9, 2011

The tower room was a sauna and even my toenails were sweating. I knew my hair had kinked into a tangle of witch locks as moisture poured from my hairline and dripped off my earlobes. The rest of me was just as sweat logged, but with Conklin due back any minute, I had no time to take a break in a cooler part of the house. I drank warm water from a plastic bottle and heaved on the window frame to open it.

Not happening. The wood had swelled in the heat and wouldn't budge.

In the distance, I spotted a series of silver flashes that pierced the stand of pine trees lining the property. Squinting, I identified the flashes as the noon sun flaring off something metallic creeping down County Road 12 toward Hammersleigh House.

"Crap."

Uncle Patrick's classic Lincoln Town Car. Even driving his usual ten kilometres per hour under the speed limit, it would take Conklin just a few minutes to turn in at the iron gates and inch his way up the bricked drive to the parking area around back. After finding the perfect shady tree to park under and removing his shopping bags from the trunk, he would enter through the kitchen door and wonder what Madam was doing.

Regrettably, I was Madam.

Turning from the window, I picked up the smelly, one-eyed moose from the floor, planning to shift it to a nearby rattan settee. The moose head was heavy and the fur greasy with age. The single, glassy brown eye stared at me as the head slipped from my grasp and crashed to the floor.

"Goddammit it all to hell."

One of the antler tips stabbed my left foot. Blood spurted from my big toe.

I hopped around the tower room, trying not to trip over glass cases full of long-dead butterflies and tiny stuffed songbirds. Out of breath, I collapsed next to a spotted leopard, grabbed my foot with both hands and looked around for something to staunch the bleeding. The only thing within reach was a roll of toilet paper I was using to clean the cloying dust off my fingers. Like grimy snowflakes, wads of tissue dotted the bodies of the hapless creatures surrounding me. Some of the animals were now extinct, all because a gang of Victorian aristocrats thought it was great fun to sit on an African plain and bag trophies to adorn their walls back home.

Way to go, boys.

While Conklin was out paying bills, shopping and visiting his sister, I had spent the morning collecting mounted beasts and songbirds entombed in glass from every room in the house. I'd brought them to the tower room until I could find a permanent resting place where I would never have to look at them again. The antelope waiting downstairs was the last of the herd, but there was no time to fetch it now.

I could have asked Conklin where the attic was, except he'd have wanted to know why, tsk-tsked at my reason and called me "Madam" again. The way I saw it, he could disapprove all he wanted after the fact, but it would be a done deal. Some wise person—I forget who—once said that it was easier to beg forgiveness than to ask permission. Worked for me.

I wrapped a strand of toilet paper around my toe and watched the thin tissue turn crimson. No time to wallow in self-pity. Conklin would be entering the house any second and I didn't want him finding me in the blood-spattered tower room.

I was about to stand when I saw something under the table in front of me. I almost missed it. The demilune table was set against what looked like a solid wall while I was on my feet. Now, sitting on the floor, I was looking at a hobbit-sized door.

"What do we have here?"

I felt a strange tingle between my shoulder blades and shrugged it off. I leaned closer to the underside of the table.

Painted white like the rest of the room, the door was about three feet high. I couldn't see a knob or handle and even the hinges were painted over, but bits of paint had flaked off to reveal the tarnished brass underneath. A nail had been hammered at an angle into each corner to keep the door from swinging open, but they had popped out an enticing quarter inch.

I forgot about my wounded foot and even about Conklin, who would be wondering why the antelope head was on the hall floor by the staircase and why the rest of the mounted heads and glass cases were missing. I forgot about everything except the anticipation of opening that mysterious door.

Over the years, I have been accused of having a short attention span, being too curious, having an overactive imagination and acting with disregard for the sensibilities of others. This last comment was the opinion of several of my older relatives, who in my view greatly exaggerated. I, Lyris Pembrooke, age thirty-eight and holding up well, was a well-balanced woman, with the standard mix of flaws and virtues.

Whichever characteristic was dominant that day, it was not within my power to walk away and mind my own business. I mean, think of it. A hidden door, nailed shut, set into the wall of a tower room in a century-old house. Who could resist the temptation to pry it open?

There could be ancient family papers or diaries behind that door. Maybe illicit love letters written by a frustrated Victorian nanny to the master of the house. Perhaps there were blueprints that pointed the way to a long-forgotten room and a treasure cache.

Shoving Bullwinkle aside and crawling over the leopard, I stood up. The blood had stopped pumping and if my gore-wrapped toe still gave me pain, I didn't feel it.

The first thing I did was pull the table away from the door. The top was covered with a half-bald squirrel posed on a branch and some other creature, maybe a mink or a weasel. The table legs screeched as I dragged it away from the wall. A couple of new scratch marks appeared on the wooden floor. I had no chance in hell Conklin would miss those on his next scheduled tour of the house.

I reached for my hammer. Using the claw end, I pried out the nails holding the little door closed, breaking three fingernails and making a few dents in the wooden wall. When I was finished, bloody handprints stencilled the white paint around the door.

I moderated my excitement. The frugal Victorian builder had likely utilized the space where the tower room wall joined the main house by constructing a simple storage closet. I was convinced of this as the door creaked open on stiff hinges, revealing my treasure.

A trio of wooden boxes.

The space behind the door was not deep, maybe two and a half feet, and no rat or other live creature pounced at me. No mouse poop and just a few cobwebs, although clouds of dry, musty air hit me in the face, tickling my nose and making my eyes water.

I reached for the nearest box and uncovered a jumble of mismatched cups, plates and other tableware items. These were utilitarian pieces for everyday use, nothing to pique my interest. The second box contained several pre-industrial age flat irons and a sinister instrument that might have been used to torture a woman's hair into ringlets.

The third box, pushed to the back of the closet, looked more promising. It was larger than the others were and so blackened with age I couldn't make out the lettering on the sides. It could have stored nails or other hardware in the pre-war years—one of the "Big Ones," like World War II or even World War I.

I pulled it into the light.

Several layers of newspaper, yellowed and disintegrating, covered the top. A local paper—the *Blackshore Oracle*. I was disappointed to note the date was July 21, 1943, only sixty-eight years ago. I had hoped for something earlier than that.

I set the newspaper aside for later. I was curious to see if any family members were mentioned. Many Pembrookes of that generation, both men and women, served in the military during World War II.

There was a piece of thick fabric under the newspaper.

A box of clothes?

If this was junk, it should be thrown out. The closet space could be used for some of the more hideous stuffed animals, like the elephant foot umbrella stand that had stood in the great hall for the best part of a hundred years—until about an hour ago when I carried it up here.

I opened the cloth. At first, I felt no alarm, merely a mild curiosity. I didn't have the slightest idea what I was seeing. Then, like a lightening bolt, understanding registered.

"No, no..."

I dropped the cloth and scrambled away.

Wave after wave of primal fear crashed over me, chilling my body, numbing my hands and feet and draining the blood from my brain.

Great-Aunt Clem always claimed I'd inherited her psychic abilities. I wish that talent had kicked in earlier, because if I had felt psychic that day, I would have shoved the age-blackened box back into the closet and walked—no, *ran*—away. Even a modest flair for precognition might have stopped me from pushing aside the crumbling cloth. But nothing had stopped me. As a result, I let loose a string of events that shaped my future and almost changed the past.

Alone in the tower room, and for the first time in my life, I fainted. Just before the darkness overwhelmed me, a long forgotten childhood memory stirred.

I knew what was in the box.

CHAPTER 2

When I opened my eyes, my head was in the hall and my feet were in the tower room, pressed against the box. I clawed at the carpet and managed to pull my legs out of the room. After several attempts, I got to my feet. It was like one of those nightmares where you are being chased by some ghastly thing, but every step takes forever.

With icy worms of dread crawling through my blood, I exerted great effort and was able to reach out and pull the door closed. I had to pry my stiff fingers from the crystal doorknob with my other hand.

With the door shut on the box, adrenaline at last flooded my bloodstream. I sped down the hallway, making no sound on the thick carpet runner and hearing the pulse beats that filled my head.

The trouble with adrenaline is you can't turn it off with a switch. In my haste to get to the telephone, I reached the stairs, but couldn't control my speed. I gained momentum on the way down. By the time I realized I was in trouble, it was too late. My feet missed a step near the bottom and I sailed into space.

And dropped like a stone to the marble floor of the great hall.

I stared up at the high ceiling of the great hall, afraid to move.

After a minute or two, I took stock. My arms and legs seemed okay. My ribs didn't hurt. I slowed my breathing and concluded that the only pain was coming from my toe. Since I was conscious, I probably didn't have a concussion.

Something smelled. I turned my head and flinched. I was nose to lips with the antelope—and it had really bad breath. I inched away.

The good news was the fall had snapped me out of shock. As a matter of fact, I was so clear-minded that everything seemed more real than usual. I decided to stay where I was until help arrived, even if it was Conklin.

Overhead, the Waterford chandelier sparked white beams of light and seemed to sway. That was odd. I saw the individual crystal drops, thousands of them.

"Boy, am I ever glad I don't have to clean that." My voice rang in my ears.

The jewel tones of the stained glass fanlight over the oak entrance doors reflected on the walls and ceiling, and mingled with the white lights of the chandelier. The colours were so bright, my eyes watered. Ruby, amethyst, jade, sapphire, amber. It was like looking through a kaleidoscope.

My stomach burbled and I had to keep swallowing saliva.

"Damn. I don't feel so well."

That's all I needed. Conklin would be displeased if I upchucked in the great hall.

Hoping my stomach would settle, I closed my eyes and sought to think of something, anything other than my discovery upstairs. The ticking of the grandfather clock a few yards away resonated in my head. I switched to yoga breathing and focused my mind.

I had moved into Hammersleigh House three days before. Great-uncle Patrick had died of heart failure a few months ago at the age of ninety-two and it was a surprise to the whole Pembrooke family when we found out he had left Hammersleigh House to me. Since the Pembrooke family numbers in the hundreds in the town of Blackshore alone, there was a lot of surprise to go around.

Uncle Patrick's wife died early in their marriage without giving him an heir and he never married again, so we all thought he would leave his entire estate to the eldest male relative. That was my father, Kevin Pembrooke, until his death in a hunting accident seven years ago. We assumed Cousin Nathan would be next in line for the inheritance. After all, Nathan was a successful financial consultant in Toronto, very much the corporate type.

We were partly right. When the will was read, Nathan walked away with Uncle Patrick's business concerns and investments.

"Hammersleigh House," the lawyer stated, "is bequeathed to Lyris Pembrooke."

Me.

In his will, Uncle Patrick stated that he knew I would cherish and protect Hammersleigh House and all it contained. I promised to do my best, although I knew nothing about caring for such a valuable estate. I loved antique houses and furnishings, though, and I had to believe my uncle knew what he was doing.

There was still a lot of rumbling from the family about my inheritance.

"Lyris, the will is valid and binding and there are no grounds to challenge it," the lawyer, John Brixton, informed me. "So move in and enjoy Hammersleigh. It's yours."

Easy for him to say. He didn't have to face the black looks and pursed lips I encountered every day on the streets, in church or at my job at the Blackshore Power Commission. I mean it, the Pembrookes were everywhere. At least my mother and brother, David, were happy for me.

However, Uncle Patrick's will was not without a string of clauses. Some good, some not so much. For instance, one clause prevented me from selling Hammersleigh House or any of its contents for twenty-five years, so it was a good thing I loved the house, because I was stuck with it. The will also established a trust that paid the maintenance and repair costs for Hammersleigh. This included the wages of casual help to keep the grounds and gardens in pristine order and the cost of the cleaning team that came in weekly. The trust also paid for a housekeeper and Conklin.

I guess this Trust business made me more of a caretaker than an owner, but on the upside, I didn't have to worry about saving for a new roof or electrical upgrades. Best of all, I didn't have to clean the place.

Conklin and I were the sole occupants of Hammersleigh House, unless you counted Jacqueline, the hell-poodle, which I didn't. And if my first two nights in residence were filled with dark silences, well, I would get used to it.

I continued the yoga stress-relieving breathing. Four breaths in, hold for four, four breaths out, hold for four, then repeat. The ticking of the clock was soft, soothing now, and too quiet to mask the sound of footsteps that came to rest beside me. Rescue was at hand.

I looked up. "Hi, Conklin."

Conklin wore his off-duty apparel, consisting of a pair of faded brown corduroys and a weathered beige jacket over a snow-white polo sweater, which exactly matched his thick shock of hair.

We were in the middle of a July heat wave—outside, it was at least thirty-five degrees Celsius. I was wearing shorts and the briefest tank top I owned, and until I'd discovered the box, I had been sweating buckets in the tower room. Now I was shivering.

I guess I should explain Conklin since he played such a central role in my new life at Hammersleigh House, kind of like an unwelcome conscience I might ignore at times, but couldn't shake loose.

Strange as it may seem in this day and age, Conklin was my butler. First, he was Uncle Patrick's butler. Then Uncle Patrick left him to me in his will. Or, to be precise, Conklin was given the option of staying on at Hammersleigh or retiring. He decided I couldn't possibly get along without him.

Unfortunately, he was right.

Conklin had served Uncle Patrick for more than fifty years and knew Hammersleigh's every whim and whimsy. He knew who to call when a section of stone lintel developed a miniscule crack. He knew what to do when one of the ancient plants in the rose garden contracted black spot. He knew where to get the special beeswax polish that was used on Hammersleigh's woodwork. He knew the name of the contractor who annually checked the stone gargoyles on each corner of the house to ensure they didn't fall off.

In short, Conklin knew everything and I needed him. Technically, he worked for me, but since I didn't pay him, he was pretty much a free agent. I think he disapproved of me and my inheritance.

There he stood with Jacqueline at his side.

"Madam?"

I had a lot of explaining to do. I searched for the words to tell him about the box upstairs.

"Madam, are you hurt?" He bent down and tugged on my arm.

I sighed. I weighed only a hundred and twenty-two pounds, but that's still beyond the capacity of one senior citizen to handle. I yanked my arm away.

He captured it again. "What happened, Madam? Please, speak to me." He made comforting noises to reassure me. He glanced from my face to the antelope's and back again.

Jacqueline planted her body within inches of my ear and barked.

"Shut up."

Since "shut up" and "get off the furniture" were the only two phrases I ever directed at her, she couldn't pretend not to understand. The racket subsided, but she sat down close to my face. I kept one eye on her, since she had a fondness for biting.

Conklin looked at my injured toe. The ream of scarlet toilet paper trailed from it, like a bloody banner of surrender. "Madam, you seem to have injured yourself. I will call 911."

"No ambulance, fire truck or rescue vehicle will be necessary. Would you please call Marc Allaire and tell him to come over right away? Right now. Tell him it is business and I need him." Conklin was a very literal man. I found it helped to be specific.

"Shall I tell him it's an emergency, Madam?"

"You can tell him it's very serious. However, no sirens or backup are required."

While Conklin was making the call from the cramped telephone closet under the staircase, I pulled myself up onto the bottom step and sat there, thinking. After a minute, I got to my feet, shuffled to the door and opened it to wait for Marc's arrival.

"Madam, Chief Allaire said to let you know he will be here immediately. I advised him you appeared to be slightly injured, but did not require medical attention at this time. I hope that was correct."

"Perfect, Conklin. Thank you."

"I hope you haven't been attacked, Madam."

I sure wished he would stop calling me Madam. I was beginning to feel like the owner of a massage parlour. I had already asked him to call me Lyris or Miss Lyris even. He just looked appalled at the idea and would have none of it. Yet he insisted I call him Conklin, though everyone else called him either Mr. Conklin or Arthur.

"No, Conklin, I haven't been attacked." I was tired all of a sudden.

My bones craved heat and I sat down in the sun. My mind drifted to the tower room. To the box. And its secret.

What could have happened so long ago to end in such tragedy? A terrible act—an *evil* act—had been committed in this house.

Selfishly, I wished the box had withheld its secret for another sixty-eight years.

CHAPTER 3

During daytime hours, Hammersleigh's gates were set wide open at the end of the long driveway. Inside the house, a button in the electrical panel set into the wall by the front door controlled a mechanism that locked the gates every night and opened them again in the mornings.

I thought the practice was a waste of time. Sure, the house was equipped with other security devices such as motion detectors, but locking the front gates when only a six-foot wrought-iron fence surrounded the rest of the property seemed absurd. There had been several break-ins around Blackshore in the past month, and there I was, sleeping in lonesome splendour on the second floor, while Conklin slept…somewhere else in the house. I had no idea where. Hammersleigh House was full of valuable objects protected by a psychotic poodle, an aged butler and one confirmed coward.

Lights flashing, but siren muted, Marc's cruiser careened around the gates and sped up the driveway, skidding to a stop ten feet from the steps where I was sitting. I stood up and waited for Marc to reach me, the bottoms of my bare feet burning from the heat of the limestone.

I had hoped to have a word alone with Marc without Conklin listening in—Conklin was not a young man, and I was afraid of shocking him into an anxiety attack or cardiac arrest—but it was not going to happen. Conklin and Jacqueline came out of the house and hovered nearby. I couldn't swing a dead cat without hitting one of them.

Marc jumped out of the cruiser and ran up the steps to meet me. I wasn't able to read his expression behind the mirrored sunglasses, but the well-shaped lips were set a little more firmly than usual.

I wondered what I looked like. Not good, I suspected. Blood-caked hands and foot, dust-streaked clothes, and God only knew what state my hair was in. Or my face. I dragged the back of my wrist down my cheek, hoping to remove a few sweat streaks. I probably still looked like three-day-old road kill.

Our relationship was new, and sometimes I wondered why Marc was interested in me. Perhaps he enjoyed enigmas. He once said I resembled a Madonna, until I opened my mouth. I wished I'd asked him what he meant—not the mouth part; I got that. But with almost black hair, dark brown eyes and olive skin that tanned from April's first sunbeam, I sure didn't look like any Madonna. And my breasts, while perfectly adequate for most purposes, would disappear from sight under the folds of a saintly robe. So far, though, I liked pretty much everything about Marc. He was hot-looking and had no major fault I could find, unless a penchant for organization and order could cause me problems down the road. His person, vehicle, office, home, yard—everything was neat and clean. And don't bother laying your sweater over a chair. It will be hung up as soon as your arm is out of the sleeve.

My ex-husband, Dennis Malinski, was a neat-freak in a different way. While Marc would hang up your sweater with a smile and help you put it back on later, Dennis would just look at it and seethe, then throw it out the back door into the fishpond. I lost a few good sweaters that way. And one Christmas turkey, but that's another story.

"So where's the emergency? You haven't been robbed, have you?" Marc took off his sunglasses and I saw the grey eyes were concerned, not angry. He touched my arm and looked me over.

I snapped an accusing glance at Conklin, but the snitch refused to meet my eyes.

"Not yet. It isn't an emergency as such, Marc." And it wasn't. The contents of the box had been in the tower room for more than sixty years.

"Lyris, I left the mayor and two councillors sitting in my office with a petition signed by almost four hundred citizens. They want more police patrols at night throughout the whole of Bruce County, and I don't have the manpower. I had to tell them I was called out on an emergency. How did you get hurt?"

I figured I'd better not mention that one of the signatures on the petition was mine. Hey, I was a home owner too. "Sorry, this honestly is serious. And I dropped a moose on my foot and fell down the stairs. I'm fine though."

His eyes flickered, but he didn't mention my injury again. That's another thing I liked about him—he didn't fuss.

"Come upstairs with me and I'll show you what I found." I looked at Conklin. He and Jacqueline were still standing close behind me, sighing and snuffling respectively. Maybe I could lose them on the way up.

"Well, after you then. I hope this is important. I should get back to the mayor and his squabbling councillors."

"Don't trip on the antelope there." I led the way up the mahogany staircase, Marc behind me and Conklin and Jacqueline trailing along at the end.

"I believe that's a wildebeest. Where are you taking me?"

"It's an antelope. It says so on the plaque. We're going to the tower room."

Marc glanced back at the antelope, then followed me along the length of the hallway. I stopped with my hand on the knob. The hand was shaking a little and I gripped tighter.

"It's in here." I threw open the door.

At first glance, the room looked like it had been finger-painted by a mob of angry preschoolers. There were round red drops on the floor, and the handprints on the wall around the hidden door opening were drying and turning brownish. Marc and Conklin looked at each other, then at my toe. The moose rested beside the demilune table.

Impatient to get this over with, I tapped my good foot and indicated the box in the middle of the floor and the newspapers scattered close by. Before my momentary lapse of consciousness, I must have let the cloth drop back into place, so it was not possible to see inside the box. Marc turned and looked at me with a questioning eye.

"Something in this box? You better show me."

I glanced at Conklin. He was sticking close to my side. Well, I just hoped he had a strong heart. Jacqueline growled low in her throat and backed away. I pushed her out of the room, and for once, she didn't protest. She lay down flat in the hall a few yards from the door.

I found I couldn't let Marc look in the box without warning him. He may have seen a lot of gruesome sights during his career, but I was betting this would be a first for him. I just wanted to get the words out and done with. "It's little Tommy."

Both men continued to look at me.

"You know, little Tommy Pembrooke."

They still showed no reaction.

"At least *you* must remember," I said to Conklin. "It was during the war. They never found him."

"Which war would this be, Madam?" .

"Lord love a duck. World War II, of course. You were here then, weren't you? How could you forget something like that?"

"Madam, during the War, I was overseas. My employment at Hammersleigh House did not commence until 1948."

"Oh, I didn't know." The way he felt about Hammersleigh, I figured he had been born under a hydrangea bush in the back garden. "You must have heard about little Tommy. Everyone in Blackshore knows. It's a legend."

"Wait," Marc said, "I remember now. He was here for a family reunion and disappeared one night. I came across the file in our archives a few years ago. The case is still open, although the file has never been appended."

Conklin cleared his throat. "The affair is coming back to me also, Madam. I did hear about it from staff who were employed at Hammersleigh House many years ago. It was a fascinating story as well as a sad one. Poor child, I believe he was just an infant."

"Two months from his second birthday. The house and grounds were searched over and over. Finally, the police decided to call it a kidnapping. They said someone entered the house in the middle of the night and took him."

Marc leaned over and poked at the top of the box with a finger. I shuddered and moved closer to Conklin.

"The federal authorities were contacted," Marc said, "but in those days they had no accurate tracking system for missing children, and no trace of the Pembrooke child was ever found. Did you come across some newspaper accounts here?"

"Marc, you aren't listening to me. Tommy is in this box. Don't you get it? He never left the house. He's been here all along."

Beside me, I could feel Conklin stiffen. "Madam, are you sure? The child disappeared over sixty years ago. It does not seem possible that he would still be recognizable." His faded blue eyes were sad. "Perhaps you have found the skeleton of someone's pet, a cat or a puppy?"

A pet. I ignored him and turned to Marc. "Look in the box. I may not be a forensic specialist, but take one look and then tell me I'm wrong. And it's no skeleton."

Marc took a pair of black latex gloves out of his pocket and pulled them on. He dropped to one knee and sorted through the newspapers, picking up each sheet by the corner with the tips of his thumb and forefinger and looking at it before replacing it on the floor. When all the papers were piled in a neat stack beside the box, he inspected the cloth without touching it. Now that I saw it again, I realized it was the remnant of a blanket. As Marc lifted it, the faded satin binding fell away from the soft blue material. A baby's blanket.

A feeling of sorrow swept over me and I brushed at my eyes. For a moment I imagined I saw a toddler running toward me on the grass at Hammersleigh, his tiny hands clutching a yellow cloth bunny...

Marc placed the blanket on the pile of papers and I kept my eyes on his face, not wanting to see the tiny body again.

Marc leaned toward the box. He recoiled and rocked back on his heels. Then, he stood up and backed away.

Conklin made a move to step forward and I clutched at his sleeve. He gently disengaged himself. "Madam, I was in the medical corps. I am no stranger to death, even in its more unpleasant forms."

After a moment's consideration of the box's contents, Conklin plucked at the neck of his sweater with trembling fingers and spoke to Marc. "How could this have happened, Chief Allaire? I don't believe I have ever seen anything like this before."

Marc looked in the closet. "The temperature and humidity must have been just right for the length of time it takes a body to dehydrate. And air current is a factor too. That looks like a ventilation pipe that's rusted apart running up the back of the closet. It isn't a large body and the desiccation process would have been quick. And the child did disappear during the summer."

That was rather more information than I needed.

He reached into the box and lifted out a stuffed toy, a rabbit that might once have been yellow. I moved uneasily and shrugged off the tingle between my shoulders.

Marc replaced the toy. He stood up, removed his gloves, and motioned us to go ahead of him into the hall. He closed the door of the tower room and took me by the elbow.

"I want you to tell me how you came to find the box. But first, I need to call Ronnie."

Marc led us down the staircase, across the great hall, through the double oak doors, and down the limestone steps to the bricked driveway. The late afternoon heat was heavy with humidity as we halted in a row beside his cruiser.

Marc called the dispatcher on the radio, asking her to contact Ronnie Guilbert, his sergeant, and instruct him to come to Hammersleigh House with his camera and other crime equipment. The radio squawked a question at Marc and he replied distinctly with a brief glance in my direction. "Ms. Lyris Pembrooke has found the mummified remains of a child in one of her closets."

CHAPTER 4

"He looked at me like it was my fault. I mean, how could I be responsible for something that happened sixty-odd years ago? I wasn't even born yet."

"Marc knows you aren't responsible. But you are a bit of a catalyst, if you don't mind me being honest."

It wouldn't much matter if I did mind. Patsy Gerard had been my best friend since preschool and had *always* been honest with me. She prided herself on it. I guess we all need a friend who will tell us when our skirt is tucked into our pantyhose, or that we possess an undesirable human attribute. Patsy was mine.

We were sitting at a table in a dim corner of Hammersleigh's kitchen, tossing back glasses of iced tea. The kitchen was cool, thanks to the dense pine bushes that lined both sides of the property and shielded the house from winter winds and summer heat. We were quite comfortable in our shorts and T-shirts. Unlike the police officers who, two days after my grisly discovery, were still trudging up to the tower room and down again.

The thunder rolled in the distance, as it had for weeks. But the moisture continued to hang heavily in the clouds, refusing to fall and cool the earth.

"I'm just unlucky. Sooner or later somebody would have looked in that closet and sorted through the boxes. Look how long the Egyptian mummies lasted. A sixty-eight-year span is just a blink of the eye. That poor baby would still have been there another hundred years from now. Why did it have to be me who found him? Or why didn't someone find him fifty years ago?"

"Well, never mind." Patsy poured another glass of iced tea with one hand and gave my arm a pat with the other. Her plump face was framed in reddish-brown hair that was tightly curled from the humidity. Between the hair and her round, hazel eyes, she looked like Little Orphan Annie, if Annie had irises. "Marc knows you aren't to blame. He's just worried you'll start digging into the past trying to find out what happened to Tommy and mess up his investigation."

"Thanks. And there is no investigation. What possible leads could there be after all this time? Most of the people involved are dead now. Anyway, I don't have time to worry about a crime that old when the family reunion is less than two weeks away."

"Sure."

"I'm serious. I'm going to put it right out of my mind. And I don't think Marc is going to spend any time or manpower on this. It was an alleged kidnapping, and the RCMP were called in, so why aren't they handling it?"

"Marc already contacted them. They said he's to let them know if they can do anything to assist."

"How do you know? Marc never said anything."

"I bet you never asked." She fluffed up her short curls. "I'm kidding. Marc called Nick yesterday to put off their golf date and mentioned what the Mounties said."

"And Nick came home and spilled everything." This was not a question.

Nick and Patsy were my dearest friends, but as a couple, they made me squirm. They shared everything, including thoughts and feelings. It wouldn't surprise me to learn they used the same toothbrush.

"Lyris, when will Marc be done here? His officers aren't searching the whole house, I hope. There can't be any evidence left."

"Why ask me? I don't know as much as you."

"Well, you and Marc must have been together since you found Tommy. What did you talk about? Or maybe..." she leered, "you don't talk at all?"

"I haven't been alone with Marc since I moved in last Saturday. This place just hasn't got enough rooms."

"What? Hammersleigh is enormous."

I lowered my voice. "It's Conklin. I think he's Nosferatu in the guise of an elderly butler. I never hear him coming, but out of nowhere, he's standing there looking at me, calling me Madam. I hesitate to take a shower for fear I'll throw back the curtain and find him holding my towel for me. Eyes modestly averted, of course."

Patsy's one-track mind was still stuck on my sex life. "Are you telling me you and Marc haven't...you know...since you moved in?"

"We haven't...you know...at all. What kind of person do you think I am, anyway? Marc and I have only been going out for two months."

"I just don't believe it. I've seen the way you look at each other. Lyris, you're almost forty. It's not like you can be deflowered in the petunia bed again. What are you waiting for?"

"The right moment. I've had sex with one man in my life, and I don't want to make another mistake. We're not all sex maniacs like you and Nick. And I wasn't deflowered in a petunia bed in the first place. It was in the back seat of Dennis's 1969 Pontiac. And I'm barely thirty-eight, three months younger than you."

She slapped the table and hooted, "No wonder Marc has been looking so grumpy. Wait till I tell Nick."

"I'll never speak to you again if you do. I mean it, Patsy, don't say anything. Let Marc and I set our own pace."

"I have a pretty good idea what pace Marc would like, but you can relax. This will be our secret."

"It better be. The chief deterrent to our unwedded bliss right now is Conklin, as I started to tell you. He sticks closer to me than a zebra mussel on a sailboat. I wish he'd go haunt somebody else."

"You're mixing your metaphors again. Conklin is lost without your uncle, so he looks to you for direction, don't forget."

"He does *not* look to me for direction. As a matter of fact, he tries his best to boss me around, in that genteel way he has. When I first moved in, I wanted to show Marc around upstairs, but Conklin followed us up asking if he could help us or bring us some refreshments. We felt like teenagers trying to find a place to park and went back outside to sit on the porch. Even if I did want to try out that petunia bed again, Conklin would find it necessary to weed it right then and there."

Patsy listened without comment for a minute. "Why don't you hire a new housekeeper? With her to train, Conklin would be off your back."

"Do you think it's that easy? Housekeeping is an outdated profession. John Brixton has advertised several times and few people have responded. He's going to eliminate the objectionable applicants and send me the rest. I have to interview them, can you imagine? I could hire a kleptomaniac or a serial killer. How would I know?"

"Ask Conklin to sit in. He'd be a good judge of character."

"Anybody that old should be. I've already asked him to help. He just looks down his nose and says it's my job, and he couldn't possibly interfere. I didn't like Marion Beadle much, but sometimes I wish she was still here."

Marion was Uncle Patrick's long-time sixtyish housekeeper. When her bequest and pension from Uncle Patrick hit her bank account, she took off for the bright lights of Montreal, never to be seen again.

"Quit whining. You'll figure something out. I have to go. Let me know if I can do anything to help you with the reunion."

"You know, Patsy, it's obvious now that nobody crept into the house during the night and kidnapped Tommy. I wonder if the family suspected it was an inside job all along."

"What do you mean?"

"Nothing. I'm just thinking out loud. Since Tommy never left the house, either somebody already here, or somebody who knew the layout, must have killed him and placed his body in the closet."

"You don't know he was murdered. It could have been an accident, then somebody panicked and hid him in the closet."

I couldn't argue with her, but I didn't think she was right.

Patsy stood up. "I'm going. Call if you need any help. With the reunion, I mean. Don't ask me to help you with any murder investigation."

I was scarcely aware of her leaving. Little Tommy's death had begun to prey on my mind, and the last thing I needed right now was to let anything deflect my attention from the reunion. Before I inherited Hammersleigh House, all I had to do was show up on the right day, picnic basket in hand. Now there were a dozen arrangements to make, with Conklin being no help at all. I didn't know where to start.

I went over to the sink to rinse out the pitcher and glasses. Suddenly, a pair of arms encircled my waist and a pair of warm lips nuzzled the back of my neck. I squealed in alarm and dropped the glass I was holding into the sink. It shattered into dozens of crystalline pieces.

"Look what I did," I said to Marc with some anxiety. "No doubt this glass is a family heirloom and I've broken up the set. Conklin will have a fit."

"I didn't mean to make you jump. Usually you like it when I kiss you there."

"I was thinking about Conklin."

"Don't tell me he's been making passes at you," Marc said with a disbelieving smile. Despite the heat, his regulation shirt was crisp and smelled pleasantly of fabric softener. His thick black hair just cried out to be touched, but I controlled myself. And the slight dimple in his right cheek, oh my.

"Hardly. But he has me spooked. You know how he keeps popping up."

His arms were around me again, and I felt the too-familiar warmth suffuse my body and begin to overcome my better judgement. Kid stuff. I moved away from his touch.

"Well, he's not here now, so why don't we take advantage of his absence. You can show me your bedroom and explain all the changes you want to make in there. And we can talk about getting married."

"Married!" Good thing I wasn't holding another glass.

Marc clapped a hand over his ear. "I think I'm deaf."

"Is this a sincere proposal, or are you just trying to take advantage of me? Because you know what a sucker I am for a man in uniform."

"Oh, I mean it. I thought I would just get the subject on the table so you can begin thinking about it, now that you're more or less used to my company."

"Well, couldn't we just wallow in lust and debauchery and leave it at that?"

He pretended to consider. "Okay. We'll start there if you like, and the sooner the better. Just think about my suggestion, won't you?"

I would think about it, not seriously, though. Somehow the thought of Marc, his two daughters, dog and cat joining my own unconventional household at Hammersleigh was almost funny. Mind you, it would be company for me at night, but I would have to sign Conklin into a rest home.

Over Marc's shoulder, I could see the kitchen door swing open. "I'll have to tell you about my redecorating plans some other time. Don't look now, but we are not alone, as the bishop said to the actress."

Marc cursed under his breath, but stepped away from me.

"I want to know about the autopsy..."

"I'll phone you and by the way, we're finished here." After a gentle tug on my ponytail and a brief word to Conklin, he was gone.

I broke the ensuing silence by asking Conklin, "Whose turn is it to make supper tonight?" I held my position in front of the double acrylic sinks, hoping to distract him from seeing the pieces of broken crystal.

"I believe it is yours, Madam. I made the eggplant quiche last night if you recall. Before that, we had the beef stew you prepared in the crock pot. And the canned beets."

And a sorry meal that had been, if I do say so myself. I had not bothered to peel the potatoes or carrots, and left the onions in chunks. The meat was the cheapest I could find at the supermarket, and it was gratifyingly tough and stringy despite twelve hours in the crock pot. The dish turned out almost as bad as Conklin's quiche—it was an unpleasant revelation to me that a quiche can be created from eggplant and cabbage.

When I moved in, Conklin and I agreed to take turns making the evening meal until we—make that I—hired a housekeeper. It was Conklin's idea. I was hoping he would do all the cooking, but was soon put in my place by his reminder that the preparation of meals, at least at Hammersleigh, was the responsibility of the housekeeper, not the butler. I was sick of everything being the housekeeper's job. He made it sound like he was doing me a favour by taking a turn at cooking.

We had been trying to wear each other down with our culinary ineptitude, hoping the other would give up and offer to cook every night. Both of us were on the lean side to start with, and growing leaner with each passing day.

"I bought a packaged macaroni and cheese dinner. We could have that with some frozen fish sticks. Oh, and I think there's another cucumber left in the fridge." Conklin hated cucumbers, especially the mutant kind without seeds.

"It sounds delicious, Madam. I will be in the pantry polishing the silver tea service if you need me."

"Fine, but I can't let you spoil your appetite with the macaroons you bought. I moved them out of the cupboard where you keep your silver polish and cloths. You can have them back later for dessert."

His brief smile failed to reach his faded blue eyes. His thin shoulders drooped even more, and I felt I was being a bit harsh with him. Just as I decided a couple of cookies wouldn't hurt, he looked in the direction of the sink. "Madam, might I suggest you exercise care in clearing up the broken glass, lest you cut your fingers?"

Straight-backed, he marched into the butler's pantry, a narrow room between the kitchen and the formal dining room. It was lined with glass-fronted cupboards from ceiling to floor and held all the exquisite, priceless china and silver collected by several generations of Pembrookes. The room was Conklin's special place of refuge, and he retreated there now to mourn the loss of his cookies.

I opened one of the two double-door upright freezer units and rummaged for the package of frozen fish sticks I had bought on the same shopping trip as the stewing beef. Both freezers were packed full of more enticing offerings such as lobster and steaks, but I stoically closed the door on them. Time enough for that later when I had either hired a housekeeper or forced Conklin to his arthritic, creaking knees.

An hour later, we were seated at the same table where I had earlier shared iced tea with Patsy. Initially, Conklin had been upset when I refused to eat alone in the dining room, but the huge Jacobean-style dining table, twelve matching chairs, looming mirrored sideboard and the ten-foot serving table unnerved me. And I wasn't going to eat in there by myself. Conklin was stiff and formal when I joined him in the kitchen, but was becoming more relaxed each day in my presence, and I felt he secretly enjoyed the company.

I left the fish sticks in the oven ten minutes longer than instructed on the package and didn't bother to add the quarter cup of milk to the macaroni and cheese. You could re-point bricks with the result. I was satisfied with the outcome of my meal, but had no intention of eating it.

Conklin took ten minutes to cut his fish into pieces manageable enough to swallow whole. I guess his teeth weren't up to the task of chewing the rock-like morsels. His macaroni was piled in a heap in the middle of his plate, and he poked at it with his fork from time to time and watched it jiggle. He didn't so much as glance at the cucumber slices arranged attractively on a side plate.

I occupied myself with moving the pieces on my plate from one side to the other, then back again. After a few minutes of silence, I asked the question that had been bothering me.

"How could Tommy have been in that closet for over sixty years without anybody finding him, Conklin? I find it hard to believe that closet was nailed shut all this time without anybody prying it open, for no other reason than curiosity."

Conklin choked on one of the fish nuggets he was trying to swallow. I watched him closely, but he managed to get it down.

"When I arrived here after the war, Madam, the tower room was full of furniture, paintings, accessories and such things. They were items of no use that were in the house when Mr. Thomas, that would be Mr. Patrick's father, purchased it from John Hammersleigh around the turn of the century, the twentieth century, that is. The pieces were gathered up and stored in the tower room, and there they stayed. You see, Madam, there were more than enough bedrooms in the house for Mr. Thomas's four children, Mr. Patrick and his brother and two sisters, so the tower room was not needed as sleeping quarters."

"But little Tommy wasn't in the closet back then."

"No, of course not, Madam. I'm trying to give you a possible explanation for the body remaining hidden for so long. You see, by the time the war started, Mr. Patrick was in sole residence at Hammersleigh. His brother and sisters were married and living in their own homes, and Mr. Patrick's wife had died—in 1941 that would be—without leaving him an heir. Therefore, from that time to this, there have not been children in the house."

I waited, not seeing any connection.

"Madam, children are inherently curious. I believe that, had there been a child in residence these last sixty-eight years, the body would have been discovered."

"Maybe, Conklin. I know if I had lived here when I was a child, I would have explored every wall surface for secret passages."

"There is no doubt in my mind you would have, Madam."

"But before I filled the tower room with the trophy heads and other stuffed dead things, the room was empty except for a few side tables and wicker chairs. And the walls look like they were painted more recently than sixty-eight years ago. Don't forget that the hinges and the nails were painted right over."

"Quite right, Madam. About ten years ago, Mr. Patrick planned to create a winter sunroom. We hired an antique dealer to clear out the furnishings and to whitewash the walls. He had no instructions to do anything other than make the room look clean."

He looked at me rather severely. "Not everyone has your inquisitive turn of mind, Madam."

"Yes, well, I have one more question, Conklin. Who is Tommy? I mean, whose child was he? He wasn't one of Uncle Patrick's nephews."

"He was the child of a second cousin of Mr. Patrick's. Miss Wisteria Pembrooke."

"Aunt Wisty? You mean Aunt Wisty wasn't married?"

"Of course she was, Madam." Conklin looked shocked. "She married another cousin, Thomas Pembrooke. He died in Italy only months after the tragedy.

My head whirled. It was hard enough trying to keep the Pembrooke lineage straight without every second male being christened Thomas. "Poor Aunt Wisty. First her child, then her husband. No wonder she spent most of her life in Lychwood."

Lychwood was an exclusive mental institution a few miles away. It was Hammersleigh's nearest neighbour to the east as the crow flies, but because both properties contained expansive wooded areas, it was easy to forget their proximity to each other, easy to forget the chain link fence that separated their common border. Lychwood was a maximum security facility, and the patients were not free to leave at will. Aunt Wisty was by no means the only Pembrooke to have been a registered guest at Lychwood, but she was the only one who had lived most of her life there.

"What are you making for supper tomorrow night, Conklin? Have you decided?"

"I believe I will attempt to make baked beans, Madam. I used to enjoy them in the army and have developed a desire to experience them again."

I looked at him. "I hope you plan to de-gas them first."

"Excuse me, Madam? De-gas?"

I explained. "Beans contain an enzyme which produces intestinal gas when they're cooked. However, there is a very simple way to avoid the problem. You may want to write this down, Conklin."

After he fetched pen and pad from a drawer, I continued, "Boil the water first, then drop the beans in, and boil them for four or five minutes. Then take the pot off the heat, cover it and leave for several hours. You may want to do this much tonight, Conklin. Next you drain the beans, add fresh water and simmer for an hour or so. Oh, and don't add any tomatoes until just before the beans are done since tomatoes toughen them. Did you get all that?"

"I believe so. Madam, this seems like a lot of work for a pot of beans."

"Believe me, Conklin, the result will be worth the effort." I was betting he would forget the whole thing and open a can of mushroom soup for dinner. At least the soup would be edible, even if he didn't whisk out the lumps.

Conklin cleared his throat. "Now, Madam, I have taken the liberty of making up this memorandum for you. It lists everything you need to see to before the reunion. Which will be," he paused for emphasis, "in less than two weeks."

"The reunion." I shot up straight in my chair. "We have to sign a guest book at every reunion. I could look at the book for 1943 and see who was here."

"The police have already thought of that, Madam. Unfortunately, the use of a guest book did not begin until 1962." His thin lips compressed and it was clear he was done with the subject.

Too bad about that, but I had other ideas and no time like the present to start working on them. First, though, I needed some real food to keep my strength up, and I wouldn't get it in that kitchen. I reached over my head and opened a cupboard. I dropped the bag beside Conklin's plate.

"I have to go out for a bit, Conklin. Here, you can have your cookies back." I spied what looked like a giant dust bunny underneath the table and walked toward the door. "It's your turn to feed the dog."

CHAPTER 5

I woke up to the clamour of birdsong. Before daylight.

The racket produced by thousands of birds was not, to me, a wondrous and mystical experience. I realized they were planning to twitter and chirp every morning, and I wanted to wring their noisy little necks. Rolling over, I pressed the pillow against my ears.

It was no use.

"Quiet," I yelled at the three sets of open windows. All were hung with stiff green and gold brocade that matched the bed curtains and canopy. The heavy fabric was meant to prevent the sleeper from experiencing a draft in winter, but they also stopped any cooling current of air from reaching said sleeper during periods of stifling summer heat.

The birds continued to celebrate with joyous abandon, as though the imminent sunrise happened just once a year like the April Revenue Canada deadline. I jumped out of bed to slam the windows shut and almost broke a leg again. I kept forgetting my bed was four feet off the ground and the one way to get on or off was by means of a two-step wooden stool that never seemed to be in the right spot for vacating the bed in a hurry.

My bedroom overloaded the senses, both by its size and by the proportions of the furniture. The bed was a four poster and matched the highboy, armoire, cabinets, bureaux, chiffoniers and several other unfamiliar pieces, all looking like some crazed woodworker had mated Gothic Revival with Late Classical to beget this Early Hideous result.

Dragons and other mythical creatures writhed their way up the bedposts and legs of the chairs and highboy, while a row of frilled and feathered pineapples crested the armoire that soared to within a millimetre of the twelve-foot ceiling. It was typically Victorian and terrifying to wake up to each morning.

In fairness to Hammersleigh, most of the other rooms contained furnishings much more pleasing to the eye, but I had chosen this room over the five other possibilities for several reasons. First were the three sets of windows that opened onto the stand of mature sugar maples. I thought it idyllic before learning about the dawn habits of bird life.

The other reason could be seen high up near the ceiling. Dozens of gilded cupids cavorted on the cornices, all with unique expressions on their carved faces. They made me smile whenever I looked up at them.

With the windows closed, the noise from the trees was reduced to a muted peeping. However, the air inside became close and still within seconds. My T-shirt clung to my body and I felt my hair corkscrew into tight curls.

Even the thick stone walls of Hammersleigh were yielding to the summer heat wave most of the continent was enduring. In the northern parts of the province, forest fires were raging out of control, and closer to home, campers were forbidden to light fires for cooking. There was even talk of prohibiting backyard barbecues. Since Blackshore sits smack in the middle of beef country in south-western Ontario, steak enthusiasts were prepared to storm the town hall if any meat-restrictive law was passed.

My own house in town had air conditioning and so far, it was one of the few things I missed. My bed was another, and then there was the lack of privacy. Living with a butler that materialized without warning was a definite minus, although I had to admit I wouldn't want to live in that house alone.

The tower room was a problem. Whenever I came out of my bedroom or walked down the hall toward it, I kept my eyes on the floor. I did not want to look down the dark length of the hall toward the door of the tower room.

It was ridiculous to feel this way. The body of a child had been hidden in there for over sixty years. I did not believe in ghosts, but I could neither ignore nor suppress the tingling sensation between my shoulders when I was in the upper hall. And even worse was the smell that accompanied the tingling.

The subtle odour was faint and somehow familiar. But I couldn't pin it down. It wasn't unpleasant and I seemed to detect it with just the first breath I took in the hall. When I stopped and breathed again to recapture the fragrance, it was gone. The tingling in my back lasted a few seconds longer, then it too would fade away.

I felt it now as I held my breath and hurried into the bathroom, which in keeping with the ambience in the rest of the house, contained a pedestal sink and a toilet with the tank suspended six feet off the ground. Everything worked, though, even the showerhead in the claw-footed tub. The shower curtain hung from a brass track that circled the entire tub and I found there was no appreciable difference from showering behind a tub enclosure, although I mopped up a lot of water before I got the hang of it.

While I readied myself for work, I thought about what I had learned the previous evening about that long-ago reunion. Not much.

Having left Conklin and Jacqueline behind in the kitchen to feed on cookies and kibble, I had headed for Ali's Pizza Emporium on Blackshore's main street and treated myself to one of Ali's deluxe personal-sized pizzas. I sat alone at a tiny table and devoured the whole pizza in minutes, washing it down with a quart of watery peach-flavoured drink. I felt much stronger when I finished my meal, and I walked the three blocks to the police station.

I planned to break my own rule and visit Marc at work, hoping he would unbend enough to give me some information about the cause of Tommy's death. With a lot of luck, I thought he might even let me peek at the police archives.

Marc was not in his office. The on-duty officer reported that the chief had left and wasn't expected back that evening. Her eyes followed me out.

The library was my next stop. It would have microfilm of newspapers from the past, and I wanted to read the *Blackshore Oracle's* coverage of the reunion and Tommy's disappearance. The library was next door to the police station, but when I climbed the steps to the double front doors, the sign stated the Public Library was closed on Thursday evenings during July and August.

I started back toward my car parked in front of Ali's and I wondered whom I could visit at eight-thirty on a hot summer's night. Someone that might have been at that reunion or at least remembered hearing about it.

In some towns that might not have presented a problem, but Blackshore's residents were notoriously mobile during the summer months. They visited back and forth, went to the air-conditioned movie theatre, lawn bowled, attended outdoor concerts given by the local pipe band in the park. You name it, the town folk did it, anything to get out of the house.

Since Blackshore was located on the shores of Lake Huron, the fiercest of the Great Lakes, about three hours northwest of Toronto, our winters were long and harsh. This might explain why the population of 7,500 felt the need to make every minute of the summer count.

I was just about to give up and go home when my eye was caught by the display in the window of Tackaberry's Antiques.

It was a Crown Derby teapot. The shape was unmistakable and the delicate colours glimmered in the light of a mock-Tiffany lamp. I admit to a weakness for teapots and was the proud owner of dozens, most not very valuable but precious to me all the same. The collection was still boxed up and piled in a corner of my bedroom at Hammersleigh, along with my computer paraphernalia. I proposed to set the teapots in a cabinet in my bedroom where they would not be overshadowed by the priceless collections found throughout the rest of the house. There was enough room in my bedroom for half a dozen display cabinets, and plenty of cabinets to choose from. The computer required a more modern setup and I hoped it wouldn't look out of place in a corner by the windows.

Through the shop window I saw Peter Tackaberry's head bent over the counter, his dark blond hair falling around his face. Since the handwritten sign on the front door was not yet turned to Closed, I took this as an opportune invitation.

Three minutes and fifty-seven dollars plus the dreaded HST later, the teapot sat wrapped in a box on the counter.

"I was going to call you about that teapot, but I figured you might have lost your taste for the merely pretty since you inherited Hammersleigh. There must be hundreds of pieces of antique china and porcelain there. At least there was the last time I was in the house." Peter shoved the drawer closed on his manual cash register and smiled at me.

"I'm always interested in an unusual teapot to add to my collection. The contents of Hammersleigh don't belong to me, you know. Not for another twenty-five years anyway."

"I hope you're enjoying yourself. When I heard about your uncle's will, I knew you were the one person who would be appreciative of the beauty and history of Hammersleigh."

"I love it. Although finding the body was a shock and it's going to take me a while to feel comfortable near the tower room again."

"Do you want to hear something odd?" Peter stopped fiddling with his cash register and moved around to my side of the counter. Nudging me into a fretwork-backed mahogany side chair—reproduction Elizabethan Revival—he pulled over another for himself and sat down.

"I was in that tower room about ten years ago. Your uncle hired me to clear out all the junk and paint it. I think he planned to make it into some kind of sun porch with plants and rattan furniture. I hoped he would ask me to decorate and furnish the room, but I never heard back from him after I finished the painting."

It had slipped my mind that Peter did painting and wallpapering on the side when his antique business was slow, which was every winter. He also had other talents and was popular with Blackshore's numerous women's clubs as a guest speaker on decorating and gardening.

"Uncle Patrick never did anything else to the tower room." I recalled all those glass eyes now staring from the walls. "I wonder why?"

Surely Uncle Patrick didn't know about the child's body concealed at the back of the closet. If he did know, he had over sixty years to find another resting place. And what if he didn't know—what if he found Tommy after Peter started cleaning and painting. He would have stopped Peter from doing any further work on the room, but then why didn't he inform the police? My brained whirred as I imagined myself back in time, back to Hammersleigh House so long ago. Who else was there in the house?

I jumped and realized Peter had been talking to me.

"I was sorry about not finishing off the room. It would have been lovely, filled with greenery and natural light with a soft area carpet on the floor and flowered cushions on the furniture."

"Do you remember the closet behind the door? It was painted over. Didn't you want to open it and see what was there?"

He shuddered. "I remember it quite well. I asked Mr. Pembrooke about it, but he instructed me to just paint the room white and not worry about prying out the nails. He wasn't interested in extensive renovations. Just think, if I had opened the door of the closet, I might have been the one to find the child."

It would have been impolite to tell Peter that I wished he had found little Tommy ten years ago and saved me the trouble, so I kept quiet.

He seemed to know what I was thinking though. "I can't say I was very curious about the closet at the time. I was there during the summer and was doing the work for your uncle at night after I closed up the store. Not everyone is as curious as you are, Lyris."

He smiled. "You were always that way. I remember your inquisitiveness used to get you into a lot of trouble at school."

"It still does. Curiosity is not an attractive trait in a woman my age, or so I've been informed more than once."

Peter had been a friend when we were in high school. He was not a member of the more popular groups, since he lacked the aptitude or interest for sports or the postgame parties. Peter was a loyal friend to me and I could trust him not to blab my confidences all over the school. Peter, Patsy and I had been close friends for several years until life took us in different directions.

"Well, it's getting late and I have to work tomorrow. I better take my teapot and get going."

When I stood up, I noticed for the first time the glass case standing on a shelf behind the counter. Inside was a doll about two feet high with an exquisite bisque face and blonde hair styled in ringlets. It was dressed in a high-necked pale-blue dress with puffy sleeves and ruffled hem. I moved closer for a better look. "Why, it's beautiful, Peter."

Peter pulled me around with him to stand in front of the case. "This is Samantha. She's a Kammer and Reinhardt doll. Mint.

"Where did you get it?"

"From my Aunt Judy. A friend left Samantha to her, and Aunt Judy bequeathed Samantha to me when she passed."

Peter opened the case and handed me the doll. I held it with careful fingers and wondered, as I always did when I looked at an antique doll, how so fragile a plaything could have survived intact for a hundred years or more. The most obvious explanation is that no child was ever allowed to touch it.

"Samantha is priced at twelve hundred dollars," Peter said, "but I kind of hope nobody will offer to pay that much. I could use the money, but I would hate to part with her."

I gave the doll back to Peter. "There's a cabinet in the drawing room at Hammersleigh full of antique dolls. Several look very similar to Samantha. If you're interested, you should come over some time and have a look. I think there's an index somewhere of the dolls and who made them."

His blue eyes brightened with interest. "I saw that cabinet from a distance when I was painting the tower room. But I never had a chance to get a close look. Mr. Conklin escorted me up and was waiting for me when I finished for the night. It was quite painful to see all those dolls from afar and never get a good look at them. I would love to come over sometime if it wouldn't be putting you out."

"Not at all." A thought occurred to me. "As a matter of fact, you can maybe help me. You still do decorating, don't you?"

He nodded.

"My bedroom needs some drastic work done on it."

"Like what?"

I explained about the horrible furniture and curtains and the special cherubs on the cornices. "I asked John Brixton. He's the executor of Uncle Patrick's will, and he says that if I pack the existing fabrics away and pay for the new ones myself, I can do what I want in any room as long as I preserve the period look of the house."

He raised his eyebrows. "What do you propose?"

"We could take the furniture out of one of the other bedrooms and you could coordinate the wallpaper and curtains and everything else. Are you interested?"

Peter beamed from ear to ear. "I have the time in the evenings, if that would be suitable. When can I come over for a look?"

"Tomorrow is Friday. How about after you close up shop?"

"Fine. About seven o'clock? I'll close early."

The air outside remained as sultry and still as it had for the past month. In the distance, I heard the low rumble of thunder, and heat lightning flashed on the horizon. What I wouldn't give for a violent summer thunderstorm, complete with crashing thunder, lightning and a torrential downpour. Like everybody else, I had stopped expecting it. A storm had seemed imminent for weeks, but it never broke.

I worked for the Blackshore Hydro Commission and was aware that the company was buying from the power grids in record quantities. A lot of the extra power was required for the air conditioners you could no longer buy for any amount of money. Even electric fans were scarce.

My car was equipped with air conditioning, and so was my bungalow on Whitsun Street. I eyed it as I passed by on the way to my mother's house a few blocks over on Queenston Heights Crescent. I thought of phoning Conklin and telling him I was staying at my own house for the night, but discarded that idea for a better one. It would take several hours for the air conditioner to cool my house, but I could stay at Mom's in my old room. I'd run back to Hammersleigh in the morning for fresh clothes before work.

I pulled into my mother's driveway and cut the engine. This house I grew up in was a bungalow too, but much more spacious and better decorated than mine. I had bought mine two years ago after my divorce from Dennis. He took the marital home, which was fine because Mitch was just starting university and I needed a change. Somehow I never got around to doing much decorating.

Just look at me now though. I lived in a mansion. The situation was ludicrous, although some might envy me if they weren't acquainted with Conklin and Jacqueline.

I opened the front door. "Mom, are you home? It's me, are you here?"

There was no answer, but I knew she had to be somewhere in the house, since the lights were on in the kitchen and living room. In case she was in the sunroom at the back of the house and couldn't hear me over the hum of the air conditioner, I raised my voice. "Mom, it's me, Lyris. Where are you?"

By this time I was standing in the living room near the hall that led to the bedrooms. I heard the sound of scurrying feet across hardwood floors. The noise was coming from the direction of my mother's room. Alarms went off in my head, but at that moment, my mother stepped out of her bedroom and closed the door behind her.

"Why, Lyris, what a surprise. I wasn't expecting you. You look hot. Come into the kitchen and I'll make you a cup of herbal tea."

She was wearing a thin cotton wrapper and her short hair tumbled around her face. She saw my glance and put her hands up to tidy it. Her face was pink and I could see that she was nervous or upset about something. A vague idea was forming in my mind. Just then, a man came into the kitchen and put an arm across my mother's shoulder.

Would somebody just shoot me? It was John Brixton, the staid lawyer who was steering me through the intricacies of Uncle Patrick's will. He wore a blue-striped terrycloth bathrobe and nothing underneath if the bare feet and legs were any indication. I didn't know where to look.

Mom flushed even pinker and moved closer to him. I felt my own face grow hot. I eyed the door, but Mr. Brixton was blocking it.

He said to my mother, "Sorry, Maureen. I didn't think cowering in the bedroom was the right way to handle this. Lyris is a grown woman and we shouldn't have to hide what we feel for each other from her."

Not so fast. Certain things could, and should, be withheld from a sensitive daughter. I had blundered into a love tryst. My insides squirmed, but I knew that the next few minutes would make or break my relationship with my mother. I couldn't afford to say something stupid.

My father and Mr. Brixton had been partners in the law firm of Powers, Pembrooke and Brixton, and the two men and their wives were personal friends as well. Dad died seven years ago and Elva Brixton a year or two later. Mom had moved to Victoria several years ago when my brother, David, and his wife had their first child. She returned for Uncle Patrick's funeral two months ago, and I knew she and John Brixton had been in telephone contact since. Now she was back for good and just when did all this happen?

Mr. Brixton offered David a partnership in the firm and was accepted. It meant that my entire family—brother, sister-in-law, two-year-old nephew, infant niece, and mother—would be together again in Blackshore. David and his family were flying in the next week and planned to rent my house until they could decide where to build. Mom had opened up her own house just days before I moved into Hammersleigh, and I looked forward to spending a lot of time with her.

I glanced from one to the other, not knowing what to say or how to get out of there and leave everybody's dignity intact. John Brixton was a handsome, fit man in his early seventies and I could understand why my mother was attracted to his physical appearance. From what I could see, and I could see plenty, he still had most of his hair and teeth. But I had always considered him the slightest bit stuffy. Not a natural companion for someone like my mother.

At the age of 71, Mom was fun loving and busy with many of the activities and clubs Blackshore had to offer its senior citizens. Five foot three, she was six inches shorter than I, and gifted with natural silvery-blond hair, light blue eyes and a flawless complexion.

My brother and I tell outsiders we take after our father, but the truth is more sinister. A dominant Irish gene mutated many generations back and created a spate of tall, dark-haired, brown-eyed Pembrookes in Bruce County. Think Children of the Corn, featuring Italian actors.

"Lyris." My mother's voice was tentative. "Do you want to sit down and talk about this?"

"No, no. There's no need to explain anything to me. I'm just sorry for barging in on you this way. I think it's wonderful that you and Mr. Brixton have found each other. I just hope you'll forgive me for interrupting…"

Wrong word. I knew it as soon as it was out of my mouth.

"Ah…walking in without knocking."

Despite the coolness of the room, I could feel sweat trickling down the back of my neck. I was desperate to make things right before I left.

They must have felt sorry for me. Mom relaxed a little and patted my arm, while John Brixton steered me over to an armchair. I collapsed into it and exhaustion overtook me. Too many dawn awakenings were taking their toll.

The lovebirds sat close together on the couch across from me and joined hands. I would have been much more comfortable if Mr. Brixton had taken the time to put his pants on, but I admired his composure. Maybe he wasn't as stodgy as I believed.

They looked at me with expectant faces. I searched my mind for something to say. I couldn't tell them the reason for my visit was to beg a cool bed for the night.

I abhorred a vacuum as much as nature did. I opened my mouth and babbled. About my visit to Peter Tackaberry's shop—I regretted not having my new teapot on my lap to show them—and Peter's proposed visit to Hammersleigh to look at my room. The subject of Hammersleigh led to Conklin and our cooking feud, although I didn't use those exact words. I merely mentioned that neither Conklin nor I were very adept at the culinary arts and were beginning to suffer.

I made light of it, but Mr. Brixton had been listening closely. "I'm glad you dropped over tonight, Lyris."

He said that with a straight face. My respect for the man soared.

"I was going to call you tomorrow, so this will save me the trouble. I have been making discreet enquiries for a new housekeeper. Most respondents were not suitable for one reason or another, but one young lady might do very well. Her name is Caroline Fournier." He paused and waited for a response.

I shook my head. "The name doesn't mean anything to me. Is she from around here?"

"Her maiden name is Hanlon. She may be distantly related to you, Maureen."

My mother, whose maiden name was Hanlon, looked uncertain. "I may know her grandmother, Letitia."

"She moved with her parents from Blackshore to Northton when she was a child. She married, but now the marriage has failed and she would like to make a fresh start. Caroline seems very well qualified and I have had her character references checked out."

Northton is a town even smaller than Blackshore, a mile or two west of us, and there are a lot of Pembrookes living there too. In truth, Pembrookes have pretty much spread themselves all over Bruce County. Hanlons were also thick on the ground.

Mr. Brixton's said bluntly, "But you will have to decide if she is right for Hammersleigh. Talk with her and make up your own mind. Remember, you and Arthur Conklin will have to live with her."

He seemed to be choosing his words with care. "I don't want to put undue pressure on you, Lyris, but remember that Caroline Fournier is the one reasonable candidate we have at this time, and I have been advertising for months. I suggest you give her a chance unless you feel that she would not be suitable for some reason. If she can leave her past behind, her employment at Hammersleigh House might benefit all of you."

No worries. As long as Caroline could cook and didn't try to order me around, she was in. I had no other criteria. I would turn her over to Conklin and that would both get him off my back and relieve me of the duties I was ill-equipped to perform. Like washing the dog and supervising the cleaning team. Maybe she would even do my laundry. In retrospect, I should have been thinking long-term, not immediate gratification.

"When can I interview her?"

"How about tomorrow at five? You will be home from work by then, I believe?"

"Yes, five it is. Thank you, Mr. Brixton."

"And Lyris, I think that under the circumstances, you might call me John."

There seemed no more to be said on that subject, and the vacuum loomed again. Just as the silence was becoming awkward, Mom asked, "Has Marc learned anything new about Tommy? I haven't heard the cause of death or if there are suspicions it wasn't an accident. It all happened so long ago, of course. But I do remember that reunion, even though I was just a very young child, because of Tommy's disappearance."

My nervousness was forgotten. "You were there? How come? You weren't a Pembrooke then. Tell me about that reunion. Who was there, what led up to Tommy's disappearance and what happened afterward?"

Mom laughed and put up a hand. "One thing at a time. First of all, I was at that reunion only because my best playmate was a Pembrooke, and I just went along for company. Why don't you let me think about it and put my thoughts in order? I was just three, but I think I have some pictures. Come over on Monday and we'll sit down and discuss it. You can tell me what you learned from Marc."

Others might deny this, but I *could* take a hint. I left, with smiles all around, and slunk back to Hammersleigh, where I was too demoralized to resent Conklin's disapproving sniff when he opened the door to my ring. I didn't even mention to him, yet again, that giving me a key to the front door would solve his problem of having to wait up for me. I didn't mind that the key to the massive entrance door was six inches long and weighed two pounds. I would gladly lug it around in my purse for the chance to feel like an independent adult again. One of these days I was going to insist on having a key.

I showered, made myself a cup of chamomile tea, and then dropped into bed. And I dreamed of a lost child—either young Tommy or my own infant daughter, I could not be sure. I remember waking up once or twice, feeling upset and alone, and it was a long while before I could shake off the feeling of depression. Finally, I was able to sleep again, dreamless this time, until the dawn chorus performed their morning concert in the maples outside my windows.

CHAPTER 6

"You can't be serious, Kelly." I looked at the clerk from the finance unit and refused to take the sheaf of papers she was waving at me. "Since when do office supervisors have to prepare a budget forecast for the next fiscal year? Doesn't that job belong to you people? Are you sure you have the right person?"

"Quite sure," she said with an attempt at firmness. She took a step backward before holding out the papers again. "All unit supervisors and section heads have to hand in next year's budget projections by the end of September."

"Whose idea is this? My clerical group always correlates the data for the budget preparations and distributes the information, but..."

"This memo will explain everything you need to know. The board of directors has mandated that the manager empower all employees to improve production, and this is Mr. Langelle's first instruction. And there will be others." Kelly's promise sounded like a threat. She held the papers under my nose.

I took them. I did not like the word empower. It was one of the new buzzwords of the new century and meant I could end up doing anything from scrubbing the toilets to making a presentation to the board of directors on the capital cost program. I would do neither well, but the presentation might come off better.

With her hand on the doorknob, Kelly turned back. "Oh, one more thing, Lyris. There will be a general discussion on budget preparation during the next staff communication meeting."

"I'm afraid I'll be away all next week. I'm on vacation." The reunion was closing in on me and I desperately needed at least one free week to do all the things I should have been working on for the past month.

"That's quite all right. The meeting is the second week of August. You'll be back by then."

She closed the door with finality and left me standing with a fistful of trouble. What did I know about budgets? What was a budget, in corporate terms? The cost of a file folder multiplied by the number I expected to use in the next year?

I sat down at my desk and shoved the papers into the top drawer. It was Friday, and I refused to think about budgets until the reunion was nothing but a painful memory, as it surely would become. I slammed the drawer closed and looked around the office to check on my staff.

Faye Amette, my competent payroll clerk, was entering data into the staff information system. Daphne Rourke filed papers like she knew what she was doing, while I knew for a fact she hadn't a clue. I was interested to see a new piercing in her left eyebrow. Yesterday there had been two, today there were three. The dripping dagger tattoo on her next-to-naked back glistened under the fluorescent lights. However, Daphne's father was on the board, so what can you do?

Sheila Overton yakked nonstop with two middle-aged customers at the front desk, putting the personal touch into her customer services job. From the back, she resembled a dandelion with her permed blonde hair and swamp-green blouse.

The customers left and were replaced by another woman of indeterminate age. She wore a wide straw hat tied under her chin with a bright orange and yellow scarf. A pair of wraparound sunglasses hid most of her face. I was about to shuffle some papers when the apparition spoke.

"Well, Lyris, this will be the first reunion without Patrick and it will be up to you to make it as successful as possible in his memory. That is quite a responsibility. If I can help in any way, please just ask."

It was evident from her voice and words that she was well past the first blush of youth and I was related to her. But in the disguise she wore, she could be any one of dozens of great-aunts and great-great-aunts, not to mention second cousins removed to the fifteenth time, all called by the courtesy title of Aunt.

"Thanks, Aunt...ah...but I have it under control. With a bit of luck, the reunion should go off without a hitch. Thanks for the offer, though." A deer had a better chance of surviving a set of oncoming headlights than I had of pulling off a successful reunion.

I stood beside Sheila and peered into the face. She could be Aunt Iris, Aunt Peony, Aunt Viola...the family tended to favour floral names a couple of generations ago.

"I will be bringing Wisty, at least on the first day. She hasn't attended a reunion for many years, but the doctors think it would be good for her to get out for a while. I'll pick her up at Lychwood and take her back when she gets tired."

Ah. Aunt Clem. Clematis and Wisteria. Tommy's aunt and mother.

"Of course Aunt Wisty should come to the reunion. I don't believe I've seen her since Uncle Patrick's will was read." And what a party that was.

I leaned closer to her. "Aunt Clem, can I come and see you? Perhaps this weekend, if you can spare me a few minutes? I'd like to talk about Tommy. I was the one who found him, you know." I made myself as small and pathetic as possible, the small part being a real stretch for me.

She didn't answer, just regarded me through her bug-eyed lenses, so I decided on the direct approach. "It must have been quite a shock when you heard Tommy's body was found and even worse for Aunt Wisty. I'm sure she's very upset."

"As to that, Wisty doesn't know about it yet. Her doctors feel I should impart the news since Tommy's disappearance was a major factor in her hospitalization, but I am still trying to find the right words. They think it may relieve her mind to know what happened to him. I have to tell her before the reunion, since someone is sure to mention it then, but I would appreciate your not saying anything to her about Tommy if you should visit her before the reunion."

I had not visited Aunt Wisty in Lychwood ever, and until this moment I had not realized I was thinking of doing just that. I felt one quick tingle between my shoulder blades.

Aunt Clem scared me. She had been a teacher at Blackshore's high school for thirty years. In my final year there, Aunt Clem had been my math teacher, and I haven't recovered yet. To be sure, I did attain my highest grade ever, but that was out of fear, not ability. She tolerated nothing but her students' best efforts and had a strange talent for knowing what we were going to do before we thought of it. *Stay One*

Step Ahead and Take No Prisoners had to be her motto. A skill no doubt honed during her years of mysterious war service at the infamous Camp X, the secret training base near Whitby, Ontario.

"And of course you must come and see me, Lyris," Aunt Clem continued. "It has been far too long since we had some time together."

She accepted her computerized receipt from Sheila and headed for the exit. Aunt Clem turned in front of the door. "Come by on Sunday for tea. You are past due for a reading, my dear."

Then she was gone in a flurry of floating garments that covered her from neck to ankles, guarding her from the nasty UV rays as efficiently as a suit of armour. And the icy prickling in the middle of my back increased. Aunt Clem always had that effect on me. She was a spooky lady. She was also the family psychic. Or Family Psychic, as I called her.

Sheila was unabashedly interested in the exchange and waited for me to explain. How could I begin to explain Aunt Clem? I didn't try.

I attempted to settle myself to some work, but knowing I would be on vacation for a week made it impossible to concentrate on anything as mundane as billing statements or customer complaints, not to mention budget forecasts.

I had been working at the Blackshore Hydro Commission for twenty years, beginning right after high school graduation, with four months off when Mitch was born. I liked my job, but sometimes I felt I needed something different, something *more*. Every year or two we were re-organized, downsized or right sized, depending on your point of view. And now it was happening again.

My entire body felt weighted down with nameless anxieties. I stood up to check on Daphne, but all her rings and tattoos jangled my nerves, so I sat back down. Perhaps I would feel better after a week away.

When four o'clock came, I left the office behind with relief. I felt like a kid released for summer vacation.

Hammersleigh House slumbered under a blistering sun and a sky empty of clouds. We had decided to stop using the underground sprinkler system for fear of running the well dry, and Hammersleigh's luxuriant lawns and abundant flowerbeds were beginning to dry out. Conklin mentioned that it usually took several weeks for the grounds to recover after a reunion, but he was worried the lack of moisture would be more damaging.

While I waited for Conklin to answer my ring, I ran a fond eye over the stone lintels and sills. They were of a contrasting, darker stone than the limestone walls, with a pattern of curlicues and swirls carved into them. Quite handsome, and more or less mine. All of a sudden, I felt cheerful again and thumped the door with the ancient brass demon knocker, just for the fun of it.

The door opened at last. I said to Conklin, "Avon calling. Do you need any moisturizer today? Or perhaps some bath oil? It's on sale."

Conklin looked down the length of his nose. "Madam."

I meant to go right upstairs to change for my upcoming interview with the prospective housekeeper, but I stopped short at the bottom of the staircase. The antelope was gone again.

I raced into Uncle Patrick's study at the end of the great hall and removed the head from the wall where Conklin had placed it, or replaced I guess I should say. I was keeping it at the bottom of the staircase for the moment when I felt I could enter the tower room again. But Conklin kept taking it back to the study. I would put it on the hall floor. He would carry it to the study.

I don't know how many trips the antelope had already made. It had more miles on it than my four-year-old Corolla. I dropped the head on the floor— today was not the day I would enter the tower room—and took the stairs two at a time.

I returned in a pair of shorts and a T-shirt. I thought about dressing more conservatively for the interview, but decided against it. *Begin As You Mean to Go On* was my motto. Or one of them. I had many mottos. It was while I was making the return descent, just rounding the turn in the staircase, when I saw it.

I don't understand how I could have missed it. On an upholstered shelf above the landing squatted the most flamboyant peacock I had ever seen. The outspread tail was dotted with dozens of dark circles, the proud head topped by a magnificent crest. My mind's eye must have been so used to the sight that it didn't register the fact that here was the most colossal stuffed trophy in the house.

"It's the tower room for you, my fine young cock." And this time I would go into the tower room. Or I could open the door and toss the peacock in, maybe the antelope as well. I was Woman. I was Invincible.

There was one problem. The shelf was much too high for me to reach. And I couldn't place a ladder on the stairs and prop it against the shelf without Conklin finding out. I'm sure he'd have noticed if I carried a ladder through the kitchen right under his nose. And where would I find a ladder?

I studied the problem for about ten seconds. What I needed was something long to shove the peacock off the shelf, and something to catch it in. A broom and a net of some kind would be just the ticket. The broom was easy, but a net? It had to be more substantial than a butterfly net, but not as cumbersome as a fishing boat net.

Ha.

I knew just the thing. There was a utility room off the summer kitchen. I had noticed a store of sports equipment in one corner of the room—stained tennis rackets, a croquet set, and more. I was sure there was a fish net too, the kind an optimistic angler would take along in hopes of bagging Old Lucky, the monster trout.

Conklin was nowhere to be seen in the kitchen quarters, and I was able to fetch the net and a broom without awkward questions being asked. Back on the stairs, I found I had to raise myself on my toes before the broom would reach the shelf.

I poked at the peacock with the broom, ensuring the net was underneath the shelf. At first nothing happened, and I feared the peacock was glued to its cushioned perch. But after a few more jabs with the broom, it started to rock. Back and forth, back and forth. Then it stabilized.

I poked it again. It leaned forward. I dropped the broom and grabbed the net with both hands. In slow motion, the bird swayed. Then, without warning, it plummeted. I held the net up and the peacock fell inside. Perfect. Direct hit.

To my surprise, the peacock ripped right through the netting, bounced off the stairs, and flew over the railing. Hearing a loud thud and a tinkle on the floor below, I looked over the banister.

The peacock had exploded.

There were feathers everywhere. On the tiered sideboard, on the tufted chairs, the cabinets, the tables, everywhere. But that wasn't the worst of it. Pieces of wire and some brown matter that looked like long curls of sawdust were scattered from one end of the great hall to the front door. What on earth did the Victorians use for stuffing? As I watched, iridescent feathers drifted past my head and wafted to the floor. I weighed my chances of getting the mess cleaned up before Conklin saw it. Not good, I decided.

It was a nightmare, nothing less. Conklin glided into my line of vision, twirling a feather between thumb and index finger. The dark eye on the top of the feather betrayed its origin. He looked around in puzzlement, shaking his head and mumbling. I froze for a moment, and then backed slowly up one stair at a time. I hadn't gone very far when he looked up, and our eyes locked.

I toyed with the idea of denying any knowledge of the mess in the hall, but since I was still holding the remains of the fish net, I knew that wouldn't work. I stepped down the staircase. I would have to face this catastrophe like a woman and the mistress of the house. I was not, after all, a child to be chastised for breaking a knickknack.

However, standing face to face with Conklin, I was a bit worried about his set expression and rigid stance.

"Quite a mess, eh, Conklin." My feeble attempt at jollying him. "Who would have thought that one peacock could contain all this…this…whatever it is. What is this stuff, anyway, Conklin? It looks like desiccated snakes."

"Excelsior, Madam. They used a wire armature and excelsior a hundred years ago in the art of taxidermy."

"Well, they sure used a lot of it. Don't worry, Conklin, I'll clean this up. You sit down and relax. It won't take me a minute."

His eyes swept the length of the hall, then fixed on the remains of the net in my hand. With a depth of bitterness that surprised me, he said, "Madam, you have managed to destroy two antiques at one fell swoop."

To this day I don't know what a fell swoop is, but I got the picture. "Antiques? Are you telling me this ratty net and that stuffed peacock are antiques?"

"What you are holding, Madam, is the remnant of a net that is at least one hundred years old. You may have noticed it was displayed with a few antique fishing rods and other sports paraphernalia. The peacock dates back even further. It was here when your great-grandfather bought this house from the Hammersleigh family. It has sat there above the landing all these years. And now, look."

His sad gaze encompassed the hall. Out of the corner of my eye, I saw Jacqueline crawling across the floor on her belly. Before I could open my mouth, she snatched up the head of the peacock, which was the only body part to survive intact, and ran into the drawing room.

I only just stopped myself from screaming at her and giving chase, but I didn't want to upset Conklin any further. A peacock's head wasn't all that easy to hide. I expected I could find it later. I turned back to Conklin.

He was stooping over a pile—one of the many piles—of debris. When he straightened, knees creaking audibly, he was holding something in his palm. He held it out to me and I saw a delicate porcelain arm and part of a shoulder. I looked up at Conklin.

"What is it?"

He bent down again, every joint cracking and popping, and rummaged among the feathers and excelsior. After a few minutes, he stood up and showed me a tiny head and another hand.

"I'm not sure, Madam. I believe this may be the Meissen shepherdess that was believed taken from the house the night young Tommy disappeared. It was an eighteenth-century figurine and stood on that sideboard over there. One of the cleaning staff conveyed this information to me many years ago."

"I didn't know something was stolen that night. But if this is it, it never was taken. It's been here all along. Just like Tommy. Quite a coincidence, it showing up now."

We looked at each other.

"Perhaps you wouldn't mind informing Chief Allaire about this, Madam?" Conklin had too much class to make further reference to a fell swoop, but I felt awful about the valuable figurine, smashed in dozens of pieces. Three antiques. Nice going, Lyris.

"Why don't you lie down and rest, Conklin? I'll clean up in here and make dinner. Even though it's not my turn." I felt virtuous in making the offer.

"Thank you, Madam. However, if you recall, I am preparing baked beans tonight. Perhaps you could trouble yourself to find Jacqueline and retrieve the head before she buries it in the furniture?"

I thought I was showing sufficient remorse for destroying the peacock and the net, both just junk as far as I was concerned. I didn't care if Queen Victoria fed one and fished with the other. And God knows I did feel wretched about the shepherdess.

The doorbell rang.

"I will allow you to answer that, Madam," Conklin said before turning away.

"Why don't I just tie this broom to my ass and sweep the hall while I'm at it?" I muttered under my breath.

"No need, Madam, I'll fetch the vacuum cleaner for you." He had ears like a bat, a vampire bat.

Jacqueline had returned to the hall, grasping her prize in her mouth. When the bell pealed again, she dropped the head and started to bark.

"Shut up!" I made a futile grab at her.

Conklin stiffened, then continued to march toward the back of the house without another word, hard as that may be to believe.

I made another move toward Jacqueline, but she dashed past me, head in mouth once more, and I lost her. The bell sounded a third time and I threw the door open.

A young woman was standing there and something she saw in my face seemed to startle her. She stepped back and looked around, no doubt to gauge if she could make it to the front gates before she was caught.

I made a conscious effort to smile and extended my hand.

"You must be Caroline Fournier. Come right in, won't you? I'm Lyris Pembrooke."

She shook hands, just a slight brushing of my fingers. I rearranged my face the best I could and ushered her through the hall, both of us wading through the mess.

Her bewildered expression called for reassurance.

"Just a slight accident. Nothing to worry about. This place is very neat, most days."

I sat Caroline down in a sofa upholstered in yellow velvet and took the cream brocade-covered rosewood side chair opposite her. Since the seat was at least an inch higher than the sofa, I felt I had a psychological advantage in case I needed it. While she settled herself and looked around the drawing room, I studied her.

She was attractive, in a rather washed-out way. With a little makeup, Caroline could be quite pretty. But she had made no attempt to show herself to her best advantage, perhaps feeling that an interview for a housekeeper position warranted a plain appearance.

Her pale brown hair was short and clung to her skull, and her eyes were a light grey, perhaps hazel in another light. I judged her age to be mid to late twenties, young for the responsibilities she would face as housekeeper to Hammersleigh House.

"Caroline, let me begin by telling you something of Hammersleigh and the duties you would be expected to perform. Then, if you're interested in the job, you can tell me about yourself, qualifications, training and so on."

"That would be fine, Mrs. Pembrooke. This is such a beautiful house. I would be honoured to work here if I was hired."

She had a soft, hesitant voice, and I had to strain to catch all she said.

"Well, this *is* a beautiful house, Caroline, but it's also a spacious estate. The grounds are cared for by gardeners who come in on contract when needed. All the plants in the house receive loving attention from a retired gentleman once a week. Four cleaning ladies also come weekly, on Fridays, to dust, vacuum, mop floors, all the usual things. They also clean the Waterford chandelier in the hall, the stained glass fanlight, the Venetian mirrors and the other larger items according to a schedule. All the collectibles, the contents of the cabinets—and there are a great many cabinets throughout the rooms in this house—are the responsibility of the housekeeper. I believe Conklin has an inventory list of everything. He can probably come up with a schedule for the housekeeper's cleaning duties, too. And by the way, it's *Ms.* Pembrooke."

"And Conklin is…?"

I took a deep breath. "Conklin is the butler. I'll introduce you to him later."

She looked surprised, as well she might. I didn't know anyone else in the western hemisphere who had a living butler, and we shall not see his like again.

"What else does the housekeeper do, Ms. Pembrooke?"

"Ah, well, many things." I was floundering. I found I had no real understanding of what a housekeeper did. Except for the things I was sick of doing. I should start there.

"The housekeeper does the cooking. That may not be usual, but here at Hammersleigh the housekeeper has always done the cooking. Just plain food, nothing fancy." I was firm about cooking.

"That would be no problem for me. I love to cook, and I think I'm quite good at it."

I breathed a sigh of relief and combed my brain for further duties. There, in that cool, dim room, I was beginning to sweat.

My glance happened to fall on the slim-legged table placed beside the sofa. A handsome Boston fern rested on the marble top. It radiated health, thanks to the plant man. Underneath the table reposed a stringy, off-white lump.

I made a quick dive across the floor and grabbed the object in both hands. She growled, but refused to release the peacock's head. The head was beginning to look the worse for wear and it made Caroline recoil when I plunked Jacqueline down beside her. Jacqueline looked a little surprised to find herself on the sofa, placed there by the person who always ordered her to get off the furniture, dammit.

"What is it?" Caroline asked, and moved a few inches to put more distance between her body and the squashy object.

"It's just the head from a peacock. You saw the slight disorder in the hall? A stuffed peacock fell off a shelf and disintegrated. It wasn't new." Another of my mottos: *Never Apologize, and Keep Explanations to a Minimum.*

"No, I mean, what is that?" She pointed at the tangle of dingy fur chewing noisily and wetly on the head.

Jacqueline looked up at her with indignation written all over her hairy face. I shared the sentiment. "That? That's Jacqueline, the housekeeper's dog."

CHAPTER 7

"A dog? What kind of dog?"

"It's a poodle." I looked at the item in question. "She's missed her last two grooming appointments. That's why she looks a bit…untidy."

That was an understatement. There's nothing quite as slatternly as a poodle that's let herself go.

"And you say she's the housekeeper's pet?"

"Well, let me put it this way, Jacqueline is the *responsibility* of the housekeeper. She belonged to my Uncle Patrick, but his former housekeeper was devoted to her and looked after all her needs. I hope that isn't a problem?" There had to be a touch of hellfire in my distant future.

"Oh, no. No. She's quite cute. Once her fur is washed and trimmed, I'm sure she'll look fine." Caroline looked far from convinced by her own words, but I decided not to notice.

Jacqueline dropped her treasure and leaned over to rest her head in Caroline's lap. She looked up and batted her eyelashes. It would have been more effective had the matted hair not grown down over most of her face, but Caroline seemed marginally charmed by this display anyhow. I was grateful Jacqueline had been too preoccupied with the peacock's head to bite Caroline at first sight, and now she knew who was going to be doling out her kibble.

Caroline rubbed Jacqueline's fur with a circular motion, the dog's favourite kind of attention. I relaxed. A major hurdle had been cleared.

"Caroline, how about telling me about yourself now. For instance, why did you apply for this job? It isn't a common career for someone your age."

"Oh, but I studied domestic science at university. And I took a cooking course too. As a matter of fact, I was all set to go to France to study at a well-known cooking school, but I got married instead."

"Tell me about that. I don't want to pry, but this is a live-in position and requires a single person. I understand from John Brixton that your marriage has broken up."

Caroline did not respond to my unspoken query. She was looking down at her printed cotton skirt, pleating the material with her fingers.

"What I mean is, if there's any chance of reconciliation, perhaps you should not be looking at a live-in job."

She said quietly, "I will not be reconciling with my husband. I am applying for this job because I want to make a fresh start and look after myself. I have a copy here of my resume. It lists my education and pertinent training as well as some personal references. Perhaps I could leave them with you? You might want to know that I grew up in my grandmother's house. Although not quite as fine as Hammersleigh, it contains many antiques and collectibles, so I know how to care for valuable pieces."

I had been glancing through her resume as she was speaking. I made up my mind. After all, she was not a complete stranger—she was a distant connection of my mother's. "If you want the job, Caroline, it's yours. But if you want to think about it for a day or two, I understand. And we should talk about your salary."

"I don't need to think about it, Ms. Pembrooke. I'll take the job. And Mr. Brixton explained about the trust and we discussed the salary. When do you want me to start?"

"As soon as you like."

"Tomorrow?"

This was my lucky day. "We'll see you tomorrow then. I'll get a room ready for you."

The pleats fell out of Caroline's skirt as she stood up. "Thank you very much, Ms. Pembrooke. I appreciate this opportunity and I'll try to do a thorough job."

"I'm sure you will, Caroline. And please, call me Lyris. Ms. Pembrooke is too formal."

"Thank you, Lyris. And what do I call the butler?"

That stopped me. "Well, I don't quite know. Mrs. Beadle, the former housekeeper, called him Arthur. I call him Conklin. Perhaps you could ask him. I'll introduce you now. I'm sure he can tell you more details of your duties too."

The doorbell rang as Caroline followed me into the hall. There was no sign of Conklin and presuming he was still pouting in the kitchen, I answered the ring myself. Standing outside was Peter Tackaberry, an eager smile lighting up his thin face, a heavy, ornate earring just brushing his neon-green T-shirt. I saw he was wearing pressed khaki shorts and clean sandals, and his dark-blond, shoulder-length hair was tied back in a neat ponytail. I was touched that he had dressed up to visit Hammersleigh.

He glanced at Caroline hovering behind me. "I'm sorry, Lyris. I know I'm early. I didn't have many customers today, so I closed the shop. Did I come at a bad time?"

"No, not at all. Come in. Caroline, this is Peter Tackaberry, a friend of mine. Peter, meet Caroline Fournier. She has just agreed to take the housekeeper's position."

"Lovely." Peter was looking at something over my shoulder and I turned around to see Conklin brandishing a wooden spoon.

"The beans are disarmed, Madam. What do I do next?"

Conklin's thick white hair was standing up in a tuft and he was wearing a bright blue bib apron. He looked so much like a Smurf, I had to stifle a smile.

He stopped dead when he saw my two visitors, but before I could introduce our new housekeeper to him, Peter spoke up. "Did you say beans, Mr. Conklin? I have a great recipe for beans. If you want, I can write it down for you."

Conklin stared at Peter for a moment. I held my breath and waited for the deep freeze to engulf us all. He threw a curve ball instead. "That would be very helpful—Mr. Tackaberry, isn't it? The kitchen is this way."

"Wait. Conklin, I would like you to meet Caroline Fournier. She's our new housekeeper and she's starting tomorrow."

"How do you do, Miss Fournier? I look forward to working with you, but if you'll excuse me now, my beans await in the kitchen and I fear they are at a critical stage." After a courtly bow in Caroline's direction, he disappeared into the kitchen wing with Peter. Peter did not react to the debris on the floor.

Well, that went not too badly. I felt Conklin would be his usual courteous self with Caroline.

"We'll tell him tomorrow that you're married, not a Miss, although he might call you Caroline." Maybe he would; maybe he wouldn't.

"Come tomorrow whenever you're ready. I'm having a few people over for dinner tomorrow night and I'll do the cooking myself. You'll need a little time to get acquainted with the house before you start your duties."

"Oh, no, Lyris. Please let me cook for your dinner party. As long as I know where everything is in the kitchen, I'm sure I'll have no trouble. I'll be here at eight in the morning."

"Great." I managed a smile. I had been hoping to sleep late on my first day of vacation. "And it isn't a dinner party. It's nothing that formal. Just my son, his girlfriend, and a few other people. I've already bought the food."

Caroline stopped at the foot of the staircase and looked down. "Did the wildebeest head fall off the wall as well?"

"Sort of, and it's an antelope."

After I closed the door on her I thought with satisfaction that tonight was the last time I would have to eat Conklin's cooking. Despite Peter's recipe, my hopes were not high for that pot of beans, and my stomach rumbled in distress. I looked around the hall and sighed.

I swept all the bits of debris into one pile—a pile much higher than the peacock from whence it came—then sorted through it to pick out all the porcelain pieces. These I set aside before shovelling everything else into three garbage bags, which I dropped outside the kitchen door. Peter and Conklin had their heads together over a casserole dish and an assortment of spice bottles. They paid no attention as I dragged the bulging garbage bags through the kitchen.

After searching through various closets and alcoves in the kitchen wing, I located the vacuum cleaner and managed to eliminate all traces of the accident. Except for more pitiful pieces of the figurine that I placed on the sideboard. I thought it prudent to save them for Marc, so he wouldn't think I was withholding evidence, although I could imagine what would run through his mind when he looked at the dozens of tiny fragments.

Ravenous as a caged lion at feeding time, and prepared to eat anything, I wandered back to the kitchen to see how dinner was coming. I was surprised to see Peter setting three places at the table. I looked at

Conklin, but he was reaching into the oven with mitts on his hands. The air was redolent with spices and cooked tomato.

"Dinner is served, Madam." Conklin turned and held out the casserole dish, the source of the heavenly smells. "Mr. Tackaberry has agreed to dine with us. I hope that meets with your approval."

"Certainly. Delighted."

Not only did we have baked beans for dinner, but one of them had whipped up a huge salad—glory be, I hadn't had anything green to eat in days—and an entire loaf of garlic bread. My money was on Peter as the creator of this bounty, but while we ate, he kept telling Conklin how wonderful the food was, as if Conklin had done it all himself. Conklin sat there and beamed—when he wasn't scooping food into his mouth—and I was so bemused I almost forgot to eat. This must have been the way Dorothy felt when she woke up in Oz, disoriented and a bit dizzy with the strangeness of it all.

I would have bet anything that Conklin would never allow Peter into the kitchen, never mind let him help cook. And to invite Peter to dinner. A dignified butler extraordinaire and a gay hand-to-mouth antique dealer who moonlighted as a painter and paper hanger? While Peter and Conklin bustled about cleaning up the kitchen, I watched the two of them, trying to figure out what Conklin's game was and how it was going to affect me.

True, they seemed to talk the same language—they discussed antiques, Conklin's war experiences and Peter's plans to create an English wildflower garden in his back yard. Conklin advised Peter on the hardier types of English plants that might survive our harsh winters. And how would he even know, since to my knowledge, Conklin had never set foot in England? Unless he spent time there during the war, when I doubt he would have had time to learn the names and habits of English flora. And Peter took notes, if you can believe it.

I hate it when people act out of character, since it suggests I was wrong about them in the first place. Could Conklin be more human than I gave him credit for? Or was he more devious? I pushed myself away from the table.

"Conklin, would you mind getting me the key for the doll cabinet? I want to show the dolls to Peter after he looks at my room." It was difficult to pry a key out of Conklin, and I was gratified that he did not hesitate this time. Gratified, but suspicious.

"Of course, Madam. I'll fetch it for you immediately." He went through his ritual of removing the key from his belt and taking himself off to the butler's pantry. There, I knew, he would unlock a drawer which contained more keys, organized and labelled by room and cabinet. In the drawer beneath was a complete inventory of each cabinet, including the value of every item at the last insurance appraisal.

After he handed me the key, I had to drag Peter out of the kitchen. He wanted to linger and continue discussing plants with Conklin.

I was afraid Conklin might accompany us upstairs like he did when I wanted to show Marc my room, but he seemed to know Peter was no threat to my virtue. And that was another thing—all the world knew that Uncle Patrick had shared his sheets with Mrs. Beadle on occasion, but I couldn't see Conklin following them around to prevent the dastardly deed being done. So why was he appointing himself the guardian of my virtue?

"Do you want me to do something with this wildebeest, Lyris? Carry it to the attic maybe?"

"No, just leave the *antelope* there for now, Peter. I'll deal with it later." And I still didn't know where to find the attic.

When we reached the upper hall, I was hoping Peter wouldn't ask to see the tower room, and he didn't. We entered my bedroom, where he went into raptures over the cherubs. "Cunning little imps, aren't they? I can see why you want this room, but I agree the furnishings are overbearing. Can we look into some of the other bedrooms and see what we have to choose from?"

We spent a pleasant hour foraging through the other five bedrooms, bickering amicably over which furniture would be the best choice. We decided on a Queen Anne suite, a style much more restrained than the others.

"Although it's reproduction," advised Peter. "Queen Anne died in 1714, and this stuff is more like 150 years old, not 275."

"Fake is fine with me. At least it won't give me nightmares."

"It's not *fake*," Peter said, outraged. "It's genuine Victorian reproduction. Very valuable."

"The subtlety escapes me. And now that we have settled the furniture question, what about the rest of the room? Walls and curtains."

"I have some sample books of Victorian wallpaper and fabrics at the shop. I'll bring them over and we'll decide on a colour scheme. First, though, I could bring some guys over and move the furniture. Tomorrow, if you like."

"Perfect." Tomorrow was shaping up to be a busy day. A few minutes later, we were standing in front of the doll cabinet.

Ten feet wide by eight feet high, the cabinet was filled with dolls of a bygone era.

"What a marvellous collection." Peter stepped closer as I turned the key to open the cabinet door.

"All these dolls belonged to Aunt Deborah, Uncle Patrick's wife. Most were given to her as a child although some, the earliest ones, were passed to her by her mother and grandmother."

Peter touched the dress of a doll that resembled his own Samantha. "This is a Simon and Halbig head, but I can't tell if the body is by Kamner and Reinhardt, not without examining her up close. Simon & Halbig manufactured their own bodies too, of course."

I indicated a doll about fifteen inches tall with dark bobbed hair and brown eyes. "This might be a Schoenhut. Look at the holes in the bottom of the feet. Schoenhut often did this so the doll would fit onto a metal stand."

"I think you're right," said Peter. "The inventory sheets will have them all indexed, but it's fun to guess."

He worked his way along the shelves, exclaiming every time he recognized a doll's make. I am not ignorant about antique dolls myself, but Peter's knowledge far surpassed mine as he identified a Kestner, a Jules Steiner, two Handwercks and an Armand Marseille. He got excited about a trio of French fashion dolls, whose costumes were perfect replicas of the fashions of the time.

There were many dolls neither of us could identify and we would have to resort to the insurance inventory lists to be sure. There was one special doll I was pretty sure was a long-faced Jumeau. She was about two and a half feet tall with long, chestnut ringlets and dark blue eyes. Her wistful expression went straight to my heart. I lifted her out of the cabinet and straightened the flounces on her faded rose dress.

"This is Amelia. When I learned I was in Uncle Patrick's will, I hoped he remembered how much I loved Amelia and left her to me."

"I imagine you were a little overwhelmed when you got the whole enchilada, not just the doll."

"You have no idea." Handing Amelia to Peter, I rearranged the dolls so her absence would not be noticeable, then locked up the cabinet.

Still gazing at the dolls, Peter said, "This collection is worth a fortune. Some of these dolls are extremely rare, and all are mint examples of their type."

"The whole house is full of collections. Most are locked up, with some odds and ends just sitting around on tables and shelves. I'm afraid I'll knock something over and break it." I didn't mention the Meissen shepherdess since that was totally not my fault.

I took the doll back from Peter. "There's no reason why Amelia should sit on that shelf for another hundred years. I'm going to keep her in my room."

I ushered Peter out and ran upstairs to deposit Amelia on one of the window seats in my bedroom before returning the key to Conklin. I was sure I would never have to explain to him why the doll was not in her accustomed place but in my bedroom. Conklin would never enter my private place, not even to save me if my bed was on fire and I was in it.

CHAPTER 8

I was up with the damn birds again the next morning and found Conklin already at the kitchen table with his bran cereal and tea. He wore his daytime butler attire of dark grey-striped pants and black jacket over a stiff-looking white shirt. And a bow tie, just in case the Queen stopped by.

I made myself a cup of liquorice root tea—good for the liver and general internal cleansing—and sat opposite him. "Conklin, where did Mrs. Beadle sleep? I have to get a room ready for Caroline. She'll be here any minute." I liked to plan ahead.

Since Uncle Patrick and Mrs. Beadle had been so...uh, close, I figured he gave her one of the upstairs bedrooms to keep her handy and Caroline might as well have the same room. It would be good to have another living body upstairs with me at night.

Conklin got up without a word and opened a door I hadn't noticed before. Assuming for no particular reason he wanted me to follow, I was right behind him as he glided down a corridor.

He opened the first door. "These are my quarters, Madam."

I didn't want to appear nosy, but one quick glance was enough to note an expansive, comfortable room that included a double bed covered by a navy and taupe spread, window coverings in matching fabric, and off-white walls. A dark blue recliner sat before a flat screen television, which no doubt was tuned to the hockey game on Saturday nights. If I had to guess, I'd say Conklin was a Leafs fan. That's all I saw before he closed the door on the hum of an air conditioner.

"These next two rooms are bedrooms also, Madam. However, they are unfurnished at the moment. Across the hall, as you can see, is the sitting area."

I stepped into a bright, airy space filled with plump sofas and ergonomically correct easy chairs surrounding a television even flatter and wider than Conklin's.

Bookcases lined the walls, while a microwave and miniature refrigerator were tucked into one corner. It was blessedly cool, thanks to another air-conditioning unit.

I was tempted to linger a while, put my feet up and maybe watch a little television, perhaps make myself another cup of tea with the electric kettle sitting on the counter by the spotless sink. But duty called.

Conklin was already back in the hall and when I caught up to him, he was standing by a door at the end of the hallway.

"This was Mrs. Beadle's room, Madam. I took the liberty of turning on the air conditioner earlier this morning."

It was comforting to know Conklin and Caroline would not be sweltering in their quarters at night like…well, like me. The air-conditioning units in this wing alone would keep one unit busy at the nearby Bruce Power nuclear plant.

"I think Miss Fournier will be comfortable here, Madam."

"Conklin, Queen Elizabeth would be comfortable in this room."

The suite was even more expansive than Conklin's and it would be strange indeed if Caroline could not be happy in these surroundings. Here there was no television to mar the pastel femininity of the taupe walls and the peach and celadon-green floral of the bedspread and curtains. The carpet was a lighter shade of taupe than the walls and extended through to the ensuite bathroom.

"It's wonderful, Conklin. Caroline will love it. Oh, and before I forget, she's a Mrs., not a Miss."

"I'll remember that, Madam. Shall we return to the main house now? By the way, there is also another bathroom here." He touched the knob. I was glad he didn't open it. I don't know if I could contain my joy if the bathroom had a hot tub or whirlpool bath. Or more air conditioning.

"And this, Madam, is the exit door. It is a requirement of the fire code." He pushed the bar and the door opened to a garden area surrounded by pines. Instantly, we were engulfed in hot, humid air that took my breath away after the temperature of the staff wing. Conklin closed the door, and another minute later we were both back in the kitchen, which moments ago had seemed so cool and inviting.

I stood there making a mental inventory of what I had just seen—four bedrooms, a sitting room with kitchen amenities, one full bathroom and at least one ensuite. I hadn't even known that wing existed until now. And there was still the third floor attic area to be explored. Again, the enormity of what I had taken on threatened to overwhelm me.

The doorbell rang. From out of nowhere Conklin appeared at my elbow and Jacqueline at my ankle. Conklin managed to get hold of the doorknob ahead of me, so it was a proper butler dressed to kill and a yapping dog who greeted the new housekeeper on that sweltering July morning. I hoped the bewildered look on Caroline's face was not going to prove permanent. She would have to get used to our strange household and become part of it, and the sooner the better.

There was a man standing behind her holding a suitcase in each hand.

Before I could open my mouth, Conklin butted in. "Welcome to Hammersleigh House, Mrs. Fournier. I hope you will be most happy here. I'm sure we will work well together. Now, have you more luggage I can help you with?"

"Thank you, Mr. Conklin. My belongings are in the car. I wasn't sure where I was to park."

She caught sight of me behind Conklin as I wrested the knob away from him and threw the door wide open. I elbowed Conklin aside. "There's a parking area around the side of the house. Just follow the bricked driveway. There's a door at the back, close to your suite. You can take your things in that way." I hoped those were the right directions and she didn't end up on Lychwood's front lawn.

I looked at the man. Caroline didn't turn in his direction. "Oh, this is my...this is Scott Fournier, my...husband."

The young man put the suitcases down and stepped forward. He held out his hand and smiled. "I'm very pleased to meet you, Ms. Pembrooke. Caroline is very lucky to have the chance to work in this wonderful place. Thank you for giving her the chance."

I pulled my hand away and looked him over. "Well, Scott, Conklin and I think we're lucky that Caroline has decided to work with us. She appears well qualified and I hope she finds Hammersleigh House interesting and fulfilling."

Scott was in his late twenties or early thirties, with short, curly, fair hair, and his eyes were a bright blue behind gold-rimmed glasses. He was an attractive young man, confident and charming, smelling of a clean, citrusy aftershave. I wondered what he was doing here with Caroline. Yesterday she seemed positive that her marriage was over, but I suspected her husband did not share her conviction.

The rest of her luggage may have been in the car, but Caroline was carrying a case by a handle at the top. It had a barred door and looked a lot like a pet carrier.

Caroline saw the direction of my gaze and clutched the carrier to her side. She lowered her eyes and blushed. "I hope you don't mind...I mean, I hope it's okay..." She glanced up at my face, then quickly back down again.

"I didn't mention it yesterday because...I mean..."

"What's in the box, Caroline?"

"My cat, Rasputin. I've had him for three years, and my grandmother was going to keep him, but now she's going to the cottage with my aunt for the rest of the summer and can't keep Raspy because my aunt has a dog and Pierre, that's the dog's name, dislikes cats..."

We were going to be there all day. "We have a dog here, too, Caroline." I looked at Jacqueline who had not stopped barking since the doorbell rang. My foot twitched.

"Pierre is a real dog. I mean, not a miniature dog."

I didn't know what to say. I looked at Conklin for inspiration and intercepted a fleeting expression of uncertainty in his own features before he arranged them into the usual austere mask.

Scott weighed in, though nobody asked. "I knew she shouldn't bring the cat. I'd be glad to keep him."

Caroline's face was paler than yesterday. I threw in the towel. "Is Rasputin litter trained?"

A nod.

"You will keep him in your own wing?"

Nod.

"He doesn't hunt birds, does he?"

Shake. "He would never hurt a bird, would you Raspy darling?"

No answer from the cat. "Well, let's try it then." After all, it was just a cat. I figured I could count on Jacqueline to keep Raspy darling under control.

With Caroline, her husband and Conklin all out of the way unloading her car at the back of the house, there was no one around to prevent me from answering the doorbell when it rang again a few minutes later.

Peter and two body-builder types stood on the threshold. Peter wore an eager smile and an immaculate purple T-shirt. His friends—both with freshly shaved heads, one with a moustache, one without—wore brief, tight shorts and no smiles whatsoever. One was fair with a peeling, sunburnt nose, and one swarthy with no tan line where his shorts hung low on his hips. Not twins would be my guess.

Peter introduced us. "This is Gordon, and this is Roddie."

We all nodded.

"We'll go right up, Lyris, if you don't mind. It should take us about an hour, then Gordon and Roddie have a job moving a household this afternoon. Any changes to what we discussed yesterday?"

There were not, so the trio trooped upstairs, Peter's thin legs leading the way, the burly thighs and calves of the other two following after.

Peter was a very organized person, I realized, as was Conklin. Now if Caroline turned out to be so as well, then it shouldn't matter that I wasn't.

I was further assured when I showed Caroline around the ground level of the house, finishing with the kitchen where we discussed tonight's dinner menu. She seemed to feel right at home in Hammersleigh's state-of-the-art kitchen and was confident she could prepare a meal for eight with the supplies I had bought. And there was no sign of the cat or the charming husband. I was satisfied.

When asked if her suite was adequate, she was adamant that she adored the bedroom, the sitting room, this kitchen and everything else about the house.

But her eyes were apprehensive as she explained why her husband had accompanied her that morning. "I'm sorry, Lyris. Scott insisted he wanted to come with me to make sure I was going to be all right. I've told him it's all over and I will look after myself from now on, but I can't seem to get through to him. I guess it will take time before he realizes our marriage is over. But I'm sorry he came with me. I made it clear he wasn't to come here again."

I put my hand on her arm to stop the flow of words. "Stop worrying about it. You're making a new start here at Hammersleigh, and you can begin by not apologizing for your former husband."

Since everything seemed to be rolling along without me, I found myself with nothing to do. It couldn't be. There must be something.

There was. The reunion.

Exactly six and a half days from that moment, the first campers and trailers would be rolling up in the field beside Hammersleigh House. All those people would be wanting…things. Where was the list Conklin had given me?

I left Caroline in the kitchen and went to look for it. It took me a half hour to find the list in the outside flap of my purse. By this time Peter and his pals were ready to leave. I gave Gordon and Roddie fifty dollars each, thanked them for their help, and waved the three of them off from the front steps. Peter promised to be back within the next few days with wallpaper and fabric samples.

I peeked into the kitchen to see if Caroline had everything she needed. If she didn't, she wouldn't find me much help. But she was moving bowls and pots around, looking less anxious than I had yet seen her. She seemed in control. Conklin had shown her where the table linens were, as well as the china and silver. Everything would be ready at seven.

I left feeling that my simple supper was turning out more formal than I had intended, but Caroline was cheerful and on a roll, and I hadn't the heart to derail her by reminding her I had been planning a casual meal for close friends and family.

I saw no sign of Conklin anywhere. Or Jacqueline for that matter. Or a cat. I wandered into the drawing room and dropped onto a velvet sofa.

Okay. The list. As the list unfolded, I straightened up. There were over a dozen items on the list. And I had to do all of it? Thank God it was Saturday and none of these places were open. I put the list aside until Monday.

I lay back on the sofa and closed my eyes. Almost seventy years ago a terrible tragedy had taken place in this house. Maybe it was murder, maybe not. Hiding the child's body could have been an act of fear and desperation, and this did not preclude accident rather than murder.

My first step should be to find out who was staying in the house during that reunion weekend. Marc would have all that in the police reports and lots more besides. But I doubted he'd let me see them. He might part with some clinical police facts, but it would be best to talk to somebody who had been on the spot.

Despite her promise to think about it, my mother would have been too young to remember details. But there must be dozens of older people who were here in 1943 and would be again next weekend. The Pembrookes were notoriously long-lived, most reaching their nineties before kicking and screaming their way into the arms of their ancestors.

Okay, I had a plan of sorts. Talk to Marc that night after dinner and find out what he knew and was willing to part with. I would have to tell him about the figurine of course, and we needed to discuss that. Something didn't feel right about the figurine.

Then, see Aunt Clem the next day, Sunday. And while I wasn't keen on visiting Lychwood, Aunt Wisty might be lucid enough to remember something. But first, the public library. They must have an archive where records were stored, microfilm of newspapers if nothing else. I could do that right away.

I was just dozing off for a much-needed rest when I felt I was being watched. And there was a crawling sensation on my skin. My eyes snapped open to behold a wizened troll staring at me from a few feet away.

"Yeek." That was the troll. He jumped back and scuttled toward the great hall, dripping water from a giant watering can every step of the way.

Now that I was wide awake, I saw that the watering can was regulation size. And the troll was merely a short, wizened man heading for the hall in alarm.

"Stop. Wait." My legs were longer and I had almost overtaken him when Conklin stepped between us and held up his hand to stop me.

"Madam. Please. May I introduce Malcolm O'Reilly." The little man peered out from behind Conklin. "Malcolm waters the house plants here several times a week. I'm afraid you frightened him."

"Well, I'm sorry. I forgot today was watering day. Sorry, Malcolm. I'm very pleased to meet you."

Malcolm shook his head, and with a reproachful look at Conklin, skittered away, leaving Conklin and me standing in a puddle of water.

Conklin cast a reproachful look of his own in my direction. "Malcolm is frightened of women, Madam."

"I said I was sorry. Why do we need somebody to water the plants anyway?" It sounded like a housekeeper task to me.

"There are over eighty house plants, Madam. Your uncle was pleased to assist a fellow veteran and Malcolm has been performing this duty for the past fifty years and more. He depends on the stipend he receives to supplement his pension."

"So Malcolm was in the army with Uncle Patrick? Then he was around during the 1943 reunion."

Conklin soon squelched that idea. "Not at all, Madam. Your uncle and Malcolm did not serve together. Malcolm sustained a serious head injury in combat and your uncle took him on out of kindness when he came to the door seeking employment some years after the war's end. I was already here by that time. Malcolm is very shy around people, and terrified of women."

He went off to the kitchen again, and I had just flopped back onto the sofa when the doorbell rang.

I shouted, "I'll get it." But it was too late. Conklin was at the door by the time I reached the hall. How he did it, I'll never know. He handed me a mop before pulling the door open.

The short, dark man on the doorstep was wearing an insolent grin and not much else. This was my day for naked men. Why do men think it's okay to take off their shirts when the thermometer soars? Never mind, that question will never be answered in our lifetime.

I handed the mop back to Conklin. "Come on in, Angelo. My computer stuff is upstairs. I'll show you where I want it set up." I had forgotten that Angelo was coming over today to run network cable and whatever else is necessary to get me online. I was a little concerned that it might be difficult to do this, given the age of Hammersleigh House, but Angelo pointed out that Hammersleigh was already set up with electronic access and other security measures, and he was sure he could hook up a simple computer.

Since Angelo Bertollini was our systems analyst at the Hydro Commission and a wizard at his work, I had asked him to moonlight for me.

Peter and his crew had done a good job in moving in and rearranging the Queen Anne furniture. Already the room looked brighter and more comfortable. I showed Angelo the nook and the workstation where I wanted the equipment.

At one time having Angelo in my bedroom might have presented a problem, but since Marc and I became friends, Angelo had desisted from making his flowery overtures. A year or two ago, Marc had caught him growing a marijuana plant in his kitchen, so Angelo was now respectful of the law. Sometimes having the chief of police for a boyfriend came in handy.

He looked around the spacious room. "I'll bet this place has seen a lot of action over the years." His eyes rested on the bed, but before he could make some other comment, I left him to it and went back downstairs.

Uncle Patrick's determination to keep Hammersleigh free of any obvious signs of the twentieth or twenty-first centuries resulted in a few inconveniences, such as having to search long and hard for a telephone. I could never remember to bring my cell phone in from the car.

There were two phones in the house that I knew about. Neither of them was upstairs. One was in the kitchen with an answering machine, call waiting, call display, call back and every other modern convenience. The kitchen was exempt from Uncle Patrick's obsession.

The other phone resided in a cubicle under the stairs. The size of a closet, the room contained a non-functioning antique wall–mounted telephone, an armchair and a roll-top desk. In one of the desk drawers reposed a serviceable beige phone.

I dialled Patsy's number. That's right, I said dialled. Don't try calling long distance—the day after I moved in, while dialling a Toronto area code, I reached Dubai, where someone wanted to sell me a hotel. Or a camel.

"Patsy, are you busy?"

"I might be. Why?"

"Meet me at the library after lunch?"

"Why?"

"I thought we could go through the newspapers and see what we can find out about Tommy's disappearance."

"What's this 'we' business? I already advised you loud and clear I wanted no part of that poor child's misfortune. I'll help you with the reunion, but not some investigation you've dreamed up to entertain yourself. Let the past alone."

"You sure are grumpy, Patsy. I don't expect to find any answers after all this time. But I think it would be interesting to read about it."

"You're not getting any psychic vibes, are you?"

"How many times do I have to tell you I'm not psychic?"

"How long would we be? You're having us for dinner tonight, I hope you remember. Why aren't you busy cooking?"

"I don't have to cook anymore. I have a new housekeeper. Meet me at the library and I'll tell you all about her. It shouldn't take more than a half hour or so."

"Fine, then. One o'clock."

I placed the thingy back on the whatsit and went in search of lunch.

CHAPTER 9

Babs Hanlon, one of my mother's cousins who worked Saturdays at the library, was nose deep in a book.

"Hi, Babs. Where do you keep your archives?"

"Archives, dear?" She tore her eyes from her paperback. It was one of those bodice-rippers, where the cover showed a man with long flowing hair clutching a woman with long flowing hair to his shirtless, hairless bosom. Personally, I was tired of looking at naked male bosoms.

"Yes, you know, records and newspapers, microfilm. Stuff like that."

"Microfilm, dear? I don't think we have any microfilm. But there are lots of newspapers on the top floor dating back to before the war."

"And how do we get there?"

"Well, you just take...Why, Lyris." Her blonde hair swayed. "I just heard Caroline is starting the housekeeper's position at Hammersleigh House."

"That's right, Babs. I guess you're related to Caroline, aren't you?"

"Certainly, dear." She patted the blonde bouffant back into an almost upright position. "Caroline is my sister's girl. Your mother's second cousin, you know."

"Upstairs, you say...?"

"What? Oh, the archives. Yes, just go past the...I know Caroline will do a good job, and Lord knows, the girl deserves a break. After that husband of hers..." Her voice trailed off just when it was getting interesting.

"Yes, her husband? I know they are separated."

"And a good thing too. The man was no good. No good at all. Why, the way he treated that poor girl was a disgrace. There should be a law against that sort of conduct."

There probably was, and I had to know more. "I'm not sure that I know Caroline's husband..."

"Scott Fournier, that's who. A good-looking young man, but evil hides behind a comely face."

"And Scott lives here in Blackshore?"

"Of course not. He lives in Northton, in the house he and Caroline bought together last year. I hear he wants her back, but Caroline is too smart to fall for that young man's lies any more. At Hammersleigh House she can get a fresh start. If anyone deserves it, she does. I'll be popping in to see her now and again, just to make sure she's doing well."

"Please come anytime. Now, about Scott, just what was it...?"

But Babs seemed to feel she had said enough. She gave us directions to the archives and returned to her romance novel. Patsy had been standing by my side throughout this exchange, dabbing at her damp forehead and silent as a mute swan for once. Not like her at all.

She followed me along the dark corridor that led to the stairs to the third floor. As soon as we were out of earshot of Babs and the two or three other book lovers who had been standing near the front desk, ears flapping and eyes avid with curiosity, I turned to Patsy. "What do you think Scott did to Caroline that was so terrible?"

"Don't know." She tore her collar open to let the steam escape. "I can't stand the heat anymore."

"Yeah, it is hot, but I bet I'll find out sooner rather than later. I have a pretty good idea anyway." I halted at the bottom of a steep flight of narrow stairs. There was no handrail. "Do you think these are the stairs Babs meant?"

"Must be, there isn't any other. My, these are steep, aren't they?"

It was impossible to walk upright. We crawled up on our hands and knees.

"Don't look down," I cautioned Patsy who was literally bringing up my rear.

The stairs opened into an attic space. We surveyed the Blackshore archives. I've been in saunas that were cooler, and no place that was less tidy. And that includes my son's bedroom during his "make my day" years.

There were rusting metal file cabinets, cardboard boxes and piles of newspapers everywhere. And nowhere did I see a table or a single chair. The heat was skin shrivelling. I looked at Patsy and watched the moisture drip from her upturned nose and run in rivulets down her round cheeks. Her hair was curled tightly again. I could feel my own hair doing the same thing.

"Look." She knocked me aside in her haste to get to the other side of the cluttered room. "Fans."

It took a minute or two to get the three fans blowing in directions that dried the sweat on our skin, but didn't send the loose papers flying ceiling ward.

"Do you think there's any order to this mess?" I didn't expect an answer. Only chaos reigned in this forgotten world.

"Doesn't look like it, but the newspapers might be stacked by year. You start there and I'll look in this corner first." Good old Patsy, her organizational tendencies surfaced despite herself.

"Well, try not to mix things up," I joked as moisture ran down my bare legs and made my feet squelch in my sandals. "We should have brought some water with us. We won't be able to stay here for long."

The stacks of newspapers *were* arranged by year, but not consecutively. The pile from 1965 was beside 1987, which was next to 1949. I finally found 1943, but not before stopping to read about the end of the Korean War in 1953 in which several Blackshore residents served, don't ask me why. I guessed they were either too young for World War II, or they were veterans of that great conflict and wanted to re-experience the excitement of dodging grenades and mortar shells.

I was disappointed in the coverage that Tommy's disappearance received. I quote the article in its entirety from the July 28, 1943, edition:

TRAGEDY STRIKES PEMBROOKE REUNION

The town of Blackshore shares the grief of the Pembrooke family as they mourn the disappearance of twenty-two month old Thomas Adam Pembrooke from Hammersleigh House during the Pembrooke Family Annual Reunion. The infant was found to be missing from his cot on the Sunday morning of the reunion weekend, and intensive searches conducted by family and volunteers throughout the house and grounds have turned up no trace.

It is believed that young Thomas may have wandered out of the house during the night and become lost in the wooded area adjacent to the lawns and grounds. Searches are continuing, but hopes of finding the child are waning after four days.

Police Chief Percival V. McPherson had no statement to give this reporter but did assert that the search parties would not give up until the child was found, whether dead or alive. Thomas is the son of Wisteria and Captain Thomas Pembrooke. Captain Pembrooke is serving with the First Canadian Infantry Division in Italy and is not yet aware of the family tragedy.

The next week's account was even briefer. There was one short paragraph stating that Thomas Adam Pembrooke, age twenty-two months, was still missing and the search had been discontinued. There was a chance he had been kidnapped. The week after that there was nothing. And there was no mention of the stolen Meissen figurine.

Patsy was still in her corner, thumbing through piles of yellowed paper with an uncharacteristic lack of enthusiasm. I read the two articles to her, but she didn't respond.

"Have you found anything there?"

"Nothing. These are just council meeting minutes from the 1960s." She raised a red and dripping face. "Let's go. I don't think we'll find anything more."

"Probably not, but you have to admit, this is kind of fun. I think I'll come back here some day when it's not so hot."

She gave me one of her eye rolls. "Come on. I'm dying."

"In a minute. I haven't looked in these filing cabinets yet." I pulled open the top drawer of the nearest cabinet and rummaged.

"No, seriously, Lyris, I have to get out of here. I've stopped sweating, which means I'm dehydrated and the next stage is death." She was exaggerating as usual. She hadn't stopped sweating at all.

"Look what I've found. Police reports. I wonder what they're doing here."

"Let me see." She shouldered me out of the way and pulled out the first file. "This is from 1951, so the rest of this cabinet should date after that. Look into that one and see if it's older."

It didn't work that way. The 1943 records were at the other end of the room near the solitary round window against which two blue bottles butted helplessly. I moved one of the fans closer.

The file we wanted was in the second drawer from the bottom, with "Pembrooke, Thomas" hand lettered in faded brown ink on the top. There were three pieces of paper in it.

A quick search verified that this was the only file on Tommy. Just one file with three pieces of paper. I pulled them out. All three were in the same handwriting and signed by Percival V. McPherson, the police chief. The writing was difficult to read, as faded and brown as that on the folder. There was little more information than appeared in the newspaper account.

Only two additional facts. The first was a list of the names of the people who had stayed in the house that weekend. *Captain Patrick Pembrooke, age 31; Lieutenant Bruce Wingate, age 29; Sergeant Clematis Pembrooke, age 21; and Mrs. Thomas Pembrooke, age 20, mother of the victim.* The other mentioned the theft of a valuable "Myson" figurine.

"Well, here's our suspect list, Patsy. Four of them."

That got her attention. "Suspects? You're doing it again, aren't you, Lyris? Trying to get me involved in some stupid scheme. Well, it won't work this time. I have enough on my mind without trying to figure out what happened well over sixty years ago. It was likely an accident, and sure, somebody hid the body. But that might have been out of fear of discovery. Can't you just for once leave well enough alone?"

She slammed the drawer shut and stomped off toward the stairs. I grabbed her by the arm and swung her around.

"Okay. What's wrong? It's not like you to get angry like this. Is it Nick? Or one of the boys?"

"No, it isn't anything." She wrenched away. I grabbed her again.

"I'm going to keep you here until you tell me why you're so upset. They'll find *our* mummified bodies in this attic fifty years from now."

Without warning, she slumped to the floor and started sobbing.

I didn't have anything to dry her with, so I wiped her face with the tail end of her cotton polo shirt. I let her carry on for a minute or two until she showed signs of slowing down.

"We've been friends for over thirty years, right?"

She nodded.

"Well, then, you know I'll do anything I can to help. If I can't, at least you'll feel better if you share it."

She took one long, shuddering breath and looked up at me. Her swollen, unhappy eyes made me want to wail, too.

"I'm losing my job. The three hospitals in Bruce County are amalgamating, and there is going to be one administrator. And it won't be me. The administrator at Northton Memorial has been given the job."

I was dumfounded. Patsy had worked at the Blackshore Hospital since graduation from Business College and had been administrator for the last five of those years.

"But won't they need assistant administrators?"

"One, and that isn't me either. I'm the most junior."

"So you're out of a job, just like that? Won't they try and find you another position?"

"There is nothing else for me. I sign a contract every year, and it's up the end of August."

"What does Nick say? Does he know yet?"

"He says not to worry, something will come up. And we can live just fine on his salary although that's not the point. What will I do after all these years? I've always worked, except for two maternity leaves."

What could I say to my best friend? Her news stunned me. Never would I have expected that she would lose her job. She was a wonderful administrator, had in fact won an award of excellence in her field two years in a row.

We bumped down the stairs on our behinds and parted at our cars in front of the library. I would see her again in a few hours and by that time I hoped I could find some words of comfort.

Back at Hammersleigh, I ran upstairs to my bedroom, almost too upset to notice the scent, again gone almost before it was there, or to feel the tingle between my shoulder blades.

After a cooling shower, I threw open the armoire where my clothes hung and surveyed the choices. Shorts were not appropriate. Long pants were too hot. I settled for a cotton sundress, red with minuscule white dots. It was too humid to contemplate a gold chain around my neck, and I decided that pearl studs were the only jewellery I could tolerate. I was pulling the dress over my head when I again had the feeling that I was being watched. This time, the hair on the nape of my neck stood on end.

I smoothed the dress in place and looked around. The trouble was, you could hide a whole army of trolls in that room. And there weren't any plants, for good reason. If a growing green thing wanted to live, it didn't live with me.

The door was not tightly closed. I must have neglected to shut it properly when I returned from the bathroom. As I watched, the door opened an inch or two wider, then another inch. I looked around the room for a weapon, but the closest item to hand was a four-inch makeup brush. Wonderful, I could fluff him to death.

Into the room lumbered the most evil-looking creature I had ever seen. It was black, with a huge head, and a tail about three feet long. The face looked pushed in, with copper eyes that blinked in my direction.

Did I mention how enormous it was? It must have weighed twenty-five pounds. Back away slowly and don't make eye contact. I shouldn't show fear.

Then reason prevailed. It was a cat, just a cat. It was Caroline's damn cat.

"Well, you must be Rasputin." My heart slowed to normal and the adrenaline stopped flowing. I felt weak and sank onto the bed.

A dusty off-white shadow slipped in behind the cat. For once she wasn't barking and acting like an idiot, and I knew why. "Jacqueline. You know you aren't supposed to be up here. Take your new friend back downstairs and stay there. And you, Rasputin, you may as well know from the start that I will not tolerate your presence in the main house. Please stick to the employees' wing or the outdoors. But you are not to hunt birds, squirrels or chipmunks either. If you do, you will be taken to the pound. Ask Jacqueline. She knows I mean it."

Both creatures turned and left without making a sound or even looking at me. I slammed the door behind them. Pets could be destructive and messy, and I couldn't take a chance with Hammersleigh's furniture or carpets. Everything in the house was an antique and valuable, except the kitchen appliances, which were *new* and valuable. And I was personally responsible for every single item.

Thinking of the kitchen made my stomach rumble. The tomato sandwich Caroline made for me at noon was long digested and dinner wasn't until seven. With all the activity going on in the kitchen, a snack was out of the question.

I gathered my hair up into a high ponytail, put on some blush, eyeliner and lipstick and went downstairs and out onto the terrace. There was no shade except for the puny shadows cast by four potted orange trees. I crossed the flagstones to a row of stone urns.

Yellow and purple pansies bloomed there, looking decidedly unhappy. Their heads drooped in the heat and I looked around for a watering can or hose. There was a rolled up hose close to the house and I spent fifteen minutes rehydrating the pansies, and even gave a squirt or two to the orange trees.

I was fingering a limp coneflower, and wondering if I dared tax the well any further, when I heard a voice behind me.

"The black thumb strikes again, I see." The familiar voice made my empty stomach churn faster.

"Well, well, if it isn't the Stud of Bruce County."

My ex-husband and I contemplated each other across the patio, practiced adversaries waiting for the other to make the first combative move.

He broke first.

"Someone pushing forty shouldn't wear her hair in a ponytail. It's very aging."

"Someone who *is* forty shouldn't wear red plaid shorts. You look like a bagpipe."

The pleasantries over, he came over and slumped on the wrought-iron bench underneath one of the orange trees. I sat on the other end. Dennis had put on at least twenty pounds since high school, and the damp white golf shirt emphasized his burgeoning belly roll. Sweat dropped from his thinning blond hair and was rerouted by his eyebrows to run down the sides of his cheeks. Although my hormones belonged to another now, I admitted he might still be attractive on a cooler day.

"So how are you, Dennis? And your daughter, and the teenage bride?"

"I'm fine, Amy is fine, and Tracey is not a teenager. She's pregnant again, though." He sounded rather gloomy for a proud father.

"Yes, I heard. Congratulations. Are you hoping for a boy or girl this time? Although I guess it doesn't much matter since you have one of each now."

He didn't answer, just gazed at the maples that bordered the lawn at the bottom of the garden. I glanced at my watch. Fifteen minutes till my guests were due to arrive. "So did you come here for something special?"

He looked at me, his eyes serious. "Well, I thought I would run into Mitch here and invite him to dinner tomorrow night before he has to go back to his summer job."

"He hasn't arrived yet, but I'll tell him to call you. His girlfriend is coming too, you know."

He nodded, then just sat there, staring at the trees. "Are you feeling all right, Dennis?" Not that I cared, but he was my son's father, so I felt compelled to pretend.

"I'm fine." He gave vent to a lung-collapsing sigh.

I was losing interest fast, but before I could excuse myself, a high-pitched "Yoo-hoo" sounded from the parking area. The next instant, my cousin Jody tripped around the corner in a pair of sandals with dangerously high heels and a black sundress with a halter top and no skirt to speak of.

Dennis brightened up at this vision, straightening his shoulders and running his hand through his hair. I couldn't blame him. Any male with an ounce of testosterone would have reacted to Jody, and most did.

"Lyris, darling. I'm so happy to see you."

"You are? Why?"

She laughed and slapped me on the arm. "Oh, you. You're always kidding. What are you doing with this handsome ex-husband of yours? Not getting back together, are you? That would break poor Marc's heart for sure and I'd have to give him another chance."

I was tempted to slap her back, harder. Marc had taken her out for a brief time last winter before he and I met over a traffic ticket I didn't deserve, and she never missed a chance to remind me that she had been there first. Jody had been *there* first with most of the men in Blackshore between the ages of eighteen and seventy. Make that eighty. Jody was an equal-opportunity skank.

"So what can I do for you, Jody?" Please, God, let her leave soon, before anybody else gets here. And let her take Dennis along.

"Oh, I just thought you might give me a tour of the house. Dear Uncle Patrick was such a recluse, I have never been anywhere except the main rooms on the ground floor. Since Uncle Patrick saw fit to leave the house to you, maybe you'll allow the rest of us to visit once in a while."

It was more likely she heard I was having guests for dinner and wanted to ruin it for me. "Not today, Jody. I'm having some people over for dinner. But another time…"

"You're having your ex-husband for dinner? How modern. Is your wife here too, Dennis? I hear she's expecting again."

"Dennis isn't staying. He just dropped by to speak to Mitch." Dennis hadn't said a word since Jody's appearance, but he was drooling a little. I had to get them both out of the grounds, fast. I gave Dennis a slight shove to get him moving toward Jody, trusting he would follow her.

Two more figures appeared from the direction of the car park. An Adonis and his goddess walked over to us, their fair heads shimmering under the late afternoon sun.

My son was stunning, if I do say so myself. He was slim hipped and wide shouldered, with his father's hair and my eyes. He seemed unaware of his looks, however, and appeared astounded that a beautiful young woman like…uh…I could never remember her name…had consented to be with him.

Tiffany, that was it. I don't know why I had trouble remembering that, since she looked like a Tiffany. Her long blonde hair hung past her shoulders, and her green goddess eyes never left my son's face. Nor did her arm release his. She clung tightly even as she greeted his parents and cousin.

Jody's own eyes were Pembrooke-dark like my own, but they glowed almost as green as Tiffany's as she beheld this beautiful younger woman. Dennis's eyes were jumping out of his head as they always did when an attractive woman was present.

After introductions and greetings were over, my attempts to move Dennis and Jody along were unsuccessful. They weren't budging and my other guests would be there any minute.

They were all talking away a mile a minute when Mitch said, "Dad, why don't you stay for supper, too? You don't mind, do you, Mom?"

I chewed the inside of my cheek. Telling them there wasn't enough food to go around wouldn't do it. I had seen the mountains of dishes being prepared in the kitchen. I couldn't come right out and say I didn't want my ex-husband and boyfriend sitting down at the same table, could I? Mitch should have been more socially apt than to suggest it.

Before I could say anything at all, Mitch turned to Jody, who was pouting and trying to look left out. "You can stay too, Jody. The dining room table will seat two dozen people at least."

I forced my teeth to separate. "Won't Tracey be expecting you?" I asked Dennis. To Jody, I said, "What about your mother?"

Dennis waved his hand. "Tracey's at her sister's cottage for the weekend."

Jody shook her head. "Oh, Mother isn't expecting me back for hours yet." With my son looking so happy and pleased, all I could do was smile with clenched jaw. "Fine. There's more than enough room for everybody."

And at that moment, the invited guests erupted onto the patio. Marc was striking in an emerald-green short-sleeved shirt and light tan pants. He was followed by his twin daughters, Eva and Cherie, and by Nick and Patsy, but I don't remember what any of them were wearing.

Nor do I recall what anyone said to anyone else before we all filed into the drawing room for drinks. And not caring if Dennis thought it was because of his remark, I did shake my hair free of its ponytail.

CHAPTER 10

I had been kicked down a rabbit hole, and the Mad Hatter's teatime guests had stayed on for dinner.

My seating arrangements were destroyed and we were breaking several rules of etiquette. I did manage to place Marc next to me on my left, but to accomplish this, I had to shove Jody to the far end of the table, where she made the best of it and was smiling up at Dennis. Somehow, Dennis had grabbed the other end of the table, which he doubtless thought was the head.

I was at the head of the table, let there be no misunderstanding. It was closest to the kitchen and that made it the head. Marc's daughters, Eva and Cherie, sat next to him, then Jody. On my right were Patsy, Nick, Mitch, and then Mitch's girlfriend. As I said, Dennis was at the other end, and he seemed quite happy between the two lovely ladies, Jody and the blonde. He believed he had the best seat in the house.

I thought that Caroline would cook, and I would be the one carrying food back and forth between the dining room and kitchen. However, both Caroline and Conklin carried dishes to the table, and offered them to the guests before placing them on the sideboard. Caroline looked flustered but pleased as she hurried in with the crown rib roast.

I had been a little concerned about the roast. Who would carve it? I wasn't used to the job and would bungle it. Asking Dennis was out of the question, even if he hadn't been a gate crasher. If I asked Marc, Mitch would be insulted. But Mitch had, to my knowledge, never handled anything sharper than a jackknife. See what I mean?

However, I should have known. As soon as the meat was placed on the table, elegant paper hats covering the ribs, Conklin stepped up with a long knife and fork. With the expertise of long practice, he cut the roast into pieces that fit nicely on the sides of our plates.

And since Conklin leaped —knee joints twanging—to offer a dish again whenever someone finished a food group, all I had to do was sit there and eat. I lifted my hair away from my damp neck.

This dinner was supposed to enable Mitch to become better acquainted with Marc and his daughters. And so I could get to know Whosit, although I was hoping Mitch would break up with her before I had to. I just didn't feel she was the woman for him. All that blonde hair and frosted fingernails had to be high maintenance.

So there we all sat, my invited guests and the two who would never be invited, even if there was nobody else left on earth. I looked toward the other end of the table. Judging by their expressions, my ex-husband and the Family Trollop were engaged in an interesting and highly private conversation. The blonde was clinging to Mitch's right arm and he was eating with his left hand, which was odd, since he's right-handed. With her hanging on a like a leech every time I saw them together, he was probably practicing to be ambidextrous.

Nick and Marc were talking across me about their golf date the next morning. Patsy was turning her salad over with a fork. She was allergic to radishes and suspected one might be lurking under the lettuce.

Eva stared at Mitch, who was having trouble with his jellied consommé, while Cherie seemed fascinated with Conklin, resplendent in his formal butler uniform. The fifteen-year-old twins were indistinguishable to many people, but I had no trouble telling them apart as long as they were looking at me.

Both were about five and a half feet tall, with long black hair and eyes as gray as their father's. They were pretty young girls and were already sending Marc into frequent anxiety states over their upcoming dating years.

Neither girl was thrilled with my friendship with their father, but that didn't put me off my food. These things take time, and since they spent the school year in Mississauga with their mother, I knew summers in Blackshore with their father were precious to them. They didn't like

Dad's girlfriend hanging around. Cherie was polite enough, but Eva—short for Evangeline—scowled whenever she was obliged to speak to me. So really, it was easy to tell them apart.

With Cherie's attention fixed on Conklin, I became acutely away of him as well. He persisted in standing behind me with the gravy boat in his hand. Every once in a while, the boat rattled faintly against the stand. To get my mind off the hot liquid just waiting to cascade down my defenceless neck, I decided it was time to break up the clusters of conversation that were happening around the table.

I cleared my throat. "So Mitch, how is your summer job going?" Everyone stopped talking to listen to his answer. Mitch was working with a construction company in North Bay.

Mitch flushed slightly and gave me a look that said he was unhappy about being singled out for attention. "It's okay. I'm working for another four weeks, then Tiff and I are going camping in Algonquin Park for a week." Mitch was an avid camper and outdoorsman, which is surprising considering neither of his parents was fond of roughing it.

All eyes swivelled at "Tiff," who continued to look composed and seemed to take the attention in stride. She didn't release her stranglehold on Mitch's arm, though.

I had to ask her. "Have you ever been camping before?"

"No, never. But I'm looking forward to getting away before school starts again. I'm working at a nursing home for the summer, you know. I'm studying gerontology and the job is part of a co-op work term."

"There's a lot of money in gemotology, isn't there?" asked Jody. "But I can't imagine those seniors having much jewellery in the nursing home. Unless they're rich of course, but in that case, they wouldn't be in a home."

That stopped the conversation. Dennis seemed to be the first to pick up on what she was saying, making me wonder if they knew each other better than anyone suspected. He laughed and waved his empty wine glass at Conklin, who placed the gravy boat beside me and went to fill him up again. I grabbed the gravy and shoved it closer to the middle of the table, where people could help themselves.

Watching the ruby liquid as it ran from the bottle to his glass, Dennis said, "That's *gerontology,* young lady. It means the study of elderly people, not gemology."

Jody lost interest right away. "Oh. That can't pay very much."

Jody held a dual title—Family Trollop *and* Family Idiot.

I steered the conversation back to camping before we got into a philosophical discussion on the merits of money versus ideals. Mitch and

Tiffany could carry on for hours on that subject, I knew for a fact. Mitch believed my job as an office manager was not beneficial to the universal community, and I have had to point out to him more than once that it had benefited him, enabling him to attend the University of Guelph, where he was studying engineering.

"Tiffany, it's pretty primitive in Algonquin Park. Are you sure you want to go for a whole week? Maybe a weekend would be better to start with."

I was thinking of my own trip to Algonquin with Dennis just after we were married. We planned on staying a week, but after four days of hell, we packed it in and came home. The details were burned into the memory stick of my brain—sleeping on uneven ground in a leaky tent, portaging over rocks and fallen trees, boiling water over a fire it took two hours to light because the matches were in my backpack. The backpack that got wet when I tipped over backwards and fell in a river we were trying to carry the canoe across. Oh, and eating dried packets of food I upchucked because I was pregnant, cowering in the tent waiting for the bear to finish eating our food, fending off the black flies whose bites raised lumps on every inch of my body…

Oh yes. I looked at Tiffany, at her long nails, the tumbled hair and clear skin.

I smiled at her. "On second thought, Tiffany, I'm sure you'll have a wonderful time, an experience you will remember forever." I ignored the suspicious look Mitch threw my way.

Dennis jabbed his fork into the table, trying to recapture a baby potato that had rolled away from him, and gesturing with his free hand to Conklin, who refilled his wine glass once again. Even though I never drank alcohol, having an unfortunate allergy to the stuff, I had no objection to others enjoying the fruits of the vine or wheat field. Dennis enjoyed himself too freely. He always had, but that night he was swallowing wine by the gallon.

His face was flushed and I could see his coordination was already suffering as the potato eluded his fork and rolled down the middle of the table. He gave up on it and speared one from Jody's plate. She giggled and slapped his hand. "Oh, you."

When all eyes turned to her, Jody giggled again and licked a tiny bit of food off her fork, her pink tongue darting in and out. It sounds disgusting and believe me, it was, but the men seemed to be mesmerized. Dennis, Mitch, Nick and even Marc watched the little pink tongue. Then again, maybe I was selling them short. Maybe they were fascinated by the sight of the breasts that promised to bounce free of her skimpy halter top every time she moved.

I leaned across and whispered to Patsy, "Do you think Dennis is having an affair with Jody?"

"I don't know about now," she whispered back, "but they had one a few years back. Maybe they're starting up again."

I grabbed for her arm, but she pulled it away. "Are you saying they had an affair while we were still married? Why didn't you tell me?"

"Quit pinching me. I didn't tell you because, well, Ann Landers always said to mind your own business. Anyway, I thought you already knew and didn't want to talk about it."

I turned my back on her and smiled at Marc. "I want to talk to you later. I have something to show you."

He looked alarmed. "The last time you had something to show me, it turned out to be a body."

"No body." Thinking of the tiny figurine, I said, "Not a *human* body anyway."

He didn't appear reassured and I patted his knee under that table. He was so adorable. His gray eyes darkened, as they seemed to when whenever he felt a strong emotion, and at first, I thought he was running his hand up my calf.

No, it wasn't Marc, not unless he was wearing a fur mitt. It had to be the cat. Now, there is nothing more pleasant than a soft cat rubbing against your bare skin, but animals do not belong under the dinner table, unless you don't mind hair in your food.

Lifting up a corner of the white linen tablecloth, I addressed Rasputin and Jacqueline. I had no doubt she was under there as well. She had a nasty trick of grabbing an ankle with her tiny sharp teeth and hanging on until forcibly detached.

"Come out of there, you two. You will not be fed from the table. Please return to your own quarters at once."

Dennis and Jody both started and reached for their wine glasses in unison.

First Rasputin, then Jacqueline, filed out and stalked from the room, making quite a show of it. The cat's indignant tail arched over his back, giving us an awesome view of his backside, and his hair stood out, making him appear even larger than he was. Jacqueline was still shabby and seemed to know it. She didn't try to bite anyone or even bark. She slunk after Rasputin.

"What a nice cat," Eva said. "What's his name and is he yours?"

I gave her the details, adding Rasputin's stay was a temporary one and he would go back to live with Caroline's grandmother at the end of the summer.

Dennis and Jody were pelting each other playfully with the paper rib hats. Dennis's free hand was underneath the table again and I didn't even want to think about what was going on down there. At least he wasn't waving his glass at Conklin for a refill anymore, but Mitch looked uncomfortable at his father's conduct and I didn't know how to help him. This whole situation was beyond my control.

"Dennis," I called down the length of the table. "You haven't said anything about the new baby. When is it due? I saw Tracey downtown last week and she looks close to term."

He pulled his hand out from under the table and gestured at Conklin. The poor guy trotted over once again, but this time, he poured a mere thimbleful of wine.

Dennis surveyed his glass gloomily. "She has three months left. She had an ultrasound last week, and it's twins. Both girls."

I couldn't believe my ears. I took a mouthful of Patsy's wine without thinking. "Twins? Twins, did you say? Let's see, that will make three babies under two, won't it?" I gestured heavenward with Patsy's glass. "There is a God."

Patsy reclaimed her glass, but not before I had another swig to celebrate the imminent birth of Dennis's twin offspring.

Jody spoke up, "Just think, Lyris. If you marry Marc, Mitch will have twin stepsisters and twin half sisters."

That was a low blow. Marc and I were not engaged, and nobody even knew he had asked me to marry him. She was just being spiteful, hoping to embarrass us. I took a little sip of Marc's wine.

Of course the idea of Marc and I joining hearts and households did not go over well with our children. They were all three scowling at us.

Caroline came in bearing a gateau—a piece of edible art. Six layers, cream filled, two inches of mocha frosting, nuts and fruit dribbling down the sides. What a treasure Caroline was turning out to be.

I was starved. I hadn't eaten much of the main course. Conklin seemed to know this and gave me a double-sized slice. Once everyone was served, I dug in with my fork.

Jody waited until my mouth was full before mentioning, "Lyris, dear, if you keep eating like that, you'll soon balloon up and look like Mother." Since Aunt Bertilla was every bit as wide as she was high, and I could be deemed willowy on my heaviest day, that was a silly exaggeration.

My son immediately leaped to my defence. "Mom eats like a horse all the time and she never puts on any weight."

"Thank you, dear." I took a sip of Marc's wine to wash down the cake. Then I took another, just because it tasted fine.

Patsy looked from Jody to me, anxious to help. "You know, you and Jody look a lot alike. I always thought there was a resemblance, but now that Jody is growing her hair longer, the likeness is striking."

I looked down the table at Jody. "I'm taller".

Jody smirked. "I'm younger."

She had me there. I took another mouthful of Patsy's wine.

"And you have smaller boobs, too," Jody added for no good reason. She was such a bitch.

"Maybe, but I could buy myself a bigger pair if I wanted, same as you did. At least I don't tip when I walk."

Tiffany's voice rang out. "I love the centerpiece. Are the flowers from your garden, Ms. Pembrooke? They're lovely."

The centerpiece had been created with my own two hands. I had used cobalt blue, white and pink hydrangeas with white and mauve alyssum. These were arranged in a low silver bowl with sprigs of tiny ferns I had found growing next to the fishpond in the shade garden. It was very simple, but anything showier would have detracted from the display of china, crystal and silver. Caroline had certainly convinced me she could handle the job.

"Thank you, Tiffany. And please call me Lyris." I closed one eye, hoping that would stop me seeing two of everybody. And seeing two of some of those seated at the table was two too many.

"Lyris always made the house look nice," said Dennis. "She was good at decorating and stuff like that. Not so good at cooking, though." He must have caught my look. "And she was a good wife and mother too."

Then why did he run around with every tramp in town? I looked at Jody. *So Many Men, So Little Time* was undoubtedly her motto.

"Harlot, thy name is Jody," I muttered. Nobody heard that except Marc and Patsy. Marc moved his wine out of my reach and Patsy finished hers off in one swallow.

I knew the wine was affecting me. I didn't break out in spots or any kind of allergic reaction like that. Alcohol just bypassed my blood and went straight to my brain, and even a drop would do it. I shouldn't even smell the stuff. And everybody should make sure I didn't. It wasn't my fault.

Marc took a turn at being heroic. "Lyris, Eva and Cherie were hoping they could have a tour of the house after dinner. Both of them are interested in Victoriana." Like I cared what those two spoiled brats wanted.

Conklin caught the ball. "I'll be pleased to show the young ladies around, Madam, and point out the various objects of interest."

"Thanks, Conklin, and be sure to show them the collection of mourning memorabilia in the green bedroom upstairs." I spoke slowly, but still had trouble with the word *memorabilia*.

"Of course, Madam."

"When someone died," I said to the two girls, "they used to cut off locks of hair and make wreaths and jewellery. There's all different colours of human hair up there—red, blond, brown." I hoped the little snots had nightmares tonight.

To a chorus of "Oh, neat" and "Can we see that first?" from the twins, and "How gross" from Jody, we got up from the table at long last. My right leg was wrapped around the chair and it took me a moment or two to untangle it.

Dennis fumbled in his pocket for his keys. "Guess I better get going."

Mitch plucked them out of his father's hand. "Tiffany and I will drive with you, Dad. We can walk back."

At the door, Dennis said to me, "I almost forgot what I came here for in the first place."

"You mean it wasn't to ruin my dinner?"

He laughed like I had made a huge joke. "No. Tracey and I want to bring Amy to the reunion, and I thought I better tell you first so you won't be surprised to see us there. Tracey discovered she's a distant relation to the Pembrookes and wants our children to get in touch with their roots or something."

"Tracey is related to the Pembrookes? When did that happen?" I vowed to investigate that particular twig of the family tree. And somehow I didn't think this was the real reason he came here today.

Jody decided to leave at the same time, and I breathed a sigh of relief when I closed the door on the clammy night air that was rushing into the hall. Nick professed an interest in mourning memorabilia and dragged Patsy upstairs with him. That left me alone with Marc.

At last.

He gave me a sexy smile and opened his arms. I pushed them aside. "Come with me. I have evidence." The floor seemed to be slanted and I had to step with care.

"Evidence of what, my dark-eyed Madonna?"

More of that Madonna shit? I refused to be sidetracked, and opened the drawer where the porcelain fragments were wrapped in a piece of paper towel. Explaining what had happened, even though it was painful to recount—that fell swoop remark still hurt—I asked Marc about fingerprints.

"If I hadn't smashed the shepherdess, would you have been able to take fingerprints from it?" It was a moot point now, but I wanted to know.

He fingered the tiny pieces, all indistinguishable except the head and hands. "There have been some instances where laser equipment has raised fingerprints up to ten years later or even more, but not sixty-eight. So you're off the hook for destroying evidence."

With that weight off my chest, I took him to the landing and showed him the padded shelf where the peacock had stood.

"The figurine must have been behind the peacock. What I can't understand is, how did it elude discovery for so long? This place is cleaned every Friday. The crew doesn't clean under or behind everything every week, but after sixty plus years you'd think that stuffed bird would have been moved a few times." With a plunk, I sat down on the top step, hoping it looked deliberate. Marc wrapped his hand around my elbow and pulled me up.

We walked down a few steps to a point underneath the padded ledge.

"I agree the peacock must have been moved," Marc said, "but never lifted down. If the figurine was stuck between the feathers somehow, the cleaning staff would have missed it. Look up there. What do you see?"

"I see a very high shelf, and yes, it would be difficult to clean up there. Which means…" I stopped and looked at him.

"Right. How did it get up there in the first place? Look how far up it is. Not even a circus acrobat could clamber up the wall and swing from the ledge while tucking the figurine in far enough to stay hidden for sixty-eight years. Which means…"

"Which means that somebody used a ladder. And had the time to fuss with the placement of the figurine." My lips appeared to be working fine, my legs not well at all.

We walked back downstairs and out into the sultry night. At the side of the house, we passed the fishpond and sat on the rustic bench that curved around the giant maple in the middle of the shade garden.

"I guess we're talking about murder, after all," I said as Marc removed my sandals and started to massage my right foot. Good thing I had had a pedicure the day before. I lay back on the bench with a sigh of pleasure. There's nothing like a foot massage to make you forget ex-husbands and trampy cousins. But my head was spinning, and I felt like I was going to roll off the bench.

"Nobody said anything about murder." His hand was at my knee. "The autopsy revealed a crushed hyoid bone. In a baby that age, it's not hard to inflict enough damage to cause death."

I had to put my hand on his own to stop its ascent. This wasn't the town square, but anybody could come springing out of the bushes—his daughters, my son, his best friend, my best friend, a butler.

"Somebody put Tommy in the closet, and somebody hid the figurine. I think that lets Aunt Wisty and Aunt Clem out. I can't imagine Uncle Patrick doing it either, so we're left with Bruce Wingate."

Marc's hand stopped working my left foot. "How do you know that name?"

"I went to the library this afternoon. I read the newspaper account, but there wasn't much information. Why are the police archives in the library attic, by the way?"

He squeezed so hard, I yelped out loud. He let go at once. "Sorry. So you read the police report?"

"I couldn't help it. They were right out there in plain view. I didn't even need to search." Hellfire beckoned.

"I see. Well, I'll need to have a word with the library board. They promised they would store those records in a secure area until we received the money from the province to have them microfilmed. And Ronnie—he went over there to photocopy the Pembrooke file and didn't mention they were accessible to just anybody."

"I'm not just anybody..." Then I stopped. I was being led off topic. "Never mind that. I must say I was not impressed by the report. Three pages. Was that McPherson guy incompetent or what?"

"There was a war on. All the young men were in the military, and McPherson was forced to come out of retirement to run the police force in Blackshore by himself. I agree the report is short on detail, but no doubt the man did his best. If there had been anything else to add to the report, he would have documented it."

"All right, don't get uppity. I didn't mean to insult your fellow peace officer. But now that the body has been found, aren't you going to launch an investigation?"

"I'll do what I can, but that won't be much given the length of time that's elapsed. Which I am still not calling a murder."

"I guess you won't mind, then, if I poke around a little on my own?"

"Go right ahead. But while you're investigating a sixty-eight year old crime, and concealing a body is a crime by the way, promise me you'll think about something?"

"Sure, what?" Will wonders never cease, I thought, swinging my legs off the bench and sitting up. My head still swam, just a little. Marc was telling me to go ahead and investigate. He must think I won't find anything. But somebody put little Tommy in the closet with his blanket and yellow bunny, and I wanted to know who, and why. Finding out why was important.

"What?" I said again.

"You aren't listening to me."

"Sorry, I am now. What did you say?"

"I said I love you and I want to marry you. I know you have an aversion to the marital state and that's understandable considering what an ass Dennis is, but I think you might love me too. So maybe you could take a chance? You might like being married to a man who worships your every little finger and toe, not to mention the most beautiful legs in town and the most elegant neck." He held my hair back from my face and kissed my elegant neck. "And there are other parts I haven't been allowed to see, but I'm sure are every bit as worthy of being worshipped."

"Yeah, well, that sounds tempting, but you know I don't like to rush into things."

He laughed, which under the circumstances I believed was uncalled for, then said when he could speak again, "The only thing you don't rush into is matrimony. And that's okay, I'll wait as long as I have to. I just want you to think about it once in a while, maybe while you're investigating Tommy Pembrooke's death."

"Okay, I'll think about it, just because you're as cute as a bug." And to prove it I hopped onto his knee and we spent a satisfying minute or two in a hot and sweaty embrace, which felt better than it sounds.

Before we got too sweaty, though, I heard the inevitable, "Madam, Madam," emanating from the darkness.

I jumped up and dragged Marc by the hand behind me. "Come on. Either I'm neglecting my hostess duties, or Conklin wants to weed the petunia bed."

"There are no petunias, and why would Conklin...?"

But there was no time to explain. The guests were standing around under the portico, except for Mitch and his girlfriend, who were walking up the drive toward us. The illumination from the tall lampposts surrounding the circular driveway made the night as bright as day. The thunder rumbled, but I don't think anyone even heard it anymore, or noticed the flashes of lightning on the horizon.

Patsy threw me a knowing smile and waggled her eyebrows at me, like a plump Groucho. Eva and Cherie did not look as pleased to see me emerging from the dark with their father. I adopted a casual air, like we hadn't been doing anything, but I knew my hair was a mess. And where the heck were my shoes? My head still buzzed.

Nick and Marc firmed up their golf date for the next morning, and everybody thanked me for a lovely time. Nick and Patsy sounded like they meant it—Nick even said it was the most interesting dinner party he had ever attended—but the twins couldn't quite pull it off.

Mitch and his blonde had already gone upstairs, and I wandered through the dining room on my way to the kitchen. It was spotless, looking as pristine as it had earlier in the day. The wood of the table gleamed, as did the rather frightening sideboard with its tortured mythical animals twisting a path up the corners.

In the kitchen, the dishwasher was shirring softly. Conklin and Caroline were having a cup of tea. Caroline jumped up to offer some to me, but I waved her back down and thanked them both for the work they had put into my dinner. The food and service had been perfect—it wasn't their fault the evening turned out so awful.

I made myself a cup of bedtime tea, a soothing mixture of chamomile, rosemary, liquorice root and catnip leaf. Saying good night, I took my tea upstairs with me, where I experienced the expected fleeting aroma and tingle.

Tonight there was something else. Another smell lingered after the first one departed. Again I couldn't identify it, but it was still there at the second then third breath. Then it too was gone, and I was left with the smell of ancient wood and fabrics. Was it my imagination or something more unworldly? I wished it would go away.

Feeling troubled, I went into my bedroom. It was the middle one at the back of the house and I had given Mitch and Tiffany the rooms on each side of me. If they hoped to get together in either one, they were out of luck. I planned to stay up all night if necessary to ensure they did not. I fired up my computer and prepared to go online for a long session on the Internet. There were lots of things I could look up and much to learn.

Once I had to go into the hall. I intercepted Tiffany on her way to the bathroom, so she claimed. After that, all was serene and at about two in the morning, I thought it safe to go to bed myself. I was wrong.

CHAPTER 11

I forced one eye open to find my bedroom filled with a yellow half-light. It must be morning. No bird noises, though.

As I struggled out of REM sleep and opened the other eye, I realized the light was not coming from the morning sun. Nor was it the moon shining in on me. That orb was just one-quarter full and hidden somewhere behind the pine woods. I remembered catching a glimpse of it while I was sitting in the shade garden with Marc after dinner.

I heard the sounds of cricket legs rubbing together in the grass and a few frogs ribbeting in the fishpond. I stumbled to the window seat and knelt down. As the sleep fog started to clear from my brain, I realized the motion detector lights mounted on the corners of the house had been tripped.

The detectors were set so that a ground-crawling animal such as a rabbit or raccoon could pass undisturbed, without alarming the household. So something more substantial had moved through the grounds, maybe a deer, or a bear. A black bear and two cubs had been sighted at the municipal dump in the spring, foraging through the garbage.

While I was trying to remember if Conklin had shown me the magic button that reset the motion detectors, I glimpsed a shadow slip into the trees beyond the edge of the sun garden beyond the terrace.

I was still not fully awake and wondering if I had seen a shadow at all, when suddenly the crickets stopped chirping. I heard a rustling noise, and a sound like twigs snapping on the dry ground beneath the pines. It wasn't a heavy sound like a bear would make, but a calculated, deliberate tread.

It had to be a man. I jerked my head back from the window in case he looked up and spotted me. Then, feeling foolish, I peeked around the window frame and saw the shadow dart from the trees around the corner of the house. I ran across the hall to the middle bedroom and pulled aside the heavy draperies.

I strained my eyes to pick out a moving shape somewhere within the blackness of the front lawns, but the darkness was total and complete. The electric lamps lining the driveway were turned off at night, and it appeared there was no motion detector set up at the front of the house. The intruder could have been turning cartwheels on the grass and I wouldn't have spotted him. But he might have slipped back over the fence, frightened off by the bright lights of the motion detectors at the back. I crossed the hall and returned to my bedroom.

I stood there for several minutes trying to decide whether or not to call the police. I didn't believe the intruder had entered the house, but if he was part of the gang that Marc was investigating for breaking into local homes, then the police needed to know about this attempt. On the other hand, Marc was inclined to think I overreacted to situations, and I didn't want to embarrass myself again.

In the end I decided to call the police station and report what I saw, like any other citizen, and let them take it from there. Marc could sleep undisturbed unless his duty officer woke him. I pulled on shorts and tee-shirt over the camisole and bikini underpants I had taken to wearing during the heat wave.

I turned on all the hall lights before waking Mitch and his girlfriend and telling them what had occurred. Not for the first time since I moved to Hammersleigh, I wished fervently for a telephone in my bedroom. As soon as the reunion was over, I would get the Bell boys in to install phones in every room of the house.

After making the call from the airless little room under the stairs, I turned toward the kitchen to put the kettle on before rousing Conklin and Caroline. A movement under the table startled me until I realized it was the devil's familiars.

"What are you doing under there? You, Jacqueline, you need to go outside." I opened the door and shooed her out, then turned back to the cat.

"Don't you have a litter box or something you need to visit?" Rasputin refused to even look at me, just carried on grooming his tail. I didn't like his attitude at all.

Conklin came to his door after a few minutes, his white hair standing on end, but quite coherent. He grasped the situation immediately, announcing he would get dressed and join me in the drawing room.

Caroline, on the other hand, opened her door at my first knock, although it was some time before she understood what I was telling her. Her pale face was blotchy, her eyes red-rimmed and swollen, poor girl. It had been a long day for her and she might have had trouble sleeping, this being her first night in a strange bed.

Mitch and his girlfriend were in the drawing room by the time I ushered Conklin and Caroline in. Mitch was wearing pajama bottoms, while the girl had a shirt. All of us looked the worse for wear.

I started to explain in more detail what I had seen from my window, when the doorbell interrupted me. Conklin beat me to it and opened the door for Ronnie Guilbert and Tammie Wilberts, two of Marc's officers. Ronnie seemed to have a cauliflower stuck to his right ankle until Mitch reached down and detached Jacqueline from his pant leg. The fur ball scooted off not knowing how lucky she was to have chosen Ronnie's leg. She would have been turned into buzzard food by Tammie who, inexplicably, was allowed to carry a gun.

Ronnie was the sergeant and Tammie the constable, but that didn't matter. Tammie took charge right away.

"Okay, Ms. Pembrooke, what is it this time?" Out came the notebook and pen. "Just give me the details."

While I was trying to collect my thoughts, she nailed me with her bead-shaped eyes. "Well?"

I cleared my throat. "The motion detectors were activated and the light woke me up."

"What time was this, please?" She drew all of her sixty-two inches up as high as possible, but I still towered above her. I felt like apologizing for being taller.

"About twenty minutes ago now."

Constable Wilberts checked her watch and made a notation. "Continue."

"I looked out the window and saw a shadow melt into the trees. It went around the corner of the house, so I looked through one of the front bedroom windows, but couldn't see any movement. I figured he climbed back over the fence..."

"Just the facts, ma'am, if you please. Let us conduct the investigation."

"Of course, *mein fuhrer*, I mean Constable Wilberts." I glanced at Ronnie, but he just stood there looking apprehensive, whether for himself or me I couldn't tell. "Anyway, that's about all. What with all the break-ins around here, I thought I'd better..."

She snapped the notebook shut and put it back in her breast pocket. She turned to Conklin, who had been absent from the festivities, but now returned to stand at attention by my side.

"Mr. Conklin, could you check to see if anything is missing from the house?"

She had to be kidding. Give him a few weeks to check the inventory sheets and he might have been able to tell. Wrong.

"Most of the valuable pieces are locked in cabinets, Officer, and it will take some time to check everything. It seems unlikely that an intruder could gain access to my keys and take items away without anyone hearing him." He cleared his throat modestly. "However, there is a piece or two missing from the sideboard in the hall."

We tripped over each other trying to get to the hall first, me trying to remember what had been on the top of that tall, multilevel cabinet. But even when I noted the empty spots on one of the ornate shelves, my mind's eye drew a blank.

The notebook was out again, and Conklin told the constable, "A five-inch jade figurine, Officer, in the style of a Chinese dragon. Ivory in colour."

"Valuable?" Tammie's freckled face was wrinkling in concentration as she wrote. I wanted to give Ronnie a swift kick. He hadn't uttered one word so far. Marc swore by Ronnie's meticulous and painstaking methods of police work, but he was no good at the upfront details, that was clear.

"The jade is worth four or five hundred dollars," Conklin said. "But it is an attractive piece, and Mr. Pembrooke liked to handle it. Also missing is a gold hummingbird, which is encrusted with semiprecious stones, valued at about a thousand dollars. I would have to consult the insurance papers to be sure of that."

Snap. The notebook went back to the pocket. "If you find anything else is missing, Mr. Conklin, give me a call at the station. In the meantime, you folks can get back to sleep now. And keep the doors locked." She gave me a baleful glance and started for the door, her short frizzy hair bristling with disapproval.

Ronnie didn't follow. He called to the departing Tammie, "Constable, I think we should have a look at the doors and main floor windows. You check the front, and I'll look at the back. The rest of you can go back to bed if you want."

I gave Ronnie an approving nod. It was about time he showed some gumption.

Nobody wanted to go back to bed, so while Mitch and the girl followed Tammie, the rest of us went with Ronnie as he checked the doors at the back of the house, including the exit into the garden from the employees' wing. There was no sign that someone had attempted to force his way into the house, and the windows were shut and locked as well. Conklin was never derelict in his duties.

Tammie's search turned up no forced entry at the front of the house, and the two police officers left at last, this time with Ronnie in the lead. The entire household stood under the portico to watch them drive away, the lights on the top of the cruiser flashing and whirling. Tammie's idea. But there was no siren, and that was thanks to Ronnie I was sure.

I gave Ronnie some thought. He was about thirty and single, with a pleasant, homely face. Just the right man for Caroline, after she had recovered from her bad marriage, of course. Both of them were too shy to get anywhere on their own, but with a little help, who knew? I had noticed Ronnie giving Caroline several sideways glances when she wasn't looking. I resolved to think of some way to introduce them properly, after the reunion was over.

The crickets and frogs were silent, and a few birds were stirring in the pines. Dawn was imminent and the heavy air promised yet another day of oppressive moisture. On the horizon, the indistinct glow of the rising sun erased the heat lightning, and thunder continued to rumble quietly. It was eerie to hear thunder while the sun shone from a bright blue, cloudless sky day after day, although the eeriness seemed almost commonplace now.

But no creepier than an intruder entering Hammersleigh House and taking a jade figurine and gold hummingbird from the front hall. While leaving behind not a trace of his passage.

After the departure of the police, we all wandered off to our respective bedrooms, but it seemed no one felt inclined to get back into bed. One by one, we turned up in the kitchen, showered, dressed and looking for sustenance.

I had instructed Caroline that she was responsible for cooking one meal per day, five days a week, and I preferred that meal to be dinner. We would all get our own breakfasts and lunches. After all, she had a lot of other duties to perform, like doing something with the raggedy mutt that was scampering around under the table, trying to attract Rasputin's attention.

However, that early Sunday morning found Caroline beating a bowl of yellow batter. I said good morning, but before I could repeat my wish that she not bother about breakfast, she hastened to assure me this was a special occasion since Mitch and Tiffany were visiting and she wanted them to have a good breakfast. Tiffany. I should remember that.

"I want to make some blueberry pancakes for the young people." That was sweet, considering she was only a few years older than the young persons in question. "And for yourself, of course," she hastened to add.

What could I do except thank her and make myself a cup of lemon balm tea? I set the table, and when Caroline turned around to hand me the maple syrup, I saw her eyes were even redder than before.

"Caroline, I want you to take the rest of the day off. You worked too hard yesterday. It was your first day and you cooked a meal for ten people before you even settled in. And I know you didn't get enough sleep." I set the flatware in place.

"But I'm fine." She handed me the butter.

"We forgot to discuss which days you'll have off each week. Sundays for sure, and that's today. What other day do you want? Or do you want to take the second day at random? Maybe we could create a monthly schedule."

"That's great, Lyris. I have no plans, so why don't you just make up the schedule. Any day is fine."

I looked at her again. She seemed more than tired.

"Caroline, are you feeling okay?"

Her eyes filled up, but before they quite spilled over, Mitch came in.

"Are those pancakes? I'm starved." He sat down and looked expectant.

I looked at him. "Good morning, Sunshine. You look like you just crawled out of a swamp full of alligators."

He gave me a sour look, which went well with his dark-rimmed eyes. Well, that made three of us so far. I was sure my own eyes were baggy from lack of sleep.

"Mom, was it necessary to patrol the hall all night? You'd think you didn't trust us or something."

"Or something." I passed him a platter of pancakes piled a foot high. "Where is…uh." Damn, what *was* that girl's name? I'd forgotten it again.

"Tiffany, Mom. Her name is Tiffany. How come you can't remember that?" At that moment, the goddess herself arrived.

"Good morning again, Tiffany. Sit down and have some breakfast." Her blonde hair was tumbled and uncombed. She had changed to cut-off shorts and a T-shirt that just reached the bottom of her perky bosom. She looked adorable to me, and what she looked like to Mitch was apparent by the expression on his face. The way she gazed back at my son made me blink and indeed made me realize I should never again forget her name.

"I wanted to tell you, Mitch, it was very responsible of you to take your father home last night. I don't know what might have happened if he had driven himself. Marc couldn't have allowed it…"

"Yeah, well, Dad had a little too much to drink, that's all." He took a bite, chewed and swallowed. His dark eyes, so much like my own, were troubled. "He's having severe financial problems, you know. His business isn't doing so well and the mortgage on the house is in arrears."

"Real estate has been in a slump, true, but it's picking up. I've noticed that several of his listings have Sold signs on them, so I'm sure he'll…"

"The problem is, Mom, that when Dad had to give you half his assets, it pretty much put him in the red. He took a mortgage on his house and cashed in his investments. And he even took out a loan. He's hurting, Mom, and now with three more kids to support, and a wife, it's no wonder he's drinking. Not that there's any excuse for getting drunk, but I can sort of understand why."

Dennis had certainly been filling his son with a lot of drivel. When we separated, we had agreed to keep our differences just between the two of us and not ask Mitch to take sides. However, it appeared Dennis had broken that pact and if Mitch was ready enough to get involved, he needed to hear both sides.

"Mitch, it upsets me to hear you refer to your father's assets, *his* house, *his* investments. Remember that I worked during my entire marriage, so anything your father and I had, we accumulated together. That made half of it mine." I took a swig of my lemon balm tea, now lukewarm, and continued.

"I don't want to say anything negative about your father to you, but his financial problems could be the result of poor planning, and perhaps trying to live beyond his means. We split everything straight down the middle. You're right, he has a new family now to support, but his income is much higher than mine and he should be able to handle his new responsibilities without difficulty. Many people live on a lot less."

Mitch had the grace to look ashamed of himself. "I know all that, Mom. And believe it or not, I know what you had to put up with. It's just, well, you have so much now."

"Your father has a wife who loves him, a beautiful little girl, and two more on the way. In the eyes of many people, your father is a rich man. And if you're thinking of Hammersleigh House, this place won't be truly mine for twenty-five years. You know that, I've explained…"

He put up a hand to stop my words. It appeared I was not destined to finish a sentence that morning.

"Sorry. I don't mean that, Mom. I'm not explaining very well. It's just that you got half of everything. Now you still have it all, plus this house. It just seems that Dad got short-changed."

I closed my eyes, frustrated with my son. Usually we were on the same wavelength, but it seemed he would have to figure this out for himself. How could I compete with Dennis, who was playing the sympathy card?

I changed the subject.

"So, Tiffany, you're studying gerontology? Which university are you attending?" I could tell by Mitch's look of exasperation that I was already privy to this information.

Tiffany flung her hair back and forked at least half of the stack of pancakes onto her plate before she answered. "I thought you knew, Lyris. I go to Guelph too. I'm going into third year in September."

Caroline saw the pancakes disappearing fast and tossed more ingredients into the bowl. She averted her face from us as she worked.

Tiffany looked at me. "The furniture in my room is very strange. Every piece has horrible animal faces on it. I had the feeling they were looking at me all night. I didn't shut my eyes."

That's not why you didn't shut your eyes, my girl. "So that's where that furniture went. It used to be in my room. Very gothic, isn't it?" Both pairs of eyes swivelled toward me, and I pretended great interest in my teacup.

I said to Mitch. "You remember, don't you, that the reunion is next weekend? Are you still going to help me?"

"I guess. I'll take Friday off work and arrive late Thursday night."

"You, too, Tiffany. You're welcome to attend the reunion and get to know all the Pembrookes." If meeting Mitch's extended family didn't scare her off, she probably deserved to become part of it.

Tiffany wrapped herself around Mitch's arm. "Thanks. I'll be here."

"It's a funny thing about last night," Mitch said. "Those things were taken, yet there were no signs of someone breaking in. If it wasn't for the fact, Mom, that you saw somebody outside last night, I'd say he was already in the house or had a key."

Behind us, something crashed into the sink. "Sorry," Caroline mumbled, "it slipped out of my hand."

"You're overtired and need some sleep. Why don't you go lie down?"

"I will. Just as soon as I clean up."

I didn't argue with her. I hated cleaning up even more than cooking.

"Mom, are you going to keep dating that cop? You know, the one who was here last night. For dinner?" Mitch qualified his question as though I had various cops dropping in for breakfast, lunch, *and* dinner.

"You mean Marc Allaire? What, don't you like him?" It hadn't escaped my notice that Mitch had not addressed one word to Marc at the dinner table or after.

"He's okay, but I don't know. I never thought you would fall for someone like that."

"Like what? What's wrong with him?"

"Nothing's wrong with him. He just seems so different from Dad."

Well, that stopped me in my tracks. Any response I made would be wrong, or worse, flippant. "I suppose there's no accounting for taste, is there?" I had to be content with that.

I quit playing with my pancake and dumped it in the garbage. Grabbing an apple on the way out, my mind was already turning over the plans for the day. I met Conklin in the hall and he gave me a half bow. "Madam." He was dressed in his butler clothes and looked in better shape than the rest of us.

"Conklin, how do you think those items were stolen without any sign of a break-in?"

"I don't know, Madam. If the motion detectors had not been tripped, it would be a simple deduction that the thief did not break in, but was already in the house. I have no theory to offer given the facts."

Aha. His lips said no, but his eyes said yes. I had some thoughts myself, but they were too formless as yet to discuss with anyone.

I went upstairs to my bed. I had a date with Aunt Clem that afternoon and needed some sleep before sitting across the table from her crystal ball.

CHAPTER 12

Cowbell Lane. Cowbell Lane

When I was a child, I liked to chant these words to myself as I walked with my mother to visit Aunt Clem at Hollyhock Cottage. I always expected to come across a fat cow wearing a bell tied around her neck with a red ribbon. The bell would tinkle every time the cow bent down to munch the grass. I never saw the cow, but the words still lifted my spirits as I remembered those sleepy summer days that never seemed to end.

Today, as I parked on Cowbell Lane and got out of my car, I felt like kicking its tires. The air conditioner had conked out, and Wes at the garage couldn't get to it until the following Thursday or Friday. The short drive from Hammersleigh had reduced me to a wilting shadow of myself. I pulled my cotton skirt away from my damp thighs and pushed my hair behind my ears, wishing I had tied the hair on top of my head before leaving home.

Referring to Aunt Clem's house as a cottage was like calling Hammersleigh House a raised bungalow. Built high above a quiet lane that went nowhere, Hollyhock Cottage was a beautiful example of Queen Anne architecture. Pale yellow with white trim, the house had a wrap-around porch that dripped gingerbread. I climbed the fifty-six steps past flower beds bursting with waving clumps of daisies, ripe pink peonies and of course, hollyhocks. There were hundreds of hollyhocks in colours ranging from white, through all shades of pinks to the darkest burgundy.

The painted wooden sign swinging from the moon gate arch on the porch read, "Welcome to Hollyhock Cottage Bed and Breakfast." Aunt Clem advertised her bed and breakfast business, but not the other one. She got all the psychic clientele she could handle by word of mouth. Sundays she reserved for family, but needless to say, we mostly stayed home and watched television instead. Not because we didn't want to know what the future held, but because she had never lost the intimidating demeanour from her teaching days. I was on her doorstep that Sunday afternoon only because I wanted to question her about the 1943 reunion.

When ringing the bell brought no response, I knocked on the wooden screen door. I heard slow heavy footsteps approaching. Last chance to cut and run, I advised myself, then snickered at my cowardly impulse.

The face that appeared behind the screen did not share my amusement at life's little foibles, and it wiped the smile off mine. Twyla Malinski was Aunt Clem's maid, housekeeper, companion, and did whatever else needed to be done. She was also Dennis's aunt, so enough said on that subject, but I was sure she was pleasant enough to strangers and anyone else not previously married to her favourite nephew.

The door was not going to open without further explanation, not for me.

"Good afternoon, Aunt...Mrs....um, Twyla. I've come to see Aunt Clem. Can I come in?"

I was pretty agile for my age and managed to sidestep the door that opened so suddenly, it just missed my nose. She left me standing in the foyer and clumped her way down the hall. Her ample backside jiggled with indignation as she disappeared into Aunt Clem's spirit room.

I turned to the cigar store aboriginal that guarded the stairway. "Do you get the feeling Twyla would like to kick me back down the steps to the street?"

The wooden statue didn't answer, being busy gazing over my head at eternity. He was a handsome devil, dressed in buckskin with applied wooden fringes and painted beads. Peter had drooled over this specimen, believing it would make a wonderful conversation piece for his antique shop. I wouldn't mind him standing close by my bed at nights either.

Leaving Charlie—my name for him since he looked a lot like a young Charlton Heston—to his Zen state, I wandered into the parlour, which was used as a guest sitting room, and was again amazed at Aunt Clem's ability to recreate the perfect Victorian ambience. But perhaps it wasn't a recreation, but a blip in time. There was nothing in that room that wasn't buttoned, tufted, ruffled, fringed or tasselled.

The room was empty of guests and I went to stand by the bay window and look around at the various sofas and chairs. Each and every one was festooned with antimacassars. On the backs, the arms—they were everywhere.

Since these things were *anti*macassars, I wondered what a *mac*assar was.

From behind me came the answer. "Gentlemen used macassar oil on their hair, so antimacassars were used to protect the upholstery. They still have their place today with so many people using mousses and gels, not to mention hairspray."

My own hair stood up on the back of my neck, and I forced it back down by sheer will power.

"Hello, Aunt Clem. Reading my mind again, are you? With all the clutter in my head, I'm surprised you were able to pick out one thought."

"Your face is quite expressive, dear, and quite easy to read. No need for me to strain myself by reading your mind."

Since my back was to her, reading my face must have presented quite a challenge, but I preferred her explanation to the alternative. Then I realized she could see my face in the ornate mirror hung between two tall windows.

"Come on back to my spirit room, Lyris. I feel quite in touch today with my guides. Since this is my day off and I am rested and refreshed, I think we could have a good session."

Whoa, back up the soul train. I was feeling unsettled enough without activating Aunt Clem's spirit guides. The less they knew about me the better.

"I wanted you to tell me about the 1943 reunion, Aunt Clem. Since you were there, I…"

"All one and the same, Lyris." She turned and led the way to her spirit room. For the first time I noticed what she was wearing. Just because she lived in a time warp didn't mean Aunt Clem dressed to match her décor.

Aunt Clem was a funky dresser. She wore black stretch leggings and a tunic top of deep purple that shimmered in silvery tones as she walked. The fabric was slinky and looked light as air. A black silk scarf tied around her short white curls, and new white Nikes on her feet completed the ensemble.

She led me along the hall to the back of the house, and into the room where the same clients returned year after year for a psychic update. I heard Hollyhock Cottage Bed and Breakfast was booked for the next twenty-five years, and that made me wonder if Aunt Clem planned to run her business from the next level of existence.

The spirit room was in a turret wing and had one stained-glass window to allow muted sunlight inside. The walls were painted ivory and the ceiling was a deep midnight blue. Some kind of luminous paint had been used to dot the ceiling with silver stars.

The bare hardwood floor was coated with a matte finish that glowed in the reflection of the light from the candles. Dozens of candles. They were in sconces on the walls at different levels, in tall holders on the floor, and several in varying sizes on the round table in the centre of the room. A dark cloth covered the table, and three plain wooden chairs waited.

Aunt Clem gestured me to take a seat, then moved the candles to one side of the table. From a chest in a corner she took out an object covered with a black handkerchief. She set this in the middle of the table and took another chair.

Under the handkerchief was the crystal ball. It was a plain globe chopped off at one end so it would sit still and not roll off the table in the middle of a discourse by one of the spirit guides. There was nothing in it. I looked. No images, no scary face peered back at me. Believe me, if there had been a face in there, Aunt Clem would have had to call for the paramedics and their defibrillator.

Aunt Clem had been trying to get me in that room for years. She kept telling me I had the gift too and needed to nurture it. Hah. Not in a million years. Correction, not in *two* million years.

From inside the filmy sleeve of her shirt, Aunt Clem pulled out a tissue and started rubbing the ball. "Just to clear it a bit, you know." Then she blew her nose in the tissue before returning it to the sleeve.

"A bit of a summer cold," she explained. "Or possibly an allergy. The ragweed is early this year, since the heat has been so intense."

I sat still as a stone.

"Now. I should explain about this crystal ball. It is merely a tool I use to focus my mind and allow my spirit guides to talk to me."

"Then how do you know things?" I was curious in spite of myself. "Don't you *see* things?"

"No, not anymore. When I was a child I used to see people who weren't there, who were dead. But not anymore. Now, my guides talk to me."

"You mean, you hear voices?"

"In my head, I hear them talk to me. Not actual sounds. It's hard to explain. We all have spirit guides, although most people do not accept them or realize how much help they can be to us."

"Well, I've never seen anything that wasn't there, and nobody is trying to talk to me, so I guess I don't have the gift."

"Lyris, psychic ability is something that everybody possesses. At least the potential is there. Everyone can use it if they work at it. And some day, I believe that all humankind will be able to tap into this ability through training and experience. In the meantime, some few are born with a greater skill in this area, call it a more finely developed psychic gene if you want. Maybe science will discover a psychic DNA, although I hope they won't mess with it too much. I would hate to see the more psychically gifted people cloned and used as weapons against another nation, for instance."

My eyes must have been bugging out of my head. She looked at my face, which I guess we all agreed was an open book. "I digress. Lyris, I know you don't want to admit it, but you have one of these highly developed psychic genes. Just because you don't see things that aren't there—and don't forget there are many planes of existence—doesn't mean you don't possess the ability to hear your spirit guides speak. You are fighting it, but why?"

I had a couple of dozen good reasons. "Who are these spirit guides anyway. Are they, like, Egyptian princesses or Roman philosophers?"

She laughed. "Certainly not, dear. Oh, I imagine that some psychics have a princess or a philosopher as a guide. Why not? Even princesses and philosophers need jobs when they pass over for the final time. But most guides were just ordinary people when they were here. For instance, one of my own guides was a stonemason who helped build Westminster Abbey in England in his final embodiment. His name is Luke. And another was a nurse in the Crimea. Her name is Florence, but not *the* Florence, you know."

With my luck, my guide would turn out to be a former juvenile pickpocket who worked for Fagan and knew Charles Dickens.

"Not so, dear." She was reading my face again. "Only souls who have lived good, useful lives are allowed to guide those still on this earth."

Now, this made no sense to me whatsoever. "Do you mean, all the nasty and evil people who die are not allowed access to the psychic hotline?"

"Certainly not. God does not allow it. You see, Lyris, the soul's journey takes it through many earthly lives, the goal being to advance, grow with each passage. Only those who have advanced enough are permitted to become guides for others."

"So these guides are kind of like angels." Why was I asking these stupid questions instead of concentrating on the reunion?

"No. Angels are something else. I will explain angels another time. Right now, just remember that your guides are sent by God to assist you. All you have to do is be still and listen."

"But you had this skill since you were a child, Aunt Clem. I'm sure I was perfectly normal when I was a child."

"That doesn't mean a thing. And who's to say what is normal? I mentioned I saw spirits when I was a child. But as I grew up I lost the ability, and by the time I was in my teens, I had forgotten all about my previous experiences. It wasn't until something happened during my service days that the ability returned. Or, to be precise, I accepted the gift and started to hone it. You do remember that I was in the service?"

Sure I did. Aunt Clem's military service took place during World War II and was supposed to be top secret. She sometimes referred to it, but never explained it, as if the Secrecy Oath she took over sixty years ago still applied.

She thought nobody knew, but her sojourn at Camp X was part of Pembrooke family lore. Camp X was a secret Allied training base in a wooded area near Whitby, Ontario. The camp trained Allied secret agents and was the planning headquarters for many European resistance movements.

Aunt Clem was part of the secret communications operations developed at the camp, in a capacity no one seemed sure of. One interesting fact about Camp X was that Sir William Stephenson, the Canadian-born super spy, nicknamed Intrepid by Winston Churchill, created it.

And one of Intrepid's best students was Ian Fleming, the author of the James Bond novels. Fleming was, by all accounts, adept at weaponry, unarmed combat, explosives and all sorts of other awful pastimes. And my Aunt Clem was part of it. The tales she could tell if she would, but alas, her lips were zipped on the subject.

"Lyris." Aunt Clem waved the black hankie in my face. "You know I can't talk about my war work, but I was going to explain how my psychic gift reappeared."

"Go ahead, Aunt Clem." I still refused to admit to the so-called gift myself.

"We weren't supposed to fraternize with the agents or other personnel. But we were young and the inevitable sometimes happened. Do you understand what I'm telling you?" She peered into my face, which wasn't as easy as it sounds, since one or two of the candles were flickering and sending up smoke signals.

I nodded, hoping that my maiden aunt wouldn't get too graphic for my tender ears. I was still reeling over my mother's sex life.

"I know what you're thinking," she said.

I didn't doubt it.

"Just because I was left on the shelf doesn't mean I was never taken down and dusted once or twice."

I attempted to hurry this along. "So you met someone and he was psychic too?"

"No." Good thing she didn't have a ruler, she would have whacked my fingers with it. Bad, bad student.

"We were...close. Then he got his orders. He was being dropped behind enemy lines in France. When he was saying goodbye, I suddenly heard a voice in my head. It said to tell him not to trust the resistance officer who promised to smuggle him into Paris. The voice said that the officer was a traitor, in the pocket of the Nazis. I was so surprised at what I was hearing, and so confused, my friend left and I didn't tell him."

My nails were digging into my palms. I suspected Aunt Clem had never before uttered these words to any living soul. And it was an un-living soul who gave Aunt Clem the warning. My shoulder blades were tingling to beat the band. Damn, I wanted out of there.

"Anyway, I heard later that he died during Nazi interrogation before he reached Paris. The false resistance officer had betrayed him."

She blew at the candle that was doing the most smoking, which made it smoke all the more. The room was so hazy I couldn't see her face, but her words came through loud and clear.

"I believe that if I had repeated the words I heard in my head, he would have lived. He may not have believed me, but when the time came, he would have been alerted. From that day, I embraced my destiny and listened to the voices of my guides. And I have helped others. Perhaps if I am very, very lucky, I can be a guide for someone else when I pass. If, that is, I have lived through sufficient passages of my own."

I was determined to wiggle out of my destiny. "Yes, well, I still don't think I have the gift. All I get is a tingling in my shoulders and a few smells."

"Those are just indications that your spirit guide is trying to communicate with you. And one of those smells is misleading. It is not from your guide. Perhaps if you learned to meditate, the voices would come through."

No way I wanted any voices coming through. I didn't want to hurt her feelings so I said nothing, an achievement which indicated how unnerved I was.

She broke through my bemused state. "Lyris, a psychic always recognizes another psychic, albeit a reluctant one. And by the way, just because most of the psychics you meet are women doesn't mean there aren't just as many male psychics. Women are perhaps more willing to accept the gift. Or some say females are the slightly higher life form. Who knows?" She smiled at her little joke.

While Aunt Clem's Queen Anne cottage was air conditioned, she had closed the door to the room, and with no open windows or other form of ventilation, the air was growing closer by the minute. I used the tail of my shirt to wipe my face. Aunt Clem pulled off the silk scarf from around her head and wiped her own face and neck with it.

"Aunt Clem, I need to ask you…"

"Time for your reading now, Lyris." From out of nowhere she produced a pack of cards. "Shuffle these then cut them. As with the crystal ball, this is just a way of focusing my energy."

I complied.

"And again."

She had me cut the deck several times, then moved them around and placed others on the ones I had turned up. She was silent for several long minutes. Then just as my anxiety level was reaching critical mass, she said, "I see you are heading into a period of potential danger."

Routine. I gave up. It was best to just sit back and let her get on with it.

"Now you must understand, Lyris, that nothing I tell you is absolute, just possible or probable. By being aware, you can change what could *possibly* happen or will *probably* happen. Use what the spirits tell you as a guideline. They are trying to help, not constrain. Take what I say to you as a warning only. You have the power to prevent or minimize the consequences."

It seemed to me this gave the spirits an out if they turned out to be wrong, but hey, who was I to criticize those who had advanced to a higher level. This would be my first existence which explained why I seemed to be screwing everything up all the time. I just needed more practice.

"This danger that is approaching you can be averted if you are vigilant. Be careful in a high place." She peered at the cards. "There is a greater danger to someone you love. I can't tell who it is except that it's a man. Tell him to watch out for someone he hasn't met yet?" This last was put as a question, and she looked at the empty chair between us. Well, I was as spooked as I was going to get and it wouldn't have shook me much more if Florence or Luke had materialized in a swirl of ectoplasm to sit down in that chair.

Aunt Clem was apologetic. "It's Luke today, and sometimes he's a little vague. He doesn't like to give out too much information in case we get the wrong impression."

"Well, get Florence in here instead. Maybe she can be more specific."

"Lyris, your own spirit guide could be more helpful to you if you let him. But wait a moment and I'll see if Florence will speak." She sat there for a few moments twirling the many rings on her gnarly fingers.

Finally. "There are many changes going on in your life. You will have to make some important decisions soon about career, love, and finances. Follow your heart for career and love, and your intellect for finances."

"That's pretty standard stuff, Aunt Clem. I don't mean to offend Florence or Luke, but can't they be more precise?"

Aunt Clem pulled out the tissue and honked into it again. "Darn allergies. It's Florence now, and she says your mind is resisting and in such turmoil that she can't get through it. You must stop resisting."

I was not prepared to stop resisting and go over to the dark side. However, if Aunt Clem could answer a couple of questions, then maybe I could put some credence in all this stuff.

"How about if I ask a question?" Aunt Clem nodded. "Does Florence know who took the jade figurine and the jewelled hummingbird from Hammersleigh? We appear to have had a burglary."

Aunt Clem looked surprised. "Perhaps not a burglary in the sense you mean, since those items have not gone far. Are you sure they were taken? Maybe Arthur moved them."

"Nope. Conklin says they were on the sideboard in the hall and now they aren't. He's never wrong about these things. Besides, there are empty spots where they used to be."

"Well, they are very close by. In a high place."

The high place again. Maybe Florence had mixed up those two objects with the Meissen shepherdess that had been on the shelf with the peacock.

"There is something else missing, isn't there?" Aunt Clem said. "A doll. Have you checked the doll cabinet in the drawing room? One of those might be missing too."

"I don't think so. I don't know how anybody could get in there without a key. And Conklin, Caroline and I are the only ones with access to it. I'll check when I get home."

"These missing objects are related to the danger around you, Lyris. I mean your personal danger and the danger to your loved one. There are animals involved too. A cat and a dog. The dog could be Jacqueline, but do you have a cat at Hammersleigh now?" Not a cat lover, Aunt Clem gave me a severe look.

"Caroline Hanlon, my new housekeeper, has a cat. He's not staying."

"Don't be too sure of that. Now, I think you have another question for me, Lyris?" Out came the tissue again. Honk.

"Yes. I'm wondering, since you have this psychic ability, why you didn't know what happened to Tommy during that reunion."

Her shoulders slumped and the lines on her face seemed to deepen as I watched. She looked her age, then some. I was almost sorry for my question.

"My gift didn't return until I went back to the camp after that reunion. Maybe the trauma of Tommy's disappearance triggered it. Sometimes that happens. I never asked, and my guides have never presumed to intrude."

"I guess I can understand that. Since there were just four people staying in the house that weekend. Whoever put Tommy's body in the box, then sealed it in the closet, had to be one of those four people."

"Four?" She looked up. "Yes, four. Some things are best left alone. The truth would help no one now."

She covered the crystal ball with the black hankie and gathered the cards together. "This session is over, Lyris. I can tell you nothing else, but there is much you can learn if you will listen. Oh, just one more thing—your spirit guide's name is Leander".

"How do you know that?"

"He has been trying to communicate with you for some time now. When you wouldn't respond, he approached Florence to pass on his name to you and ask that you allow the channel between you to open."

Hah.

When I reached the door, she spoke once more. "I let Wisty know about Tommy being found. I don't know if she understood me, but I am going to bring her to the reunion next Saturday. If you talk to her, please remember that her grasp on this world is tenuous at best and we don't want to drive her further within herself. Tommy's funeral is Tuesday morning and the burial is in the family section of the cemetery. I would like it if you came. Just don't tell anyone else. We could have a media circus if the time and place are known to the public."

On my way out I ran into Twyla again as she was ushering in a family client, Challis Pembrooke. A few years ago, I had attended her wedding to a cousin, another Thomas.

I said to her, "You might want to come back another time, Challis. Florence and Luke are having an off day.

My rear end escaped trauma by a hair when Twyla slammed the screen door.

CHAPTER 13

I was rockin'. The Crystals, my favourite female band from the sixties, was belting out "Da Doo Ron Ron" on the CD player, and I put the pedal to the metal as I turned off Highway 22 onto County Road 12 that led to Hammersleigh House. The windows were open and I hung my left arm out to catch the wind. You can't get that feeling with the windows closed and the air conditioner blasting in your face.

With about two hundred yards to go before reaching Hammersleigh's iron gates, I slowed down and glanced into the rear-view mirror. Something I should have done a bit earlier. A blue and white cruiser passed me and pulled up in front of the gates, blocking the entrance.

How fast had I been moving? I hadn't paid attention. And what was the speed limit on the concession road anyway? I couldn't remember that either. I mean, I was normally a lawful driver.

The lights on top of the cruiser were whirling, and when I turned off the music and the ignition, I could hear the last low notes of the siren fading away. I knew the officer was going to be Tammie Wilberts even before she stepped out and strode toward me. And it wasn't clairvoyance either. Given the way my day had been going so far, there could be no alternative.

She stuck her frizzy little head in my window. "Do you know how fast you were going?"

"Eighty?"

She snorted and pulled out a summons book and pen. "Try a hundred and four."

"Oh, surely not. I never…"

"Do you know what the speed limit is?"

"Eighty?"

Another snort. The officer was a woman of few sounds.

"Okay, seventy?"

"The speed limit on all county roads is sixty kilometres per hour. So let's see, a hundred and four in a sixty. Do you know how many demerit points that is?"

"One?"

"You wish. I should take you in for dangerous driving. Let me see your driver's license and registration. And proof of insurance."

I dug the stuff out for her, all the while thinking how unfair this was. The police never ticketed a speeder for the full clock. Everybody knew that. If they caught you doing a hundred and four in a sixty, they wrote you up for seventy-five, eighty tops. Not only would this get me a whopping fine, but I'd lose most of my points. If my license was suspended, it would be a long, frosty walk into town and out the other end come winter to get to my job. Maybe Conklin would chauffeur me in Uncle Patrick's Lincoln.

Maybe in another plane of existence.

I located the insurance information in the glove compartment and was handing it to her when another cruiser pulled up behind my car. There were no lights or sirens this time, and Ronnie Guilbert got out and walked up beside Tammie.

With a glance at me, he pulled Tammie away a distance and talked to her in a low voice. Whatever he said, she wasn't buying. At one point, I thought she was going to hurl her hat to the ground and stomp on it. She gestured at me, then back up the road, then back to me again. I wondered what lies she was telling Ronnie about my driving.

Flinging both arms up to the heavens, she strode back to me and snatched the insurance, license and registration information from my fingers. The freckles stood out lividly on her pale face. She scribbled on her little pad, signed it and thrust it at me. I used her pen to sign my name and was relieved to note she had ticketed me for doing seventy-five in a sixty. I was afraid to thank her.

Grabbing her copy of the ticket and her pen back, she galloped to her cruiser, turned the vehicle around and sped off. I figured she was doing over a hundred by the time she reached the highway.

I got out of my car on shaky legs and waited for Ronnie to join me. I saw a lecture coming on, not that I didn't deserve it, but I wasn't in the mood.

"I know, Ronnie, I'm sorry. I don't know why I was driving so fast and I won't do it again. I'm not a speeder, you know. And thanks for intervening for me."

He took off his hat and wiped his forehead on his sleeve. His hair was damp from the humidity and his pleasant face was almost as red as his hair. "Okay, Lyris, I won't chew you out, but I hope you'll stay out of Tammie's way in the future. You seem to bring out the worst in her. I've never seen her try to write someone up for the clocked speed before. Not that she wasn't within the law." He looked at me to satisfy himself that I got the picture.

"She seems to hate me. I wish I knew why?" That was just a fishing expedition. I knew full well why. I just wondered if he did.

Ronnie gave me a look that said he knew I knew perfectly well Tammie had a thing for Marc and didn't appreciate me cutting her out before she even let Marc know how she felt.

"Just try and stay out of Tammie's way, will you Lyris?" Then he, too, made a U-turn—I thought they were illegal?—and drove off even faster than his comrade.

A half hour later, I watched Caroline taking out objects from one of the cabinets and dusting them with one of those feather duster things, except it was bright green polyester. Or maybe parrot feathers. Yes, Ronnie was a distinct possibility. But was she ready for another relationship yet? If she hadn't recovered from her current relationship, then she could hurt Ronnie, and that would not be acceptable. Or Ronnie could toy with her affections and hurt her. That wouldn't be so great either. Maybe I should just mind my own business?

That last thought just popped into my head, and I liked to think it was my common sense talking, not a guide from the astral plane.

I had changed from the denim skirt and white cotton blouse I wore to Aunt Clem's into black shorts and a sleeveless, pink T-shirt. The house was cooler than outside, but not as comfortable as I knew the employees' air-conditioned wing would be. How I longed to stretch out on the couch in the lounge and relax. Anything would be better than this brocade sofa, which was never meant to be sprawled on. I eased my upper back away from a sprung spring. You couldn't see it, but it was there waiting for someone to try and relax on it.

We were in the parlour, which was across the hall from the drawing room, and as far as I was concerned, the two rooms were interchangeable. Both had ornate fireplaces, eight-foot windows and lots of beautiful antique furniture to sit on. As long as you sat on it, you were fine. Just don't lie down.

I felt a little guilty watching Caroline work while I loafed. But then everybody had his or her job to do, except...

"Hey, Caroline. Why are you doing that today? This is Sunday, your day off, remember?"

"I know Lyris, but I thought since I only started yesterday, I didn't need a day off so soon. I'll just finish this cabinet, then maybe have a nap. Since I didn't get much sleep last night." She gave the tiny glass globe a final flick and returned it to the cabinet. The globe reminded me of Aunt Clem's crystal ball and I shuddered.

I sat up so quickly I gave myself a head rush, my blood pressure being on the low side. When the spots in front of my eyes cleared, I ran across the hall to the drawing room. A missing doll?

The doll cabinet was still locked, and nothing looked disturbed. There were no gaps or empty places in the rows of beautiful faces that looked out at me. Unless someone had moved them, like I did when I took Amelia out.

Amelia.

I raced past a startled Caroline and took the stairs two at a time. As soon as I entered my room, I knew she was gone. The window seat was empty, as were the bed and the chairs. Just to make sure, I opened the wardrobe and searched through all the drawers, under the bed, everywhere.

I spent a frantic five minutes looking through the five other bedrooms, both bathrooms and I even stuck my head in the tower room. No Amelia.

Downstairs, my luck was no better. Amelia was nowhere to be found. She couldn't disappear into thin air. Caroline was making a cup of tea in the kitchen, and she dropped her tea bag when I grabbed her by the arm. "Have you seen Amelia."

"Who's Amelia? Is somebody here?"

"Amelia is an antique doll, a Juneau. She was sitting on my window seat and now she's gone."

"To be honest, Lyris, I haven't been into the bedrooms upstairs yet. I thought I would look around tomorrow. When did you see the doll last?"

"I don't know. I can't remember." I was beside myself. Not only was Amelia a very valuable doll, but I had loved her ever since I was a little girl and first saw her in Uncle Patrick's doll cabinet. And it was my fault she was missing. I should never have taken her out of that cabinet.

"Caroline, would you look through the employees' wing, just in case Jacqueline or Rasputin dragged her out of my room? And where's Conklin?"

Conklin was in his pantry counting the silver or polishing it, whatever it was he did with it. The three of us searched the house from top to bottom. Conklin even looked through the empty former servants' bedrooms on the third floor.

Conklin wore his prune face the whole time and cast disapproving glances in my direction. I was too upset to care. After an hour, we had to concede defeat. Amelia was nowhere in the house. Somebody had taken her.

"Perhaps you should call the police, Madam. The officer, if you remember, asked us to contact her if we found anything else was missing." Conklin was looking less immaculate than usual, a trifle dry and dusty in fact. And I noticed he didn't offer to make the call himself.

"I think I'll go to the police station in person."

Since Tammie Wilberts was recently on patrol, harassing innocent taxpayers, she was unlikely to be in the station now. Didn't the woman ever sleep? She was here last night too. But I wasn't going to chance her answering the phone. And Marc had said he was planning to be in his office for a few hours that afternoon.

I drove a virtuous sixty on the county road, enraging the driver of a red pickup who pulled out of the Gates of Heaven Cemetery behind me, then a lawful eighty on the highway into town, where it changed to forty or fifty. I couldn't remember, so I drove forty with the same red pickup tailgating me all the way, wanting to pass, but finding no suitable spot. The driver parked half a block from the police station, while I stopped right in front. When he got out, I noticed it was Scott Fournier. He gave me a friendly wave.

I returned the gesture. "Right back at you."

He turned and walked away from his truck in the direction of Spangles Bar and Grill. Funny. I wondered what he had been doing in the cemetery. His family would be buried in the Northton cemetery.

Tammie was not on dispatch duty. It was a kid about seventeen with a buzz cut and a pimple on his chin, and someone had given him a policeman's uniform. He had the phone crunched between ear and shoulder. "Yeah, yeah, go on." He wrote on a printed form.

He didn't notice me, so I walked behind him and slipped into Marc's office. Some security. I closed the door and leaned back against it.

Marc looked up in surprise, and then his wonderful smile transformed the handsome features. God, he was a babe. I still couldn't believe he wanted me when he could have any woman in town.

I felt like having a little fun. It was the devil made me do it. If there were spirit guides, they weren't on the job, or they would have stopped me.

"I've come to confess." I fluttered my eyelashes. At least I hoped they were fluttering flirtatiously, but it probably looked like I had a nervous tic in both eyes. I was not a flirty girl.

"Oh, really. What have you done now?"

Good, he hadn't heard about the ticket yet.

He put his pen down and swivelled his chair toward the door. He was wearing shorts and a black T-shirt with a police logo and a caption that read "Speed Kills."

I couldn't take my mind off his thighs. I swear you could bounce a quarter off that man's thighs. Or his stomach. I clicked the lock on the door.

I moved over to sit on the arm of his chair. "I've been a bad girl."

He glanced at the door. His skin flushed.

"It's locked. I'm a bad girl and you're the good cop, and I have to be punished." I slid off the arm of the chair onto his lap and put my arms around his neck.

He froze. With his eyes glued to the door, he pulled on my arms to unwrap them. "What's got into you? You better sit on the chair over there."

"I like it better here. Haven't you ever played games in this office before?"

"Just Hangman. Lyris, cut it out and get up. Someone might come in."

I clung tighter. "Relax. The door is locked. And this is more fun than Hangman. Are you telling me you never played Bad Girl/Good Cop with anyone else in this room?"

"I never heard of Bad Girl/Good Cop. And I never had a woman sit on my knee in my office. I could get fired for this."

"Nonsense. You're the chief. You're the chief policeman and I'm a very bad girl. So what are you going to do about it?"

With a mighty heave, Marc stood up and pried my fingers loose. He took me by the shoulders and pushed me into the visitor's chair. "Now sit there and don't move."

He sat back in his own chair and pulled the neck of his T-shirt to loosen it. I reached over and ran my fingers down his thigh.

He brushed my fingers aside and looked at me. "Why don't you ever do that when we're alone? I wouldn't say no under other circumstances."

"We're as alone here as we are in my Conklin-infested house. Or in your twin-filled bungalow. But okay, I'll just sit in my chair and be good. I have a crime to report anyway. Amelia is missing."

"Who is Amelia?"

"What."

"I said, who is Amelia?"

"No, I mean Amelia is a what. She's a doll."

I thought I saw his left eye twitch. Probably a trick of the light, but I figured it was time to cut the kidding and get down to business. I explained about Amelia.

He pulled a folder from his in-basket and added the information. "How much is the doll worth."

"About forty-five hundred dollars."

He looked up in surprise. "Would this be general knowledge? That's a lot of money for a doll."

"Probably not. But all the items taken were all sitting around, not locked up. The two pieces from the sideboard in the hall and Amelia from my room. And there were so many people in and out of the house in the past couple of days—the cleaners, the plant man, Peter and his friends to move the furniture, Caroline and her husband. I can't remember who all."

I didn't mention the dinner party guests, but I'm sure he remembered there were eight extra people in the house last evening alone. It was unthinkable that any one of them would have taken the doll and the other pieces.

"Lyris, I want you to make a list of everyone who has been in the house since the last time you saw the doll. Everyone." He gave me a look that was meant to be stern, but merely stirred my blood. "And quit looking at me like that. At least until later."

"We'll see about that." I got up and moved toward the door.

When my hand was on the knob, Marc asked, "Lyris, how do you play Bad Girl/Good Cop?

I opened the door. "Let's just say it involves a jar of jasmine massage oil and a string of twinkle lights. The white mini ones. Oh, and a peacock feather." I closed the door behind me with a soft click.

On the way home, my mind kept switching back and forth between two dilemmas.

First, when *did* I last see Amelia. I couldn't for the life of me remember. Before the dinner party? After? Or after Peter and his friends moved my bedroom furniture?

Second, why did I make up that stupid game? One day, I would have to come up with a bedroom frolic that included jasmine massage oil, twinkle lights and a feather. The massage oil was plausible. I could see a use for that, and maybe even the feather. But the twinkle lights? And all in keeping with the theme of a very bad girl and an officer of the law.

Once again, my mouth runneth over.

CHAPTER 14

Nothing disturbed my rest that night, and I showed up for breakfast eager to strike items off my reunion list. I crossed the kitchen to the cupboard, where I kept my tea collection.

A movement from the corner by the window startled me. I turned, but saw nothing more threatening than Caroline holding an ice pack to her chin.

"What happened to you? Are you hurt?" I gently pried the pack away from her face, unable to restrain a gasp when I saw the livid bruise on the left side of her jaw.

She covered the injury again. "I'm fine, honest. I'm so clumsy. I walked into my bathroom door this morning. Don't worry, Lyris, it will fade in no time."

"Funny, the time I walked into a door, it was my nose that connected first. Guess mine sticks out more."

She got up and fussed around the sink, although there was nothing left to clean. The kitchen was immaculate.

"Let me fix you a cup of tea." I placed two miniature teapots and two metal tea balls on the counter. Standing in front of my tea cupboard, I considered if Caroline needed something calming or energizing. Ah, ginseng was just the thing to help protect the body against stress and give it a little boost.

I explained this to her. "For myself, I think I need some burdock root this morning. It's a powerful purifier and cleanser. Maybe I'll put a little in with your ginseng as well, since burdock also aids in skin healing." I filled the tea balls with the loose herbs and placed them in the teapots. The loose pieces were more potent than the processed herbs you buy in bags.

Caroline looked at me a little strangely, but I was used to it. Many people are inexperienced in herbal remedies and doubtful of their healing properties. Mother Earth has given us a wealth of natural cures and restorative plants, but we are so trusting of anything that comes out of a prescription bottle, we no longer even think to consult Her.

At that moment Conklin came in from the employees' wing, dressed for another day of polishing things and harassing the Madam.

"Good morning, Conklin. I'm going to make you a nice cup of cascara sagrada tea. It's good for —"

"I know what it's for, Madam, and I don't need it. Thank you anyway."

"Oh. Are you sure? Okay then, how about ginseng for—" Once again I was not destined to finish a sentence.

"Ginseng will be excellent, Madam. I'll get a cup for myself."

Caroline had been staring at the open cupboard where my tins of tea were stacked. She moved over to look at them. I had labelled each tin carefully and was proud of my collection.

"Lyris, do you have a tea for everything here?"

"Not everything. Most of these herbs are to calm, energize, detoxify, regulate body functions, that sort of thing. I steer clear of anything potentially harmful or dangerous. There are people who are trained to mix herbs for treatments of specific ailments, but that requires specialized training and I'm afraid I'm just an interested amateur. However, if you have an occasional headache, cramp, indigestion, or if you just want to cleanse your system, I have the herb that might help. I get my supplies from a Chinese herbalist in town. Well, she's not Chinese. She has a degree in Chinese medicine."

Caroline still looked dubious. "Well, okay, thanks Lyris."

I took a sip of my burdock root and managed not to shudder at the bitter taste. "Now, I'm going to make the three of us a tasty omelette. Nothing like a good breakfast to start off the day."

The omelette turned out well, to the surprise of all three of us. Even Conklin lost his horrified look at the prospect of eating something I cooked and cleaned his plate. And I made sure they drank up every drop of their tea before leaving the kitchen. I even cleaned up the dishes, and that alone proved how well rested and take-charge I felt.

An hour later, my enthusiasm faltered as I laboured in the claustrophobic telephone room. Quite a few check marks decorated my reunion list, but there were many more to go. First I had called Wooter Sanitation to arrange for six porta-potties to be delivered on Friday morning. The Neanderthal I spoke to argued that since past Pembrooke reunions required four porta-potties, then four porta-potties I was going to get. "Six," I insisted. We settled on five.

Then I phoned the town offices to arrange for periodic inspection of the recreation vehicles, which would park in the field beside Hammersleigh. I remembered a few reunions ago there was talk about several out-of-towners dumping their sewage in the field. They insisted it was an accident, but Uncle Patrick had to pay for the cleanup and no way was I going to. The health inspector promised to drop around twice on Saturday and again on Sunday morning before the campers pulled out. I wrote a note to myself to post a sign to that effect on one of the few trees in the field. The wrinkle was that the inspector couldn't remember which bylaw forbade dumping raw sewage, so I would have to make one up to quote on the sign.

I staggered out of the telephone room, dizzy and dehydrated. A cup of ginger tea and a tomato sandwich restored my stamina enough to allow the short drive to my mother's house. Mom was alarmed at my appearance and made me sit in her cool living room and put my feet up. She brought me a glass of icy lemonade and a plate with two cinnamon buns.

I drained the glass at one go and then turned my attention to the buns. Mom had left the room again, and when she came back, she was carrying a battered shoebox. She glanced at the empty plate and glass and put the box on the coffee table in front of me.

"There should be a picture of the 1943 reunion somewhere in here." She upturned the box on the table and dozens of photos spilled out, all sizes from tiny pictures a couple of inches square to eight by tens. All were labelled on the backs by year and subject matter.

"I know it's here somewhere." While she was shuffling through the pictures, I pulled a notebook and pen out of my purse and wrote "Call photographer, make arrangements to come Sunday morning for official photograph." Forgetting that little item would seriously annoy the people who loved to have their picture taken with their arms around each other or holding up a beer while pinching their fourth cousin on the butt.

"Here it is." Mom handed me one of the eight by tens, then came around to sit beside me.

She pointed to a tiny girl sitting cross-legged in the front row with other tots. "That's me."

I dug into my purse again and found the magnifying glass I carried to read the small print on labels in the grocery store. One of these days I was going to have to buy a pair of glasses.

The sepia-toned photo was surprisingly clear, and with the magnifying glass, I could see every face in detail, including the blonde pigtails on the toddler who became my mother.

"Pretty cute." At least a hundred people had gathered for the photographer that summer day so long ago, happy and carefree. A couple of the men were wearing uniform caps, and by scanning the rows with my magnifier, I could make out many more in the telltale wool khaki pants and ties which they had pulled loose. Those clothes must have been murder in the heat.

At least one of the women should be in uniform too, I figured. "Which one is Aunt Clem?" I asked.

Mom took the glass from my hand. "This one." She indicated a young woman in the back row. She was shorter than the men on either side of her and I couldn't make out if she was wearing a uniform or not. Her face was tilted toward the man beside her, her hair dark and glossy, her lips red and inviting. The man's arm was encircling her waist and she leaned into him. He was suggesting they slip away after the photographer was finished, to the pine wood where it was cool and private. She laughed and whispered to him that her mother would notice, they didn't dare. Maybe tonight…

"Lyris. What's the matter?" Mom put her hand on my arm and I shook my head to clear it.

"Nothing. Just one of those flights of imagination I'm so fond of." I laughed, but my heart was thumping and the magnifying glass was shaking in my hand. I put it down. "Which ones are Aunt Wisty, Uncle Patrick and what's his name, Bruce Wingate?"

She gave me a look of concern, but didn't mention my lapse again. "In the back there is Patrick, then Clematis. I don't know the next man. I guess he could be this Bruce Wingate, then Wisteria. She's holding little Tommy."

I peered at the grouping and saw the young, unlined faces. Aunt Clem was looking straight ahead and not leaning against either man. She was smiling gaily.

Patrick's short dark hair framed a face unmarked by time, unrecognizable as the shrunken, elderly man I had known. Bruce Wingate, if indeed it was he, was gazing down at Tommy, who reached up with his little hand to pull on his mother's necklace. Wisty seemed not to notice, just looked back at the camera like her sister. Unlike her sister, she did not smile.

Just a few short hours later, their world would change in such a terrible way. Tommy would be dead, his grief-stricken mother well on her way to the madness that would force her imprisonment in a mental hospital for the rest of her life.

Uncle Patrick? He went back to war and returned a changed and reclusive man. He died of natural causes at an advanced age, so you could say he lived his allotted span. But was it a full and satisfying life? Did what happen at this reunion shape his future in any way?

Aunt Clem returned to her secret war work, loved, lost, and then rallied to pursue a teaching career and her psychic gift. I wondered if the summer of 1943 had anything to do with her decision not to marry. There was no reason to think so, but I felt she was not as forthcoming about the reunion as she might have been. Could she truly have felt no psychic twinge about Tommy's fate?

Bruce Wingate was an unknown factor. I would like to think it was his hand that caused Tommy's death rather than a family member— Tommy's mother, aunt or uncle. That was too awful to contemplate.

"I wonder who Bruce Wingate was? And what happened to him after the war, if he survived it?" I looked at my mother, but she had no answers.

"I never heard much talk about any of this over the years. Until Tommy was found, I had forgotten all about it."

"What are people saying now? The women in your book club and lawn bowling group must be talking."

"Everybody is talking, although nobody knows anything. Of course they are all too young." She picked up the picture. "All the older people are long dead. The younger ones, the ones who survived the war, are almost all gone as well. Even the children are past middle age now."

"And children who weren't born yet *are* middle-aged." I was thinking of myself because, let's face it, thirty-eight was crowding middle age. "If Tommy was still alive, he would be almost seventy. Yet, because he died as a little child, we can't think of him as grown up."

Mom started gathering up the pictures that were scattered on the table and put them back in the box. "Come now, Lyris, we're getting too introspective and morbid. Forget about what happened that summer. Let's talk about something else."

That suited me. I had started to identify too much with these people and had given myself a headache to boot. I grabbed the reunion picture before she could put it away. "Can I borrow this for a while?"

She released it into my hand. I dropped it into my purse before she could change her mind.

While she was in the kitchen getting us more lemonade, I called to her, "When are David and Denise and the kids arriving?"

"Thursday, I think. They're going to stop here first for the key to your house, so if you want to leave it with me today, it might save you a trip. And I could get a few staples into the fridge to save them having to shop right away."

I removed the key from my ring. "It's here on the table. The house is ready for them. I even put clean sheets on the bed and dragged Mitch's crib out of storage and set it up."

"Thanks, dear." She handed me a glass and another plate of buns. For some reason, my mother thought of me as a hearty eater. "I admit I'm happy that David is moving back to Blackshore with his family. I've missed them and I know John is looking forward to David joining the firm and taking over some of his workload."

She looked at me over her glass. "John would like to do some traveling." She pushed the plate under my nose and I took another bun, just to be polite. "And he wants me to go with him." Anxiety filled her blue eyes.

I chewed my bun while thinking of a response. I had no problem with people traveling together in an unmarried state, but Blackshore was a conservative town. The gossip network, captained by my Aunt Bertilla, Jody's mother, would eat my mother alive.

"…and we thought we'd get married in the New Year, which would give David enough time to…"

"What? What did you say?"

I wished I would stop spacing out. Maybe I had a neurological problem, like a brain lesion or something.

"I said, John has asked me to marry him and I said yes."

I put the remnants of the bun down and threw my arms around my mother. I was so happy for her, I felt tears run down my face. Her reputation was intact. "That's wonderful, Mom. I can't tell you how pleased I am."

She looked pleased too. "I'm glad you're not upset, Lyris. I was afraid you might be. I know it's sudden, but when you're over seventy, you don't have time for long courtships."

"If you're sure, Mom. That's all that matters."

"Oh, I'm sure. I just wish I had met John a long time ago." She stopped speaking and looked nervous again.

"What do you mean? Dad's been gone only seven years and I know how devastated you were when he died."

"Of course I was, Lyris. I loved your father very much. You know that." She gathered up glasses and plate.

"No, wait, Mom. Do you mean you wish you had married John Brixton instead of Dad?"

She didn't answer, so I continued. "Because now that I look back, I have the sense that you weren't as happy as you should have been." I didn't know why I was saying these things. My father had been a wonderful man.

"I thought I was happy. I know I was well looked after by your father, and he was faithful to me always."

"But?"

She sat back down and looked at me. "Lyris, I want you to remember that there is a reason I'm telling you these things. My marriage and yours had many similarities."

I jumped up and walked to the window to stare out at the shimmering heat rising from the pavement in front of the house. "Mom, you just said that Dad was a faithful husband. And that's something that Dennis never was. How can our marriages be the same?"

"I said there were some similarities, Lyris. Here's one—your father never hit me, and Dennis never hit you, but there are other types of abuse. And we were both victims of it."

What was she saying? My mother never suffered from abuse, and I know I didn't.

"Sit down, Lyris, and let me explain. I'm sorry to bring this up now when you have so many other things on your mind, but I only just figured it out for myself, and I've been watching for the right time to talk to you about it. Your father did everything for me. He picked my clothes, he made out a weekly menu, decided when we could take a vacation, how many children we could have."

She paused for a moment. "He handled all our finances—I didn't know anything, didn't even have a chequebook and if it wasn't for John helping me after your father died, I don't know how I would have managed. John made me learn all those things for myself and showed me that I was capable of looking after my own affairs. He convinced me I was a worthwhile person, who could do *anything* on my own. I was terrified when I moved to Victoria to be near David. It was the first time in my life I did anything alone, but John kept in touch and encouraged me one step at a time."

I was stunned. "Why didn't I know this? I must have been blind."

She took my hand between both of hers and squeezed. "You can't blame yourself. You were going through a bad time with Dennis when your father died. I'm sure he didn't mean to, but your father chipped away at my self-confidence all the years we were married until I was incapable of functioning without him."

She looked away for a moment. "I don't know whether it was a control or power ploy, or whether he truly believed I was helpless. I have thought a lot about it, and I still don't know the answer. Sometimes I blame myself. Maybe I somehow brought it on myself by *being* helpless. All I know is, I have to fight every day of my life not to take the easy way out and look for someone else to take care of me."

"Are you sure John isn't that person?"

She smiled. "I'm sure. He's my friend and my lover, and he wants me to be an independent person. We have so much fun together, but I also enjoy my time alone or with my other friends."

I thought about Mom and John Brixton for a minute. I couldn't think of any downside.

"Okay, but what makes your situation the same as mine? Are you saying that Dennis treated me the way Dad treated you?"

"I'm afraid your Dad set the stage for you to allow Dennis to control the important aspects of your life."

"I don't know what that means."

"Lyris, looking back, this is the one thing I feel the most guilt about—that I allowed your father to undermine your and David's self-confidence. I told you both how much I loved you and how proud I was of your accomplishments, but I don't know if it was enough."

I felt I should defend him. "Dad always wanted us to do better. He just wanted the best for us, and I know he was disappointed that I didn't go to university, but he was proud of David."

"He loved both of you—and me—very much. He had no idea the damage he was inflicting by not acknowledging your successes and achievements, ever. He thought that to do so would make you content with less. Do you ever remember him telling you he loved you, or that you had done a good job of anything?"

I shook my head. I had never thought about it before. If I got an A at school, he wanted to know why it wasn't an A plus. And anything other than an A wasn't even mentioned. The report card was just signed in tight-lipped silence, while I squirmed in humiliation. When I informed him I was pregnant and had to marry Dennis instead of going to university, well, my mind refused to even retrieve that memory. It turned out he was right, though.

Mom touched my arm. "You and David are both strong people, and that is why David is a successful lawyer and you managed to survive an abusive marriage and find the strength to finally end it. But if you had valued yourself more, you wouldn't have stayed with Dennis and put up with his infidelity for so many years. I'm glad you seem to have found a man who respects your qualities and doesn't want to change you."

I didn't want to discuss Marc. "Yes, well, I understand what you're saying. And I don't disagree about Dad, though I know he meant well. But how can you refer to my marriage as abusive? We had some pretty loud fights, but I did as much yelling as Dennis did."

"There is such a thing as emotional abuse, Lyris, and you were a victim of it. Dennis was unfaithful many times and somehow made you believe you were at fault. He made you feel inadequate, that you were unlovable and deserved to be treated so shabbily."

"I didn't know for a long time…"

"You didn't want to know. You refused to talk about it for years. I just thank God you left him."

I had to smile at that. "I didn't have much choice, Mom. He got Tracey pregnant. I had to do the honourable thing and release him to her teenaged arms."

"He got what he deserved. I just hope that now you don't think your father didn't love us, because he did, very much. It just wasn't a constructive type of love. But we survived and we go on."

"Mom, are you going to have this conversation with David?"

"I already have, when I was in Victoria. He confided that he had attended some counselling sessions when he was in university, so had worked through most of it then. He was waiting for one of us to mention the subject and was very happy that I had come to terms with the past. Now we're waiting for you." She looked at me.

"Me?" I was surprised. "I left Dennis, didn't I? I realized that the bastard was playing me like a violin. Mind you, it took Tracey's pregnancy to give me the final push, but I was ready to get out by then anyway."

She gave my hand a final pat and stood up. "You know what, dear? I think we've been through enough today. This was very hard for you, but until you can open up and communicate your feelings to another person—whether it's Marc, or me—without making jokes about yourself, then you won't be healed. I know your strength of character will allow you to do this, and if you decide you need some help, let me know and I'll give you the name of a wonderful woman I see every week. She's helped me very much."

Partway home I had to stop the car and throw up in a plastic grocery bag that I fortuitously found stuffed under the front seat. Even my iron digestion was no match for three cinnamon buns. Okay, make that four.

Of course, an emotional bloodbath could produce enough excess stomach acid to upset the digestive process. Not to mention my mother suggesting I needed the services of a therapist.

When I got home, Caroline met me at the door with a note from Aunt Clem. Written on it were the time and place of Tommy's funeral the next day.

CHAPTER 15

I yawned and swayed on my feet. I eyed a rectangular raised tombstone nearby. The incumbent wouldn't mind if I stretched out for a bit, but the few mourners in attendance might.

It was 5:30 a.m., and the rosy sunrise threatened us with yet another hot day. The funeral mass had lasted fifteen minutes in the cool stone church in town. Afterwards, the hearse had sped the tiny white coffin to the old section of the Gates of Heaven Cemetery, so very close to Hammersleigh House.

I had followed in my car with Father Conners by my side and Aunt Clem, Aunt Wisty and Conklin buckled into the back seat. That was it. No one else watched the cemetery staff lower the coffin into the hole.

Aunt Clem insisted that the funeral had to take place early in the morning so that no newspaper reporters from the city would catch wind of it and harass Aunt Wisty. I looked around, but couldn't see a single person with or without a camera, so I guess Aunt Clem had outsmarted them.

Aunt Clem was clothed head to foot in black—wide-brimmed hat, loose gauzy ankle-length dress with empire waist, sandals. All black. Except her lipstick was bright red and a cobalt silk scarf was wrapped loosely around her neck and thrown over one shoulder. She looked too good for a funeral.

On the other hand, Aunt Wisty seemed to be holding on to her earthly existence by a thread. She was all bones and angles, her mauve pantsuit hanging on her tiny frame. Her unfocused eyes fluttered from sky to tree line to tombstones, anywhere but at the rectangular depression in front of her.

I suspected she was drugged and wondered why her doctors felt attending her son's funeral would be good for her. The poor soul didn't appear to be aware of where she was or why she was there.

And Conklin? Conklin was just himself. Dressed in his butler uniform as befit that solemn occasion, he was standing between the two elderly sisters and supporting each by an arm. Not that Aunt Clem needed any support. And I couldn't figure out why he was there since, by his own admission, he hadn't been anywhere near Blackshore when Tommy died.

And why was I there? Beats me, unless Aunt Clem felt that, since I was the one who found the body after so many years, it was my responsibility.

Looking down, I found I was dressed in a bright red denim skirt and white sleeveless blouse. Scarlet toenails erupted from thong sandals. Maybe not funeral attire, but after all, it was still almost the middle of the night. I would still be in bed if Conklin hadn't knocked on my bedroom door with a cup of tea at 4:30 a.m. My inherent respect for the elderly barely prevented me from throwing my pillow at his noble head.

I yawned again and eyed Aunt Wisty. I wanted to talk to her, to ask her about the 1943 reunion, but would have to put it off until later when the drugs wore off. They couldn't keep her zonked all the time.

The graveside ceremony was soon over. I pulled Conklin aside and asked him if he would drive the ladies home while I walked back to Hammersleigh through the field. He gave me a courtly half bow.

"I would be honoured to drive Miss Clematis and Miss Wisteria to their residences, Madam. Would you like me to drop you off first?"

I declined and handed over my keys. After reminding him not to forget Father Conners as well, I watched the group disappear among the gravestones on the crest of the hill. The cemetery staff followed behind. I hoped they were going somewhere for breakfast and would be coming back to fill in the grave.

I looked around. Why was I standing in the cemetery on a midsummer's dawn? All alone with the acres of dead.

I moved over to stand at the tidy mound beside Tommy's final resting place. But I knew somehow that he wasn't resting. Not yet. There was a secret, a secret that I felt had to be discovered before the child could sleep in peace. No, not the child, that wasn't right...

Giving myself a shake, I moved away. Sometimes I give myself the creeps.

Tommy's grave was no more than a few feet away from where my own tiny daughter lay. If I were more fanciful, I might have felt comforted that my little Jessica had someone close to her own age for company. Jessica's tiny heart had never beat in this world, and I still missed her very much.

I never came here without feeling a consuming rage—at fate for taking Jessica before she drew a first breath, at Dennis for talking me into a tubal ligation when my grief was too fresh for coherent thought so that there would be no other little girl for me, and at myself for being too weak to resist his selfish will. I was too aware that he had a young daughter of his own now, with two more on the way. If this was part of the universal master plan, I failed to see the point.

I wandered through the cemetery without purpose. When I reached the top of the steep incline where gravity tipped the grave markers to an impossible angle, I stopped.

This cemetery was as familiar to me as my backyard had been when I was a child. Patsy and I had played among the tombstones for hours at a time on sunny days, and this would explain why the cemetery held no dread for me. There was soft green grass to walk on in bare feet, tiny wild flowers to pick under the aged maples lining the perimeter, oak benches scattered here and there to read or dream on. And everywhere there was family, from both sets of grandparents back to the pioneers who settled this area a hundred and fifty years ago. Those early grave markers were still legible, thanks to the work of the Blackshore Preservationist Society who had traced the eroded letterings with black paint so history would not be lost.

It was time to pull myself together and get home. First a few more hours of sleep, then back to the reunion list. There was no reason I couldn't complete it today, and then spend a few days working on the murder before the first campers rolled into the field on Friday afternoon.

As I walked down the eastward slope toward the maple boundary between the cemetery and the field, I felt a light tingle between my shoulders. I ignored it and picked up my pace. The tingling increased in intensity until it felt like invisible fingers were poking me, prodding me.

I was more angry than frightened. This tingling sensation came and went with no seeming relevance, and I was sick of it.

Now I imagined a bony finger shoving me in the back, urging me on. *Don't be so obdurate, Lyris, it is right there in front of you. Be still and look...*

I halted abruptly. "Okay, knock it off. Stop." To my surprise, the sensation ceased and for some reason, that did frighten me.

I was standing less than a foot from a tall obelisk-like gravestone. It was nestled in the shade of one of the giant maple trees near the edge of the cemetery. I stepped back to see it more clearly and recognized it as a memorial to those Blackshore men who had fallen during World War II. Their bodies lay in foreign graves, in France, Holland, Belgium and Italy. But the town had erected this monument to honour their sacrifices and provide a link to the future. Their future that was now our past.

I had seen this stone a hundred times in my life and never paid it any attention. An empty tomb is not attractive to a child, and as an adult, I haven't been much interested in past wars. Other than what I was forced to learn in history classes, I knew little of the causes or consequences of world conflicts. I bought a poppy and observed the two minutes of silence on Remembrance Day and felt nothing more was required of me.

I walked all around the obelisk and read the names. There were eight altogether and under each one, their age, date of death and location of their final battle were recorded. Three of the eight were Pembrookes and one was a Hanlon, so at least half of Blackshore's World War II dead were my family members, and maybe a couple of the others shared my gene pool as well.

William Kevin Pembrooke, age twenty-seven, died July 5, 1943, in Italy, and Jonathan Martin Pembrooke, twenty-three, on March 21, 1944, in the Netherlands. The third Pembrooke, Harold Cyril, was only eighteen when he was killed in Germany on May 1, 1945. The poor kid almost made it back.

No Thomas Pembrooke. William Kevin's date of death would be about right, but I was positive Conklin said Tommy's father was a Thomas as well. That would be easy to check through any of the great- and great-great-aunts or uncles. Some of them might not remember where they left their lawn bowling ball last Monday, but they would be able to recall every detail of the family tree back to the eighteenth century.

A dry, rustling noise startled me out of my half stupor. I turned around, expecting to see the cemetery staff with their shovels and cardboard coffee cups. But the cemetery was empty and silent except for the songbirds in the maples.

Just as I decided the faint noise was made by a squirrel or chipmunk running among the branches, the rustling and crackling resumed. Out from behind a nearby memorial, Rasputin appeared. He was pursued by Jacqueline who jumped and barked in rapture.

I pointed my finger at them. "Quiet."

Jacqueline stopped yapping, but continued to run around my feet in joyous welcome. Rasputin's tongue hung out and he wheezed as though every breath were his last.

"What are you two doing out of the house?" I had let Jacqueline out the kitchen door for a few minutes before leaving for the funeral, but I know both animals were in the house when Conklin and I left. Caroline must have got up early, and not knowing Jacqueline had relieved herself already, let both of them out—whereupon they had made a beeline for the cemetery, somehow knowing that's where they would find one of their humans.

Rasputin and I locked eyes. I blinked first, but refused to look away.

"Come on. We're going home." He didn't budge and I wasn't leaving them there with an open grave not twenty yards away. Jacqueline cavorted in coquettish glee.

"Let's go". I walked a few feet and looked back. No takers.

Deciding the weaker vessel was my best bet, I said to Jacqueline. "My, you look beautiful today. The shampoo and cut has done wonders for your looks. And those bows in your ears suit you perfectly. Pink is *so* your colour."

She was suspicious at my tone, but followed me anyway. I continued to talk to her in a soothing voice, and we headed for the line of trees.

Then the fingers were at my back again, sharp and insistent. Instinct made me turn and my foot must have caught in a tree root. Before I could catch myself, I was on the ground with the wind knocked out of me.

As I bent my elbows and pushed my face off the ground, I felt something hard—harder than the earth—under my knees. Scrabbling to one side, I noticed I had landed on a stone almost covered over by grass and moss. What an odd place for a grave. I started pulling the vegetation away from the marker.

I had never noticed this grave before. I thought I knew every name and every grave in the cemetery. This one was almost outside it. Still, how could I have missed it?

Because it had been protected from the elements, the engraving on its surface had not eroded. I saw there was no name on the stone, just the word *PEACE*.

I pulled myself to my feet and stared down at the marker. The tingling between my shoulder blades had stopped. I became aware that Jacqueline was whimpering and rubbing against my leg.

"Okay, let's go." I turned for one last look at the grave, sad and forgotten, so far from the bones of others.

Once we broke through the line of trees and were in sight of Hammersleigh, Jacqueline rushed across the field to where a cold drink and some treats waited.

I turned to see if the black cat was coming. Through a gap in the trees, I was relieved to see the two gravediggers filling in Tommy's grave. It seemed sad that no one from the family was there to watch the black earth settle on his tiny coffin, but the sight brought back the vivid memory of my own baby's funeral. I couldn't look any longer. Before I turned back, I caught a movement on my far right. A figure was fading into the trees.

It was a man, and from the fairness of his hair and the way he carried himself, I was almost sure it was Scott Fournier. I stopped where I was and watched for him to step into the cemetery. But he must have followed the tree line toward the other side of the cemetery because I didn't see him again.

If it *was* Scott, he was spending a lot of time in the cemetery. And so early in the morning too.

In the center of the field stood a lone, splendid elm. Possibly the very isolation had protected it from the death beetle. It had watched the nineteenth century turn over to the next and the next after that. The soaring branches still provided a welcome shade from the early morning sun and I stopped there to wait for Rasputin to catch up and to let him rest a moment.

The cat didn't even glance in my direction as he trudged along.

"You're too fat to run around in the sun, and I use the verb advisedly. You couldn't run if a pit bull was chasing you. Black attracts heat too, you know." He passed me with a languid swish of his tail.

We walked in single file back to Hammersleigh, where Rasputin waited for me to open the side gate for him. He took a drink out of the fishpond and swiped at one of the goldfish cruising among the water plants. It swam unhurriedly away.

The kitchen was empty and I made myself a cup of milk thistle tea to keep my liver in shape. Caroline came in silently a few minutes later as I sat at the table with my tea and a bran muffin liberally spread with red pepper jelly.

She stopped short when she saw me and said in surprise, "Oh. Lyris. I didn't expect to see you up so early. Let me make you a proper breakfast. How about a nice poached egg with a slice of ham?"

"Not for me, thanks. This is all I can handle, and in any case, you're not supposed to be cooking breakfast or lunch for me. Just pretend I'm not here."

"I don't mind, honestly. My plan is to make a light breakfast and lunch for Conklin and myself anyway, so one more would be no trouble."

I wavered, and then shed my self-imposed directive without a modicum of guilt. "How about this, then? If I'm around, I'll share your meals, but don't bother to save anything for me if I'm not here." God, I was so weak where my stomach was concerned.

She agreed and proceeded to whip up some breakfast, enough for three. I watched as her hands moved from refrigerator to stove and noticed the injury on her face was that purple-red colour of a bruise at its zenith, just before it starts to fade to yellow and green.

"How did you sleep last night, Caroline? It's not easy getting used to a strange bed, and your personal problems must be affecting your rest too. I hope you know you can talk to me if you want. I may not have had quite the same issues in my marriage as you have, but I think I can understand how a break-up can affect your life."

She kept her face averted. "Thank you very much, Lyris. I appreciate that more than you can know, but I have to work my problems out on my own. For now, anyway."

I ran words through my mind, trying to find the right ones. Before I came up with anything sensible, Conklin appeared at my elbow. He had changed from his butler outfit to a more casual one—light wool pants, dazzling white shirt and, of course, the black bow tie.

"Madam, I noticed that you have not checked off the facilities firm on your reunion list. This is not at item that should be left to the last. It would be very serious, indeed, if there were no facilities for the number of people…"

I grabbed the list out of his hand. "Don't worry about it, Conklin. I'm on it. I just forgot to check it off. Everything is going great. I even have a few surprises up my sleeve."

That worried him. His wrinkles took on a life of their own as his face puckered in concern. "Madam, the facilities…"

"...are under control. Everything is under control. Just sit down here, Conklin. Caroline is fixing you some eggs and ham. And if you'll excuse me, Caroline, I won't wait for breakfast after all. I have a lot of phoning to do."

Snatching a bottle of water out of the fridge to combat dehydration, I headed for the telephone room. Once seated on the tiny velvet armchair with the telephone book in hand, I remembered it was still just seven o'clock in the morning. It would be at least two hours before any business would take my call.

Throwing the book on the desk, I did what I should have done in the first place. I went back to bed. And couldn't sleep. That secret grave at the edge of the cemetery disturbed me. I had to find out who was buried there.

CHAPTER 16

A few hours later, I was back in the kitchen where I drank a cup of green tea and ate a few chocolate chip cookies someone was thoughtful enough to leave on the counter.

Refreshed, I settled in the telephone room with the now-tepid bottle of water and prepared to dial. Before I could begin, however, it rang.

It was Sheila Overton. "Sorry to phone you on vacation, Lyris, but I thought you'd want to know."

"That's okay, Sheila. What's going on?"

"We're being downsized." She said this mournfully, as if the world were coming to an end.

I laughed and took a drink of water. "We're downsized every six months or so. Nothing ever happens. We're all still here, aren't we?"

"Not for long. They mean it this time."

I sighed and settled myself into my velvet chair. I pushed the door open a little wider. "How do you know they mean it?"

"They've issued an information package. Twenty percent of the staff are over complement. They're offering a financial incentive to leave, based on your seniority. If not enough people take it, they'll start laying off the junior people, with four weeks' termination pay."

I sat up straight. "Twenty percent. No way. Are you sure?"

"Positive. I'm holding the package in my hand. You'll be okay, you've got lots of seniority. But I'll be gone, and Daphne. Faye too."

After I hung up I sat there without moving until the heat forced me from the tiny room in search of more water. As I drank a glass of tap water laced with ice cubes, I pondered my job without Sheila or Faye, or even Daphne. They drove me crazy, but they knew their jobs, except for Daphne, and the thought of training an entire new staff left me mentally exhausted. I couldn't even imagine the consequences of being laid off on those who needed to work to survive.

I had to put my job worries aside for the rest of the week. The success or failure of the reunion rested on my shoulders and there were few enough days left until blastoff. Putting the Blackshore Hydro Commission at the back of my mind, I returned to the telephone room and managed to check off a few more items from the list.

Caroline called me for lunch. After a plateful or two of macaroni and cheese, I felt rejuvenated. It was real macaroni and cheese, creamy and flavourful, as unlike the orange mess I had served Conklin before Caroline's arrival as night and day. The dish was accompanied by fresh green beans and sliced tomato. I felt blessed.

After lunch I decided I could spare a little time from reunion business and drove around the concession road to Lychwood. It had been necessary to call ahead, and after announcing myself to the security guard at the gate, I was waved in and instructed to drive to the administration building and park where another guard waited for me.

He escorted me to the main office and left me in the hands of a formidable woman in a purple and pink flowered sundress. Her clothing notwithstanding, she was cool and authoritative enough to wring every last morsel of information from me, from my relationship to Aunt Wisty to my reasons for visiting her.

This last took some verbal manoeuvring, as I could not deny I had never visited Mrs. Pembrooke before. I managed to convince Miss Olga Venhuiss that my motives were pure and that Mrs. Pembrooke really was my second cousin once removed, a kinship which may or may not have been true. We Pembrookes never bothered much with accurate lineage— it was enough to know we shared DNA, how much was not important and best not to know in certain instances like marriage proposals.

Miss Venhuiss passed me over to a younger lady, who chatted as she led me through a colourful flower garden to a row of fairytale cottages. She walked to one near the middle with a discreet brass plaque on the door engraved with the number 7. A clump of black-eyed Susans on either side of the step bowed their heavy heads in the afternoon heat.

The door was opened by an even younger female in a white smock and pants who took me through the air-conditioned cottage. I scarcely had time to register the sitting room and a miniature perfect kitchen before I found myself stepping out the back door.

These accommodations and the excellent care did not come cheap. Uncle Patrick had paid the bills for over sixty-eight years, and his estate would continue to pay until Aunt Wisty's death.

My escort indicated a reclining lawn chaise under a soaring oak. "I'll wait for you inside when you're ready to leave," she whispered. Then she disappeared into the cottage.

I moved with tentative steps to the recumbent figure in the chaise and sat down on a nearby bench. I watched the slow rise and fall of Aunt Wisty's chest. Her thin white hair waved in the almost nonexistent breeze. In spite of the stifling heat, she was covered in a pale yellow knitted afghan. She appeared to be asleep and I was reluctant to disturb her.

I looked around the well-groomed yard. It was separated from its neighbour on either side by a high, heavy chain-link fence. Across the back, the fence was even higher and angled inward. I felt a shudder of anxiety. There was no escaping this prison.

Aunt Wisty stirred and brushed away a fly that had landed on her cheek. She opened her eyes and looked around in bewilderment, as though she found herself in a strange and unfamiliar land.

"Aunt Wisty," I said softly so as not to startle her.

Her fluttering eyes finally settled on my face and she showed no fear or even surprise. "Hello. Do I know you?"

"I'm Lyris. Lyris Pembrooke. My father was Kevin."

"How is Kevin? I haven't seen him for a long time. Can you ask him to come and see me?"

"Aunt Wisty, Dad is dead. He died about seven years ago." I wasn't sure if she even remembered who my Dad was, and I didn't know if I should tell her he was dead. But if I wanted her to tell me about that reunion weekend, the here and now had to be clear. Or so I reasoned, although I knew nothing about what went on in Aunt Wisty's mind. Had time stopped for her in 1943?

"Dead. Everyone is dead."

I thought I should leave. Raking up the past, a past that cost her so much pain that she retreated into her own mind, could not be helpful to her. But I stayed. It was not just the living that deserved rest.

I cleared my throat. "Aunt Wisty. Do you remember we saw each other yesterday? At the cemetery?"

"Cemetery?" Her face changed as she looked at me. The eyes had faded to a colour more translucent than blue, reflecting some green from the leaves above. "Clem was there, and a gentleman. I saw you too."

"Yes, that's right. Do you remember why we were there?"

"Yes. Yes. My baby, my little Tommy. Clem told me."

I sat still as I could.

"It's been a long time now, hasn't it?"

"Yes, Aunt Wisty. More that sixty-eight years".

"Sixty-eight years? I never thought it would be that long."

"Did you know where he was?"

She was still staring into my eyes, and although it was almost painful to me, I held her gaze. I knew it was the only way to maintain a connection.

"It was a different world back then. They had the death penalty. Hanging, you know."

"Did somebody do something to hurt Tommy?"

"Nobody would hurt Tommy, not on purpose. Everybody loved him. He was so sweet and funny. He laughed all the time and he talked too. So smart."

"Somebody did hurt Tommy, Aunt Wisty. And somebody hid him in the closet in the tower room."

"It was different back then. A woman had to do what her husband said, and she couldn't tell. No one would listen."

I was wishing I had brought a tape recorder. Some of this didn't make sense and I wasn't sure I could remember every word. I didn't want to break her concentration by rummaging in my purse for pen and paper either.

"Your husband, Aunt Wisty. He was in the army, wasn't he?"

"Thomas? The army? Yes. Yes, he was. He hated it too. It was very hard on him, the killing and the noise. He was so cold all the time, he said."

"Why isn't his name on the memorial in the cemetery, the one with the names of the men who died in the war?"

"I don't know. I don't know." She sat up straighter and rocked back and forth.

"Aunt Wisty, do you know anything about the grave at the edge of the cemetery, the one that has no name?"

She continued to rock and did not answer.

I changed to another subject. "Aunt Wisty, can you remember who was staying in the house that time. Remember, it was during the reunion."

She pulled the afghan up to her chin and lay back again. She was watching the leaves of the oak stir above her head. I wasn't sure if she heard me.

"Clem was there, wasn't she, Aunt Wisty? And Patrick. You were there too, and a man named Bruce Wingate. Can you remember him?"

"Yes, we were all there. We were all so young. The men were going back to their outfits. Clem too. She loved her work, and took it very seriously. She said the things that went on there would win the war for us, that's how important it was."

"Why were you and Clem staying at Hammersleigh House, Aunt Wisty? Your parents had a house in town, Hollyhock Cottage. Why didn't you stay there?"

"Tommy and I were living with my parents while Thomas was overseas. That weekend we had a lot of relatives staying with us, so Patrick said that Clem and I, and Tommy of course, could stay at Hammersleigh."

"What about Bruce Wingate?"

"Bruce Wingate?"

"Yes, was he a friend of Patrick's? Why was he there?"

"I don't know. I don't remember any more." Her head moved back and forth on its cushion.

I glanced at the cottage door expecting the young aide to fly out to protect her charge.

I knew I didn't have much more time. I leaned over and took both her hands in mine, trying to capture her gaze. But her eyes were closed. Her hands were twitching and trying to pull away from me.

"Aunt Wisty. Please listen to me. Who hid Tommy in the tower room? Was it Bruce Wingate?"

"Hanging. Hanging."

She keened low in her throat. Before the sound could reach the ear of anyone in the cottage, I reached over and patted her shoulder to soothe her. "It's okay, Aunt Wisty. It was a long time ago. Just forget about it now and try to sleep."

Her hands stopped moving and her breath came low and even, like it had when I first entered her little garden.

The aide smiled and opened the front door for me. I saw no one else on my way out except the security guard at the gate.

Minutes later, I sipped a cup of oolong tea in my shade garden. I sat on the same wooden bench where Marc and I had spent those few romantic moments after the dinner party. I lay back and stared up into the cloud of green leaves. Much as Aunt Wisty had gazed upwards in her own little garden. A die-hard robin squawked at me from somewhere high above. I was too close to her nest, although her babies should already have left her.

Aunt Wisty had said some peculiar things about hanging and a wife having to listen to her husband. But she didn't admit knowing where Tommy's body had been all these years, and she didn't admit harming him herself. Nor did she blame anyone else.

But I was convinced that the tragedy played out in Hammersleigh in July of 1943 happened because of some interaction between one or more of the four people staying here that reunion weekend. Aunt Wisty knew all or part of it.

I had to either tackle Aunt Wisty again or get what I needed from someone else who was there. Uncle Patrick was dead, so that meant Aunt Clem or Bruce Wingate.

Bruce Wingate was the unknown factor. Was he still alive? And if he were, would he or could he help me? My best bet seemed to be to wait until the reunion and talk to Aunt Wisty and Aunt Clem. Whether together or separately remained to be seen, I would have to wait for an opportunity.

On my way up to bed that night, Caroline called to me from the bottom of the stairs. "Lyris, in case you're wondering, I moved the wildebeest into the tower room. I knew that's where you put the rest of the heads and such, so I figured the wildebeest might as well go there too. Hope that was okay?"

I assured her that the tower room was exactly where I wanted the antelope to be stored, and feeling that I wanted to be proven right about something—anything—I sat down at my computer.

Ten minute later I hoped I would never have to think or hear about antelopes or wildebeests again as long as I lived. What had at last found its way into the tower room was indeed an antelope as the little brass plaque on the back proclaimed. However, it appeared that *antelope* was an encompassing term for many species, such as gazelle, buffalo, goat, and yes, wildebeest. My curly-horned head belonged to the wildebeest species, a black wildebeest to be exact, which was now almost extinct. It was also known as a gnu.

So I was correct in calling it an antelope, but everyone else was more correct in calling it a wildebeest. After admitting to this, I lost interest.

In disgust I almost terminated my Internet connection, but on impulse, initiated another search.

By entering "veteran," then specifying "Canada," I was led through Veterans Affairs Canada to the Canadian Virtual War Memorial. On this website, a last name could be entered and a list of all those with that name who died during the First or Second World Wars appeared onscreen. When a particular name was chosen and entered, all known information on that veteran appeared.

If, that is, the veteran died from war-related causes either in battle or after. The date of death was recorded, as well as the names of his parents or wife, his age, regiment and any medal he may have won. The burial place was also specified.

From the site, I was able to access the various Commonwealth War Graves cemeteries, in Holland, Belgium, Malta, Italy, France, England and various other locations around the globe where Commonwealth war graves are revered and maintained to this day.

I keyed in "Wingate" and in a blink, discovered three Wingates had died during World War II. One of them was Bruce.

Bruce died on September 16, 1943, two months after the reunion. His burial place was listed as the Vimy Memorial in France and this seemed to mean his body was never recovered or buried.

At this point my imagination took wing for a minute or two. Maybe Bruce Wingate killed Tommy, then returned to his war in France where he arranged to disappear and make it look like he had died in battle, except there was no body to bury. He made his way to Switzerland where he waited out the rest of the war, then created another identity for himself and was now living in peaceful retirement in a veteran's home in the Alps.

I couldn't sustain this fantasy for very long. Although something was niggling at my memory, I had to let it go. I had hoped Bruce was responsible for Tommy's death. Now I was sure he was not. The truth was still waiting to be unearthed, and the name on the Vimy Memorial was not a significant piece of the puzzle.

Next I typed the name Pembrooke and got twenty-four hits. Ten of them died during World War II and I recognized among them the three names from the memorial in the cemetery. The other seven were from various places around the country, and any one of them may or may not have been related to the Blackshore Pembrookes.

But there was no Thomas Pembrooke. Of the ten Pembrooke men who fell during World War II, none was Thomas Pembrooke, husband of Wisteria, father of little Tommy.

I spent some time looking through the lists of names in the Commonwealth war cemeteries and memorials. There were so many names. I looked until my back ached and I had to squint through blurred eyes. I searched until there was no place else to search.

I glanced at my watch and realized that five hours had passed since I sat down at my terminal. As I shut it down in the darkest hour of the night, I knew that Thomas Pembrooke had not perished in battle during that terrible world conflict.

CHAPTER 17

I wasn't quite as dumb as I looked. There was something nasty going on between Caroline and her husband.

So when I appeared in the kitchen on Thursday morning, still thinking about my Internet marathon the night before, and noticed a fresh abrasion on Caroline's cheek before she could turn away, I decided to speak up.

I hoped she would confide in me without prompting, but we had met just a few days ago and I understood that she wanted to keep her personal problems from me. But I could not ignore that sort of mistreatment. I waded into shark-filled waters.

"Caroline, let's talk." I wrested the teapot from her fingers and pulled her over to a chair. She dropped into it with a fatalistic sigh.

"You can't go on this way. Scott is abusing you. You know it, I know it, I'm sure Conklin knows by now. We can stop it. Let me call Marc."

"No." She started to get up and I stepped in front of her. I might not be good at that kind of thing, but I knew if she didn't admit it, no one could help her.

I was no expert, but Patsy had seen her share of abuse victims at the hospital. According to her, statistics showed the main roadblock to helping these women was getting them to admit that first, there was a problem, and second, it was not their fault.

"You're letting Scott into the house at night, aren't you Caroline? Why are you doing that? If you don't let him in, he can't hurt you."

"It's not that simple, Lyris. You just don't understand how it is."

"Tell me, so I do understand. He hasn't been coming to the front door and ringing the bell. If he wants to see you, and you want to see him, why doesn't he come to the front door? Why wait until the middle of the night and then sneak around the back?"

She wouldn't look me in the eye. "It's not quite like that, Lyris. Our separation has been hard on Scott. I have to make him understand that we can't be together anymore."

Bull crap. Caroline needed to talk to an expert and I had to get her to one. Fast.

"Have you explained to him that you don't love him anymore, that you deserve better, and that you won't tolerate physical abuse anymore?"

"No, not exactly."

"Why not? Maybe he needs to hear the truth."

"He needs to get used to the idea first. I explained that we needed a trial separation, then when he gets used to me not being around, I'll tell him it's permanent."

"Caroline, I am going to get you some help. You must know that your behaviour is enabling Scott to continue with his abuse. He isn't going to change so you must break free from him emotionally. That is, if you are serious about ending your relationship. This isn't just a plan to try and get him to change, is it, because you must know…"

"I do know, Lyris. I've read a lot about abusive marriages and I realize I will need some help to distance myself from Scott. I know it isn't…wasn't my fault he hits me, but I still have all these feelings of guilt."

"Which is why you continue to let him in at night and let him continue to hit you. Well, it isn't going to happen anymore. No one is going to get hit in this house if I can help it. And I can."

I patted her shoulder as I got up. "Leave it with me for now. I'll find you some help. In the meantime, don't let Scott in. If he causes a fuss, come and get me."

I didn't tell her to call the police because she wasn't ready for that step yet. Better to get her to a counsellor first. Patsy would know someone, I was sure. And then we would deal with any charges. If he was the one taking things from the house, he would pay.

Since I couldn't remember when I last saw Amelia, it was just possible Scott had come into my room while I was sleeping Saturday night and taken her. The thought made my skin crawl. He was going to pay for that too.

I couldn't think of a motive for his taking things and I didn't want to upset Caroline by asking her. She had to know about his thieving, but maybe he was a kleptomaniac, who had to take a souvenir during each visit...

"Lyris."

"Oh, sorry, did you say something?"

"Yes. I'm making some eggs for Conklin and myself. Can I do some extra for you as well?"

"Thank you, no, I'm not hungry just yet. I'd better get back to my reunion work. They'll be rolling in tomorrow around noon."

I paused at the door. "You will remember what I said about Scott, won't you?"

"I'll remember. I won't let him in again."

For the first time that morning she looked directly at me. "Thanks for offering to help me, Lyris. I feel lots better now that you know what's been happening."

I waved away her gratitude, not a bit convinced that Scott wouldn't still be prowling through Hammersleigh come midnight. But it was a start, and the sooner I got her to abuse therapy, the better for all of us.

In the drawing room, I woke Jacqueline and Rasputin and kicked them off the furniture. Not literally, though I was tempted.

One item remained on my reunion list and it could be ticked off with a visit to town. I took a few minutes to write up another list for Marc of the people who had been in and out of the house on Saturday. Then I wandered back into the kitchen for a bite before heading for Blackshore.

Conklin and Caroline were companionably sopping up gooey egg yolk with whole-wheat toast. When I headed for my tea cupboard, they both pretended great interest in the contents of their cups.

"I think perhaps a little balm tea this morning. It will help with the slight indigestion and nervousness I'm suffering from, no doubt due to the reunion kick-off tomorrow. Join me?" I waved the tin at them.

Both heads swivelled from side to side. For some reason, most people were scared of herbs other than for flavouring foods. I found that very odd. *Less Drugs, More Herbs* was another of my mottos.

As well as teas, my cupboard held various tinctures, also prepared by my Chinese doctor. I added a few drops of gingko biloba to my cup to improve the circulation to my brain. I would need any mental boost I could get for the next few days. A banana completed my breakfast.

As I parked my car across from the police station, I saw Jody standing on the curb. This was noteworthy because Jody was known for her idle lifestyle, and any sighting of this wannabe socialite before noon was indeed rare.

By the time I put my quarter in the meter and crossed the road, the Family Trollop was hightailing it down the street in the direction of the Donut Delite coffee shop. She had been standing on the sidewalk between the police station and Dennis's realty office and no telling which she had visited. That a man was the reason for her morning appearance on the main street of Blackshore was a given. But which man? Well, I intended to know the answer to that before the sidearm was over the lamppost, or however the saying went.

Inside the police station I had to ask Ms. Constable Wilberts if I could see Marc, then convince her it was business, whereupon she wanted the list and was not happy when I insisted I would release it into Marc's hands alone.

Just before we came to blows, Marc came out and ushered me into his office. He shook his head at me like I had caused all the rumpus. That woman was just a born troublemaker and should never have been placed in a position of authority.

"Was Jody in here just now?" I winced. Some days I just did not know what would come out of my mouth. Certain topics needed to be led into, slowly.

"Jody?" He looked surprised.

I was relieved. So the little tramp hadn't been hitting on Marc that morning.

He was waiting for more.

"I saw her out on the street in front of the building and thought she might be paying a fine or something."

"She might have been. I didn't see her."

The hell with subtlety. I wasn't good at it. "Marc, you went out with Jody last year, didn't you?"

"Twice."

"Twice? Twice?" The slut acted like it was the grand passion of the decade. "Why did you stop seeing her?"

"She wasn't my type. Anyway, maybe she stopped seeing me, did you ever think of that?"

"So are you over her yet?"

"I think so. Lock that door and come over here. We'll find out."

"Very funny. You'd just unlock it again."

He smiled. "Maybe so. But why all the questions about Jody? It took two dates to find out we had nothing in common, and I didn't sleep with her in case you want to know that."

Well. I was shocked he hadn't slept with Jody—everybody else had—and relieved he was more discriminating.

He sent me another sexy smile. "Besides, once I saw you, every other woman just disappeared."

"There were other women? What other women?"

When he opened his mouth, I said, "Just kidding. I don't want to know about them. Now, I'm here on business. Here's your list of visitors to the house on Saturday."

He took the list from my hand. "I see our friend Angelo Bertollini is here. He might be worth a look."

"No. I told you before he isn't a thief. Growing pot on his kitchen window sill is different."

"Barely. Did you see him leave on Saturday?"

"No, but I know it isn't Angelo."

"We'll leave him for now. I know Peter Tackaberry, but who are Gordon and Roddie?"

"Two near-naked men who came to move furniture. Just trust me on this—they didn't carry anything out in their shorts they didn't come in with."

"I'll take your word for it. Now who's this?"

I knew he was looking at the final name on the list that I had printed in caps and underlined. "Scott Fournier. Who is Scott Fournier?"

"Caroline's husband. It's an abusive relationship. Caroline has been letting him in at night."

"Why? I thought they were separated. Did you know this was going on?"

"She's only been with me for a few days, remember. Caroline feels guilty for leaving Scott so she's trying to let him down gradually. The thing is, when she lets him in, he hits her. Then I think he steals something."

Marc regarded me. "This is a dangerous situation. Anyone who gets in the way of an abusive husband and the object of his so-called affection can be hurt as well. I want you to stay out of it."

"Sorry, it's too late. And I wouldn't anyhow. I promised Caroline I would get her some help, which to my mind means counselling and police protection. In the meantime, I made her agree not to let Scott in anymore."

He came around his desk and put his hands on my shoulders. "You should have let me know as soon as you suspected. These men can and do kill." He gave a slight squeeze and released me.

"This is dangerous for you and Caroline. Fournier lives in Northton, doesn't he?"

When I nodded, he added, "I'll find out if they have any record on him. In any case they can have a talk with the gentleman and warn him off. If I see him in Blackshore, I'll do the same."

He punched at the keys of his computer. "I don't like this. Caroline needs a lawyer right away, and if she comes in and signs a complaint, we can take steps to protect her."

"No, Marc. Not yet. Caroline has only just admitted there's a problem. If we move too fast, she may go back to Scott."

"Don't you understand, Lyris, an abusive spouse will not let anything stand in the way of his goal. Usually he won't harm anyone other than his spouse, but if you are seen to interfere, he might go after you. I've seen it before. Sometimes these men even assault counsellors or lawyers."

It seemed the air conditioner in the police station had broken down. A solitary fan swished lazily back and forth across Marc's office. In spite of the closeness of the room, I felt a chilly hand on my neck.

"I want to get on this right now, Lyris. Don't forget. Call me if you even catch sight of Fournier around Hammersleigh."

I didn't like being scared, so I put Scott Fournier out of my mind for the moment and bought a heavenly hash ice cream cone from the little variety store beside Dennis's office.

I was licking and dripping on the sidewalk when I heard a thumping sound behind me. I turned around to see Dennis through his office window, all smiles. He motioned me to come in.

What the heck, I figured I might as well drip on his office as the street.

Inside the door, several clerks were busy filling out computer forms, and a youngish couple was seated around a desk in one corner, where one of Dennis' agents was showing them a book of listings.

"Looks like things are going pretty well in the real estate business."

He handed me a roll of paper towel from his bottom drawer. "The market is picking up some."

"Glad to hear it." I wiped brown ice cream from his desktop and dabbed a few drops from a file folder. He looked pained, but didn't say anything. That made me suspicious.

He was wearing navy twill pants and a pale blue sports shirt. Blue tones went well with his eyes and tanned skin. There was no denying he was an attractive man, and if Jody hadn't been in the police station, I was betting her cute little derriere had been parked in this very chair a few minutes ago.

"Can we have a serious conversation about something, Lyris?" He laced his fingers together and leaned forward over the desk. I recognized this as his sincere posture, useful for convincing prospective buyers that the house they were thinking of buying didn't have termites or toxic mould.

"Sure." I went down the front of my tank top with the paper towel after some ice cream. I'd have to remember next time not to get the double scoop.

"To be honest, I'm having some financial trouble right now. Temporary, but if I don't raise some capital soon, I'll lose the house."

"That's too bad. Maybe you could take out a second mortgage."

"I already did that. The bank won't loan me anymore."

"Then maybe you should consider moving to a smaller house. In your business you should be able to find a good deal on a more modest place."

A vein in his left temple was pulsing to beat the band, I noticed with some interest.

"In a few short months I will have three children to support. Do you expect me to move my family to a tiny hovel somewhere?"

"There is a world of difference between the house you live in now, with its five bedrooms, four full baths, a swimming pool, sauna, and guest cottage, and a tar paper shack. But I don't think that's what we're discussing, is it?"

"I just need you to return a portion of what you took when we divorced. You took unfair advantage. I didn't mind so much at the time, but now I could use the money."

I threw the remains of my cone in his wastepaper basket where it landed with a wet thud. "I got half, you got half. How you manage to convince yourself you deserve more is beyond me."

"I have a family to support. I'm forty years old, and as you pointed out the other night, I am soon to have three children under two."

"And you think that, out of the goodness of my heart, I'm going to give you some of my hard-earned investments? Because you have a family to support?"

"You could show some consideration. We were married for almost twenty years."

For a minute I felt Dennis and I existed in parallel universes. We were talking to each other, but we were out of synch by a heartbeat.

"Tell me Dennis, when did you start being unfaithful to me? Was it five years after we were married? Ten? Whenever it was, any consideration I owed you stopped right there."

We were by this time hissing at each other, but I was aware that all was silent from the outer office. I kicked the door closed and waited for his answer.

His voice was hard with anger. "I don't deny we had problems in our marriage and I didn't always treat you as well as I should have, but it wasn't all me. If you had been different, I wouldn't have had to look elsewhere."

As soon as he said it, he knew it was a mistake. His eyes shifted to my face, hoping I had missed the statement. Not likely.

He reached across for my hand. I jerked away, hearing my mother's words clearly in my mind.

"One thing I will not do, Dennis, and that is take the blame for your philandering. You made me feel inadequate for as long as I can remember. I may not have been blameless, but my main flaw was putting up with you. I should have kicked your ass out years earlier."

"You didn't kick me out. I left you."

"Because you got a young girl pregnant, you moron. You're just lucky you didn't find yourself in court on a statutory rape charge."

"Tracey wasn't that young, bitch. And keep your voice down."

I got up and prepared to leave. "Here's a piece of free advice for you, Dennis. If you are at all tempted to start up with Jody again, don't. You can ill afford another divorce and subsequent split of your remaining assets. Not to mention child support for the next eighteen years. And you'll be lucky if Tracey lets you off with half. She's not as easygoing as I am."

"Will you at least think about what I asked you?"

I slammed the door on my way out.

That evening, after a delicious dinner of stuffed turkey breast and oven-roasted vegetables, I picked up the *Blackshore Oracle* and scanned the obituary page. I was hoping to find a name there that I called kin.

As it turned out, none of the deceased was a close family member, but one obituary listed several Pembrookes among those left behind to mourn. It would have to do.

I called Patsy. "Put on your pantyhose and a black dress. We're going to a wake."

CHAPTER 18

"How was I to know you'd put pantyhose on? Seriously, come on, it's still thirty degrees Celsius at eight o'clock in the evening. You must know I was kidding."

Patsy had almost gone ballistic when I picked her up in my car and she saw I was wearing a sundress.

By the time we pushed our way through the crowd in the foyer of the Lavette Funeral Home, I was sweating like a stevedore, and I shuddered to think how Patsy felt in her black shift with matching jacket. And tasteful taupe pantyhose.

She kept throwing accusing glances at my navy and white striped sundress and muttered about going home. But I wasn't worried. Between the heat and the pantyhose, she knew she'd never survive the eight-block trek. There was also her questionable choice of shoes to consider—an inebriated thirteen-year old in her first pair of stilettos would be steadier on her feet than Patsy with her three-inch sandals.

"Just who is this Clive Ainsdale anyway?" she asked, her voice ringing through the foyer.

About a dozen people were milling inside the front door, and I scanned the foyer trying to locate the queue to sign the visitors' book.

"There." I grabbed Patsy by the wrist and dragged her behind me. As we took our place in line, I whispered, "I can't remember ever meeting him, but he's related somehow to the Pembrookes. I recognize a pack of distantly related family in there. So we have a legitimate reason for coming here."

"You mean you do. And why are we here? You didn't tell me. I thought you wanted some company to pay your respects to an uncle or something."

I signed the book with a flourish and handed the gold pen to Patsy. "I need some burial information, and I think it might be in the records. Remember, I worked here one summer, Grade 10 if I'm not mistaken."

For the next fifteen minutes, she whispered in agitation as we waited our turn. I ignored her. Sometimes I wished I had a friend who wasn't such a scaredy cat. But my other friends weren't as loyal as Patsy. I knew she wouldn't leave me, no matter how nervous she was.

When we reached the elderly widow and middle-aged children at the foot of the coffin, I merely introduced myself. The fact that I was a Pembrooke seemed to be sufficient reason for being there. They thanked me for coming, and I moved past them to stand at the open coffin, leaving Patsy to sink or swim on her own. She was more socially adroit than I, so I figured she would say the right things.

Gazing down into the coffin, I saw that Clive Ainsdale had been a veteran. His service beret rested on his chest along with a medal that I recognized as the Victoria Cross.

"A pretty high honour, Clive," I said to him silently. "My generation acknowledges your service and thanks you. I hope the next one never forgets the sacrifices our soldiers made during World War II."

Once Clive was young and courageous, anxious to serve his country. And he left his new bride behind to help stop the terror of Hitler's demonic campaign. We're more sophisticated now, not so quick to trust politicians, faster to empathize with people half a world away. But in 1939, they had no reservations. They had to save democracy and the free world from the Beast of Berlin, although the cost to young Canadian lives was enormous.

And what about Clive? He came back, but what horrors did he see when he closed his eyes at night? Did he look at his wife and wonder if she sought comfort in the arms of another man during those dark years? Did he look at his young son and count the months, wondering if conception had occurred before or after he went overseas?

"Lyris. Move along. You're holding everybody up." Patsy pushed me away from the coffin, and we squeezed our way through the crowd back into the hall.

"Come on, this way." I led Patsy into another reception room, this one empty of both coffin and mourners. The carpeting and draperies were similar in both parlours, beige to blend with the earth tone fabrics of the various sofas and easy chairs.

"You're not going to look through confidential funeral home records, are you?" Patsy asked in a plaintive whine, just a hop and a skip from whimpering.

"I sure am. Give me a minute to get my bearings. The room where they used to keep their files is down this hall and downstairs. As long as the door isn't locked, we should be in and out in a couple of minutes."

"I'll wait right here." Patsy plopped herself in a beige floral armchair and crossed her arms.

"Did I tell you why I'm going to look at the funeral home's records? It's a very interesting theory." Wheedling often worked on Patsy.

"You have one minute to explain yourself." To my surprise, she stepped behind the drapes. While I outlined my suspicions to her, the drapes billowed and bulged like a stage act was about to come bursting out.

When she emerged one minute later, she was without jacket or pantyhose, having stuffed these items into the carryall she always slung over one shoulder.

"Why don't you just tell Marc about this theory of yours? He can look through the records, legally. We can't. And it's a pretty wild theory, by the way."

"Marc isn't interested in Tommy's murder. He says he'll look into it after he catches the gang who's robbing all these houses in Blackshore. And he doesn't mind if I do some investigating. He said so."

"I'll bet he didn't suggest you perform a felony break and enter at the funeral home."

I felt exhausted. I wasn't doing this for the fun of it. Contrary to Patsy's belief that I liked to live on the edge and take wild chances for no other reason than the thrill of it, I preferred a quiet life free of strife and turmoil. It wasn't my fault things happened to me all the time.

"If you don't want to help, I understand. You can wait outside for me. I shouldn't be more than ten or fifteen minutes."

"Oh, knock it off, you over-grown baby. You know perfectly well I'll help you. If we wind up in jail, it will just be embarrassing, not the end of the world I guess. It's not like my job can be jeopardized"

"Thanks, Patsy." I gave her a hug. "Okay, here's the plan. I'll go in alone, and you wait outside in the hall. If anybody comes along, you say you were looking for the bathroom and follow the person back upstairs. I'll make my own way out later. Any questions?"

She opened her mouth, but I didn't wait. We found the door to the basement. It wasn't locked, and we were able to descend the stairs without being noticed.

Luck was with me. The door to the office at the far end of the corridor was unlocked as well. A flip of the light switch inside the door verified that the room was just as I had remembered it more than twenty years ago—filled with a row of filing cabinets and a scarred oak desk. I had spent my fifteenth summer filing little cards and folders into these cabinets, and it was obvious that the Lavettes still believed in hiring student slaves during summer months.

Before I closed the door on Patsy, she asked, "What are you going to do if you find proof in there? You know you can't use illegally obtained evidence. You'll have to tell Marc anyway..."

"If I'm right, we won't need proof. Nobody is going to be accused of anything. It's too late. Now, if somebody comes, let me know by knocking once on the door. Then get out of here."

I was relieved to see that the Lavette family still maintained organized business files. Every funeral and burial transaction was documented both by name and by plot.

First, I went to the filing cabinet marked *P* and thumbed through until I found the name Pembrooke. In fact, most of the *P*'s were Pembrookes, and they were broken down further by initial, not date of burial.

Seven Thomas Pembrookes were buried in the Gates of Heaven Cemetery, spanning many years. None of them were buried between 1941 and 1946. I scanned through the whole *P* group again in case a student had misfiled the relevant Thomas.

He wasn't there. Undecided where to look next, I was jolted by a strong tingling between my shoulders. I felt like I had been stabbed by a cattle prod.

"Stop it." I looked over my shoulder, trying to locate the cause of my discomfort. There was no one there. I was momentarily relieved until I considered the alternative. Was an earth-bound soul trying to get my attention? What better place for a spirit than a funeral home?

The pressure between my shoulder blades increased. Shit. Were Luke and Florence following me around now?

I raised my head to discover that I was standing in front of a map that covered one entire wall.

I moved closer. The map was a schematic drawing of the cemetery layout. All plots were numbered, and when one was filled, the initials of the occupant were printed beside the number.

It didn't take long to locate the plot where the memorial to Blackshore's World War II fallen stood. It was plot 176 and marked with a simple *M*. All around were other numbers and initials, but no *TP* appeared anywhere in the vicinity, including the perimeter of the cemetery.

I carried a chair over to the front of the map and checked my watch. Ten minutes had passed since I first entered the basement office. Patsy would be beside herself by now. Climbing onto the chair, I put nose to map.

At the exact spot I expected would show Thomas's hidden grave was the number 153 pencilled in, and beside it was a black daub, like something had been inked out. I scratched at the spot with my fingernail, but a sharp rap on the door interrupted me.

I jumped from the chair and extinguished the light. I stood quietly and listened to Patsy ask someone where the powder room was, then waited while two sets of footsteps faded away.

I stayed where I was for a few minutes longer. Then I snapped on the light and resumed scratching at the blotch.

"Damn." A tiny piece of paper from the map fluttered to the floor.

I retrieved the torn piece, wet my finger, and stuck the scrap back on. The map was no doubt an antique, and I had damaged it. I shouldn't be allowed near anything old.

I lowered myself onto the chair and looked around while I considered my next move.

Another shock struck my back. And a muffled voice said, *How's it going, Lyris? Call me Leander.*

What the hell. I stood up and whirled about, scanning the room, expecting to see a body to go with the voice. I was alone.

Don't mean to scare you, Lyris, but I can't wait any longer. I drew the short straw and was assigned as your spirit guide. I've been trying to get your attention for years, but you've refused to open the channel and let me through. I can see you're going to be a pain in the ass to work with.

I felt light-headed, and I sucked some air back into my lungs so I could make a break for the door. Nothing doing, I felt as if my feet were immersed in hardened cement.

Go look in the desk, Lyris. And make it snappy.

I can't. I'm paralyzed. Oh God, I was hearing and talking in my head.

Don't be melodramatic. You aren't paralyzed.

It...he—whatever—was right. I wasn't. My eyes darted around the room, still hoping for something, anything, to explain the voice. There was nothing.

If you want what you came for, go to the desk and open the top drawer.

Looking warily around, I obeyed. The voice was inside my head, and I wasn't really hearing it, more like feeling it.

The only thing in the top drawer of the desk was a key. I picked it up and waited for further direction. No response. I pulled on one of the left bottom drawers and found it locked. My fingers were trembling badly, but I found the keyhole. With a twist of the key, the drawer opened. I reached in and lifted out a long metal box.

Get with it, kid. You're running out of time.

Inside the box were sheets of paper, of various quality and age. My eyes skimmed the top document, dated 11 years ago.

The burial of a male infant, stillborn, in plot 534 was detailed. No parents were listed, just the name of the baby, Alexander Pembrooke. I looked over at the map, trying to spot another inked-out plot.

Quit dawdling. You have one minute left before you're interrupted.

I snatched up the next piece of paper. A female infant, unnamed, was buried in plot 477, on October 21, 1967. The initials "SH/PM" were the only identifiers. Despite my panic and fear, I was fascinated by those papers.

For crying out loud, will you get a move on?

Then I found it. The cream-coloured page in my hand stated that Thomas Charles Pembrooke was buried in plot 153 on July 24, 1943. No other information.

The metal box held records of secret burials. I was tempted to fold up the papers, lift my skirt, shove the papers down my thong, and run like hell. This evidence proved that the Lavettes had been party to mysterious burials for generations. Perhaps all funeral home directors helped out their clients with such unorthodox requests.

You're out of time. Go.

Reluctantly, I thrust the papers back into the box and returned it to its drawer. Locking the drawer, I replaced the key and stood up on shaking legs.

From the door, I cast one last glance around the room and shut off the light. How could I have missed finding the metal box that long-ago summer?

Move it, move it.

I moved it. Upstairs, I saw that if I had waited a few minutes longer, I would have had to break out of the building. A few stragglers were taking their leave of the family. I managed to slip around them and out the door into the oppressive heat. The night was black and I stopped under a lamppost to glance at my watch. Ten o'clock. I jumped a foot when Patsy's form detached from the trunk of a nearby tree.

She appeared wilted and a little cranky. "Where have you been? You've been hours in there. I thought I would have to go back in and tell Mr. Lavette where you were."

"Good thing you didn't, Patsy. He might have had to add two more files to the metal box."

"What? What are you talking about? Did you find what you were looking for?"

"Yes. And then some." It was lucky for me Patsy was so agitated, and it was too dark to see clearly. Otherwise, she would have noticed I looked like I had seen a ghost, which was closer to the truth than I cared to acknowledge. And the contents of the metal box were going to haunt me for the rest of my life.

Life before Leander was so simple, when I only had Conklin to contend with.

CHAPTER 19

Two colossal tents arrived on Friday morning at eight o'clock. One was set up on the sunniest part of the front lawn, as close to the gates as possible, and the other in the empty field, where the motor homes, tent trailers and pup tents would sprout like toadstools right after lunch.

I drank a cup of ginseng tea and allowed Caroline to feed me an egg salad sandwich to give me energy, and then dashed outside again at the toot of another horn.

The Wooter Brothers Sanitation flatbed truck was backing under the pines, and I sensed Conklin wince as the tires sank into the still-green grass. It seemed he was determined to stick to me like Velcro.

Mitch and Tiffany rounded the house from the car park, and I called to them to put their things in the rooms they had used last weekend, then rest for a while. I would see them at ten o'clock in the drawing room.

I turned my attention back to Benny and Donny Wooter, who were setting up the ramp they used to roll down the units. They did this in an efficient manner, while I avoided looking at Benny's butt crack. His jeans hung low under his enormous belly, and when he leaned over to secure the unit on the rollers, Conklin and I were treated to a sight only Benny's wife should have been forced to witness.

Other than a pair of work gloves, the sagging jeans were his only garments. I sighed to myself. At least his brother Donny wore coveralls with his gloves.

"There you are, Lyris. Three units. We have to get going. We got to deliver these others to the Pedofsky farm. Their young Lisa's getting married tomorrow. We got a lot of weddings this weekend. And there's a granddaddy of a coon on the road back to town."

The Wooter brothers had a sideline to their sanitation business. They picked up road kill and were paid per head, or per carcass. Sometimes the head was gone. I'm not sure if they had to show the county clerk the bodies or just sent in an invoice each month.

Anyway, Benny wasn't slipping by me that easily. "We agreed on eight units. I want another five, please." If he could renege on our deal, I would lie with a clear conscience.

He took off his Oilers ball cap and scratched his woolly black hair. "Can't. I already said there's a lot of weddings this weekend. I can't spare you more than three total."

"You listen here, Benny Wooter. Three porta-potties are not enough for three hundred people. I want another five."

He looked pained and shook his head. If a two by four had been handy, it would be upside Benny's ear.

"Benny, if you're looking for more money, I'll..."

He held up a meaty hand, now devoid of glove. "It has nothing to do with money, Lyris. I just can't spare them." Sincerity filled his eyes and threatened to overflow in tears. What a phony.

Conklin was beginning to rattle and stir beside me. Before he could jump in, I said, "I know where you live, Benny."

"Huh?"

"I know you have rows of porta-potties sitting in your back field."

"Those are spoke for. There are lots of weddings..."

"If you don't give me five more, I will have no choice but to arrange a regular shuttle service to your field. Every twenty minutes ought to do it. These folk will have to go, and I can't have them going in the bushes or on the grounds."

"But you can't..."

"If they can't go here, they'll go at your place. I see no alternative."

The brothers glared at one another, then at Conklin for help. Not happening.

"Okay, I might give you two more. Absolutely that's it."

"Three. Two here and one in the field." We stared into each other's eyes. I won.

Benny said to Donny, "Unload Tintagel and Brigadoon. Shangri-la goes in the field."

One of the more charming facets of the Wooter operation was the name gilded in gothic script on the door of each porta-pottie. They had already off-loaded Camelot, Avalon and Xanadu. I was touched to see one called Hammersleigh on the truck, but Benny didn't offer me that one.

With a baleful glance in my direction, Benny sped off with Donny by his side to drop Shangri-la in the field. Conklin winced even harder as a few clumps of grass flew into the air.

"Don't forget the coon," I yelled after them.

I viewed the row of five porta-potties with satisfaction. The one in the field was a bonus I hadn't expected.

"Well played, Madam," Conklin said. "Two more than last year. This should help considerably."

Things started to happen fast. The spring water arrived in the form of seven cooling systems and a hundred five-gallon containers. An electrician installed a portable generator to run the coolers and strung up some temporary lights in the field. Throughout this activity, teenagers slouched up the driveway in twos and threes and were directed to wait for me in the sitting room.

I was writing cheques with abandon. It was Uncle Patrick's money, so I felt nary a twinge in my cheap bone, as Mitch used to call my disinclination to part with hard-earned cash to pay for hundred-dollar athletic shoes.

I took a minute to run upstairs to change my T-shirt for a tank top. On the way down, I paused to sniff. There had been nothing last night when I went up to bed, and there was nothing now. Somehow I knew it was gone for good. And Leander had better keep his bony fingers to himself from now on.

In the sitting room I surveyed the sullen crowd of fifteen young people standing or sitting apart from Mitch and Tiffany. They were all related to each other, and to me, in one way or another. I had recruited them by calling their parents who were more than happy to offer their children's services for the weekend. That way, they figured I would be responsible for the kids and leave the parents free to enjoy the reunion.

Of course I planned to pay the kids, and without exception, they perked up when they heard that. They were all younger than Mitch and Tiffany, between fifteen and seventeen.

They were a motley crew, dressed in everything from baggy jeans and expensive sneakers to bicycle shorts and mesh T-shirts. A few of the young ladies were blossoming right out of their halter tops.

"First of all, does anyone here have St. John's Ambulance training? Six of you? Good, move to the other side of the room, please. Now here's the deal. Mitch is in charge of security. Everyone on this side of the room will report to him. I have baseball caps here in this box, black with white lettering." I held one up for all to see, then passed them out. "They say 'Security' on them."

I outlined their duties. "I do not want anyone smoking on the grounds, either regular tobacco or wacky weed."

A few of the little pot heads groaned, but whether at the thought of enforcing the no-smoking signs I had posted or the ban on the weed itself, I didn't stop to ask. The grounds were too dry to risk a fire from careless smoking.

"Tiffany is head medic. The rest of you will report to her. You will wear these caps." I showed them the white ball cap with a red cross on the front. Much eye rolling ensued.

"We will have many elderly people and children at the reunion. They are at greater risk of dehydration and heat prostration. Tiffany will explain to you what to watch for and what to do. I'll talk to Tiffany later, but your jobs will consist of watching for problems, making sure young children are wearing hats and taking them back to their parents if they don't, handing out sunscreen, making sure the elderly are seated in the shade and that they have liquid refreshment of their choice."

"Now." I paused for effect and lifted the last box onto a low table. "This is a two-way radio." I picked one out of the box and held it up. "It is not a cell phone. You will carry one at all times. Each of us has a number. I have lists that designate our names and the corresponding numbers. Take one, please. You will note that Mitch is number two and Tiffany is three."

"And I..." I needed them to realize the importance of my next statement. "I am Number One."

Out of the hat box I took a fluorescent orange cap and set it on my head. I had thought of having the word Boss lettered on it, but settled for the number one. Kids that age didn't have a sense of humour where authority was concerned.

"I will be everywhere. You can call me on the radio any time, day or night. And yes, we will have a night patrol. Medics will become security after eight p.m. You will work your schedule out with Mitch and Tiffany in a minute. By the way, they will both carry a cell phone as well as their radios for emergency use only. Please stay off your own cell phones, iPods or whatever else as much as possible. Now are there any questions? Oh, one other thing. If you lose or damage your radio, the cost of replacing it will come out of your pay."

Standing outside the sitting room a few minutes later, I could hear the raised voices right through the heavy pocket doors. I left them to it, confident Mitch and Tiffany could handle any insurrection. Last year, a lot of the kids in that room had been responsible for much of the mischief and misery that had occurred at the reunion. I couldn't do anything about the out-of-towners, but this year I hoped these local delinquents would be too busy calling each other on their radios and enforcing the rules to break them. Time would tell.

I walked down to the front gates to make sure they were open just enough to let people walk through. Now that everything was delivered and set up, no vehicle need pass through these gates until the reunion was over.

I turned at the gates and looked back at Hammersleigh, pulling my orange cap further down on my nose. The heat caused the house and grounds to shimmer in the sunlight.

The blue and white striped tent top was a sharp contrast to the greens of the lawn and trees and the soft grey of Hammersleigh's stone walls. The row of turquoise porta-potties not quite hidden in the pine border was another jarring note. Well, by Monday afternoon, the tent and porta-potties would be dismantled and taken away. And I would be back at work.

The thought of returning to another downsizing depressed me. I took off the cap and wiped the sweat from my forehead. My eye was drawn back to the house and I admired again the dignified Georgian façade, the mellow limestone walls rising to the cupola and widow's walk.

Since moving into Hammersleigh two weeks ago, I had been too busy to explore the attic floor or the cupola. From the widow's walk it would be possible to see the countryside in every direction, perhaps even into Blackshore's main street.

I strolled up the driveway again, then came to an abrupt stop. I craned my neck to look up at the cupola, and Aunt Clem's words came back to me. Or maybe they were Florence's words or Luke's.

In a high place. Something to that effect. Look in a high place. I couldn't remember what for. That whole episode at Aunt Clem's was so spooky, I wasn't sure I understood half of it. I wondered if Luke and Florence were acquainted with Leander. Aunt Clem's guides seemed a little too high-toned to associate with the caustic Leander, but everyone must know everyone else on the other side. My mind couldn't even get around that concept.

After a light lunch of turkey breast sandwiches and homemade cream of mushroom soup, I stood up and addressed Conklin and Caroline before they could run off.

"We are on red alert until Sunday afternoon. Conklin, forgive me for mentioning these points. I know you have directed more reunions than I can even remember, but bear with me, if you please."

I looked at their faces and was reassured by the serious expressions. "Conklin, you will of course ensure that all doors are always locked. Please patrol the house on an hourly basis during daylight hours. I have asked Peter Tackaberry to take the night shift." I paused for Conklin's reaction. He nodded his approval.

"Now, Caroline. First of all, thank you for giving up part of your Sunday off to help us out. You will be responsible for Jacqueline and Rasputin. When Jacqueline needs to go out, put her on a leash and take her yourself, locking the door behind you. We can't take the chance of a lawsuit if Jacqueline goes berserk and bites someone. Other than that, just remain attentive and assist Conklin."

I strode up and down the length of the kitchen. "Except for Mitch and Tiffany, don't let any of the security or medic teams in unless it's an emergency. In that case, accompany the delinquent, I mean young person, every single minute. You can provide sandwiches, fruit and pop, which they will consume in the garden."

I had one more thing to say. I handed each of them a two-way radio. "At the first sign of trouble, call me. I am programmed in as Number One." I looked at Conklin in case he had a problem with this, but he nodded and pocketed the device. I thought I saw his lips twitching, but chose to ignore it. Caroline looked uncertain, so I took some time to reassure her and show her how to use the radio.

A few minutes later, I was changing my tank top for a fresh one and my shorts for a long skirt with a split side to facilitate movement. Through the open window I heard a rumble in the distance.

Not the thunder we had all grown used to. This was something else, a mechanical rumble. I recognized that sound and I straightened my skirt and stiffened my spine.

I picked up my radio and pressed the button that would alert all other devices within a one-kilometre radius. I pressed it again, guessing that my rag-tag army would be fumbling and swearing at this very moment as they searched for the audio button.

I spoke into my radio. "Attention. Everyone stand by. Recreational vehicle entering the field."

The reunion had begun.

CHAPTER 20

The vehicles continued to roll into the field throughout the afternoon and evening. At the same time, other campgrounds and private residences in and around Blackshore filled up with reunion attendees.

There were no major incidents to that point. A few scraped knees and bug bites, and a gentleman from Calgary who took personal offence to the no smoking policy on the grounds. Mitch sorted him out and he retired, grumbling, to light up in his own RV.

Around four in the afternoon, Aunt Bertilla managed to lock herself in Tintagel. Since she lived in Blackshore, I don't know why she didn't use her own bathroom before she left home. I wanted to leave her in there until we could call Benny Wooter to come out and free her. I knew if we sprung the lock Benny would make us pay for a replacement, but Tiffany said she would be overcome by either heat or fumes within minutes. And the noise from Tintagel was astounding, drawing a curious crowd of twenty or more, most of them wielding beer cans and watching the fun.

Mitch removed the hinge pins and lifted the door off. Then he re-mounted it and it was as good as new. I stayed behind a tree when this was going on, and a good thing as it turned out. When Aunt Bertilla came bursting out, she looked around for somebody to lay the blame on, and I would have done very well. I spent the rest of the evening keeping a lookout for her glittery green muumuu.

By eight o'clock on Friday evening, the guest book set up in the tent just inside the front gates contained two hundred and ten names. Since more family would arrive on Saturday, it looked like we had already exceeded the two hundred and three count from last year.

I didn't expect to see Aunt Clem or Aunt Wisty until the next day. Nor Mom and David and his family. Most of the locals would make an appearance late Saturday morning with picnic baskets and stay until after the campfire sing-along that night in the field.

I used my radio to remind the security team to keep special watch on the field throughout the night. It wouldn't take much for a spark to ignite the grass and spread to Hammersleigh. And there were to be no campfires or barbecues within Hammersleigh's gates.

Things settled down around 10 p.m. The children stopped shrieking and screaming, and the drunks passed out in their tents and trailers. After a word with Mitch—I hoped he had scheduled some sleep time for himself—I knocked at the kitchen door.

A few minutes later, Caroline admitted Peter. After Conklin and Caroline retired, I made the rounds with Peter and gave him my radio.

"You don't need to patrol upstairs. You can even take a nap on a sofa if you want." Let him try and sleep on one of *those*. "Somebody needs to be handy in case there's an emergency during the night, medical or otherwise."

"No problem, Lyris. I'll look after things, you just get some rest. You're looking a bit drained." Peter, in contrast, looked fresh and ready for anything. I hoped he wouldn't be too bored.

"I'm not too concerned about tonight, Peter. It's Saturday night we have to worry about. That's when local family socializes with family from out of town. Then, anything goes. And the kids will be out of control."

I should know. When I was a teenager, I spent all of Saturday night running through the fields and the cemetery, smoking a little pot, generally making a nuisance of myself with the rest of the teenage Pembrooke clan. Parents threw in the towel around midnight, and the night belonged to us.

When you're young, there's something about a hot summer night that promises excitement and adventure. Even now, my blood stirred as I remembered. Hence the security precautions inside and outside. There would be a lot of stirring of young blood tomorrow night.

I was too wired to sleep, so I took a tepid shower to cool my hot skin and put on a camisole and thong. Anything less would have been indecent. The computer held no appeal, and I was not up to unpacking my teapot collection and putting it in the cabinet Gordon and Roddie had moved in for me. I picked up a new Mary Jane Maffini mystery, but found my sweaty fingers were wrinkling the pages. I put the book back on my bedside table to await the return of some normalcy in my life so I could focus on the story.

The music coming from the field was distracting me. It sounded like a song from the war years, and I found myself straining to hear the words. I was restless and starting to sweat again. Even the crickets sounded tired and fed up with the heat.

I thought about the widow's walk. It would be cooler there. A staircase led from the kitchen to the third floor and from there another set of stairs should lead up to the cupola. Easy.

In the hall I stopped. This house was built when materials and labour were cheap. The original owners must have constructed another access to the cupola. I looked at the tower room door at the end of the long hallway. It could be right through there.

My fear of that room was gone. I believed the reason lay in my commitment to finding out what happened to Tommy, but maybe that was just my imagination again.

I could have turned on the lights as I went, but didn't want to illuminate the house like a beacon for any party-hearty types who were looking for excitement. Instead, I flipped on the flashlight I had taken from my bedside table.

The enclosed staircase was behind an inconspicuous door. I had hung a mountain goat head over it without even noticing the door. Mind you, the head could have been a domestic Billy goat, since you never knew what the Victorians would shoot, and it was hard to tell the difference in the dark.

The stairs were narrow and steep and made a couple of turns on the way up. As a result, I wasn't sure which direction I faced when I got to the top. I had climbed forty-two steps and knew I must have bypassed the third floor.

So I had to be in the cupola. I had no idea where the light switch might be even if I had wanted to flip it on. It was impossible to get a sense of the size and condition of the cupola by the feeble light in my hand. I gave it a shake and it brightened, but not much.

I played the light around the room at chest level and spotted the door to the widow's walk. I stepped through to the balustrade-lined walkway about five feet wide surrounding the cupola. I couldn't see a thing and that had to mean I was facing the pine wood on the east side of the house, or perhaps the maple wood at the back.

I switched the flashlight off and moved right, hanging on to the belly high railing. It felt solid enough under my fingers.

Far below me I saw the flickering campfires and the dull yellow lights in the field. Ghostly snatches of conversation and music reached me. I could see shadows of movement that I trusted were my security team on the job. Beyond the field were the streetlights of Blackshore, and in the far distance, I made out the faint greenish glow of the Bruce Power nuclear plant.

It wasn't much cooler up there after all. A faint breeze stirred the leaves in the woods below but didn't survive the climb to the widow's walk.

I sank down on the floor to rest. The air felt soft and damp on my skin and I was sorry I hadn't brought a pillow and comforter to lay on. Afterwards, I believed I must have fallen asleep.

At first it was the music I heard. I recognized Vera Lynn singing about a nightingale in Berkeley Square, and her words were crystal clear, like she had a microphone set up in the garden beneath my perch on the widow's walk.

The music faded until I could no longer make out the words. Instead, I heard a man's voice. It sounded like he was standing right in front of me, not far, far below.

"You can't go on this way, darling. Nobody expects you to stay with a man who treats you so shabbily."

A woman was with him. Her voice was low and hopeless, with a pain deep and unending.

"I must. He needs me more than ever now. And there's the baby."

"I'll take you both away. It doesn't matter what everybody thinks. We deserve to be together. We deserve some happiness."

A short, despairing laugh. "Happiness? While the whole world is exploding and burning? There is nothing except pain for all of us. You will soon be gone again, and I must look after him. He needs me."

"You must listen to me. The war can't last forever. They expect it will be over in months. Then we can go away from here. I can run my business from Toronto. There will be many opportunities when the war ends. We'll just go and leave this other life behind."

"Our family is here. You, especially, can never turn your back on them. And how can I leave my parents, my sisters? No, it's best if we end this now. I'll be fine, truly, and you will find someone else."

"No. I won't let that happen. Stay with me."

A new voice interrupted. Another man, older than the other. "I knew I would find you together. Get away from her. I know what's been happening while I was in hell over there. You have everything else, but you won't have her. Or my son."

The woman was hysterical. "My God. What have you done? My baby. Let me have him. What did you do to him?" She moaned, and the grief was the grief I felt in my own heart for my lost baby girl.

My head bumped against the balustrade. The voices and music were gone, and my hands shook as I turned the flashlight on and aimed it below. The feeble beam would not reach the shadowy centre of the shade garden and I could detect no movement or murmur of retreating voices.

Even the campfires had been extinguished. The darkness was complete except for the streetlights and the nuclear plant several miles away. I must have been asleep longer than a few minutes.

My flashlight faded and died in my hand. I gave it an angry shake, but it refused to emit even a glimmer. Either I stayed there until dawn, or I could feel my way back the way I had come.

I didn't want to hear more of that disturbing conversation. I felt for the doorknob and stepped back into the cupola. I dropped to the floor and crawled on my hands and knees until I found the gap in the floor.

I went down the stairs on my rear end, then picked my way through the tower room. I was doing fine until I tripped over a table and landed face down on the floor. I smelled something horrible and my fingers grasped course fur and curly horns. I realized it was the antelope—excuse me, the *wildebeest*—which somebody had carelessly left on the floor. It smelled different from the moose, but worse.

A minute later I was back in my own bed. Despite the heat, I pulled the sheet over my head and stayed there until the alarm woke me at six.

I don't kid myself. What I had heard the night before was some sort of flashback, the opposite of a premonition. Maybe it was Leander's idea of being helpful, but I planned to have a word with him. Allowing me to see or hear the past was one thing, making me *feel* it was going too far. I was a sensitive person and could not tolerate high levels of negative emotion. Everyone knew that.

While I showered and folded my hair into a twist, I went over the conversation in my mind. When I finished dressing and grooming, I got a pen and pad of paper and wrote down everything I could remember, and unlike a dream, I remembered quite a lot.

The reference to a baby confirmed that the woman was Wisty, since she was one of the two women staying in the house, and the only one with a baby. The man, the first man, I wasn't yet sure who he was. Either Uncle Patrick or Bruce Wingate. The mention of business and family fit Patrick's profile, but I would have to find out more about Bruce Wingate's life to be sure.

The other man was Wisty's husband, Thomas. There was no doubt in my mind he was in the house that weekend, the fifth person. I wondered when he had arrived and how many people knew he was here. And it seemed he was responsible for Tommy's death.

I put the pad back in the desk drawer to think about later and I picked up the picture of the 1943 reunion. As I held it, I almost hoped it would shift and change the way it had before, to perhaps make clear what I heard last night. But the sea of faces, many long dead, looked back at the photographer and did not speak to me. It was just a snapshot of a long-ago time. I was on my own from here on.

I went downstairs to face the present. Yesterday was the dress rehearsal for the reunion. Today, the curtain rose.

CHAPTER 21

Peter snored on a wingback chair in the drawing room, his bare feet resting on a flowered ottoman. He clutched my radio to his chest and didn't awake when I pried it gently away.

The kitchen was empty except for Jacqueline hopping about near the back door, and Rasputin watching her with a condescending expression on his broad face. I snapped the leash on Jacqueline and took her beyond the terraced gardens to the maple wood at the back of the house. Rasputin joined us, making heavy work of the walk. Not that I blamed him. The air hadn't improved through the night.

"You're too fat. Caroline is far too indulgent. Maybe I should take charge of your diet for a while. "

Rasputin sat down with his back to me, his tail flicking. Jacqueline yelped and ran around in circles, as was her habit before finding the perfect spot.

The woods were silent once Jacqueline was settled in front of a hapless maple sapling. The heat had penetrated even this fragrant place, but at that early hour, it might just have been the coolest spot on the continent. Reluctantly, I gathered up the pets and headed back to the house.

I was glad to be alone with my thoughts. I opened my herb cupboard and took out a canister of loose green tea. After some deliberation, I added twenty drops of gingko biloba tincture to the pot. I needed my brain cells firing on all cylinders.

Conklin stepped in from the pantry. "Good morning, Madam." He gave me his courtly bow. "It appears all was serene last night."

"No major incidents anyway." The ethereal conversation on the widow's walk didn't count. "Today will be different. And tonight."

He bowed again. I wished he would quit it. He never did it to anyone else. It was just another sign he considered me a separate species. He accepted a cup of green tea and sat down. I didn't tell him about the gingko biloba in case he balked, but figured any man his age could use some help with his circulation.

"Madam, I regret that another item is missing. An ornate paperweight in the shape of a globe on a gold-plated stand dating to the early nineteenth century."

"Shit. I mean darn it. Missing from where? And when did you notice it last?"

"It was on a gateleg table in the upstairs gallery. I'm afraid I noticed its absence just this morning, but as I make rounds on the upper floors only once a week after the cleaning team have left, it could have been taken away a week ago."

Upstairs. I wondered if the thief had taken the globe and Amelia at the same time. I hoped so. One intrusion was better than two.

"Way up on the second floor where I sleep all alone?"

Conklin looked pained, but nodded at me. "We must call in the police again, Madam. For the first time ever, I feel we are unsafe here at Hammersleigh."

I thought his expression was accusatory, like I had brought a thief along when I moved in. I swallowed my uneasiness at the thought of someone prowling around Hammersleigh while I was asleep a few feet away.

Maybe it wasn't Scott Fournier at all. It could be the gang of teenagers Marc was after for breaking into houses in the Blackshore area. Or, and the unwelcome thought jumped to the forefront of my thoughts, it could even be someone closer to home.

When I had a chance, I would have to write out a time line. I already had the list of visitors to the house during the past week. Now I had to remember the exact time each person was in the house and who else was around at the time. I felt sick when I realized the list included Patsy, Peter, Caroline and a lot of other people I trusted.

"Conklin, would you mind calling the police station and making sure the paperweight goes on the list of missing items?"

"Certainly, Madam." He bowed again. "Might I take the liberty of reminding you that the facilities will need pumping out this afternoon before they become...offensive?"

So I was in charge of the sewage. You could bet Uncle Patrick never called Wooter Sanitation himself to ask them to pump out the outhouses.

"Fine." I stomped off to the telephone room to make the call. It seemed I woke Benny from a deep sleep. I looked at my watch and was astonished to note it was 7:30 a.m. and the cock hadn't crowed yet, at least not at Benny's house. Apologizing, and almost meaning it, I asked Benny to pump out the porta-potties and was surprised when he related that he always came on the Saturday to do so and didn't need me waking him up in the middle of the night to remind him. And by the way, if I had a man of my own to look after, maybe I wouldn't be so nitpicky with other men.

I slammed down the phone, more angry at Conklin than at Benny's rude parting comment.

Conklin had reminded me to do something that was already arranged, part of the service in fact. It was obvious he thought I was a half-wit.

Still steaming, I stood under the portico and used my radio to call in the night shift. They straggled in, and I dispatched them home for some sleep, asking them to return by 4 p.m. I waited while the day shift mooched through the gates to receive their instructions, which were just a reiteration of what I had said the day before. I took Tiffany aside and reminded her that today was supposed to surpass all temperature records and to make sure that no young child or senior was running or standing around in the bright sunlight.

The campers in the field were stirring. Children cried or screamed, depending on their ages, while the door to Shangri-la creaked and slammed at two-minute intervals.

Inside, I found Caroline scrambling eggs and Peter buttering toast. Conklin was sitting alone at the table, drinking his tea like the Grand Poobah of Somewhere. When Caroline turned from the stovetop, I was relieved to see she had no fresh bruises. I hoped this meant she had refused Scott entry last night if, indeed, he had even been on the grounds.

I sat down and thought about that for a minute. Conklin had noticed the globe missing this morning. He was right, though. It could have been taken any time since last Saturday, even the same time as the hummingbird and the jade dragon. And Amelia. Unlikely the cleaning staff would notice one item missing among thousands since they didn't dust the collectibles. I sighed and dug into my eggs. There were such a mob wandering through Hammersleigh at any given time, I could no longer remember who they all were.

The field was thick with campers, and vehicles belonging to Blackshore families lined the county road. Lawn chairs sat beneath the trees and under the tent. Children chased each other over the grass and were yelled at by parents who just wanted to sit and gossip or drink beer with people they may not have seen since last year. The whole area was taking on the atmosphere of a ploughing match. And it was just 8:30 a.m.

I walked up to a young couple trying to unfold a mesh playpen. "Need any help?" I captured the struggling toddler who was doing his best to escape his father's one-armed grip. "Hey there, Trevor. Remember me? I'm your Auntie Lyris."

Trevor wiggled out of my hands and dropped to the ground, where he viewed me with round-eyed suspicion. A rare Pembrooke indeed, he had his mother's blue eyes and blonde hair. As a westerner from Whistler, Denise had not a drop of Pembrooke blood in her veins, and I for one welcomed any dilution of the dominant Pembrooke strain.

The sleepy-eyed infant cradled in my sister-in-law's arm stirred and peeped. Denise smiled and handed over my new niece. "Here, meet Grace Emily. She's just waking up."

I cradled the baby and felt a dull ache in the middle of my chest. It happened every time I held a new baby, and I thought the spot near my heart must encase my soul.

David dropped his end of the playpen and engulfed both of us in a hug. "So what do you think of her? Isn't she beautiful?"

"She is," I agreed, looking down at the tiny face. Just then, Grace peered at me with her milky eyes that nonetheless promised to be as dark as her father's.

"I'm sorry I haven't been around to the house to see you, but I've been busy with the reunion. I hope you found everything you need."

"Everything's fine," Denise assured me. "We appreciate the loan of your house."

"You can stay there as long as you like. As a matter of fact, I would have asked you to move into Hammersleigh with me, but I figured you'd want to be on your own while deciding where to build your new house."

David and Denise looked at each other and smiled.

"What? You two have done something."

"We've bought a house," Denise blurted.

"Go on. Already?"

"Yep." David seemed proud and not at all unsure of their sudden decision. "We bought Hollyhock Cottage from Aunt Clem. We don't get possession until the middle of September, so I hope you can stand being our landlady until then."

No way. Hollyhock Cottage had been built by Aunt Clem's grandfather around 1890. Her family had always owned it. But Aunt Clem had no children to pass the house to, Aunt Wisty would never leave Lychwood, and their two sisters were dead.

"It's great that Hollyhock Cottage will stay in the family, but where is she going to go? I can understand her wanting to give up the bed and breakfast business. She's still a vigorous woman, though. Where will she live?"

"She wouldn't say." Denise reached over to shoo a bug away from her daughter's miniature ear. "She says she has her plans, but didn't want to talk about it yet."

"Why am I always the last one to find out anything? I didn't even know you liked century houses." I shot an accusing look at David, who had seemed genuinely happy he hadn't inherited Hammersleigh House.

He pushed his glasses further up his nose and grinned at me. "There's a world of difference between Hammersleigh and Aunt Clem's house. I think our little family can be very happy at Hollyhock Cottage."

"And you couldn't at Hammersleigh?" I held up my hand as he started to protest. "It's okay. I know what you mean. Hammersleigh is more a museum than a home."

I thought of the many lonely nights ahead of me. Somehow, I couldn't picture Marc beside me in the Queen Anne bed on the second floor, and felt I was destined to spend the next forty or fifty years alone.

Spying Aunt Bertilla moving in our direction, I said to Denise and David, "Well, duty calls, so I better get on with it. I'll see you later." I bent to kiss the top of Grace's downy head, and a powerful reaction made me catch my breath and take a step backwards.

The smell. I sniffed Grace again, then handed her back to Denise without giving myself away. I made it to the porch and dropped into a white wrought-iron chair under the portico.

The smell of Grace, the smell of baby powder, was the first smell I had noticed in the upstairs hall outside the tower room. It was familiar, but I had never used baby powder on Mitch, since it caused a reaction on his fair skin.

Now it was gone from the hall, and I would bet my pension portfolio that Aunt Wisty had used baby powder on Tommy. I guessed that the odour was meant to focus my efforts on finding out the truth about Tommy's death. Leander strikes again.

Well, it hadn't been necessary. From the moment I found that pitiful body in the closet, I needed to know what happened to him. Now I knew who caused his death, but the reason was still a secret. And until I learned what happened that night in 1943, Tommy would continue to haunt my dreams.

It has often been said that the past should remain buried, that if you dig it up, only the living can be hurt. Well, I didn't believe that was always true, and I just knew somehow that Tommy needed his secret uncovered. Even Leander seemed to think so. Otherwise, why was he helping me? Or pushing me, rather, as I didn't seem to have any choice about his participation.

Somewhat recovered, I looked up just in time to see Aunt Bertilla charging up the drive. In deference to the temperature, she was clad in a pair of mid-thigh shorts and a tank top of matching orange cotton. The colour reminded me of my hat, and I touched my head to reassure myself I was still Number One.

Then, I took the coward's way out and leaped off the side of the porch and headed for the back of the house with the idea of losing myself in the shrubbery. By that time, Aunt Bertilla was so close I could see her huge underarms wobble. I was forced to jump over the temporary snow fence. It had been erected across the house to the ends of the property on either side to keep people from tramping through the parking lot on the left, the shade garden on the right and the back terraced garden areas.

I knew she could never heave her bulk over the fence, and I sighed with relief as I moved through the sun-drenched terrace and rounded the side of the house to collapse on the wooden bench. I figured Aunt Bertilla would soon get over her porta-pottie adventure, but until then, she was best avoided.

Relaxed for the moment, I gazed up at the canopy of leaves formed by the ancient maples. When I felt a touch on my right foot, I squawked and jumped up, thinking Aunt Bertilla must have sprouted wings and flown over the fencing.

Not Aunt Bertilla, but someone just as unwelcome.

"Hello, Dennis. So you came."

"Just for a short while. Tracey's ankles are swelling up in this heat."

"That's too bad." I had nothing against Tracey. I even felt grateful to her for saving me from another twenty years with Dennis. I wasn't sure if I would have had the courage to end our marriage on my own without the added impetus of a knocked-up, teenage girlfriend.

I sat back down on the bench and wiped my face on the bottom of my tank top. My hat had had fallen off while I was sprawled out, and I picked it out of the hosta bed and put it down beside me.

Dennis, too, looked damp all over. Cotton shirt and shorts clung to his skin, and his fair hair was limp. His face had turned pink with heat or sunburn, and he looked like a candidate for blood pressure medication.

I felt a slight concern for him, so didn't make my usual comments about his weight or thinning hair. He was still an attractive man if viewed objectively, and I congratulated myself that I was able to do just that. Now I preferred dark hair and storm-grey eyes, not to mention a dimple and firm thighs. Oh, dear…

"What are you staring at?" Dennis sat uninvited on my bench.

I sidled over until I was on the extreme edge. "Nothing much. We didn't want guests to come back here, you know. That's the reason for the fence."

"Only the lady of the manor can sit in the garden, I suppose," he sneered.

"Well, what bit your ass? If it's too hot for you, go home."

He seemed to make a great effort at control and reached over to pat my knee. I pulled away just in time. If he was trying to charm me, he had forgotten all the basics.

"I just wondered if you had a chance to think over what we discussed the other day in my office."

For a moment, my mind was blank. Then I remembered. "Oh, yeah. You want me to give you some of my money. I thought I said no."

"Lyris, I'm just asking you to be reasonable." His eyes swept the high stone walls of Hammersleigh House. "You fell into a gravy train here, and it's fair you return a portion of what you took."

"Do we need to have this conversation all over again? I don't know which concept you're having trouble with, that we split everything even-steven as the law dictates, or that I'm not parting with my half."

"It may have been legal, but it wasn't morally right. That you got half, I mean."

I looked at him in disbelief. "Get a grip on reality, Dennis. You have some nerve. As a matter of fact, now that I think of it, I deserved more than half for putting up with your idea of morality."

The humour escaped Dennis. His hands curled into fists, which should have been a warning to me. I did look around for a rock or something he might be able to throw. I saw no potential missiles and relaxed. Dennis was fond of throwing things when he was angry.

"Lyris, I am about to lose my house, and my wife will soon give birth to twins. How can you be so bitter and jealous that you won't return some of my assets?"

"Bitter? Jealous? Your assets?" I was astounded. Then, a tiny doubt probed my conscience. Was I wrong in taking half of our mutual holdings, mostly investments and half the value of the house? It wasn't a fortune, just enough to prevent me from ending my days in the county nursing home. Should I let him have more now because he had a growing family to support?

In the nanosecond it took for this doubt to cross my thoughts, Dennis was on his feet and stood in front of me. He put his hands on either side of the tree trunk and loomed over me. I don't believe he meant to appear threatening, but that's how I felt. I slipped off my seat, ducked under his arm, and stepped away from him. He moved closer.

Even though Dennis was four or five inches taller, this was an old game of ours. Confrontation head to head. That time, however, I underestimated the depth of frustration and anger built up within him.

"You have no right. Hand back some money, at least half of what you took from me, or I'll take you to court and the law will force you..."

I laughed. I couldn't help it. It was part nervousness and part astonishment that he would even contemplate such a ridiculous plan.

His hand came up and I thought he was going to hit me, something he had never done, even in the midst of our most acrimonious battles. I raised my own hand to protect my face, so I didn't see Dennis' expression as he gave my shoulder a hard shove. I fell back into the bed of hostas.

My landing was painful. It turned out there was a rock under the broad green and white striped leaves of the hostas, one with a pointy top. My left buttock connected with it, and the pain caused me to fight down a sudden wave of nausea.

Good thing it was just my butt. I eased that region off the rock. By the time my stomach stopped doing flip-flops, Dennis was gone. I don't know if he even waited until I hit the ground before disappearing.

I got to my feet and stood there for a minute. The pain seemed to be centralized in the muscle, and when I started walking, it didn't extend into my hip or spine. I think I was suffering from slight shock, because when Caroline opened the kitchen door and let me inside, I went straight upstairs and climbed into my bed.

I huddled in a ball while my rear end throbbed. After a half hour, I decided to get up and find some aspirin. I didn't think anything in my herb cupboard would help. As I slid off the bed, two pairs of eyes observed me from just inside the bedroom door.

"Why are you two here again? You know you're not supposed to be upstairs. Away you go now." Jacqueline and Rasputin had started to trail around behind me whenever I was in the house. I herded them out the door and followed after them.

"I'm sure both of you must be lonely. Caroline will have more time for you after this weekend. Just be patient. And stay off the furniture."

I checked all three upstairs bathrooms. No aspirin. Maybe in the employees' bathrooms, but I didn't feel I could intrude, and Conklin and Caroline were not in the kitchen to ask their permission.

I had left my hat in the shade garden and went to retrieve it. Then, I focused my thoughts and gave myself some instructions. Stay out of the sun, avoid Aunt Bertilla and Dennis. Talk to Aunt Clem and Aunt Wisty. I needed to know which lady was paired off with which gentleman during the 1943 reunion.

And talk to the old warrior. He can tell you a thing or two.

CHAPTER 22

I waited, my heart thudding, but Leander did not speak further. I looked around at the greenery and into the leafy ceiling above my head. If Leander ever did appear in a wisp of fog, I would drop dead on the spot.

Rear end pulsing with pain, I climbed back over the snow fence and surveyed the front lawns from the corner of the house. Groups of elderly people had gathered in the shade of the pines, as far away from the facilities as possible. The majority were women, but one or two groups of men sat together having a great time, judging by the whoops and table slapping. It didn't occur to me at the time to approach any of the women. My internal radar zeroed in on the men and I watched them for a minute or two.

I wondered if any of these men were discussing their war adventures as they talked and laughed. Not likely, since most veterans of the great conflicts did not appear to have enjoyed the experience. Just try and get granddad or great-uncle to tell you what he did during the war.

It was going to be tricky, digging information from someone who had spent a lifetime concealing his most terrible memories. On the other hand, I just wanted to know about that long-ago reunion, and didn't plan on asking about actual war experiences.

Still, I had to choose the right person, and it would be best if he was alone. I stepped away from the house and walked through the hazy sunlight toward the pines, trying to pick out a suitable candidate.

Stopping beside Avalon, I watched one trio who looked like they were set for the day with coolers of beer and cell phones. Two of them were in shorts and tank tops, while the third was bundled in his navy wool blazer and long trousers. They all wore combat berets and looked overheated.

There didn't seem to be anyone sitting alone, and I figured I would be spending most of the day lurking behind the outhouses. I kept my eye on the fun-loving trio.

Just when I was thinking of trying my luck under the tent by the gates, or perhaps among the recreational vehicles in the field, the gent in the cold-weather garb got up abruptly from his lawn chair and marched toward another group nearby. His set features and pursed mouth hinted that his conversation with his partners was upsetting or distasteful. Almost immediately, one of his companions wandered away down the drive.

The man left sitting alone was a wizened little soul who looked like he had been dipped in salt and left out in the sun too long. As I watched, he removed his beret and scratched a mottled bald head. The vacant chair beside him beckoned. I was afraid I couldn't lower myself down that far, let alone plant my posterior in it.

As I hesitated, the door to Avalon swung open, hitting me in the butt. The pain caused white spots to fly across my vision and I clutched the nearest pine for support.

When the spots disappeared, I let go of the tree's rough trunk and took a few steps away from the outhouse. A tingle between my shoulder blades propelled me toward the little man who was reaching for the beer can on his portable table. I caught his bright-eyed glance and realized he had witnessed the incident. I thought I detected a malicious bent to the gleam in his eye, but since he was the sole elderly man sitting by himself, I ignored it and limped over to the empty chair.

By the time I was seated, the sweat was trickling down my chest, not all of it from the heat. "Hello. I'm Lyris Pembrooke and I live here at Hammersleigh now."

"I know you. I heard you're taking over from Patrick." His bright glance slid over me, but it was assessing rather than lascivious, I preferred to think. "My name's Bert Pembrooke. You've grown into a fine-looking woman. A bit skinny, but that's the fashion nowadays it seems. You were a right nuisance when you were a young one, I remember"

I crossed my legs, then immediately regretted it. Easing my weight off the left side of my body helped a little, but I felt that shivery-spine thing that happens sometimes when you've injured yourself.

"Well, Mr. Pembrooke, I hope you're enjoying the reunion so far. Don't forget to come for the official picture tomorrow morning. We want to make sure everyone's in it."

"I'll be there. I'm staying in Billy's camper." He looked over at the man who had left so suddenly and was pointedly not looking our way. "He's mad right now, just because I said he stinks at bridge, which he does. He'll get over it. And Arnie there takes it in his head to be someplace else. He's getting old. Anyway, you can call me Gunner, although I think I'm your uncle or cousin or something. Because I was a tail gunner in the war, did you know that?"

"No, I didn't. Just what does a tail gunner do? Were you in the infantry?"

He appraised me like he expected a second head to pop up beside the first. "You don't know much about the war, do you, Missy?"

"Not really, I'm afraid. Will you tell me about it, about your part?" Well, there I went asking about war experiences, when I had promised myself I wouldn't.

"Not much point. You young people aren't interested in what happened to us then. Once we're all dead, and that won't be long now, nobody will remember the war or what really happened."

"There are history books. We studied the Second World War in high school."

"History books." He spat into the grass near my feet. I yanked them under my chair, causing another wave of pain to radiate down my leg.

He leaned closer. "I'll tell you what a gunner is. I sat in the back of a Lancaster bomber and operated the gun. I shot at the enemy, Missy, and got a few of them too."

"I see. That sounds dangerous, Gunner. Were you ever wounded?"

Gunner reached out and wrapped a tiny, gnarled hand around my wrist. "I was shot down once. Lucky for me it was over France, in the country. I parachuted out and landed in a ravine. Some resistance found me and I got back to my company."

"I'm sure there was more to it than that, Gunner. Did the resistance have to hide you from the Germans? How long did it take you to find your company?"

He released me and leaned away. "No need for you to know all that. It's over and done with. It's not seemly for a young lady to know about the things we had to do to survive."

Although I had started this conversation with Gunner in hopes of leading up to the 1943 reunion, I felt some frustration in his refusal to talk about the war. I wasn't so naïve that I didn't realize there was much the history books didn't tell us, so much we needed to know from these former soldiers before it was too late.

"As you say, Gunner, pretty soon there will be no one left to tell about it. Don't you think it's your responsibility to make sure your experiences, even the bad ones, are remembered by the following generations?"

He hitched his lawn chair back a few inches and looked across the expanse of Hammersleigh's vast lawns. I felt him withdrawing his memories from me.

"Gunner?" I shook his arm until his eyes returned to me and I saw awareness in his face again.

"Gunner, were you here in 1943 for the reunion? During the War?"

"I know when 1943 was, Missy. Do you think I'm senile or something? And of course I was here. I may not remember all the reunions, but I sure won't forget that one."

"Did you hear that I found little Tommy's body in the house"?

"I heard." He looked angry. "Poor little tyke. Funny thing, I remember him running around that first day, getting into everything. Some young girls were looking after him. There was no sign of his mama. Under the weather or something, I guess. It was real hot that summer, kind of like this one. Usually I don't feel the heat any more, but it sure is hot now. Just like it was back then."

Looking uneasy, Gunner lifted the neglected beer can to his thin lips. I needed to think of some questions that wouldn't shut him down for good.

"I don't suppose you remember who was staying in the house at the time?"

This time the scorn was unmistakable. "You're a ninny, aren't you?"

There didn't seem to be a safe answer to that, so I waited.

"When you get to be my age, Missy, you'll find out that you can remember what happened sixty years ago better than yesterday."

"So you do remember who was in the house then?"

"Missy, you deaf or something? I said I remember just fine." His voice carried across the still air. The people sitting nearest to us looked our way.

"Well, who was in the house, if you remember so well?" I was raised to respect my elders, but Gunner was pushing it.

"Why do you want to know?" A cunning expression crossed his face. He took another swig of beer, and on finding the can empty, expertly popped the tab on another from the cooler at his side.

I suspected Gunner was drunk, not just suffering from age-related irascibility.

I modulated my voice. "Since I found the body, I feel a responsibility to find out what happened. I believe Tommy needs us to know why he died."

"Huh. Don't know about that. Sometimes it's best to leave the past alone. The truth can hurt people, you know. Or maybe you don't know, you're such a ninny."

For a brief moment, I thought about screaming. Or crying. Or maybe drowning the old coot in his cooler of melting ice. I decided to try another approach instead.

Extending my leg to try and ease the pain, I said in a casual tone, "I guess you don't remember the 1943 reunion after all, Gunner. Don't worry, that's to be expected at your age. I'll find someone a bit younger and ask him."

Gunner had been gazing at my leg, but at this statement, his head snapped up and he squeezed his beer can in one gnarled fist. He almost dented it too.

"I remember everything about that weekend. Don't try playing games with me, Missy. Since you're such a nosy parker, I might just tell you a thing or two you don't want to hear."

"Go ahead, try me," I challenged. "First of all, who was in the house, how many people I mean?"

"Who do you think? Wisty, Clem, Patrick and that friend of Patrick's. I don't remember his name, but I will in a minute."

I supplied the name. "Bruce Wingate. So there were just the four of them?"

"The baby, too, of course."

"And that's all?"

He wore a crafty look now. "Why, do you think there was more?"

There seemed to be no point in keeping my suspicions secret from Gunner, or anybody. I was pretty sure that most Pembrookes over the age of eighty already knew how many souls were staying at Hammersleigh

House that weekend. It was even possible there was an unspoken conspiracy to ensure that particular family secret died with their generation.

"I think Thomas Pembrooke, Wisty's husband, was here. I don't know for how long or what happened to him. Maybe he went back overseas to the War for a time. But I know his body is buried at the edge of the cemetery and there is no official record of it at the funeral home."

"Well, you don't know everything, Missy. Thomas never left here..." He stopped in midsentence, perhaps aware of his imprudent words.

"I guess maybe I'll have to ask somebody else." I looked around me at the many seniors seated nearby, some of the men with berets similar to Gunner's, some with medals pinned to their light blazers or checked shirts.

Gunner pointed a shaky finger at me. "You quit upsetting people. What happened to Thomas and his little boy was a long time ago. There's still people who can be hurt by your nosy questions."

Sure, I felt like a bully. But something spurred me on nonetheless. Not Leander, just a sense that it was important for the truth to be known, maybe for Tommy who had died much too soon, and who had to wait more than sixty years for a peaceful grave among his family. Or maybe there was some other reason.

"If you tell me what you know, I won't have to bother anybody else," I said with ironclad logic.

"I only know what I heard, and the rest I guessed for myself."

"Didn't you see Thomas at all?"

"I thought I did, once. It was out back of the house." He looked at me, accusation in his eyes. "There wasn't a fence put up to keep us out back then."

I shrugged and waited for him to continue.

"I was under those maple trees, trying to cool off. They weren't so big back then. Had a nice little second cousin to keep me company, too." He waited for a reaction and I rolled my eyes obligingly. Gunner was probably his own second cousin.

"A man came out of the back door, kitchen I think, and stood in the sun for a while. He looked around like he didn't know where he was, then went back in. I thought it was that Wingate person at first, but later when I heard the stories, I figured it was Thomas himself. I didn't see him too clear."

"Then what?"

"Then nothing until the next morning, Sunday. Then Patrick came out of the house and said the little boy was missing, and a statue or something was gone too. The police came and organized a search of the woods and fields around the house, but nobody ever saw the boy again. Not until last week, that is."

Gunner seemed to be tiring. We sat in silence for several minutes before he spoke again.

"Some of us were late getting back to our outfits. Got in a lot of trouble because of it too. We were here until Monday evening, searching. They said a thief got into the house during the night and did something to the boy to keep him quiet."

"Didn't you hear anything after that? When the war was over and you were here again for another reunion."

"We talked. We heard things. The chief of police's brother-in-law or some such started telling people that Thomas was here and that he died somehow right after. It was said that he had something to do with his boy's disappearance, but nobody knew for sure."

"What was he like? Thomas, I mean."

"Thomas? Thomas was a fine man. He was older than some of us, but that didn't stop him joining up. He'd been a captain in the previous war, so they were glad to get him back."

"But what was he like as a person?"

"I told you. You *are* deaf, aren't you? He was a hard man, but a good man. He took good care of Wisty and was right fond of that little boy. He was proud as punch when he was born. Said he had to help restore the world to its proper order so his son could grow up safe."

"Were any of the others paired up at the reunion before Thomas came? Was there anything going on that Thomas's sudden appearance at the house interrupted?"

I had gone too far.

Gunner gazed past me. "Did you know some wood parts for the Mosquito fighters were made right here in Blackshore at the furniture factory? I often thought about that, back then. When I was over there." He popped another beer tab and closed his eyes.

They opened again and this time there was a malicious gleam there. "I have to have an operation, did you know that?"

"I'm sorry. I hope it isn't too serious."

"It's a hernia. The size of your head. Do you want to see it?" He pulled his shirt out from his shorts.

"No. Thanks. I'll take your word for it."

I slunk away like the ninny I was, hearing his delighted cackle behind me. During the half hour I had been sitting there with Gunner, my leg and hip had seized up. I had to force myself to keep walking as I crossed the grass and reached the circular bricked driveway.

The sun beat down without mercy, and a flickering haze rose from the bricks, obscuring the house. I looked upward at the widow's walk, barely visible from this angle. Danger in a high place. Aunt Clem's guide had struggled through the cosmic curtain with that cryptic warning.

The bright sunlight was making my eyes water and I started to look away, but a slight movement on the widow's walk caught my attention. A figure was bending over the railing, watching the grounds. Bright hair glinted in the sun, but the rest was just a shadow.

I thought I was having another flashback to 1943 and looked around to check on my surroundings. Everybody was dressed in the current fashion, and I recognized a lot of them. I wiped my damp forehead in relief. When I glanced back up, the figure was still there. As I watched, it moved slowly out of sight, probably through the door into the cupola. I decided it was Conklin. Or could it be somebody else, somebody that had no business being up there? The safety precautions I had put in place should have prevented any outsider from getting through into the house.

A touch on my arm plucked me away from that troublesome thought. I turned to see Patsy steaming and dripping on the bricks. Her sleeveless dress was a riot of primary colours, the red parts clashing with her round, flushed face.

"Holy mama. It sure is warm out today. What's the matter with you anyway?"

"Nothing. What are you doing here? Don't tell me you've discovered you're related to the Pembrookes too? Everybody else claims to be."

"Don't be silly, I just came to see how things are going, since this is the first reunion you're responsible for. I had to park half a mile down the road and walk. And you're in pain, I can see by your face. What happened, do you have cramps or something?"

"No, I do not have cramps. I bruised my butt in the shade garden."

I ended up telling Patsy all about the incident with Dennis, trying to make light of it. I was sorry right away. She typically blew it all out of proportion.

"Marc should speak to him. For Pete's sake, that's assault."

"Just forget it, Patsy. I made him mad…"

"Are you listening to yourself? That's the first thing an abused person says. That it's somehow her fault for being assaulted. You should know better."

"I do. That's not what I meant. Calm down, will you? And stop overreacting. Dennis is frustrated and desperate right now. I shouldn't have been egging him on. You know how my mouth runs away with me sometimes."

"Your mouth isn't any worse now than when you were married to Dennis, or on the day you were born for that matter. We'll talk about this later. Right now I want to see that injury. It could be serious if it causes you so much pain."

"I'm not pulling up my dress in front of 300 people and showing you my bare ass. Besides it feels better already. Anyway, listen to me."

I pulled her off the scorching bricks into the shade. "I want to get some counselling for Caroline. You're involved with the Women's Shelter and I know they provide assistance to victims of abuse."

"Caroline? I didn't know. I'll set her up with an appointment on Monday."

"That's great. Thanks, Patsy. I'll make sure she goes."

"You should come with her, Lyris. You might learn something, like why you let Dennis treat you this way."

"Get a grip, Patsy. Can you see me putting up with that kind of crap? Dennis just took me by surprise. Next time I'll be ready for him and knock him on *his* butt."

"Brave words from a hundred-pound princess, but we'll talk about it when this circus is over. Right now I have to get home. Nick is taking me out for dinner to cheer me up."

"You're acting pretty cheerful already. Did you get another job?"

"No. Well, not exactly. Later, dude."

I watched her as she picked her way through the crowd. She didn't look like she needed cheering up. She was acting more like her usual self and I had to wonder at the change since the last time I talked to her.

I looked around to see if Aunt Clem and Aunt Wisty had arrived yet. Yes, there they were, close to the tent at the bottom of the drive.

I hobbled over as fast as I could in the direction of my two great-aunts. Aunt Wisty was laying in a lawn lounge while Aunt Clem sat with straight back in a plastic chair. Hovering over both of them was Conklin. He had doffed his corduroy jacket and draped it over the back of his chair. In place of the turtleneck was a soft cotton shirt buttoned at the wrists. If it had been him on the widow's walk a few minutes ago, he would have had to hop it to get down to the front lawn so fast. I felt uneasy again.

I moved toward the trio, but was destined not to reach them, for at that moment, my radio beeped. I answered it to hear Peter's voice asking me to come to the house at once. There was an emergency. Conklin must have been watching me. He was right beside me as I reached the front door. It opened before my hand could touch the demon-knocker and I fell into the great hall, while Conklin performed a fancy step dance to avoid tripping over me. Peter steadied us both and led us down the hall toward the kitchen.

"What are you still doing here, Peter? I thought you went home to bed?"

"I decided to stick around in case you needed me tonight."

"Well, what's the emergency?"

"It's Caroline. I found her slumped over the table. It looks like she's taken something, but I don't know what. And she won't let me call an ambulance."

Caroline was sitting at the table with her chin propped up by both hands. She was trying to focus and making a poor job of it. Her eyes refused to follow the same path, and they circled in opposing directions.

My entire herb cupboard appeared to be spread out before her on the table. Tins were tipped over, the contents mixing together, and glass bottles added their tinctures to the mess. Teapot, spoon, kettle—all these littered the tabletop. A ceramic mug contained two metal tea balls and an inch of liquid the colour and texture of septic tank sludge.

"My God, Caroline, what have you done? What have you taken?" Surely she hadn't mixed up the herbs into a poisonous combination? However, that was not impossible and I had to know what she'd ingested.

Caroline's eyes, one of them anyway, rolled in my direction. "I used it all. I was nervous and upset and didn't know which of them would help, so I took some of everything."

These were not Caroline's actual words. I have loosely translated her mumbles and hesitations.

I looked at the labels on the tins. Valerian, passion flower, hops. So far, so good. All just mild remedies for nervousness. Then...uh-oh.

Burdock root, stinging nettle. Beneficial in their own way, but I didn't know if they could interact with the others.

"Madam, I will call an ambulance." Conklin started toward the telephone, but Caroline made a Herculean effort to speak again.

"No, please. No ambulance. I'll be okay. I don't want a fuss."

I was inclined to go along with her. It was self-preservation to be sure. I could see the headlines: "Amateur Herbalist Charged with Practising Alternative Medicine Without a License." Frantic, I looked at the labels again, trying to determine which could cause side effects when taken with something else. I had no idea.

I was just about to tell Conklin to phone for the ambulance when a prescription bottle rolled out from beneath the kitchen table, followed by Rasputin and Jacqueline. Peter picked it up before Jacqueline could bat at it again. I snatched it from his fingers and peered inside. The bottle contained tiny, white oval pills.

"What's this?" I held it up in front of Caroline's wandering eyes, trying to get at least one of them to see the plastic container. "It has your name on it and says to take one or two before bedtime as required."

"My doctor gave them to me to help me sleep. They relax me. I took some, but they didn't help, so I decided to try your herbs."

"How many did you take? Come on, Caroline, how many?" I pulled her hands away from her face and held her chin with one hand, while shaking the pill container in front of her with the other. If she took too many we would have to call the ambulance for sure, should have already.

"I don't remember." She groaned and pulled away from me, dropping her head onto the table again and proceeding to snore. I thought about slapping her, like they do in movies.

Instead, I opened the container and dumped the pills on the counter. The label was dated three days earlier and indicated there should be thirty tablets. I counted them. There were twenty-seven.

I sighed with relief. "Even if she didn't take any the last couple of nights, the most she can have taken today is three. That can't be enough to hurt her."

"Unless," replied Peter with unwelcome logic, "she had a previous prescription and took some of those too."

Conklin's hand was inching toward the telephone again.

I wasn't heartless, and if the poor girl was in serious trouble, I would be the first to make sure she got medical help. On the other hand, I didn't want to disrupt the reunion unless it was necessary.

"Caroline, listen to me. Did you have any pills other than these? Tell me the truth."

"Honest, Lyris. I just got these the other day and took one last night. I took one this morning because I felt so upset, and when it didn't work, I took another one, then the herb tea. That's all, honest. Please don't call an ambulance. I feel better now." Indeed, her eyes weren't rolling so indiscriminately, and she made an effort to smooth back her hair.

I looked at Conklin and Peter, and they looked at each other. When all this silent conferring was done, we seemed to have reached a consensus. No ambulance.

"Peter, would you take Caroline to her sitting room and watch television with her or something? Don't let her fall asleep or drink anything more except regular black tea, maybe Earl Grey."

I put the pills into my pocket. "I'll take these for now." Some people shouldn't be allowed out alone, much less left in charge of drugs.

I started cleaning up the mess on the table, vowing to get a lock installed on my herb cupboard the very next week. Who knew what dangers lurked therein?

By the time the kitchen was pristine again, the afternoon was well advanced. The emptiness in my stomach reminded me that I had missed lunch. Since the cook was suffering from an overdose.

I made egg salad sandwiches for the four of us and took them into the staff sitting room. Caroline didn't eat much and it took all our efforts between bites to keep her awake. She kept trying to doze off, and while maybe it would have been best to let her sleep it off, I was still a little uncertain of the effects of the herbs combined with sleeping pills.

When I was free to go back outside, the heat was more oppressive than earlier. I brought out two plastic pitchers of lemonade and a stack of disposable cups into the shade garden and called my teams in for a cool drink.

I was pleased that, although hot and tired, they remained enthusiastic. That is, they showed up when summoned, didn't whine much, and hadn't lost or disabled their radios. It was good enough for me.

I gave a pep talk about the good job they were doing, and reminded them that the night would bring all sorts of situations I was counting on them to handle. They perked up at that, and I chose not to believe this was due to any intentions they might have to participate in said situations. I emphasized that fire remained a significant risk, and both the security and first aid teams were to be especially watchful that no bonfires were started in the field too close to Hammersleigh's tree line. A couple of volunteers from Blackshore's fire department had promised to drop by during the evening to make sure the fire code was adhered to, but a little extra vigilance by my posse wouldn't hurt.

Once the kids melted back into the shrubbery, I headed around front to talk to Aunt Clem and Aunt Wisty. But they had gone from their shady spot. I wandered around looking for them before conceding defeat and settling down with my mother, her new fiancé, and the rest of my immediate family. I spotted Tracey down by the tent with her little girl, but Dennis was not with them. Tracey moved with ponderous care, and I thought it was typical of Dennis to go home and leave his pregnant wife and toddler to their own devices.

The heat had forced everyone to slow down and even conversation ceased. The children seemed content to play quietly among the pines or sleep on blankets at their parents' feet. Thus, the long afternoon passed peacefully and after supper—which I had to cook again as Caroline was still *hors de combat*—I went to my room for a nap, knowing that I would need to be awake and alert most of the night.

I woke up at eight-thirty, sore and worried. I believed I had all foreseeable risks covered, but still, I admitted to a sense of unease about the coming night hours.

As daylight passed swiftly through a blood-red sunset into dusk, then into total blackness, I moved back and forth between the lampposts, sensing something elusive, something out of place.

Perhaps it was merely a remnant of time from that summer night in 1943, oppressively humid and hot like this night, when a child and a tortured soldier died so tragically.

CHAPTER 23

I thought of the Gene Pitney song, the one about the night having a thousand eyes.

Stepping carefully through the trees, I was aware of shapes just out of my range of vision, shadows that stopped moving or murmuring when I passed by. The lampposts lining the circular driveway would be left burning tonight, but their shafts of light only randomly penetrated into the thick grove of pine trees where I stood. I turned off my flashlight so my eyes would adjust to the darkness.

No one was supposed to enter the grounds of Hammersleigh House once the gates were shut and locked for the night. In reality, I knew the young people would be here, and would go anywhere else they wanted. Fences or gates would not stop them, and at this moment, their senses would be quickening at the thought of the night ahead. These grounds, the cemetery, fields, meadows and woodlots—all would belong to the young tonight.

And I wasn't about to go crashing through the darkness to chase them away. My teams were briefed to watch out for fire and vandalism, but otherwise not to interfere. I hoped my reluctant recruits would not yield to temptation, abandon their flashlights and radios and cross over to the side of adventure and danger. But if even a few stayed with me, I knew we could survive the night.

I looked out across the lighted driveway and watched the shadows flitting through the trees on the other side. I hoped the kids were indulging in nothing worse than pot smoking and protected sex. A beam of light and a form appeared in my peripheral vision. I whirled to face it.

"Pardon me, Madam, I did not mean to startle you."

"Conklin. Don't worry, it's quite all right. My heart should start up again any minute."

"Madam. I thought it prudent to patrol the grounds tonight. Past reunions have caused some…incidents."

I felt rather than saw his disapproval. He couldn't be referring to anything I was involved in during my teenage years? Not that those *incidents* were serious, and I was pretty sure no one knew about them anyway. But who could tell, considering Conklin had eyes in the back of his head and a memory like an elephant?

"However, Madam, between the two of us, we could cover more area if you were to walk about the field and I stayed on the grounds close to the house in case Peter needs me."

"I'm on my way, Conklin." Before moving on, I thought of something I wanted to ask him.

"Conklin, didn't I see you up on the widow's walk this morning? When I asked if you would patrol the house regularly, I didn't mean the cupola too. That's a lot of stairs."

"The widow's walk, Madam? I haven't been up there for a week or more. There are, as you say, a lot of stairs. Perhaps it was Peter. He kindly offered to go over the house today in my place."

"Oh." I wasn't quite convinced. If that hadn't been his silver head up there, I was my grandmother's cousin. Although, silver or blond, it might have been either, come to think of it. "I guess it may have been Peter or Mitch, or even a trick of the sun reflecting off the windows."

"Quite, Madam."

After a few minutes of small talk made even more boring by my mention of the heat and would it ever rain again in our lifetime, Conklin aimed his flashlight on his watch and melted back into the trees, murmuring about his security patrol of the grounds.

Hammersleigh's lawns and pine groves were separated from the field by a six-foot wrought-iron fence, a fence easy enough to shinny over if you were young and lithe. On a good day, I could still do it, but not with the pain that shot through my leg and hip at every step. The other easier way to get to the field was through the wooden gate by the goldfish pond in the shade garden.

Near the pond I picked up a T-shirt that had been left in the middle of the flagstone path. I draped it over a nearby hydrangea bush so the owner could find it later and received another severe fright when the bush started to thrash and emit odd noises, much like a bobcat giving birth to a full-grown gorilla.

"This is too much." The noise and movement didn't subside, so I kicked at one of the four bare feet protruding from the foliage.

"I'm leaving now. But I'll be back in one minute. If you're still here, I'll pull you both out, and I don't care if you're buck naked. And pick up your clothes when you leave."

It looked like a laundry basket had exploded on the path. I hoped that both participants had reached the age of consent and had sprayed themselves liberally with insect repellent before crawling under the shrubbery.

"And don't smoke anything in there, either," I called over my shoulder at the bush.

I scratched my bare arms and wished I had used repellent on myself. It was too late in the season for black flies, but mosquitoes abounded. The only way to elude the voracious insects was to keep moving and stay away from plant life.

I found the gate more by memory than anything else. I opened it and walked through a portal into another universe. I had to blink once or twice before my eyes adjusted to the panorama before me.

Here the night was almost as bright as day. Strings of lights hung from one RV to another, while Coleman lanterns hissed and flickered with a surreal radiance. In the middle of the field, one oversized bonfire sent sparks flying skyward. The fire was a little too close to the solitary elm to suit me.

Lawn chairs of every hue and material surrounded the blaze, each one occupied by a senior reveller. In the rosy glow, I recognized many townspeople, who had come out to test their stamina against visiting relatives. They were drinking and eating and tossing more wood on the fire. As I watched from the gate, the flames roared and shot higher into the night sky. Music from the war years erupted from lusty throats.

These elderly family members knew the truth, I was sure of it. Maybe not everyone knew everything. But the full and true story of the 1943 reunion was collectively stored in those memories. One fact perhaps in that white-haired head, another in that gentleman's bald pate.

If I could tap into the knowledge, the final pieces would tumble into place.

Tonight was not the time. They were here to enjoy what could be their last family reunion. It wouldn't be fair or kind to ask questions about a time in their lives that was at best difficult, at worst a nightmare. But each month that passed, their ranks would decrease—until soon, there would be no one left to remember.

I checked my watch. Eleven o'clock, still the shank of the evening for this crowd. As the night wore on, many of the revellers would turn in or go home, and I was concerned that the fire would not be safely doused. If even a slight breeze came up, the elm was a goner.

They started on the "White Cliffs of Dover." I grew up hearing such songs at every reunion, and listening to them again brought back memories of dozing in my grandmother's lap as we sat around the campfire.

The woman singing the lead was no Vera Lynn, and soon, they changed to "Harbour Lights" and this tune seemed to suit the mixed chorus better. I couldn't understand why the party animals weren't grilled to cinders standing so close to the bonfire, although the heat did keep the bugs away. But I had to move after a few minutes.

"Mom." I turned to greet my son, who stood behind me out of range of the crackling blaze. His arm was draped over the goddess's shoulders, and she was squeezing his waist like a tube of toothpaste. Their hair gleamed in the light of the fire.

"Hi, Mitch. Hi, Tiffany. How are you guys holding up? Another twelve hours and we'll be home free, so let's hope we can keep our teams on the job until then."

"I think we're doing okay, Mom, but I'm a little concerned about this fire. Do you think we should ask these people to let it die down a little?"

"That elm tree is going to get scorched," Tiffany chimed in.

A redundant comment since anybody could see the tree was in mortal danger, and if it ignited, some of the trailers and tents were going with it. The bottled gas stored in every camper would fuel the conflagration. And it would turn out to be my fault. I already knew that.

"I know. Do you want me to speak to them? Or we could get one of the volunteer firemen to make an announcement."

"No, let me try first," said my son. "We'll try and keep it low key, then if they don't listen, we'll call in the fire department. Some of these people are getting kind of wasted."

"Sounds good." I moved away so Mitch wouldn't feel I was looking over his shoulder. The strains of "Red Sails in the Sunset" followed me for a while as I ambled through the camping paraphernalia that covered most of the available ground within the field's boundaries.

At the far end of the field near the cemetery, a group of middle-aged relatives were having their own party. There were about twenty or thirty of them, and instead of a bonfire, they clustered around a couple of kerosene lamps that threw out enough light to enable them to see each other's faces fading in and out of the blackness. A few were incinerating marshmallows with the aid of a camping stove and pointed sticks. Most of them were drinking either beer or coolers, but I recognized the glint of Royal Crown and Johnny Walker bottles clustered on the ground.

While their parents were singing numbers from the war, these former flower children were playing sixties protest songs on a portable CD player. Bob Dylan was blowing in the wind.

We seemed to have missed the fifties and early sixties altogether, and since early rock and roll was my favourite music, I soon lost interest and wandered away into the cemetery.

Everything seemed to be under control and I relaxed a little. Conklin was more than capable of handling anything he might turn up on Hammersleigh's grounds. Mitch and Tiffany had the field in hand. With any luck at all, both security and medic teams were out there somewhere, mingling with the enemy, discouraging anarchy and chaos, not contributing to it.

Well, if my crew turned on me now, there was nothing I could do about it. I decided to take a break for a few minutes and rest. With the aid of my flashlight, I was able to locate a flat rectangular tombstone. It was Aunt Rose, one of the younger sisters of Aunt Clem and Aunt Wisty, and I figured she wouldn't mind if I stretched out for a bit.

Although Aunt Rose rested a few feet from the cemetery boundary, close to Thomas's secret grave, the lights from the field did not penetrate that far, and the narrow slice of moon in an overcast sky permitted only shadows to loom out of the darkness. Thunder rumbled while Janis Joplin wailed about something or other. Could Simon and Garfunkel be far behind?

I lay back on the cool marble and gazed up at the sky, trying to make out the big dipper. Or the little dipper, since I didn't know the difference.

Somewhere in the distance, I heard the sounds of running feet and whispered giggles. If any of those kids passed closer to my bier, I planned to sit up and give them a good scare.

I turned my thoughts away from that other reunion. The pieces were all there and they almost fit—I felt they would come together very soon. Instead, I decided to think about Marc. I thought about me and Marc together, yes or no. I didn't know if I loved him as he deserved to be loved. Even if I did, how could the two of us live together—and where?

For Hammersleigh was my burden. I had to admit it. The grand house I considered such a treasure a few short weeks ago, my own personal museum, was just that—a museum. It was not a home for a family, especially a little family of two. I thought with longing of the wing where Conklin and Caroline lived, and for a brief moment, I considered kicking them upstairs and taking over their quarters for my own use. Of course, I'd install air conditioning for them first...

"God damn it, Lyris," a loud voice announced over my head, "what the hell are you doing here?" The voice echoed through the now empty— I hoped—cemetery.

As so often happens, the thought was father to the deed. I twisted around on my marble bed and was almost blinded by a flashlight. I turned my own on and aimed it back into the face of my perhaps beloved, my maybe lover. If I could make up my fickle mind.

"Marc." I didn't move—well, I couldn't. My leg and hip had seized up again. "What are you doing here?"

"I asked you first," he replied, rather childishly in my view.

Rolling over and pushing myself up on my elbow, I looked at him. He was so easy on the eyes, even in the unkind brilliance of the flashlight. "I'm just resting for a minute. It's been a long day, and the night holds much temptation for young blood." I waggled my eyebrow at him, but he apparently wasn't in the mood.

"Don't you have a bed at home to sleep on? I thought I had found a dead body. It's a good thing I have a strong heart."

"I'm patrolling. The night is alive, and evil lurks in every dark corner."

"I won't dispute that, although I still think this is a strange place to take a nap."

"Okay, at the count of three, we'll both turn out our flashlights."

Both lights went out in unison. I managed to get into a sitting position on Aunt Rose and patted the marble beside me. "Here, have a seat and tell me what you're doing in a cemetery, shouting at an innocent woman. And in your uniform yet. You know how uniforms affect me."

He didn't sit. "I'm on duty. This reunion madness spills over into the town, you know. I have almost all my staff on overtime, and was driving around the concession myself when I...thought I spotted some kids running into the cemetery from the road. And what do I find instead? A body draped over a tombstone."

I got the impression that Marc had started to say something else, but thought better of it.

He peered into the gloom toward the field. I could tell he itched to be on his way. He looked back at me. "Would you believe I never swore until I met you?"

"I believe it, but I don't understand it. Dennis used to say I drove him to drink, but what is there about me to drive a man to cuss words? I am the most inoffensive of women, truly a Madonna, to use your own description."

He smiled. "Dennis is an ass. And you only look like a Madonna, specifically like a print I have at home—dark hair, delicate, heart-shaped face and long, graceful neck. But I doubt the lady in my picture was half as interesting as you."

"Can I see that picture sometime?"

"Anytime. It's hanging in my bedroom." He smiled again, and we both laughed.

Then he went serious on me again. "I have to get back to work. If you're going to the house, I'll walk you back."

"What about your car?"

"Ronnie is waiting outside the cemetery with it. I can radio him to pick me up at the front gates of the house."

"Let's go, Officer." Conklin had made it clear my post for the night was in the field, but I could walk Marc to the front gates first. Even though I doubted the depth of my feelings for Marc, I still found him exciting. I even liked the sound of his leather holster rubbing against his belt. I was pathetic. The Family Procrastinator.

A rustling in the dry grass off to our right caused Marc to drop my hand, turn his flashlight on and put one hand on his gun, all in one swift motion. He sure was jumpy.

"It's just some of the kids…"

Marc shushed me with a quick motion. Even that stirred me. Pathetic.

A ghostlike figure floated out from behind a tombstone that was crested with a stone angel wielding the sword of judgment.

"Don't shoot," I shrieked. In the harsh gleam of Marc's flashlight, I recognized the otherworldly wraith.

"Okay, I won't. I generally consider elderly ladies fairly harmless, unless of course they're packing." His tone was a mite sarcastic if I wasn't mistaken.

"It's my Aunt Wisty. She must have broken out of Lychwood."

"She doesn't look strong enough to walk."

And indeed, Aunt Wisty, barefoot and clad in a long, pale nightgown, looked as ethereal and insubstantial as a real ghost.

I rushed over to my bewildered aunt and put my arm around her to lead her closer to the light. She looked around at the cemetery, then directly over to where her baby lay, although that fresh mound was in darkness and she could not have seen it.

"Who are you?" She didn't sound scared, just bemused and curious.

"I'm Lyris, Aunt Wisty. Lyris Pembrooke. Do you remember me?"

"No. What is this place? It's not home."

"We'll take you home, Aunt Wisty. Just sit down over here." Have a seat on your sister Rose, my dear.

"I'd carry her to the car and have Ronnie drive her back to Lychwood," Marc said in a low voice, "but I need to follow up on something first. I'll carry her as far as the house and you can notify Lychwood to come and get her."

"I don't think she'd like to be in Hammersleigh House tonight." I pulled out my radio. "We'll stay here and I'll get Peter or Caroline to call Lychwood and ask them to come to the cemetery. They may have missed her by now." I hoped this was an isolated incident and Lychwood's residents weren't allowed to wander the county roads in the dead of night.

With suspicious haste, Marc disappeared into the shadows rimming the cemetery in search of his "kids." After talking to Peter on my radio and explaining the situation and our precise location, I turned to Aunt Wisty.

"Why did you leave your...home, Aunt Wisty? Were you looking for something?"

"Looking for my baby, my little Tommy."

The hair on the back of my neck stirred, and I edged closer to my frail aunt. "Do you know where he is?"

I didn't know if she thought Tommy was alive and still at Hammersleigh House. Or if she accepted he was dead and had come to visit his grave.

She looked in the direction of Hammersleigh House. Although no glimpse of the house showed through the trees and shadows, she stared at the dying bonfire visible in the distance. Vera Lynn was singing "A Nightingale Sang in Berkeley Square." The haunting melody should not have been audible this far from the fire. Maybe the flower children were playing the song on CD.

"Over there," she said dully. Now the hairs on my arms were erect too.

"Did you leave him…over there, Aunt Wisty?"

"He didn't mean to. They had the hanging back then, you know. That's why I did it. He wanted me to, rather than let them hang him."

She was staring intently across the darkness to the edge of the cemetery, to the line of trees where it was darker still. I realized her eyes were locked on the spot where her husband was buried in his hidden grave.

A wave of fear gripped me as I wondered how Aunt Wisty knew where the grave was. It was my impression that Wisty had become almost catatonic right after Tommy's death.

"Did you put Tommy in the closet?"

She looked down at her bare feet, and when I looked down too, I could see they were scratched and bleeding. But if they hurt her, she didn't seem to notice.

"I'm sorry," she said with such sadness my heart broke for her. "I meant it for the best."

She was staring at her husband's grave again, and much as I didn't want to follow her glance, I couldn't help myself.

What I did not want to see, what I should not have seen, there at the edge of the tree line near Thomas's grave, was a shape. At first, it was the merest outline, a shadow. But as I watched, it took form until I saw it more clearly than I have ever seen anything before or since. A man, gaunt and haunted, dressed in the uniform of the last Great Conflict.

His eyes, which I could not have seen in the darkness, were full of longing and hopelessness as he gazed at the thin, old woman sitting beside me. He lifted one emaciated hand toward Aunt Wisty, and his agony was so impelling I could feel its powerful force reaching out to embrace us, pulling us in.

She stared back at him, and I knew her eyes mirrored the same emotions. Paralyzing fear held me. I was sitting on a tombstone in the cemetery, but at the same time, I was caught between two anguished souls, who were trapped in another time.

It was impossible to detach myself from the energy of despair that crackled like a thing alive all around us. I clapped my free hand over my eyes. Aunt Wisty cried out and the sound seemed to break the gossamer thread that held us suspended between reality and dreams.

The air around us shifted. I took my hand away and looked back to the dark tree line.

There was no one there. I had seen nothing. Aunt Wisty slumped silently in my arms, her thin body shivering. I was shaking as well, and we clung together and let the hot night air warm our bodies.

The last notes faded away and I was never sure if I had imagined the music.

A few minutes later, two attendants from Lychwood appeared on the bricked path leading from the new part of the cemetery. Aunt Wisty was borne away, wrapped in a blanket by a husky young man, who whispered kindly to her as he lifted her in his arms.

I was right behind them as they crossed through the old cemetery and the new, out the gates to the road. I returned to the field via the county road. Nothing in this life could have enticed me to cross the boundary between the cemetery and the field. Sometimes we see what we do not want or expect to see, real or not, and I had seen enough for one night.

When I found myself planning to have a recriminating word with Leander about allowing me to experience such a distortion of time, I knew I should check myself into Lychwood right along with Aunt Wisty.

CHAPTER 24

I shook Hammersleigh's massive gates until my teeth rattled right along with the iron bars. I had forgotten the gates would be locked and was frustrated with my memory lapse. I wanted to either smash the gates down or throw myself in front of them and howl.

Of course, since I was a mature adult, I did neither. I walked back along the perimeter of the property to the wooden gate and found the catch was stuck. With the help of a brawny young man who was passing by, I managed to shinny over the top and drop to the ground on the other side. My landing wasn't pleasant.

The hydrangea by the fishpond was motionless and silent as I passed by, and most of the scattered clothing was gone from the path. A lone tube sock rested at the side of the pond, as though it had managed to crawl out, and I left it there to be scooped up by the security team who had been instructed to remain after the last camper had pulled out of the field on Sunday afternoon. I proposed to have them scour the grounds for garbage and junk left behind, one last duty I was leaving for tomorrow to mention.

I rounded the front corner of the house, jumping back when I glimpsed two figures under the portico. Peering between the leaves of a sweet-smelling vine that climbed upward to the roof, I realized the two men were Marc and Conklin. Nothing weird about that maybe, except they were leaning toward each other and talking in such low voices I couldn't make out a word, and I have pretty keen ears.

There was something furtive about the scene, odd since the gentlemen in question were both beyond moral reproach. Before I could extricate my hair from the vine and join the party, Marc clapped Conklin on the shoulder, the way men do when they're up to something, then turned and strode down the steps. He was halfway to the gates before I reached the steps and Conklin was nowhere to be seen. He must have accessed the electronic panel in the hall to open the gates. They opened seconds later and Marc exited the grounds. I could see the rotating lights of the police car roll up the county road and stop in front of the gates.

The front door was now locked, and rather than risk Conklin's disapproval by bringing him back to let me in, I uttered a silent profanity and went around back. Through the kitchen window, I could see Peter making a pot of coffee.

As soon as he opened the door, Jacqueline and Rasputin made a break for freedom. I grabbed Jacqueline, and Peter managed to tackle Rasputin before the cat got more than a foot outside the kitchen.

"Go to bed," I ordered.

With a long, disgusted look over his shoulder, Rasputin plodded toward the employees' wing with Jacqueline yipping and skipping behind him.

"So Peter, how is everything? Where's Caroline?"

He poured non-fat milk into his mug and sat down at the table. "She's gone to bed. I thought the drug had mostly worn off, so around ten o'clock I put her down in her room, and she's fast asleep. I'll check on her every hour or so, but I think she's fine."

"Don't you need to get some sleep yourself? I can stay up and look in on her."

"No, you go to bed, Lyris. You've had a busy day, and I caught a nap this morning before Caroline took the pills, so I'm okay. Actually, I'm having a good time."

Then he added, "Except for the incident with Caroline, of course."

"Of course. Well, if you're sure you don't mind, I am a little tired."

"You go ahead. I'm just going to take my coffee into the drawing room and read for a while. I promise I'll make my rounds every hour, including Caroline."

"Thanks, Peter."

Then something occurred to me and I stopped him at the door. "Peter. Were you up on the widow's walk this morning? I thought I saw someone, and since you were making rounds for Conklin…"

"Sorry, it wasn't me, Lyris. I would like to go up there sometime—I know the view must be phenomenal—but I haven't had a chance so far. Who do you think it could have been?"

"Maybe nobody. It could have been a trick of the light."

Once Peter left, I did a quick inventory in my head. The sun had glinted off a blond or silver head. If it wasn't Conklin and it wasn't Peter, then it might have been Mitch or Tiffany. Although those two were supposed to be sleeping at that time of the morning.

I would have to ask the both of them where they were between ten and eleven. I don't know why it was so important to me to know who had been on the widow's walk. I guess I was afraid it was someone who had no business being there. And only one other light-haired person came to mind.

Almost dropping from exhaustion, I turned to my herb cupboard and surveyed the mess. While I had cleaned the rest of the kitchen, the cupboard itself was a jumble of overturned tins and bottles. I plucked a box of valerian teabags from the second shelf and hoped the bitter tea would relax me enough to get a few hours sleep.

A movement behind me turned out to be Conklin as he glided in through the pantry door and blinked at me in surprise. Before he could back out as silently as he arrived, I spoke up.

"Conklin. Can I make you a cup of tea? Rose hip, or perhaps nettle if you're concerned about your calcium uptake."

He flicked his eyes to the chaos in the cupboard. "Perhaps you have something among those various containers to promote forbearance, Madam."

"Ah, Conklin, I'm sure you think that remark went right over my head. That's okay, though, I understand I'm a trial to you. I know you think I have no business living here at Hammersleigh and trying to look after such a special place with no experience." Exhaustion had loosened my tongue, but I didn't care.

"On the contrary, Madam, I find you a formidable and capable young woman, who will do more than a satisfactory job of overseeing Hammersleigh for the next half century. In my humble opinion, Madam, Mr. Pembrooke made the correct choice."

"Well, thanks, although I hear a *but* in there, Conklin."

"If there is a *but*, Madam, it is that I do not wish to see you spend your life in service to a house, even Hammersleigh House. There is much for you to experience and enjoy, many other things."

"Well." I was flabbergasted. Was this just another way of saying he wanted to get rid of me, or was he being truthful about his concern for my future? "But I have you to help me, Conklin. Between the two of us, we can do anything, right?"

"Indeed, Madam." He suddenly looked sad. "However, I will not be around forever, and when I am gone, you will have the burden of Hammersleigh House on your own shoulders."

His words alarmed me. "What do you mean, you won't be around forever. You'll be around long after I've succumbed to some stress-induced disease." Some Conklin-induced illness, I could have said.

"Time is on your side, Madam."

"You can't be more than…" I cast around in my mind for a number that was less than his actual age, but not low enough to be unbelievable. "Seventy-one?" Geez, my mother was seventy-one.

"I am eighty-eight, long past the normal age for retirement."

Holy shit. "You're not going to retire, are you?" He had me on the ropes now—if this was a mind game, he was winning.

"Madam, you will have to prepare yourself for the day, not long now, when I will be forced by time and age to give up my duties here at Hammersleigh House."

"No, I can't do this without you. You have to stay." Then I stopped the wail fest. I wanted to get something else cleared up while we were at it. I wasn't so far gone that I forgot all his shenanigans when Marc was around.

"Another thing, Conklin. What have you got against Marc Allaire?"

"Madam?"

"Well, you act like you don't think it's a good idea for Marc and me to be together or alone."

"Madam. I hope I don't interfere in your relationships…"

"Come off it, Conklin. You follow me around when Marc's here like I have some honour left to defile or something. Or Marc has."

The poor guy was speechless and turned an ominous shade of pink. I caved, again.

"Come and sit over here, Conklin. I'm sorry. I didn't mean to say all those things. I just want to know how I can change your opinion of me. Is there something specific I'm doing wrong, other than my attitude I mean? I don't think I can change my personality."

He held up one hand. "No, Madam. You are perfectly right. I haven't been fair to you. You are more than capable of caring for Hammersleigh and I will attempt to assist you as long as I am able to."

"Well, you can't go anywhere just yet. We both know I'm not ready to solo, so put any ideas of retiring out of your head. Please."

He bowed his head, which meant yes, no, or I'll go when I'm damn good and ready.

"Anyway, you haven't explained why you keep trying to keep Marc and me apart."

"Madam, I sense your ambivalence about Chief Allaire. It is not my place to interfere, I know, but I would like you to be sure about your feelings before making a physical commitment."

Physical commitment? Yikes, that sounded like another term for sex.

"Well, I appreciate your concern, Conklin, but I'm a big girl and need to handle that aspect of my life by myself."

"You are correct, Madam. My concern for you has overcome my inherent disinclination to involve myself with the relationships between others. I know you had an unfortunate experience with your first husband, and while Chief Allaire is a fine man, I am most concerned that he be the right man for you. And you seem unsure of that."

I sighed. "You got that right, Conklin. I'm glad we had this talk, and I hope from now on we can be honest with each other."

His eyes shifted fractionally and that pretty much nailed my suspicion that there was something up between him and Marc. I was too tired to pry it out of Conklin then—a decision I was to regret later when I thought back to that moment.

On the landing, no essence of baby powder assailed me. But the other odour, faint and spicy, was present. No tingle between my shoulders accompanied this smell, but I felt it too was familiar, something I should recognize.

After a quick, cooling shower, I sank into a sleep so deep and dreamless that the light of morning caused my awakening to be painful. I could sense the brightness of the sun behind my closed eyes as I was dragged from unconsciousness.

I resisted, and was on the verge of drifting away again, when a muffled sound forced my eyes open wide. The light was not from the rising sun, that much I could tell from the shadows that still filled the corners of the room.

The motion detector had been tripped again. I assumed that either Conklin or Peter would have turned it off tonight. I groaned and felt a thousand achy places in my body.

Voices, urgent and loud, pushed my unwilling body out of bed and onto the window seat. One glance woke me up but good.

Fire!

Flames in the distance. It had to be one of the outbuildings beyond the brick patio area. And far too close to the house. I smelled smoke and looking across the grounds, I could make out a smoky haze escaping into the night sky. Human shapes were running either toward the blaze or away from it, and I hoped at least one of them was Mitch or Tiffany with their cell phones.

Just in case, I stumbled back to the bedside table and reached for the phone to call the fire department before remembering. No phone in this room or anywhere on this goddamn floor. And my radio was with Peter.

I knocked over a table on the landing—breaking another antique I found out later, an enamelled snuff box—and cracked my knee on the railing before reaching the telephone room under the stairs.

The dispatcher responded at once and informed me the fire had already been reported by the volunteers who were still on the grounds. The trucks would be there immediately.

I dropped the phone and ran through to the employees' wing shouting fire, almost mowing Conklin down as he came out of his room, tying the sash of a bathrobe around his waist.

"Fire." I yelled at him again, in case he didn't hear me before. "Outside. The fire trucks are on their way. Get Caroline up, will you, in case we have to evacuate. Then make sure the gates are open for the trucks."

"Quite, Madam." He knotted his sash and hurried to Caroline's room.

I ran out the door at the end of the corridor, into a night filled with heat, smoke, flames and the shouts of what seemed like dozens of people.

I got as close as I could to the fire which was, indeed, coming from the shed where we kept the garden equipment. I almost fainted with relief when I found Mitch and Tiffany counting heads and calling on their radios for the rest of the night team to come in.

Mitch saw me and yelled, "Mom, I called the fire department and the police. I don't know how this started. We've been watching for anything suspicious and the volunteer firemen are still around..."

"Never mind that now. The important thing is to determine if all team members are accounted for."

"It's okay. They are." He gestured to where Tiffany was herding a group of teenagers into a disorderly cluster. "Jason and Todd are the last, and I've just reached them by radio. They're coming in too."

"Thank God. See if you can keep them away from the fire until the trucks arrive."

I looked around behind me and spotted Conklin and Caroline standing together near the house. Conklin had turned on all the outside lights and the bulbs shone onto the scene, harsh and surrealistic. I had no doubt the gates were open to receive the fire trucks.

"I wonder if the garden hose will reach the fire," I said to Mitch. Before I could act, Peter was unrolling the hose and stretching it to its full length. It stopped short of the fire by about twenty feet. Peter turned it on anyway and sprayed water over the grass and patio.

"At least I can wet down the area close to the house," he shouted at me.

I said to Mitch, "I wonder if we should move these orange trees."

He looked at the heavy concrete pots. "No."

The tool shed was completely engulfed, and flaming ashes scattered into the air. I could do nothing except pray that they would extinguish themselves before landing. But everything was so dry. I looked anxiously at the house, wondering if I should organize a squad to start carrying things onto the front lawn. Or maybe we could dig a trench to contain the fire. But the shovels were probably part of the conflagration. The heat was unbearable and the smoke was stinging my eyes.

Sirens had been audible for some time and now five or six yellow-slickered firemen ran toward us, carrying one gigantic hose. With a series of shouts, water erupted from the spout.

One firefighter handled the crowd, which I was not surprised to see, included members of the camping brigade. Well, what could we expect with the gates set wide? Soon the whole town of Blackshore would be standing on Hammersleigh's back lawn.

The volunteer fireman pushing the spectators back was none other than my Grade 12 lab partner, Andy Finney, although you wouldn't know we were ever friends by the way he barked at me to move behind the lines. Andy was threading a thick rope in and around trees, bushes, benches and whatever else he could use to set a barrier between the fire and the house. Its purpose was not immediately apparent since the flames were beginning to fizzle under the onslaught of the super hose, but at least it kept the teenagers—and other people mature enough to know better—away from the smoke and flames.

Conklin moved up and wrapped a blanket around me. I pulled it off. "Geez, Conklin, I'm almost cooked. But thanks anyway."

Indeed, the heat was crippling and I was glad of the rope barrier to keep me—and everyone else—from getting too close. There's something mesmerizing about a fire and I'm sure most of us would have been standing too close, if allowed, despite the heat.

I noticed Marc and Ronnie Guilbert in a group with one of the firemen, the chief I thought. Ronnie unwound a roll of yellow police tape, following the path of the rope.

There were no visible flames now. The shed had been reduced to a stinking, smoking pile of twisted metal and wood ash, but the hose continued to spew water. I realized that the water to fight the fire likely came from a tanker truck parked on the front driveway. Since the house was located outside of Blackshore, we couldn't rely on municipal fire hydrants, so they would have had to truck the water in. I groaned and pulled at my hair—I would get a bill for the water.

I felt something warm and scratchy being wrapped around me. I looked up into Marc's face. He looked grim and I hesitated to tell him I was pretty warm already, thanks, so please remove the blanket. I just shrugged and let the blanket fall to the ground.

He hung it back on my shoulders.

"It's too hot for that, Marc."

"It's not for warmth, Lyris. You're next to naked."

Hell's bells, he was right. I looked down at myself and remembered I was wearing what I went to bed in—bikini underpants and a short cotton camisole. Thank God I wasn't wearing my usual thong.

Bending down, I picked up the blanket and wrapped it toga style around my body. Well, everyone was too busy fire gazing to notice one woman past her first youth parade around in her underwear.

"Where did you get that injury?"

"What? What injury?"

"Come on, Lyris. You're bruised from waist to knee. How did you do it?"

"I had a little accident in the garden. I fell on a rock yesterday, but it's almost healed already."

"Have you seen a doctor?"

"No, of course not. It's a simple bruise. Do you always show up at local fires? Not enough excitement for you in police work?"

"I was still in the vicinity. Too bad I wasn't still on the grounds. I might have caught the fire bug."

"You think the fire was started by someone?" That explained the rope and police tape barrier.

"I don't think this shed spontaneously combusted. There was a lot of metal there and I suspect it started on the inside. Is the shed always locked?"

"I don't know. I don't think there was anything stored in that shed other than gardening tools, maybe fertilizer. The riding lawn mower and the leaf sucker and the weed whacker are kept in that building on the other side of the trees…"

"Never mind," he interrupted me. "I'll talk to Conklin and have another word with Jamie." Jamie Petrowski was our fire chief, another friend and golfing buddy of Marc's.

I looked at the activity going on around me and the crowd that had now swelled to fifty or more. I eyed Tiffany resentfully. She was prancing around in very short shorts and a little bitty tube top, but nobody was trying to cover her with a blanket.

Caroline and Conklin, with Peter assisting, were serving coffee to the firefighters. Most of the men—there were no female firefighters in Blackshore yet—had stripped off their helmets and yellow slickers, and some were even removing their rubber pants.

The coffee was accompanied by cookies and slices of Caroline's marble-swirl pound cake. The whole scene was starting to look like a party. Over by the shade garden, my team members were under the loose control of Mitch and Tiffany. I saw a suspect cigarette being passed around and the kids were starting to act silly, bonking each other on the head and rolling in the wet grass.

I looked around. Here we had a police chief, a fire chief, and the formidable Conklin. Any one of them was more than capable of quelling a riot using gun, hose or attitude respectively. Was I needed? No damn way.

With that decision under my blanket, I made for the kitchen door, scooping up Jacqueline and Rasputin from under one of the stone benches on the patio, where they had been watching the show. The back door wasn't locked and I left it that way so the others could get back in when they were ready.

A whiff of my smoke-saturated camisole propelled me into the bathroom for another shower. I shampooed my hair and scrubbed my body until I was sure the smell was gone.

Jacqueline and Rasputin were waiting for me outside the bathroom door, looking forlorn as only a dog and cat who are locked inside while all the fun took place outside can look. I felt sorry for them and let them come into my bedroom.

"Okay, you guys can stay here for a while, but no barking, purring, or any other noises. Got that?"

They soon settled down together on the floor at the foot of my bed. The fans were still whirring in the corner and I positioned them so they were aiming a tepid current of air at all three of us. I climbed the steps into my bed and closed my eyes.

A few minutes later I opened them again. My mind was spinning with colours and sounds, and sleep would not come.

I lay there trembling with fatigue, my skin scorching hot but clammy. I set my mind to think mode, not a good idea as it turned out.

CHAPTER 25

I slipped out of bed to shut the windows on the smoke and sounds of merriment drifting up from the back lawns. At once the air was heavier, and I directed all three fans toward the bed and climbed back in. That was better. Not comfortable, but better.

But I was not alone. Snuffling and wheezing sounds emanated from the end of the bed, and my foot touched something soft and furry—cat fur. Undoubtedly doggy fur was there as well, taking up my valuable breathing space.

"Get out. You have an entire air-conditioned wing to stretch out in. Why stay up here where it feels like high noon in hell?"

They continued to wheeze and snuffle pathetically, like that would move me. Boy, catch me sleeping up here if I was allowed in the employees' wing.

"It's too hot for you two in this room. Go back downstairs."

I have never understood the habit some people have of allowing their pets to sleep with them. It could not be healthy. Just think of the fleas joining the dust mites in the mattress, a living layer between the sleeper and the coil springs. Eesh.

"Okay, how about if you move to the floor and I'll give you your very own fan. How's that."

No deal. Jacqueline and Rasputin continued to gasp as if every inhalation were their last. I could pick them up one by one and toss them out in the hall, then close the door on them. Frankly, I was too exhausted and sore to exert myself in a physical battle with a poodle that for sure bit and a cat that might very well bite too. And a closed door was unthinkable tonight.

I pleaded with them. "Come on, guys. Don't you know that the higher up you go, the hotter it is? Think of your nice cool tile floor downstairs."

The sounds of impending expiration continued, but I had stopped caring. My own words stopped me. I couldn't exactly remember everything Aunt Clem had said during my visit to her reading room last Sunday. I should have taken notes.

I slid off the bed and walked back and forth in the darkness. Two pairs of eyes glowed at me from the rumpled sheets. Something about a high place. The objects missing from the house were not far away, and in a high place, according to Aunt Clem. Close and high. Well, the highest place in the house was the cupola and the widow's walk which surrounded it. Or even the third floor, a place I had not yet ventured to.

I hadn't noticed anything when I was in the cupola the previous night, but it was dark and the flashback or dream had distracted me. There could be anything there. Nobody seemed to have made a point of checking the cupola during the reunion. Or nobody who's admitted to it. I remembered the figure I had seen that morning.

Of course the whole idea was crazy. No way could Aunt Clem know where the stolen articles were stashed. The loot was undoubtedly being fenced in Toronto at that very minute. And now was not the time to go exploring. It was night and I wouldn't be able to see any more than the last time I was up there. I would wait till morning.

But Aunt Clem, or one of her spirits, was right about the missing doll. And then there was Leander, and the flashback on the widow's walk, and the shifting photograph—it was getting harder to deny the psychic forces gathering me in.

I lay on the bed and ignored my bedmates. Which wasn't easy, with all the racket they were making. I did my best to think of something else, but my mind refused to host thoughts of little Tommy and the mystery surrounding his death, which I thought I had solved, by the way. And my heart was in no mood to think about Marc. My job was no source of comfort either.

"Okay, guys, how about this. I'll take you downstairs to the kitchen and give you a snack. Then you can find Caroline and Conklin and sleep on their beds." After that, I would go upstairs to the cupola and look around. I grabbed my bedside flashlight again and we started out. Much to my surprise, Jacqueline and Rasputin jumped off the bed and followed me. As we passed the drawing room, I could see Peter's blondish head propped up on some cushions on one of the settees, and I tiptoed past on the black and white marble floor. He must have come back into the house right after I did. He had been a great help to me during these last few days. The least I could do was let him sleep.

In the kitchen, there was no sign of Conklin or Caroline. Either they were still outside or they were snug in their air-conditioned rooms. I poured some dog and cat treats into their bowls, refreshed their water and then, with one eye on the gobbling animals, looked around me. I thought about the layout of the house.

The grand staircase in the great hall reached only to the second floor. The enclosed stairs from the tower room on the second floor led directly to the cupola. As far as I knew, you could not reach the third floor from the second floor, and equally strange, you could not reach the cupola from the third floor. It didn't make any sense.

In the kitchen, I opened the door to the staircase I had not yet explored. I flicked the light switch and peered upward where the steep steps disappeared into the darkness, a black hole the low wattage bulb did not penetrate.

Conklin had mentioned that these stairs led to the third floor, the former servants' quarters. That wouldn't get me to the cupola on the roof level, and I couldn't get past this odd architectural fact. It appeared that sole access to the cupola was by the steep winding staircase from the tower room on the second floor. Well, maybe Conklin would have an explanation, but for now, if I wanted to poke around in the cupola, I would have to get there via the staircase from the tower room, like last time.

If I had known where to find batteries, I might have recharged the flashlight. Or not, as I was so focused on my quest, a mundane safety matter like light just wasn't a priority. Besides, the flashlight emitted a feeble glow after I banged it on the kitchen floor a few times, and I figured I would be in and out of the cupola within a minute or two.

The Family Pets followed me back up the grand staircase and into the tower room. I thought they would stay there, but halfway up the narrow stairs to the cupola, I heard their laboured breathing and didn't bother to try and send them back. If they wanted to climb through that airless tube with me, it was their own lookout.

In the end, I had to carry Rasputin up the last dozen steps, with Jacqueline huffing and complaining behind me. Once in the cupola I dropped the cat on the floor and looked around me, but by the fading shine of my flashlight, I wasn't able to see the walls. I turned it off and stepped out on the widow's walk, curious to see what the smouldering shed looked like from this vantage point.

The animals followed me onto the narrow walkway, and we stood in a line gazing down on the back lawn and gardens of Hammersleigh House. The motion lights under the eaves illuminated the scene below where dozens of people still sat on the grass or stood around in groups. I heard their voices, but couldn't make out any words. The remains of the shed still smouldered, and the smoke hung thick and heavy in the still air, detectable even from where I was standing.

The widow's walk was somewhat cooler than my bedroom or the cupola, although not enough to tempt me to linger there and breathe in the smoky air. I thought I could see Marc still talking to Jamie Petrowski, but I was so high up and far away, I wasn't sure.

In the cupola I turned the flashlight back on and started to play the faint beam around the room. The light would not reach into the corners, and there were plenty of corners in the hexagonal space. I had to examine every inch of floor.

I felt uneasy, but since Leander's spectral finger wasn't poking me between the shoulder blades, I figured there was no danger. My skin felt crawly and I blamed that on a very long day plus an overactive imagination. I ventured into the blackness.

At first I saw nothing. The painted wooden floor seemed clear of any kind of clutter. Not a chair or even a cushion to sit on.

At that moment my beam of light fell on a cardboard box shoved against the east wall. I cried out and took a step back. I trod on a tail— Rasputin's since Jacqueline sported a mere stub on her behind—and heard an answering howl of indignation.

"Sorry. Sorry." In my fear, I forgot myself enough to grab the cat and squeeze. I was only seeking comfort from another living creature, but Rasputin took exception to my gesture and scratched the back of my hand.

I released him and ignored my first impulse to throw myself down the steep staircase to the tower room. I aimed my flashlight at the box again. My light was fading fast and I shook the flashlight.

I was understandably a little nervous around boxes. I crept up on that one. The cowardly duo stayed behind me, and I knew they would be no help if I needed it.

My heart nearly failed when I was close enough to look down at the contents of the box. I thought at first I had found the body of another baby. The little head was topped with an over-sized bow and the tiny hands hung outside the box. I patted my chest to try and regulate my racing heart. I refused to faint again.

Then recognition struck. Amelia. I reached down to pull her out and into my arms. By the feeble light, I checked her over and found no sign of damage.

Tucking her under the arm that held the flashlight, I examined the interior of the box. The rest of the missing articles were there—the jewelled hummingbird, the little ivory jade dragon and a water globe paperweight. As far as I could determine in the dim light, all three objects were undamaged as well.

Well, Florence was right. Or maybe it was Luke. In any case, the missing items *were* close by and in a high place. The question was, who put them there and why? My money was on Scott Fournier.

Thinking about Florence and Luke, not to mention Scott, gave me the creeps again. I put Amelia back on top of the other articles and lifted the box in my free arm. It was light enough.

"Come on, you guys, I'm taking this stuff downstairs. Let's go."

Have I mentioned that the staircase between the tower room and the cupola twisted and turned so that it was impossible to know which direction you were facing at any given time? The enclosure was also very narrow and I was forced to hold the box in both arms close to my body. For this reason, the flashlight pointed to the left. I cautiously started down.

I was concentrating on my feet and nearly missed the door halfway down. It was set into a curve of the wall. There was no handle as such, just a handgrip cut into the wood, which was likely why I hadn't noticed it on my last trip. This had to be the door to the third floor servants' quarters.

I stood still, contemplating the wisdom of following my impulse to see what was on the other side. The third floor was an area I had not yet explored in Hammersleigh, and I was curious. I wanted to see what condition the rooms were in and if there were storage rooms to house the animal heads and the other objects I had left in the tower room.

Common sense dictated I take the box and go back to my room. As usual, curiosity triumphed over common sense. Ignoring a shiver of dread, I juggled the box until I could insert my fingers through the handgrip. I pushed.

The door swung open on creaky springs. I stepped forward and let it shut behind me, but not before Jacqueline and Rasputin edged through as well. I was glad to have their company.

My feeble light displayed a long corridor ahead. Many doors, some open, others closed, faced the hall at intervals.

Which way? The staircase that led down to the kitchen was behind one of these doors. Which door? I had no idea which end of the house I was facing, north, south, even east or west. All were the same to my directionally-challenged brain. I felt around on the walls beside me, but couldn't locate a light switch.

Rasputin headed out, tired of waiting for me to make up my mind. I followed, figuring he might know which was the right door. I felt Jacqueline's wet nose on the back of my calf.

I respected a take-charge cat, but a thought occurred to me. "Wait a minute. You've never been up here before. What makes you think you know the way out?"

We passed several closed doors, and I hoped I wouldn't have to open any to find the stairs. Ahead, I spotted Rasputin's dim form as he paused in front of a partially opened door.

He froze. His fur straightened until he looked twice his normal size. He emitted a grating, mewling noise. Hearing this, Jacqueline growled deep in her throat. My skin tightened.

Both animals faced the door, heads down. Jacqueline growled again, unmoving—strange behaviour for her since she usually ran in circles when she was frightened or excited. On one or two memorable occasions, she peed as well.

My skin contracted. "Come on, you two," I whispered. "Let's go back."

I sensed a threat. I had to run, but I couldn't leave the pets there to fend for themselves. I set the box on the floor. The flashlight was nearly dead and it was impossible to see anything but the shapes of the two creatures in front of that door.

"Come on." With every nerve in my body vibrating in alarm, I bent over to pick them up. And the door was yanked aside.

Half expecting something to happen, I was already twisting to one side so the blow just glanced off my temple. It didn't knock me out, but I was dazed and helpless to avoid being dragged down the corridor by one arm.

I suspect Jacqueline was fixed to the pant leg of the intruder by her teeth. I heard a muttered profanity and then she yelped. I think he kicked

Rasputin too. The thud of a well-padded body hitting the wall was followed by a crying sound.

He stopped dragging me and opened a door. By this time my head began to clear, and I kicked out. I grabbed onto a forearm with my teeth and bit down. With a muffled scream of pain, my attacker hit the side of my face with his fist until I released his flesh. I kicked out again and flailed at him with my arms, but it was too little, too late.

"Bitch." He gave me a shove and I rolled through the doorway and down the stairs. Aunt Clem's words of warning flashed across my brain like a mantra. *"There is danger in a high place."*

CHAPTER 26

I remember screaming at the top, and they say I screamed as I lay on the kitchen floor, so I deduce I screamed all the way down as well. With the narrowness of the staircase, you would think I'd get stuck part way down, but you would be wrong.

I hit every step, bumped down on every uncarpeted, wooden stair. By some miracle, my head escaped serious injury, and I didn't break any bones. I didn't know that as I lay flat out on the kitchen floor. If I hadn't forgotten to close the door when I was in the kitchen, they would have had to peel me off the inside of the door with a spatula.

As I lay there, screaming if you will, although I remember it more as calling for help, I was sure I was mortally wounded. Everything hurt. It was worse than my little tumble down the few last steps of the grand staircase after I found Tommy's body. And far worse than my exploit in the hosta bed.

I heard Rasputin and Jacqueline plummet down the stairs, and felt them run across the entire length of my body, including my face. After that, I presume they raced into the employees' wing. I did not see them again that night.

Peter reached me first. He just had time to register that an emergency was in progress when Caroline and Conklin came at me from the direction of their own rooms.

All three bent down, fussing and hovering. I believe I tried to tell them that an intruder had pushed me down the stairs and he was still on the third floor, but they wouldn't listen. Cries of "Call an ambulance," "Get Marc," "No, the fire chief is trained in CPR," bounced off the walls and shattered my already sensitive nerves. Next, Mitch and Tiffany arrived.

Peter muttered something into his radio, then plucked a cell phone from another pocket and spoke into that. They all tried to shush me, when all I wanted to do was explain what had happened and get them to *catch the goddamn intruder.* Mitch patted my sore head and someone covered me with a blanket. I was underdressed again.

Next, Marc joined us, closely followed by Ronnie Guilbert and Officer Tammie, her frizzy hair frizzled even more by the humidity. Or maybe she got herself a perm, I remembered thinking.

Marc quickly grasped what I had been trying to communicate to everybody else, namely that an intruder had assaulted me and thrown me down the stairs. He ran up the stairway with drawn gun and working flashlight while Tammie raced out the kitchen door to the back yard and Ronnie headed in the direction of the great hall.

At that point I wanted to get up, but dozens of hands held me fast to the floor. Somebody, I believe Peter with his assorted pieces of technology, had summoned the ambulance, and by George, there was going to be a customer when it arrived.

Thirty minutes later I found myself face down in a treatment room at the Blackshore District Hospital. Medically-trained hands had stripped me of every stitch of underwear and I was clad in a paper gown that displayed my posterior parts to a roomful of doctors, nurses, interns and I think cleaning staff, since I noticed a string mop tucked under an arm.

It must have been a slow night for emergencies. Whoever they all were, they took an avid interest in my butt. Turning my head as far back as it would go, I took a look.

I have to say it was quite a sight. My buttock, hip and leg had all the majestic purple shine of an eggplant. Having determined that I had suffered no injury in my fall down the stairs other than superficial bruises and a laceration or two, the entire staff of Blackshore District Hospital, medical and otherwise, were concerning themselves with a fading bruise.

One white-coated individual, whom I took to be a co-op student barely into his teens and standing only five feet, pushed his glasses farther up a snub nose.

"You have some soft tissue damage there, Ms. Pembrooke. You'll be a few months healing. Try not to overextend the muscles of the leg and hip for a while, but stay as active as possible to prevent atrophy."

"You a doctor?" It paid to be careful.

The Doogie Howser look-alike drew himself up a full extra inch. "Excuse me, I neglected to introduce myself. My name is Dr. Michael Grammett. I am a resident physician at this hospital."

"Nice to meet you, Michael. Now, since I haven't any life-threatening injuries, I guess I'll get dressed and go home."

He poked my purple ouchie with a forefinger. "This appears to have happened earlier than your other injuries. Twelve hours ago?"

"Pretty close. I guess I'll leave now."

The audience was spellbound. Nobody moved.

"Thank you very much, all of you. You can go." I spoke with more hope than expectation, but they turned away at last.

I was alone, but no sooner had I painfully struggled into a seated position than Marc entered the room. Patsy, Nick, Conklin, Caroline, Peter and Mitch were right behind him. There were a couple of other people in the hall, probably media, but the room was too full to contain them. And who had called Patsy?

I hastily pulled what was left of my paper gown around my thighs. "What the hell is everybody doing here? With a maniac running loose through Hammersleigh House, one would think a few of you could have stayed on the scene to prevent other innocent people from being battered within an inch of their lives."

"Relax, Lyris," Marc responded. His voice so soothing I could listen to it all night. "I've left three of my officers in the house and Tiffany has your group of teenagers watching from under the trees. Nobody is going to slip through again tonight."

"Which means he got away. If you bunch had listened to me in the first place when I told you what happened to me, maybe Marc could have caught him."

"Lyris," replied Peter, "we couldn't understand a word you were saying at first. You were mumbling about dolls and dragons and ghosts and other stuff. It took a while before you calmed down enough to tell us you were attacked on the third floor and pushed downstairs—"

"I wasn't mumbling," I snapped back. "I found a box in the cupola with Amelia, the jade dragon and other things and was bringing it down through the third floor when he jumped out at me from one of the doorways." The ghost was none of their business and it wasn't real anyhow.

"I found the box," Marc said, "but there was no one on either the third floor or cupola by the time I searched."

"Well, he had to have gone back down the tower room staircase to the second floor, then down the main staircase and out the front door. There's no other way except the same stairs he pushed me down, and I would have noticed that."

"Madam, you quite worried us." Conklin spoke with an air of understatement. "I do not understand why you would put yourself at risk by wandering through the house at night."

I shook my head at him. "It's my house, more or less, and why shouldn't I go where I want? How could I know there was a violent presence wandering around on the third floor?"

"With everything that's happened, Lyris," Marc interrupted, "I think a little more caution would have been prudent."

I ignored him. "I'm going to get dressed now. So you can all go except Patsy, and thanks so much for coming out. Hold the flowers, but send chocolate."

As they dribbled away, Caroline's pale face caught my attention for a second, but she was gone before I could speak to her.

"Lyris, I know how you got hurt yesterday." Marc's voice echoed close to my ear.

I jumped and looked at him. Then I looked at my shifty-eyed friend who was busy arranging the tongue depressors in their metal jar on a stainless steel trolley.

"You know Patsy exaggerates. A little accident does not constitute assault. Pay no attention to her. It was just a clumsy little fall, far less serious than what occurred tonight. Now, *that* was criminal intent."

"Don't try to distract me, Lyris. Tonight's events are being looked at. It's yesterday's *accident* I want to talk about." His grey eyes were trying to pin mine to the wall, but I evaded them and spoke to Patsy.

"I'll need some help getting dressed, and I could use a ride home if you can tear yourself away from those medical supplies."

"I'll drive you home," Marc said in clipped tones. I guessed he wasn't also offering to help me dress since he appeared to be in official mode. His mouth was tight and this was the first time I had seen his ears turn a bright pink. I acknowledged I had overstepped the bounds of common sense this time, but wasn't going to admit it to anyone else.

"Do you want to press charges," he continued when I didn't speak.

"Of course not. God." I was appalled at the thought. "This is much ado about nothing. Can't we just drop the whole thing?"

"No, not really. I don't like to see this happening to you and I won't permit it to continue. I will have a talk with Dennis and make sure it doesn't. Now, I'll wait outside for you." He left abruptly, his shoulders straight in the pale blue shirt.

"I think he's mad at me," I mentioned to the heretofore silent Patsy. "He'll get over it, though. He always does."

"One of these days you're going to push him too far and he'll dump you like you deserve. Here, let me help you with that."

She could have been a little gentler, but finally I was dressed. And not a moment too soon, for the fragile gown had disintegrated under my nervously plucking fingers. With a little persuading, the hospital staff supplied me with a pair of green cotton drawstring pants to wear home over my underwear. I had to promise to wash them and bring them back the next day. Right.

While I was signing the release form that absolved Michael and the hospital from any blame should I expire in the next year due to undiagnosed injuries suffered that night, Patsy stared at me, her eyes wide with disapproval.

"I don't understand why you aren't a total basket case, Lyris," she said, shaking her head. "Yesterday, your ex-husband throws you into a flower bed, then tonight you have a fire and get shoved down a flight of stairs by a home invader. And the reunion is in full swing. Yet you're still making wisecracks and pretending you aren't black and blue from head to toe. Your face is a mess. You're either a very courageous or an extremely insensitive person." The last sentence was delivered at full volume.

I blinked in surprise, but decided to ignore Patsy's outburst. I knew she was very stressed herself over losing her job.

"I prefer courageous. And you forgot the purple."

"What purple?"

"Me. I'm black and blue and also purple if you include yesterday's injury which everybody seems to want to do."

She moved away from the counter where I was signing the release. The young night clerk was listening to our exchange with keen curiosity. Patsy closed her mouth and marched away without a backward glance.

I sighed. No doubt I was at fault in some way, but I was too tired to figure it out. Patsy was going through a rough personal crisis and I should have been more understanding. As soon as the reunion was over I would apologize for my insensitivity, since courage probably wasn't a factor here.

The lobby was deserted except for Marc. He was standing with his back to me, staring at a head and shoulders portrait of the first hospital administrator. Except for his mutton chop sideburns, the gentleman staring back at Marc looked quite a lot like Conklin. I made a mental note to ask Conklin if they were related.

Marc turned as I stopped beside him. We looked at each other long enough for me to be uncomfortably aware that I was being scrutinized, judged and found wanting. I shifted from foot to foot.

"How are you feeling?"

"Great. Considering all this body has been through in the last day or two, I'm surprisingly well." *As You Think, So Shall You Be* was another of my mottos. Plus, *Mind over Matter* and *Stiff Upper Lip* and all that.

"Funny, you look like hell. And if you feel only half as bad as you look, you must feel like hell too."

Maybe I was a little rusty on courting etiquette, but I was sure my boyfriend should be assuring me how lovely I looked, not telling the truth. I had just seen myself mirrored in one of the glass doors leading from the lobby to the treatment area and knew what that truth was—wild, tangled hair, dirty T-shirt, baggy pants and complexion devoid of any colour except a few red lumps. Oh, and a scratch or two where Rasputin's toenails had gouged me when he ran across my face while I reclined on the kitchen floor.

Still, Marc was right. I had again shown no common sense whatsoever when I explored the third floor. In light of everything that had been going on around Hammersleigh in the last while, I showed poor judgment at best. He would be less than human not to wonder at this point if I was worth bothering about. And where the heck had Leander been when I needed him?

We made the short trip back to Hammersleigh House in silence. I was too depressed to tease Marc by asking to play with his siren or talk on the radio. Marc's lips were pressed tight together like he was afraid of unleashing harsh words of truth and condemnation. He was too nice a guy to utter those words out loud, but there was a numb spot in my chest that suggested I was soon going to get dumped, like Patsy suggested.

The iron gates were closed, and I hoped Peter was near the great hall and would hear the buzzer. I could face Peter tonight, but not Conklin. And certainly not Caroline. Remembering the question shining from her eyes at the hospital, I knew I could not give her the answer she wanted.

I clutched the door handle and prepared to disembark from that ship of quiet reproach. Marc put his own hand on my arm to stop me and I thought, okay here we go. I resolved to accept the next few minutes with dignity.

"Did you recognize the man?" he asked. "And are you sure there was only one?"

I was unable to answer at first. Then my brain made an abrupt turn and I breathed again.

"No, but it was Scott Fournier and he was alone."

"If you didn't see him, how do you know it was Scott?"

"Process of elimination mostly. It couldn't have been anyone else in the house, and he's been creeping around at night. Caroline admitted that."

"What about Peter Tackaberry? He was the first to reach you after you fell. Could he have had time to run down the other way, down the main staircase?"

I pulled away. "It was not Peter. Even in the dark I would have recognized him, or any other man I know."

Marc wrapped his fingers around my wrist to stop me from jumping out of the car. For some reason, I had a hard time taking in a deep breath. Icy sweat was springing up on my forehead, and I realized that I had been chilled since leaving the hospital. The hand Marc had hold of jerked, all by itself it seemed, and my other hand soon followed suit. I needed to get out and run, but I couldn't get any air into my lungs.

"I...can't breathe," I managed to tell him. My chest was tight and my fingers were going numb.

I was having a heart attack.

CHAPTER 27

Marc turned the cruiser around and headed back to town. He put the lights on, but refrained from using the siren. I felt this was a bit cavalier of him and would have related my displeasure if I had been able to breathe. If this wasn't a flashing lights *and* siren emergency, I didn't know what would be.

Within an hour the medical staff had unplugged all the wires and monitors and diagnosed me as suffering from a stress-induced anxiety attack. They gave me a wonderful blue and yellow pill that made me feel all liquid and boneless inside and floated those nasty anxieties right out the window.

Michael was my attending doctor again and left me with some words of advice about learning to relax. He even gave me a brochure on stress reduction, and more or less suggested I seek professional help. I was so mellow I didn't ask if he had reached puberty yet, just smiled maternally and thanked him in all sincerity for the major tranquilizer. He didn't offer me any to take home, and when I asked, he said no.

Marc's presence at my side throughout this second medical ordeal of the night was comforting and I wasn't too stoned to be appreciative. You could always count on Marc to be supportive and the fact he carried a gun didn't even scare me. The fact he was so incredibly good looking was a bonus. I let myself lean heavily on his arm when we walked out of the hospital.

"Well, quite a lot has happened today, hasn't it?" I observed on the way home. "I fell into a hosta bed, saw a ghost in the cemetery, survived a fire set by an arsonist, was injured by the same evildoer when he threw me down the stairs and courageously evaded a heart attack. Yes, quite a day." I didn't mention Caroline's overdose, because I had forgotten about it. I shifted off my sore cheek and patted the hard, muscular thigh next to mine.

Marc looked at me out of the corner of his eye. "What ghost?"

I hadn't meant to mention the ghost to him, or to anyone. Ever. Even though it was only an imaginary ghost, I never wanted to talk about it. I realized the drug had loosened my lips, so closed them tightly and went to sleep.

Marc shook my arm gently and I opened my eyes to see the stone steps to Hammersleigh's front door appear beside the cruiser.

"Before we go in, Lyris, I want to say something to you."

I thought he was going to ask me to marry him again and was wondering how I would reply this time. So it was a shock to hear his next words.

"You've been under a lot of strain lately. Running Hammersleigh, dealing with Dennis, Caroline's problems, not to mention everything you had to pull together for this reunion. Add the incidents taking place in this house recently and your various injuries, it's all more than one woman should be dealing with. So I'm going to back away for now and stop pressuring you to make a commitment."

I stared at him. My lips were numb and would barely open. "What?"

"I've been pushing you. Trying to force you to make a decision before you're ready. I told you once I would wait as long as it took, but I got impatient. I love you and want you, though the closer I try to get, the faster you run in the other direction."

"What?" I licked my dry lips.

He took my hand and brought it to his own lips. "You don't have to worry about making a decision regarding us, not now."

I couldn't figure out what he was saying.

"Obviously, you don't feel you have any control over this situation. I think it would be best if you decide to come to me on your own. That is, if you want. I'm not going to mention marriage or any other alternative again. You let me know when you're ready."

I wanted to tell him that Conklin and I had talked about the alternative, and it was alright with Conklin. I barely got started when I found myself standing in the great hall being handed off like a football to Conklin and Caroline. Marc explained my second trip to the emergency room and suggested I be allowed to sleep off the sedative. Caroline and I exchanged glances, and I thought, okay sister, I know what you were going for this afternoon. I felt good.

Then Marc was gone and it took me a few minutes to make Caroline and Conklin understand that I was not—no way, no how—willing to sleep upstairs. This involved me wrapping my arms around the newel post and aiming a backward kick at Conklin when he tried to pry my fingers loose. So they bedded me down on a sofa in the employees' wing, where I spent the rest of the night in drug-induced euphoria, with no dreams or fears or catastrophes to disturb me.

I still felt great when I woke in the morning. The room was cool, the sofa just firm enough and...there were two mounds of fur at my feet. I pulled my feet away, then fell back gasping for air.

Whoa, that hurt. I wasn't even sure where the pain originated. My whole body was a pulsing, throbbing organism of agony. I staggered to a bathroom and turned on the shower. After I emerged, clean if not energized, I looked in the mirror. One hasty glance was enough and I turned swiftly away before I could burst into tears of delayed shock.

To top it all off, I had no clean clothes to put on, not even a robe forgotten by a previous guest. I had no recourse but to slip upstairs wrapped in two bath towels, and this I managed without anybody seeing me and commenting on my hideous bruises.

A few minutes later, clothed simply but neatly in a T-shirt and capri pants to hide the worst of my injuries, I went into the kitchen.

"Good morning, Lyris. How are you feeling? Did you sleep okay on the couch?" Caroline was laying cutlery at two place settings, moving a cozy-topped teapot to the middle of the table. She politely looked elsewhere as I made my way to a chair and lowered myself into it.

Glancing at her averted face, I wondered if I was up to a frank discussion about Scott and decided I wasn't. Not right now, maybe later when the reunion was over. Or maybe tomorrow or the day after. I was pretty sure Michael had given me medical orders to take it easy and not stress myself ever again.

"I slept great, actually. It's so cool down here, I'd forgotten what it was like not to sweat myself into a puddle every night."

She smiled, very faintly. "The photographer is here. Or he's in the field I mean. He's waiting for you to tell him how you want to arrange everybody."

"What's in the pot on the stove? I hope it isn't oatmeal."

"Well, yes it is. I'm sorry, but Conklin says it's good for..."

"I know it's healthy and all that, but I can't eat anything with lumps in it. I'm not hungry anyway." I pulled myself up. "I'll get something later." I couldn't be bothered even making myself a cup of herbal tea with healing properties.

Every time I look at the group photo from that reunion, I feel a pain in my shoulder, leg, chin, and especially my butt. The picture was snapped a microsecond after second cousin Harris Pembrooke from Sarnia squeezed my soft tissue injury, and my image was captured for all time—two startled eyes in a pale face, hair sticking out at a 20 volt angle. I managed to step on Harris's toes as we were descending the makeshift scaffolding that held four tiers of Pembrookes, but it was scant retaliation for the stomach-churning pain I suffered for the next two hours.

The reunion was officially over. As the trailers and fifth wheels rocked their way out of the field, they left behind a couple of dumpster loads of trash, including McDonald's wrappers, Horton's coffee cups and doughnut boxes and other less identifiable garbage. The grounds of Hammersleigh were less impacted, but not litter-free.

I convinced my security and medical teams to stay and clear up the mess by withholding their pay until I was satisfied the grounds and field were as clean as they were Friday afternoon when the first family members arrived. After collecting the two-way radios—all except mine as I couldn't remember where it was right then—I paid them off with an adequate tip and my thanks for a job well done. I believed in positive reinforcement for the young.

Catching sight of Mitch and Tiffany waving off an RV with Manitoba license plates, I realized they were not part of the reception committee when Marc delivered me home the night before. And I had forgotten that the two of them were sleeping upstairs, ostensibly in separate bedrooms on either side of mine. Well, that horse had almost certainly kicked the barn door open and escaped.

Rounding the front of the house, I caught sight of the Wooter brothers' flatbed truck and signature butt-crack down by the porta-potties.

"Hey, Benny," I called, "what are you doing here today? I thought you weren't coming to pick these up until tomorrow.

"Can't wait till then," he grunted, helping his brother shove Tintagel toward the hydraulic scoop. "Got another family barbecue over in Northton Tuesday and we got to clean these up and take them over by tomorrow afternoon."

"Well, I appreciate you leaving me six units for the reunion."

"Don't pay me no compliments, just pay your bill." Donnie snickered at his brother's witticism and watched appreciatively as Benny pulled a piece of paper from his back pocket and held it out.

Considering where that hand had just been, I took the invoice between two fingers and held it away from my body as I checked the total to make sure Benny had deducted the deposit I had given him earlier in the week. "I'll send you a cheque if that's okay."

"Hear you had a fire last night," observed Benny, scratching his grimy bare chest. "Lucky it didn't get the house."

"Yes, lucky," I repeated and turned away.

"Too bad about your aunt. But probably the best thing, considering everything."

I turned back and walked to within six inches of Benny's personal space. "What aunt? What are you talking about?"

It was Donnie who answered me. "You know, that aunt that's been in Lychwood most of her life."

"What about her?" I think I already knew.

Donnie looked uncomfortable. "I thought you woulda heard. She died last night in her sleep. I heard talk at Timmie's not an hour ago."

Aunt Wisty. Dead only a few hours after our shared experience in the cemetery. Now it was too late for her to tell me anymore about her husband or what had happened during that other reunion. The only one left was Aunt Clem, and I didn't know if she could or would tell the truth. It didn't seem fair, not after all I had gone through, to know so much, but not all. For Aunt Wisty, I felt relief. I could mourn her life, but not her death.

I wanted to go back to bed. Not the one upstairs in Hammersleigh. To my bed in my own bungalow in town. I was beginning to hate Hammersleigh. It was too big and there were too many secrets enclosed within its handsome limestone walls.

Instead, I walked around to the back of the house, where a few firefighters still probed and poked within the ruins of the tool shed. A tall middle-aged man in shorts and high rubber boots waded with the firemen, stooping once in a while to pick something up, then dropping it into the smoky rubble again. He carried a handheld device, and spoke into it every once in a while. I took him to be the fire marshal, but it was the taller man in summer uniform that made me stop, then back step into the rhododendrons separating the rear lawns from the rose garden.

Initially, I didn't know why I reacted that way at the sight of Marc. Something about the night before. It was a few seconds before it came back to me. Well, not all of it, I couldn't remember his exact words. But I distinctly recalled the bottom line.

I had been dumped.

CHAPTER 28

Okay, maybe Marc hadn't dumped me in so many words. That's what he meant, though. And I didn't blame him.

I realized that I had expected that very thing to happen, and now that it had, I felt almost relieved.

I knew I had lost a good man, a man who would have shared the good times and stuck by me through the bad times. But this was better for Marc. He deserved someone more stable. And stable I was not. My talk with Mom the other day made that clear. I had to admit that my father, then Dennis, had left me with insecurities I wasn't even aware of until now. And if that emotional baggage wasn't enough, I also had a *spirit guide.*

Thinking of Leander made me remember Aunt Wisty. I felt a dull ache in my chest, and since I had a certified healthy heart, the pain had to be emotional.

What a wasted life. I hoped Aunt Wisty had found at least a few minutes of happiness with Uncle Patrick, since the rest of her years had been filled with such pain. She had an abusive husband, her only child died by violence, and she spent the next sixty-eight years in a cage—a physical cage and a mental one.

I wandered to the shade garden and sat on the bench beneath the ancient maple, a few feet from the hosta bed. My soft tissue injury throbbed at the sight. The hostas were pretty enough, their leaves variegated with shades of green and white. Just my luck I landed on a rock hidden beneath those perfect leaves. Like the serpent in Paradise.

I felt angry at Dennis, even though I knew he hadn't really meant to hurt me, not physically anyway. He never had, but now I realized he had spent twenty years undermining my feelings of worth. And I had let him.

Dennis betrayed me with other women, and then convinced me his infidelities were due to deficiencies in my own character. And because my father unintentionally raised me to think I could never succeed in his eyes, I enabled Dennis to perpetuate this belief. There, I had figured that all out without the help of a shrink or a support group.

But *knowing* was no help to me. And knowing I pushed Marc away because I was afraid of failing him, too, didn't give me satisfaction. All in all, I was a hunk of self-pity sitting on that hard bench.

Quit feeling sorry for yourself, Lyris. You got to move on. You must fight on the beaches, on the landing grounds, in the fields and streets. You must never give up.

I jumped to my feet and looked around. The still air shimmered in the heat, and my head swam. I sat back down and closed my eyes. I had to quit expecting to see Leander.

Leander? You sound like Winston Churchill.

Winston? That's classified information. I'm here to tell you that your Aunt Wisty is now safe and happy. Soon, she'll be reviewing her earthly life to determine if her goals were met.

My guess would be no.

Lyris, a soul can choose a life of unhappiness to further a higher purpose. We can't know. Or, at least you can't. Hah.

I was in no mood to discuss the higher purpose of life. I had a bone to pick with Leander.

I saw a ghost. The ghost of Wisty's husband. I'd rather not see such things, if you don't mind. I'm far too sensitive...

You only saw an imprint. An imprint from time past. Wisty's tortured memory reflected the last sight of her husband in this lifetime. And I can't stop you seeing such things. Sometimes they are necessary and you better get used to it.

Well, how about this then. I think Wisty killed Thomas after Thomas murdered his own child. That can't be part of a plan. Murder is a crime, a sin.

True enough, Lyris. Taking another human life is serious shit and can jeopardize the soul's evolvement. But when a soul takes on mortal form, the human baggage isn't always pretty. No point trying to understand another soul's motives.

I remembered Aunt Wisty's words about hanging. And then last night in the cemetery, she had said something about not being able to let them do *that* to him.

Leander, I think Aunt Wisty shot Thomas with his own service gun after he killed Tommy, but not for revenge. I think she did it to save him from hanging. Are you saying his murder was justified because her motives were unselfish?

Of course not, Lyris. It's obvious that her life's plan went astray that night. The emotional trauma she suffered over her child's death overcame her higher self. She succumbed to a very human compulsion, as did Thomas when he took the life of his own son. Now they will be judged by a merciful and understanding Source.

Better luck next time, you mean?

Exactly. And if you don't mind me saying so, Lyris, sarcasm is not always helpful.

Look who's talking. Anyway, I'm just exhibiting a mortal weakness.

Touché. Remember, you can call me when you need me. If I don't answer on the first ring, don't give up. I have a lot on the go right now.

Well, answer this. How come I'm such an emotional mess, unable to sustain a healthy relationship with a wonderful member of the opposite sex?

You got me there. Maybe you should ask your mother.

Are you sure you don't know Winston Churchill?

Can't tell you that.

Another thing I want to ask. Why didn't you warn me—

But he was gone and someone was shaking my arm. I opened my eyes. Marc was bending over me. His shirt was clinging damply to his arm and chest muscles, and there were dark circles beneath his eyes.

"Are you okay, Lyris? You've been sitting there with your eyes closed, and your back as straight as a poker. I didn't think you were asleep."

"I'm dandy, thanks. What were you doing still poking through the fire? I figured you'd be out looking for Scott Fournier. You know, the diabolical wife beater who threw me down the stairs and almost killed me."

He laughed, for God's sake. "Take it easy. I have an alert out for him, and I'm quite certain we'll catch up with him sometime today. Are you positive it was Scott? You said yourself it was dark in the attic."

"I am sure."

"You'll have to swear to it in court. If you didn't see his face, how can you be sure it was him? Not that I doubt you, but you must see from a legal standpoint we need more than just an assumption from a witness who went into shock after the attack."

"I never. I was totally lucid the whole time."

Marc looked dubious. "I think we'll have to prove that in court. Is there anything else you can think of? Did you see his face at all with your flashlight? I found it in the attic, and it didn't work."

"It died on me. But I know my attacker was Scott."

"It's certainly possible. Well, we'll just have to find him first and see if he'll admit it. Not very likely, but it happens."

"Maybe you should talk to Caroline."

"I already did. She admits to letting Scott into the house nights, just so he wouldn't cause a fuss—she was afraid you would fire her—but she says she didn't see him last night. If that's true, how did he gain access to the attic? None of the doors or windows were forced."

"I don't know, but I'm pretty sure I saw him yesterday morning on the widow's walk." I looked at Marc. "Maybe he didn't leave Friday night. Caroline may have thought he did, and he could have pretended to leave the house, but hid upstairs in the attic until I found him."

"Maybe. We didn't see signs of anyone bedding down in the attic, but he could have slipped down to use one of the bathrooms on the second floor. And this house has two staircases, so it would be easy to take food from the kitchen."

He peered into my eyes. "You're sure it couldn't have been Peter Tackaberry? He was in the house the entire day and evening."

I shook my head. I thought we had settled all this. "Not a chance. I would have sensed Peter. I know him. It was Scott."

"Then, what about Angelo Bertollini? I wouldn't put anything past that young man. Actually, I never considered him a physical threat to anyone, but I've been wrong before. He's an electronic genius and could have found a way to bypass the security system."

"It wasn't Angelo either. He's not tall enough, for one thing."

Marc sighed and stood up. To my surprise, he leaned over and kissed me on the mouth, moving back afterward like he thought I might bite him. He sat down again.

He took my hand rather gingerly. "Have you thought about what we discussed last night, Lyris?"

"Last night? You mean when you dumped me? That discussion?"

"Dump you?" He dropped my hand and leaned back against the tree. "I knew I was wrong to say anything. You were drugged, and I should have waited. But I thought I could take some of the stress out of your life by backing off for now."

"Oh? It sounded to my Valium-fogged brain like you were telling me something quite different. That stuff was great, by the way. I wouldn't mind keeping some on hand for emotional emergencies."

"Last night was exceptionally distressing for you, and since you seem to promptly bounce back from the many odd situations you find yourself in, I doubt you'll need Valium on a regular basis."

I decided not to take offence, even if he didn't know half of the justifiable reasons I often found myself in so many *odd situations*.

"I've got to go, Lyris. I need to check that my staff is doing everything possible to find Scott Fournier. Make sure you get some rest and stay out of trouble." With another hasty kiss, on my eyebrow this time, he was gone.

So Marc hadn't broken up with me. I should have been relieved, yet I just felt empty inside. Lonely and anxious. I didn't know why exactly, but I put it down to too many days and nights of stress and worry—the reunion, Tommy's mystery, Caroline, Scott, Patsy, Dennis, not to mention Leander. Even Conklin was causing me to worry if I would be left to manage Hammersleigh House alone, on into my solitary senior years.

I felt a momentary chill and shivered despite the cloying air. I had to give myself a break. It was natural to feel such a sense of foreboding, of impending danger, under the circumstances. With all the separate little dramas swirling around me, it was a wonder I could function at all.

Peter, Caroline and Conklin were gathered around the kitchen table eating tomato soup and salmon on whole wheat bread. I joined them for a bite, then announced I was going to bed for the rest of the day. They didn't argue when I said I was going back to the couch I slept on last night.

I was afraid I would be too strung out to fall asleep. However, the Valium must still have been in my bloodstream. I slipped effortlessly into sweet, forgetful unconsciousness. Just before going under, I was aware that two warm, furry bodies had joined me, walking back and forth over me to find just the perfect spot. Since the room was cool enough for a blanket and since the three of us had been through the same war, I let them stay. I forgave them for the toenail scratches on my face.

A whole regiment of intruders could have rampaged through the house that afternoon and night for all I knew or cared. For eighteen hours, I slept that deep, healing sleep that happens only when the body and mind have reached their limits and the one solution is oblivion.

I wouldn't say I felt as good as new when I awoke in the morning. My backside still hurt, and there were aches in almost every muscle and bone I possessed. Well, when you're creeping up on your fortieth birthday, you can't expect to hit every step down a flight of stairs and not feel it.

There was no clock in the room and I didn't know where my watch was, so I had no idea of the time. I limped quickly into the kitchen and was horrified to note I was due at my desk in thirty-five minutes. I made it in thirty-three.

By the time my tires hit the road, I had spent twenty-five of those minutes showering, dressing and grooming. No eating, no time, and my stomach rumbled as I careened into the parking lot, making Angelo skip aside as he, too, rushed toward the staff entrance.

There was always coffee and doughnuts available for a nominal fee in the break room. I consumed a cup of sugared, milky coffee and a donut that oozed synthetic cream from its middle. I had to eat it or pass out from low blood sugar. My last meal was that light lunch yesterday afternoon.

I was wiping the pseudo cream off my face at exactly 8 a.m. when Sheila rushed up and grabbed my arm. "Come on, Lyris. We have to go to the cafeteria and hear Amory tell us about the severance package."

We were among the last to enter the cafeteria so had to sit in the front row. I set myself carefully into the rigid plastic chair beside Daphne. To her left was Faye, and I could hear Angelo in the row behind making a nuisance of himself with the finance clerks. Sheila dragged a chair over and squeezed it in beside mine. The legs of the chair screeched as it scraped along the vinyl floor. My nerves twanged in unison.

At the front of the room, Amory Langelle cast us an exasperated look. "Up yours," I said under my breath and shifted my own chair closer to Daphne. The noise was gratifyingly high pitched.

Amory was our CEO, and it was his bright idea to pull the Commission out of the red by reducing the staff by one fifth.

The cafeteria wasn't air conditioned, and fifteen minutes into Amory's stumbling, tongue-tied address, I was forced to tune out. My clothes were sticking to me, and I was astonished to see I had dressed myself in a long-sleeved red blouse and a pair of jeans. At least I had had the presence of mind to wear sandals on my feet, even if they were Birkenstocks.

"…our mission is to take this company into the next decade with the ability to serve our customers with integrity and economy…"

I tuned out again. Sheila poked my arm. "What does he mean?"

I shrugged, trying to envision another twenty years of this. Once a company started to downsize and reorganize, it didn't stop until a new owner came in and bought up the remaining pieces for a song. Looking around, I could see everyone else was doing the same thing—looking around and wondering what the hell Amory was saying.

I was tired. Physically, of course, I was battered and overstressed. Mentally, I had too many balls in the air, too many unfinished or unresolved conflicts. No wonder my life at the Hydro Commission seemed to extend unendingly into the future, seeing my staff and friends leave one by one, finding myself rushing from one task to another with no time to do anything thoroughly or satisfactorily.

I thought of the people around me—Sheila, Kaye, Daphne, Angelo, Kelly from the finance department, the cafeteria workers and the lines personnel. So many of them would be gone, and all of them depended on their paycheques to support themselves and their families.

I would still be there, probably. I had over twenty years of seniority. But Sheila had only ten, and Daphne, not even two.

"…vision of sustainable energy we will achieve first-class commercial performance…"

Sheila's sharp elbow dug into my bruised ribs again. "Do you understand what he's saying, Lyris?" she whispered.

"Nobody does," I answered and earned a venomous glance from Amory's secretary, Susan Laurent. Her job wasn't in jeopardy either.

"We will experience profit through progress, and if progress means we must sacrifice jobs, then we shall…"

Amory blathered on, and I closed my mind to his endless monologue. It was no use. My mind was not to be sidetracked by my other troubles. It skittered away from Scott Fournier, from Hammersleigh House, from Tommy, even from Marc. As a matter of fact, the state of my stomach was overriding everything.

The coffee and donut had been a bad decision. The combination created a conflict that was erupting into warfare in my gut. I broke out in a sweat, quite different from the sheen that coated the face of every other captive in the cafeteria.

"Each individual will have until the end of the month to accept this opportunity. The Board of Directors has empowered me to offer two years' salary to each and every one of you, a most generous proposal. If, by August 1, the criteria have not been met, terminations will commence with the most junior…"

Sheila whispered again, "What happens if more than a fifth of the staff takes the offer?"

I couldn't even respond to her. I was experiencing that feeling you get just before you throw up. Reacting for once before it was too late, I jumped to my feet and raced for the door. I just made it to the ladies' washroom.

Afterwards, pale and shaken, I lay down on the couch that management had thoughtfully provided in the anteroom. Maybe the filling in the donut was real cream and had been sitting in the heat too long. Maybe my stomach needed pumping.

A few minutes later, Sheila and Daphne came in. Struggling to a sitting position, I anticipated a spate of questions on my well-being. Not so.

Daphne plunked herself down on one side of me, Sheila on the other. Faye came in, looking disconsolate and weepy.

"I think you're all right, Lyris. But I guess I'll have to take the offer." Sheila pulled a tissue out of the pocket of her denim skirt and wiped the mascara off her cheeks.

"Where will I get another job?" Daphne wailed, searching for a tissue of her own.

Good question. Blackstone hadn't many industries. Working for the town or county paid the best, but those jobs were usually passed on from father to son or mother to daughter. Nepotism was alive and thriving in Blackshore.

"You'll find something, Daphne," said Sheila. "You're young. But someone my age will have a tough time finding another job." She sniffed and pulled out another tissue.

Sheila had a point. She was in her early fifties and any jobs not going to the friend or relative of someone in a hiring position, went to a young person.

I stood up. "I'm going home. I'm sick. I'll be back tomorrow."

In the parking lot, the heat radiating from the asphalt was almost comforting, at least for a few minutes. My car pointed itself toward town, away from Hammersleigh.

I should have stayed. My staff needed me to be strong and help them through this ordeal. At least as long as they were my staff. After that, they would still be my friends.

I parked in front of the library. It had been weeks since I had enough free time to read a book, and I thought I might slip in and grab the latest Barbara Fradkin or Rick Mofina. I glanced across the street to the police station. My heart yearned to go in and talk to Marc, but my head forbade me. He deserved better, and I had to let him go.

Someone was waving at me, and I saw with sinking heart it was Dennis. He was standing outside his office and waving me over to his side of the street. I shook my head and started up the library steps. Before my hand could reach for the door, I sensed someone running up the steps behind me.

"Lyris, I need to talk to you. Can you come in to my office for a minute?" Not waiting for a possible refusal, Dennis took my arm to steer me back down the steps.

I shook free. "Not today, Dennis. Sorry, I'm not up to it. I just want to get a book and go home."

"This will just take a minute. If you won't come to my office, we can talk here."

I squinted up at him. My jeans were clinging damply to my thighs, and I felt sweat dribbling down my chest. Even my feet were sticky and swollen in my sandals.

Dennis looked just as uncomfortable. He had forsaken his usual short-sleeved polo shirt and instead was wearing a dark denim shirt with long sleeves. His face was bright red and puffy, and the vein in his forehead was throbbing. Only the eye tic was missing, but give me time.

Alarmed at his appearance, I said, "I'm not coming to your office, but I'll spare you a few minutes over on that bench. At least it's in the shade."

We made our way back down the library steps to the parkette in front of the building. A drooping tree overlooked a wooden bench and a flower bed filled with wilting impatiens. I was relieved to sit down again.

"I was worried about you. You know, after the other day in your back garden. I heard you had to go the hospital."

"You caused me some soft tissue damage, but that's not why I was in the hospital. In case you haven't heard yet, I was assaulted on Saturday night and thrown down a flight of stairs. My body is one colossal, painful wound, but I'll heal. It's nice of you to be concerned. Unlike you, but nice."

He said stiffly, "Why wouldn't I be concerned about you? We were married for a long time. I will always want you to be well and happy."

"And I, you," I replied, not believing a word he said.

I got up, steadying myself with one hand on the back of the bench. "Well, it's too hot out here to linger, Dennis, so see you around."

Then he struck. "I have to ask you one more time, Lyris. I need money. Bad. And I mean it." He cleared his throat, that irritating habit I had always detested.

"We've been all over this, Dennis. Too many times."

"Listen to me, Lyris. I'm serious. Tracey found out about me and...someone. She wants to leave me, and she wants a monthly maintenance payment. For her and Amy and the twins."

He cleared his throat again, and I winced. "Not again. Your wife is hugely pregnant, you dope. You and who, Dennis? Is it Jody?"

"It doesn't matter, does it? The point is, I don't have a dime. The house is remortgaged, my line of credit is maxed out, and so are all my credit cards."

"I believe you conveyed this information to me already. I don't see how this is my problem." Sweat dripped from my upper lip.

"It's partly your fault I'm in this situation. Just please give me back what you took during the settlement."

"Last time we talked, you wanted half back. Now you want it all? I'm not going to argue with you any more about this, Dennis. I don't owe you anything. Your extramarital affairs are no longer my business. Now get out of my way."

"How can you do this to me, to Mitch...?"

"Leave Mitch out of this. I'm paying all his university expenses and providing his living allowance. Do you think that's easy on my salary? You were supposed to supply half. You're not, so don't bring him into this. Your second family is not my responsibility. That's the bottom line."

"I'm desperate, Lyris." Indeed, he looked it. The tic under his left eye was now in evidence and pulsed with every heartbeat. The hand he held up to me had a marked tremor, but I had to harden my heart if I was ever to break free of this man and our shared past.

"No, Dennis. Your problem. Your responsibility." I managed to squeeze past him and make my way to the car, library book forgotten. I should have warned him to expect a visit from the Chief of Police about the flower bed incident, but part of me hoped Marc would let that slide.

I thought I was going to pass out and leaned my head back against the seat. I was so afraid at that moment, afraid that Dennis' desperation would cause him to do something irrevocable. I wondered how I would feel then, if Dennis took his own life. Would I feel guilty, responsible? I almost followed him back to his office to offer him everything I had.

If I did that, I would lose control of my life forever. I would have to take a chance that his life force was strong enough to prevent self-destruction. Hadn't Aunt Clem told me not to follow my heart regarding finances? At this point I didn't know which way my heart was leaning.

After a few minutes, I felt able to start the car. I drove to the hospital where I found a parking spot in the shade of a spreading Russian olive tree. My luck must be changing, I thought without humour.

Patsy was writing furiously on a pad of paper on her desk when I walked in. She looked up and a smile crossed her face. In spite of the air-conditioned office, her reddish hair had rolled up into loose curls, and she was dressed in a tank top and long cotton skirt.

"So...how's the Family Nut? I take it you survived Saturday night?"

"Excuse me. I aspire to be known as the Family Character. When I'm eighty, I will be riding my bicycle down Main Street, wearing a purple hat and ringing a bell to make everyone jump out of my path. We'll see who the Nut is then."

"Whatever you say. We create our own futures."

We looked at each other and broke into silly grins. Patsy got up from her chair and came around to the front of her desk. We hugged and at that moment, all was well between us. What was said on Saturday night was no longer important.

"You're dressed like you don't give a damn about your job. You better watch out, or they'll fire you."

"Hah. I'm gone in a month anyway, so I might as well be comfortable. If they don't like how I dress, well, they can just lump it."

"My goodness. You seem very cheerful for a lady who will be out of a job in a few short weeks." The irony had not escaped me. Patsy loved her job and was losing it. I had come to hate mine and got to keep it.

"Yes, well, I have a few irons in the fire, as they say."

"What? Have you found another job?"

"Not quite, but it's coming together. Why aren't you at work?"

I related a bit of Amory's proposal and my inability to cope with it after my week of unrelenting stress.

There was a gleam in her eye. I didn't like it.

"Lyris, have you thought of taking the termination package?"

I hooted. "And do what? I'm a little young for a pension, and after I spend the two years' salary on, well, living, what do I do then?"

"You might use the money to invest in a business."

"What business? I don't know how to do anything else."

"You just might surprise yourself."

"Yeah, right. Anyway, I came to see if you want to go to lunch." The thought of eating made me want to retch all over again, but I needed company and reassurance that the world beyond Hammersleigh House and the Hydro Commission was still revolving.

"Sorry, I can't. I have a lunch meeting with the board members about turning over to my replacement. Maybe tomorrow?"

I still believed she was acting too happy for someone on the brink of the unemployment line. And that returned me to the thought of almost everyone I knew at work who would lose their jobs. Except me, I wasn't losing mine.

The thought was not comforting.

CHAPTER 29

I had another stop to make, then there would be no more reasons to avoid going home. I still felt uneasy, but couldn't decide if it was some sort of premonition or just a reaction to the past few days of pain and terror. I almost laughed out loud at the choice.

Cowbell Lane was dozing in the afternoon heat. The late nineteenth century houses were shuttered against the sun, and if their occupants were not indoors with air conditioners or fans, they were paying condolence calls at Hollyhock Cottage.

I had to park half a block from Hollyhock Cottage's steep front steps. Visitors were climbing up to the front porch and coming down, sometimes arm in arm with another middle-aged or elderly lady. Most wore flower-print dresses with beige hose and light-coloured pumps. There were even a few wide-brimmed hats and white gloves in the crowd. I felt underdressed and overheated in my jeans and long-sleeved shirt.

At the front door, I slipped around a trio of octogenarians who were chatting on the porch and managed to get into the front hall without talking to anyone. Spotting Twyla Malinski emerging from the kitchen with a silver teapot, I stood motionless behind the cigar store aboriginal hoping she wouldn't see me.

As soon as she disappeared into the parlour, I hot-footed it to the end of the hall into Aunt Clem's spirit room and closed the door. I figured it was the one room in the house where guests would not be welcome. I planned to watch through a crack in the door for Aunt Clem to wander by, and then nab her.

A few candles glowing in a far corner created enough light for me to make out the shapes of table and chairs. I waited for my eyes to adjust to the shadowy gloom.

The hair stood up on the back of my neck. A figure was lying on a couch pushed up against one wall. I thought Aunt Wisty would be laid out at the funeral home, not there at her sister's house. I sensed the body looking at me and yelped.

The body on the couch sat up. Before I could rush out of the room, it spoke.

"Lyris Pembrooke, is that you?"

My first impulse was to deny it. "Maybe."

"Turn on the light. The switch is beside the door."

I obeyed, and sighed with relief.

Aunt Clem pushed her hair back into shape and adjusted her turquoise shift. She picked up a matching bolero jacket and draped it around her shoulders.

"I came in here to have a little rest. I'm beginning to find all this company very tiresome. Visitors have been arriving all morning, and I finally left Twyla to manage alone. I don't know what I'm going to do without her once I turn Hollyhock Cottage over to David, but I suppose I'll have to get used to looking after myself."

"Where are you going, Aunt Clem? Can't Twyla go with you?"

She turned evasive. "Oh, now, that's not quite settled yet. Early days, my dear."

She moved over to a chair near the table. A pack of tarot cards was scattered across the navy tablecloth and she gathered them up. As she shuffled the deck, I moved closer to the door. I didn't think I was up to another reading or a visit from Luke and Florence.

"What brings you here today, Lyris?"

"Well, I wanted to pay a condolence call."

"Is that all? Are you sure?"

"Pretty sure. What other reason could there be?"

"Well, let me see. You're dressed for raking the lawn, for one thing. For another, you look ill. Come and sit down."

Against my better judgment, I did so. I sat on the edge of the second chair. "I got pushed down the stairs Saturday night and I'm a little sore, I guess."

"I heard about that incident, but I think it's a little more than that. When did you eat last?"

"Yesterday lunch." That morning's coffee and doughnut didn't count since they didn't stay with me long. "And I'm not hungry anyway."

"Wait here." Aunt Clem left the room and I took the opportunity to take a quick glance at the cards on the table. Not that I knew anything about tarot, but I wanted to make sure the hanged man on a rope wasn't on top. It wasn't.

Aunt Clem returned with a tray laden with tiny sandwiches on a plate and a glass of milk. "Eat up, Lyris. You look half-starved. I swear you've lost weight this summer."

I thought I might manage some milk and picked up the glass. The cold liquid felt good going down my dry throat. Then I selected a sandwich and bit into it. The filling was tasty so I finished it and picked up another.

Aunt Clem watched me eat. "I think, Lyris, that you have experienced something that has changed you."

"You might say that. I've had quite a few exciting experiences lately."

"Have you allowed your spirit guide to speak?"

"I couldn't stop him. His name is Leander as you said, and I don't care for his attitude. Do you think I can turn him in for another one?"

"No, he's yours for good," she said absently. I was pretty sure she was making a mental note to ask Florence and Luke to brief Leander on my quirks and shortcomings.

I jammed another sandwich in my mouth and chewed. "At least the smell in the upstairs hall has gone. I know what it is anyway."

I explained how I discovered by smelling my new niece that the scent was baby powder and believed it was Tommy's way of telling me to make sure the truth of his death was uncovered.

"There's something I don't understand, though, Aunt Clem."

"And what is that, dear."

"Several things, as a matter of fact. First of all, why doesn't Leander just tell me exactly what happened to Tommy? He must know, and it would have saved me a lot of work. Yet all I get are nudges and the odd hint although, since the words are just sort of in my head, I can't say I really hear him. Still, he can be very pushy."

"Lyris, Leander is not always with you. He has other duties and needs time for himself, for his studies and recreational pursuits. And except for an emergency, if he happens to be nearby, it isn't his role to tell you what you don't ask."

True, I hadn't got the hang of this spirit guide thing yet, but I couldn't get past the mental image of Leander engaged in a rousing game of racquetball or attending a rock concert with headliners John Lennon and Jerry Garcia. Or Elvis and Michael.

"How am I going to learn all the rules, Aunt Clem? I don't even understand this world. How will I ever understand the other, up there, wherever?"

"I will help you as much as I can, Lyris, and you must also talk to Leander. After all these years, I am still learning myself, and none of us here can ever know all there is. Leander is your guide and your teacher too, for as long as you are in your present form."

"Aunt Clem, you were here when Tommy disappeared. You must know what happened. Aren't you the logical person to make sure the truth is uncovered? So Tommy can rest."

"I know some of it, certainly. What makes you think that Tommy needs closure? His soul was born into an earthly body for two short years. That was his plan and he may already be back in this world in another form, or perhaps waiting. He may even have finished his journeys and been elevated to another level."

She was confusing me. I didn't want to think about reincarnation right then. My brain felt like it was going to burst with concepts most people never needed to think about. Maybe I could find a way to get rid of Leander and carry on like before, oblivious to any other level of existence.

"So if it isn't Tommy, who can it be? Maybe it's just simple human curiosity—mine. I should forget about the whole subject and let the past die." At this point I meant every word. I was so sick of everything and just wanted to take a two-week Alaskan cruise.

"There is no going back, Lyris, once the cosmic energy has stirred for you. I will tell you what I know, but not what I believe, and you must discover the rest for yourself. Just remember, you may never know why you have started down this path. Those of us who have been granted the gift of heightened intuition are not always privy to the reasons."

We were silent for a moment while I finished off the sandwiches. I jumped when Aunt Clem spoke again.

"Perhaps this has something to do with Wisty. She suffered a great deal for most of her life, and it could be that someone else will benefit if the cause of her suffering is revealed."

"Or maybe," I said, surprising myself, "maybe it's because of Thomas himself. Following your logic, since his involvement in Tommy's death was not according to plan, he may have wanted to ensure the truth was finally recognized, maybe so the plan could get back on track."

What I had just said made no sense to me. I needed to stick to my own plan.

"You say you know part of what happened, Aunt Clem. Why don't you know it all? You said your psychic gift didn't reappear until after the reunion when you went back to your war job, but why don't you know the rest now."

"As I mentioned before, Lyris, we are told only what we specifically ask. And I never asked anything about that weekend I didn't already know. I never asked because I didn't want to know. It appears you have been chosen now to reveal the rest."

"Do you think you can tell me your part now?"

"How much do *you* know about what happened?"

"Aunt Wisty's husband was at Hammersleigh that weekend, wasn't he? And she and Uncle Patrick were in love."

Her face showed no emotion, and it was as though her disembodied face floated free, watchful and waiting. "The three of us—Patrick, Bruce Wingate and I—were on leave for the weekend. My parents' house, this house, was full of out-of-town guests, so Patrick invited me and Bruce to stay at Hammersleigh House. Wisty and Tommy came along as chaperones so the proprieties would be observed."

As she spoke, I fancied Aunt Clem's face appeared younger, without lines. I saw her as she must have looked sixty-eight years ago, as she looked in my mother's photograph. Did she, like Gunner, remember that time like it was yesterday?

"We all arrived at the house on Thursday afternoon. Although Bruce had been Patrick's friend since private school, he was also an agent in training at the Camp." She looked sideways at me to see if I understood the reference to Camp X.

I nodded.

"He was also the man I loved," she said. "I knew he was ready to be sent into enemy territory and I was very much afraid for him. That weekend...well, it's difficult to explain to someone who hasn't lived through those terrible years. We knew our time together could be cut short instantly and forever, so we did what young people do under those conditions. And I have never regretted it for one minute." She looked at me. "I'm telling you about Bruce and me so you will understand that we were absorbed with each other and didn't realize what was going on in the house until it was almost all over. Bruce and I took every opportunity to slip away, either deep into the wood, or upstairs to the attic floor. The servants' rooms were unused by then, but still furnished."

I closed my eyes. It was as if the words I were hearing unfolded into images in my mind. I was seeing all those young people, moving with them, feeling their experiences. The bittersweet love that might end at any moment.

"On Friday morning we were all having breakfast, including Tommy. When Thomas walked into the dining room, we were all shocked. Wisty most of all. There had been no word from him for months, and she had confided in me her fear that he must be dead. To have him materialize like that without warning was indescribably upsetting. His appearance horrified us too. He looked as though he had been through a terrible illness, as we later found out he had been. His uniform was dirty and hung on his frame like it had been made for a much heavier man. But his eyes, his eyes were the worst I ever saw in a war survivor, and I have seen more than a few."

My skin tightened as I remembered the terrible *imprint* in the cemetery, those haunted eyes.

"He never explained to us how he had come to find his wife and child at Hammersleigh. No one ever admitted to seeing him in town and directing him there. Indeed, he spoke only to Wisty and asked her if he could lie down as he was very tired. Wisty got up at once and led him away. And that's the last I saw of him. Dead or alive."

Aunt Clem paused, and I opened my eyes, not sorry to look away from the sight of that tortured man and the four horrified people at the breakfast table. Or the little boy playing contentedly in his high chair. He didn't even recognize the tall, gaunt stranger whose dreadful eyes never left his mother's face.

"I should have found out what was going on in the house after that," she said, "but I didn't. Time was passing quickly, and Bruce and I wanted to spend all we had left with each other. It was hot in the attic, so we stayed in the woods most of the time. I enlisted my two youngest sisters to look after Tommy without telling them Thomas was back."

"Why didn't you tell anyone?"

Aunt Clem shrugged. "I don't know why. It seemed important not to let anyone know. I do remember Patrick looking worried and pacing the hall, looking up the staircase to the second floor, where Wisty and Thomas remained all of Friday and Saturday. I let everyone know that Wisty wasn't feeling well. The one time she came down was Saturday afternoon for the reunion photo. If she wasn't there, my mother would think she was seriously ill and insist on seeing her. So Wisty came for the picture, then went straight back to Thomas."

Her eyes held that faraway gaze as she stared past me. "There wasn't a breath of air on Saturday night. At midnight the bonfires were lit in the field and people started singing the tunes that were popular at the time, then some of the World War I songs. Bruce and I stayed outside until all the fires were put out and everyone had gone to bed. We went in through the front door. Patrick was sitting there on the bottom step of the staircase with his head in his hands. He looked up and said, 'He's dead. Thomas is dead.' At first we thought Thomas died from whatever illness he was suffering from. I ran up to Wisty. She was just sitting on the bed, her face blank."

Aunt Clem looked at me again. "She never came out of it. Not once in all these following years. And there was no sign of Tommy in his crib. When I asked her where the baby was, she didn't say anything. And I never knew, not until you found him last week."

"What about Thomas? How did he die?"

"It was a gunshot wound to the head. Patrick was upset, but he took charge and Bruce had to help him. He called Percy, who was the chief of police then, and Marcelle Lavette from the funeral home. Both of those men had been close friends of Patrick's father."

"But Thomas," I persisted, "what happened to him?"

"I never saw the body. The four men took him away and buried him. They dug the grave there on the edge of the cemetery where it wouldn't be obvious. There was no coffin. Later on, after the war, Patrick had a stone set into the ground. He didn't put Thomas's name on it. Still, I didn't think it was a good idea, but Patrick didn't want Thomas to lie in a completely unmarked grave. Patrick said that Thomas killed Tommy without meaning to, but he didn't know where the baby's body was. He thought maybe Wisty took it away and hid it in the woods, where no one ever found it."

"She did hide Tommy," I said. "But not in the woods. She wrapped Tommy in his favourite blanket and hid him away in the turret room with his toy bunny."

That part had been bothering me since I found Tommy's body. Either Patrick had no idea the body was in the house, or he did know and was the one who had pounded the secret door shut with nails and caused it to be painted over years later. While I could imagine Wisty in her agony hiding Tommy tenderly away from the world, I didn't think she was capable of nailing the door shut. Then again, how could Patrick bear to live in the house the rest of his life with that secret tucked away in the turret room?

I would never know this part of the puzzle, not unless I could wring the information out of Leander. The men involved were all dead. And now Aunt Wisty was dead too.

Aunt Clem nodded at me and I realized I had been speaking aloud.

"The men decided to say that someone got into the house and took the baby," she said. "They launched a search for him. They hoped the searchers would come across the body and at least put an end to the tragedy. But they never did and eventually, Patrick went back to his company and I returned to Camp X with Bruce. You know the rest."

"Did you and Patrick ever talk about that night, Aunt Clem? Didn't you try and figure out what happened?"

"After the war, with Bruce gone, it didn't seem important to me. Wisty was lost to us forever, and Thomas was dead. The sins he committed were due to his illness. Otherwise he never would have harmed his son."

"Exactly what was his illness?"

"All I know for certain is that he was in a hospital in Italy. He had a breakdown, probably what we would now call post-traumatic stress disorder, and while he was hospitalized, he received a medical discharge from the army. For some reason, Wisty was not notified, but that may have been his wish. He was sent back to Canada on a supply ship and was supposed to enter the Christie Street Veterans' Hospital in Toronto for further treatment. Instead, he just walked away and came home. I don't know what the army was told about his absence, but since he had technically been discharged, I don't think they pursued it. Maybe Patrick reported to them that Thomas was recovering at home."

I felt I had to tell her what I knew.

"Wisty killed Thomas." I related Wisty's remarks about hanging. "I think she killed him to save him from prosecution and execution. Then she went into that catatonic state because she couldn't stand thinking about what she had been forced to do. And because of what happened to Tommy."

Aunt Clem was silent for a moment. She seemed to be turning ideas over in her mind, taking the facts and our surmises, and arriving at the most logical solution. I wasn't ready to share my conversation with

Leander about the plans and progression of Thomas's and Wisty's souls, so I kept silent too.

She gave a nod. "You may be right, Lyris. Wisty was a woman of her time. She was completely under Thomas' control in every way and she would have believed it was her duty to save him from further torment. Even though he had murdered her baby, and she was putting her own soul in jeopardy by killing him."

"She and Patrick were having an affair."

Aunt Clem looked surprised, but didn't ask how I knew. I would share with her my experience on the widow's walk eventually. Right now I wanted the facts without too many side trips.

"Thomas was a physically abusive husband," she said. "When he went away to war, she didn't mean to fall in love with Patrick. But Patrick was so completely different from Thomas, gentle and loving. It just happened. It happened quite a lot during the war."

So many untold stories, so soon to be forgotten.

Depressed, I got up without a word and went home.

With a sturdy Georgian chair securely tucked under the doorknob of my bedroom door, I felt...insecure.

I was sure Conklin wouldn't have said anything if I decided to sleep in the employees' wing again, especially if I limped a little and looked pathetic—not much of a stretch by Monday bedtime. But I knew I had to face my fears sooner or later, and I was tired of feeling like a wussy. It was time to take charge again.

I was pinned like a rat in a trap. I had the chair under the knob, three fans blowing the hot air around the room with no improvement, and the company of Rasputin and Jacqueline to keep the bogeyman away. Before letting them stay with me, I made it clear that they better not need a bathroom break during the night, or I would be forced to open the window and drop them out. No way was I venturing into the hallway that night, not until Scott Fournier was apprehended.

Marc had phoned after dinner to say he had stationed an officer at the front entrance and another in the field near the wooden gate. We both knew this would not stop Scott from getting into the grounds if he wanted to. In point of fact, Marc avoided mentioning Scott by name, referring to the *intruder*, but I knew he meant Scott. And if Scott rapped on the door at the end of the employees' wing, I wasn't sure Caroline would be strong enough to resist him.

All in all, I was pretty jumpy by the time I barricaded myself inside my bedroom. I played with the Internet for a while, searching for *psychic* and *spirit guide,* but all I came up with were websites devoted to the occult that promised to tell me about my past lives or offered to give me a reading over the phone. I shut the computer off and climbed into bed.

I thought about trying to contact Leander, just for somebody to talk to. Up to now, he had called on me without an invitation, and I wondered if I could get in touch with him somehow by just mentally requesting his presence. But the last time we talked, I had the feeling I wasn't quite up to snuff in Leander's eyes and I was not in the mood to hear any more of that.

Even if all my senses weren't on red alert, my bedmates made it impossible to sleep. Jacqueline walked around on the bed, and Rasputin made a loud droning noise that in no way resembled purring. I got out of bed again and sat on the window seat with Amelia for a few minutes, peering into the trees and shadowy gardens. Not even a breath of a breeze moved the leaves or plants in the gardens below.

I went back to bed for the umpteenth time, and despite all the noise and twitching going on around me, managed to fall asleep.

CHAPTER 30

Staccato bursts of thunder jerked me back from the black hole of dreamless sleep. Flashes of light penetrated my closed eyelids, and at some level of my exhausted brain, I knew the lengthy drought had ended. The rain was pouring from the clouds to beat against the windows and fall onto the thirsty earth.

Then another sound overwhelmed the thunder. I sat straight up, wide awake, my heart pounding. A high-pitched shriek pierced through the thunderclaps. In seconds I was tugging at the chair under the doorknob.

When the second scream was still at its zenith, I threw the door wide and looked into the hallway. The next scream was almost overpowered by loud shouting and banging, as if furniture were being knocked over.

In the three or four seconds it had taken me to wake up, jump out of bed, open the door and call myself an idiot for not having my cell phone, I had somehow come to a decision. I had to go downstairs no matter what.

I raced down the hall, turning left toward the staircase. Simultaneously I heard a sound of pounding feet behind me and the air was forced out of my chest as something substantial tackled me from behind.

A pair of strong, hard arms encircled me. A hand covered my mouth and I was powerless to breathe or to move. I was dead. I knew it. I had been foolhardy once too often.

"Shhhh, Lyris. It's okay, it's me."

"Marc?"

I sagged in his arms. With his hand over my mouth and nose, I wasn't able to breathe.

When Marc took his hand away, I leaned against the wall and willed the dizziness to pass. "Marc, what are you doing here?"

"I'll explain later. Stay here."

He spoke into his shoulder radio as he started down the hall. I was close behind, but not close enough to hear what he said. I caught up to him as we neared the bottom of the stairs. For the rest of my life, I will wonder if things would have turned out differently had I listened to Marc and stayed upstairs.

The noise level increased. There were still shrieks and shouts and banging. Marc flattened himself against the wall of the great hall just outside the drawing room.

He looked at me in annoyance and whispered, "Go back upstairs and wait. I've called for backup."

Without waiting to see if I obeyed, he moved his head enough to look into the drawing room. By then, I was on the other side of the doorway doing the same thing.

At night, one or two low-wattage lamps were left burning in the drawing room, just enough to eliminate total darkness. I couldn't distinguish one piece of furniture from another or how many people were in the room. Marc moved swiftly inside, and I was close enough behind to hear the creak of his leather holster. I remembered the light switch was beside the doorway and flipped it up. Immediately all the lamps in the room glowed. Or, almost all.

The drawing room was in shambles. Several lamps were lying on the floor, glass fragments everywhere. A plant table had been knocked over, with earth and pieces of lacy fern scattered across the oriental carpets.

Near the centre of the room, Scott Fournier held Caroline by the shoulders and was shaking her. Her head snapped back and forth, and she had at last stopped screaming.

Conklin was pulling at Scott's arm trying to make him release Caroline. Another shoulder radio hung from Conklin's snow-white lapel.

I knew then that Marc and Conklin had been plotting together to catch Scott in the act of entering the house and inflicting more damage to Caroline or the property.

Scott was in a rage. No one watching him now would call him pleasant or good-natured. His lips were drawn back and his teeth looked longer, sharper than they had the few times he had smiled at me with such sincerity.

He pushed Caroline back onto the sofa so hard that later, when I thought about this scene, I was amazed the antique sofa hadn't buckled under the force. At the same time, one arm came up and he hit her in the face with a closed fist. He lifted the arm a second time, but Marc was there by then and grabbed it.

"Okay, Fournier, enough."

Marc was a larger man, and when he pushed, Scott fell back. At that point, although I would never presume to criticize a police officer as experienced as Marc, I believe he should have whipped out his gun and smacked Scott with it, then handcuffed him. But he didn't, maybe because he didn't think Scott a serious threat. Or maybe he meant to after telling Conklin to unlock the kitchen door to let in the other police officers.

By the time Conklin turned swiftly in the direction of the kitchen, Scott had pulled something out of his jacket pocket and was pointing it at Marc.

"Stop, you," he commanded Conklin over his shoulder.

It was a little gun. It looked so much like a toy that I almost laughed. I was glad I didn't after I saw Marc's face. It was as drained of colour as I had ever seen and his fingers moved spasmodically. I could tell he was cursing himself for letting this happen. The pounding at the kitchen door increased. Underlying the din were the sounds of thunder and the rain as it slammed against the windows.

I was seated on the sofa beside Caroline, trying to comfort her. I could see that Scott had hit her more than once. Both eyes were mere slits in her swollen face, and a thin trail of blood trickled from a cut on her lip and ran down her chin and throat.

"All of you, get over there."

Scott stepped back a few feet and with the ridiculously tiny gun, motioned Conklin and Marc over toward the sofa. I had stood up at his words, but Caroline sat rigid and still.

"Pull out your gun and put it on the table," he ordered Marc.

I knew that any police officer would rather lose an eye than give up his or her gun to anyone, and I could tell by Marc's set face and the clenching and unclenching of his hands that he was thinking about tackling Scott, gun or no gun.

I willed him to look at me, to tell him to hand over the gun. I didn't think Scott was prepared to shoot all four of us, plus the police officers outside. If Marc refused to give his gun up, I felt certain Scott would lose the rest of his thin strand of control and shoot him.

And Conklin. Conklin was leaning forward as thought he, too, wanted to throw himself on Scott and take him down to the floor and pummel him until he was bloody and motionless.

Okay, that's what I wanted to do. But I was worried about Conklin doing something foolish and getting himself hurt. The racket at the kitchen door had settled into a rhythmic pounding as if a battering ram were being used to break through. And I could hear fists beating on the front entrance as well. Maybe I should have been concerned about Hammersleigh's ancient front door with its demon knocker, but I wasn't. I just wanted them to break it down and help us.

The sounds distracted Scott, and he turned one way and then back the other like he wasn't sure where his most immediate threat was located. The gun moved back and forth too, back and forth, first pointing at Marc, then Conklin, then Caroline and me. He seemed to have forgotten Marc's gun for the moment.

Marc appeared not to notice the pounding from either the back of the house or front. He kept his gaze on Scott and moved almost imperceptibly toward him. His arms were hanging straight at his sides and he made no attempt to get at his own gun.

"Scott, right now all we can charge you with is assault on your wife. And if you give me the gun that's all we'll charge you with. We can work this out if it doesn't go any further." His voice was calm and deliberate.

I realized in that moment of danger that I loved him without reservation, hoping it wasn't too late to matter.

Scott wasn't buying it. Either he knew the many charges he faced included the more serious firearm violations, or he was beyond reason, or he didn't care about his life or freedom. Whichever it was, he didn't put down the gun. He stepped closer to Caroline and me.

Reaching across in front of me, he pulled Caroline to her feet and dragged her farther back from the rest of us. She stood still as a dead woman, beaten both physically and emotionally. Her eyes stared at the pale intricate pattern in the carpet and as we watched, the essence of her, the last bit of strength and defiance, dissipated and I knew she would not fight him back ever again.

I couldn't stand any more. I walked over to them and pulled her by the other arm.

"Let her go. She doesn't want to be with you anymore."

The gun was pointed at my chest. I think I still believed then that this was just silly, plain and simple. People in Blackshore didn't have little guns that they frightened other people with, and they didn't shoot real bullets at anyone.

"Lyris…" Marc moved a half a step closer. From the corner of my eye I could see Conklin inching away toward the kitchen. He was out of Scott's sight.

"Get back." Scott shouted. The gun moved from the level of my chest to Marc's abdomen. I didn't like that any better so I spoke again.

"Caroline is not your property. She's made it clear she doesn't want to be your wife anymore and you must respect that. You should go away and leave her alone."

"Shut up, you interfering busybody. She's coming with me now." He pulled Caroline away from me, and swung the gun in Marc's direction again. I noticed that Marc was now about a foot closer to Scott. Conklin was still backing away behind Scott. If he made it to the dining room he could dash through the pantry and from there to the kitchen.

I tried to distract Scott from Conklin and also from Marc, who inched forward whenever Scott's attention was on me or Caroline. "Can't we talk about this before you leave? You can see Caroline is hurt. You wouldn't want to take her away before we fix her face, would you?"

"Can't you shut up?" Scott was almost crying. "I love her. And she loves me. I know I lose my temper sometimes, but she knows I'm sorry, and if she wouldn't make me so mad, it wouldn't happen."

"Lyris…" Marc warned. I shut up.

Conklin was not quite out of sight. It was almost impossible to ignore the racket coming from both ends of the house, but Marc and I managed not to react. The kitchen door was a solid slab of steel and I wasn't sure it was penetrable by human hands, and I knew it would take a tank to batter down the front door. Why didn't they just break a window and crawl in?

Caroline was beginning to sag at the knees, and I was afraid she was going to collapse and force Scott into a desperate act. He couldn't carry her and manage the gun at the same time.

"Can't you just leave us alone? Caroline needs to lie down and there is no place you can take her where the police won't find you."

My blood froze when he answered."It won't matter if they find us."

Marc's expression changed, and I knew he had understood Scott's words too. He attempted once more to make Scott listen to him.

"Scott, put down the gun. We can get you some help from people who know and understand what you are feeling. Your life can be good again."

"My life has never been good," Scott snarled. He turned his body fully to face Marc. The two men were only a foot or so apart by this time, but Marc made no attempt to grab the gun.

Scott shifted his attention back to Caroline. I had my arms around her again and realized that Scott had turned his wrath on me. Although the thunder was still breaking the sound barrier, I could hear his words very clearly.

"You...if it wasn't for your interference, my wife would have come back to me a long time ago. You turned her against me."

The gun wavered in his hand as his eyes darted back and forth between Marc and where I stood with Caroline.

I was scared. I should have been scared before. Now I was for real. I was scared for myself, for Caroline and mostly for Marc, who was almost imperceptibly moving in on Scott. I wanted to tell him to run away, save himself.

At that instant, the universe shifted and everything changed forever, for so many of us.

Marc must have decided that Scott was going to shoot me, and it was now or never. At the second that Scott's arm and the gun moved once again toward Caroline and me, he lunged.

Scott saw the movement. He turned and pointed the gun at Marc. The sound of the shot was drowned out by yet another clap of thunder, so loud the house shook.

At the same instant a flash of lightning turned the room white, and time seemed to stand still. Marc's eyes met mine and I thought he said something to me. Then he dropped to the floor.

Time resumed, and in the after flash of the lightning, I almost missed the movement in the hall.

A black streak was airborne. At the very instant that Scott turned the gun toward me, Rasputin jumped onto his back and dug in his claws.

Scott yelped in pain and flung his arms wide. The gun flew from his hand as he spun around, trying to throw the cat from his back. Rasputin hung on and Scott whirled around the room, tripping over tables and knocking over objects that had escaped his earlier rage.

I don't clearly remember the next half hour in correct sequence.

I know I flung Caroline aside and crawled over to Marc. He had fallen on his side, and as I reached him, a final tearing, wrenching sound from the kitchen preceded the arrival of Ronnie, Tammie and two or three other police officers.

Several of them chased after Scott who had run out toward the hall and the front door.

Somebody called for an ambulance. I watched in horror as blood spread across the carpet from beneath the spot where Marc lay, still and motionless. I was sure he wasn't breathing. I couldn't see his chest rise and fall. I knew at that moment he was dead.

I was pushed aside and other, urgent hands surrounded Marc. Conklin pulled me away to where Caroline sat staring at nothing. The three of us grouped close together as if for warmth—I was shivering uncontrollably and could feel Caroline's body trembling beside me. I was scarcely aware that a wet nose pushed into my hand and a white furry body climbed into my lap. I wondered what had happened to Rasputin. He saved my life, Caroline's too. I never would know whether he leaped on Scott with intent or by accident since Scott was the only moving object in the room at the time.

Later, when I would have climbed into the ambulance with Marc, they wouldn't let me. I stood in the driveway with the thunder booming and the unrelenting lightning flashing around me. The cold rain plastered my shirt to my body and mingled with the tears I knew were running down my face.

I could feel them. Because tears are hotter than rain.

CHAPTER 31

Rasputin slipped inside just as I was closing the door on the storm. He must have clung to Scott's back as far as the driveway and either jumped or was shaken off before Scott got into his car and disappeared into the darkness. The cat was wet through to the skin and looked half his normal size. He slunk past me and slowly climbed the staircase, looking back once with his enormous copper eyes.

Conklin stood at the foot of the stairs, standing out of the way while the police went about their business in the drawing room. I didn't want to know what they were doing and I didn't want to see the enormous, dark stain on the carpet.

"Conklin, I'm going to the hospital. Have you seen my purse?"

"Madam, you can't drive yourself, and you can't go looking like that." He pointed at my shirt.

I looked down, at the thin fabric, wet and pink.

"Go and change, Madam. I'll drive you to the hospital."

I didn't take the time to shower or even dry off. I just swiped at the blood and pulled the shirt over my head and threw it on the floor of my bedroom. I was aware that Jacqueline and Rasputin were in the middle of the bed and I didn't have any comfort to give them.

Neither of us spoke on the drive into town. Conklin drove with his usual care, and a few times, he almost stopped completely. I couldn't blame him. The wipers couldn't keep up to the sheets of water hurled at the windshield by the storm. But it took all the self-control I possessed not to wrench the steering wheel from his hands and slam my own foot down on the gas. Conklin turned on the heater, but I still couldn't stop shaking.

I was at the point of screaming by the time we reached the emergency wing of the hospital. I opened the door and jumped out as Conklin slowed the car.

Inside was systematic chaos. Nurses and doctors in blue and green scrubs ran in and out of examining rooms. Three or four police officers, including Ronnie and Tammie, stood in a group in one corner of the hallway. I could hear a quiet sobbing from one of the treatment rooms and knew it was Caroline.

She had been taken away by a second ambulance, but since her wounds were far less severe than Marc's, she was not getting much attention. I should have gone to her, but my whole focus was on Marc. Was he even alive? I wondered if he had died alone in the ambulance on the way to the hospital.

That was the moment of my deepest despair. If I had stayed upstairs when Marc instructed me to, I wouldn't have antagonized Scott, and Marc would have controlled the situation from the beginning. And he wouldn't be here now, dying or dead.

Ronnie saw me standing there and came over. Tammie turned her back and continued talking to the other officers.

Ronnie pulled me away from the middle of the room and pushed me into an empty chair. "He's still alive, Lyris."

Good thing I was sitting down. Still, there were spots in front of my eyes and I felt my head wobble.

"He's lost a lot of blood, but all of us have stored three pints of our own blood here at the hospital. They're giving it to him now. And if he needs more, we'll get it. Don't worry, Lyris."

"I love him, Ronnie."

"I know you do, Lyris."

The freckles stood out in stark contrast to his pale skin. I could tell he was as scared as I was.

"Once Marc is stabilized, he'll go into surgery so they can repair some of the damage. The bullet went right through his shoulder, but missed his heart."

The spots danced again. When they cleared, Ronnie was gone and Conklin sat in his place. He patted my shoulder and murmured words of hollow comfort. I heard Ronnie talking to Caroline, and while she didn't answer, at least she had stopped crying.

A sudden flurry at the front door broke the silence. My heart leaped again in my chest, and seemed to stop.

Another stretcher was wheeled in through the double emergency doors. The storm might bring several accident victims in for treatment and I felt a furious resentment at the idea. I didn't want any medical attention directed away from Marc. I didn't care about any of those other people. Marc was important. No one else mattered.

A high-pitched wailing nicked my consciousness. Caroline ran out of the examining room and hurled herself on the accident victim. The man on the stretcher was Scott. He was accompanied by the two police officers, who had pursued him as he fled Hammersleigh.

By the state of his body, I guessed he had lost control and crashed. He didn't look like he had been shot. Not like Marc. I looked at Scott Fournier lying there bloody and broken, and I hoped he was suffering more than Marc.

Conklin sat beside Caroline, trying to calm her. He wasn't having much luck, and there was nobody left to treat her. The few medical personnel not assigned to Marc were bent over Scott in a nearby treatment room.

It took only a few minutes before a young intern came out of the room and walked toward me. "Are you related to Scott Fournier?"

I didn't answer, just gestured toward Caroline and Conklin. Then I averted my eyes from the intern's blood-encrusted scrubs. I was so relieved it wasn't Marc's blood.

They had to sedate Caroline. Her wailing filled the emergency waiting room for what seemed like hours before finally ceasing. In the meantime, I watched as they rolled Scott's body away, to the morgue I guessed. I felt no pity or compassion.

After that, time passed, must have passed. I sat there wishing I had a blanket over my jeans and sweatshirt to warm me.

Police officers came and went away again. Ronnie alternated between me and Caroline, who remained unconscious on a nearby stretcher. I wanted to be oblivious too, but was afraid to close my eyes. I knew if I fell asleep, Marc would be dead when I awoke.

Believe, Lyris. Life is full of endless possibilities.

I sat straight up in my chair.

You, Leander. Where have you been? You should have let me know this would happen. I could have done something to stop it. I would have listened to Marc.

I'm so sorry for your pain. However, as I mentioned before, I am not always within reach. And there is no way you could have prevented this.

What good are you to me, then? You must at least know if Marc is going to live. Can you tell me that, Mister All-Knowing?

I understand how afraid you are. Marc's recovery depends on his own soul's journey, whether he will take advantage of this exit point. Or stay.

Well, if you can't help Marc, then go away.

I shut Leander off and looked up. Several people, including Conklin, were looking at me although I knew I hadn't spoken out loud. I'm sure anybody could read the anger and anguish there. I turned my eyes to the floor and thought about nothing.

Marc went into surgery. He came out several long hours later, still alive, and was sent to the ICU. I spent a few minutes watching his still form and listening to the sinister bleeping of the heart monitor by his bed before a nurse hustled me out.

Soon, Marc's daughters, his parents, his Great-Aunt Martha for all I knew, went in to see him. When they came out and retired to a nearby waiting room, I slipped back in. Rita Pembrooke, the head nurse on duty, caught me and sent me away. I had met Marc's parents, Gilles and Therese, several times including a barbecue on Canada Day, but now we sat within the circle of our shared fear and said nothing to one another. The twins clutched their grandparents' hands.

Conklin found me and stayed with me. Other people came and went—my mother, David, Peter. Patsy and Nick stayed a long time, and then went home to feed their sons. But they came back. There was always a police officer or two hanging around, drinking coffee and telling macabre police jokes to keep their spirits up.

My own spirits were so low, they should have thrown me into the psych ward for being clinically depressed. If my mother hadn't brought me clean clothes, and a nurse hadn't tossed me into a shower, I would have sat there dirty with Marc's dried blood on my skin for more than twelve hours.

I missed Aunt Wisty's funeral. Aunt Clem stayed with me for a while and described the service. She was certain her sister was now at peace. I heard her words, but I just didn't care.

In the afternoon, I walked over to the desk.

"Listen, Rita. I don't know if you heard that Marc and I are engaged. I am going into his room now. If you have a problem with that, take it up with the hospital administrator." Which was still Patsy, my best friend. I should have thought of that before.

"You and the chief are engaged? Why didn't you say so?"

That's all it took. And it wasn't much of a lie. Marc had asked me several times to marry him.

He was lying still and pale. A massive bandage covered his naked chest, and an IV dripped antibiotics and fluids into the veins of his left hand. The heart monitor continued to bleep beside the bed.

I sat down and took his free hand in mine. There was no response and my empty stomach contracted even further.

I looked at his motionless form and didn't know what to do or say to make a difference.

"You'd better not die, Marc. I don't think your soul's journey is completed yet. Don't ask me how I know. I just do."

That wasn't helpful. I had to try something else.

"I think I figured out what happened to Tommy. It's a very sad story. Shall I tell you about it?"

I just started talking. I spilled my guts. All about how Aunt Wisty had fallen in love with Uncle Patrick, while her husband Thomas was overseas. How Thomas returned, sick and disoriented, and in the grip of despair and pain, smothered his baby son to save him from a merciless world. Wisty, mad with grief over her child's death and conditioned to always think of her husband before herself, killed Thomas to save him from the hangman, who still stalked our society.

"Today, neither one of them would have been prosecuted for murder. Back then, they wouldn't have stood a chance in the judicial system. Now, all of them are dead, everyone who participated in the cover-up—Uncle Patrick, the Chief of Police, the undertaker, Aunt Clem's lover, Bruce Wingate. All dead, except Aunt Clem, and she played a minimal part. I think she's spent the last sixty-eight years trying to pretend the whole thing never happened."

Marc continued to sleep. His fingers didn't move in mine, but the heart monitor displayed a steady, rhythmic pattern. At least, I prayed it did.

"I don't think you'll be able to close the file on Tommy's murder since I don't have any proof that it was his father who killed him. I'm satisfied the truth is known, if only to me and Aunt Clem— and now you. You probably don't believe me anyhow and that's okay because you wouldn't believe how I found out. I guess I should tell you about Leander, but even I have a hard time with that part."

Then I shut up for a while. A nurse came in and fiddled with the monitor and the IV. She smiled and left.

I pulled my chair closer to the bed so we wouldn't be overheard. "Life is funny, isn't it? You've been open with your feelings about me all along, and all I've done is pretend not to hear you, or act like you were joking. Now it may be too late, but I'm going to be honest with you anyway."

I took a deep breath and let it out slowly, hoping to find a place of calm and courage somewhere in my heart.

"I'm kind of screwed up, in case you haven't noticed. It seems that Dennis, and even my father, have contributed to my inability to commit to you. Not that I blame them, not really. We have to take responsibility for our own lives sooner or later, despite our past traumas, and I think I can get past mine. I might need some help, though, professional help. So I hope you won't consider me a total nutcase if I start seeing a therapist.

In the meantime, I am going to tell you I love you. And that I'm sorry I haven't said it before now. I hope somehow you know I love you. I don't want you to...to leave...without knowing that."

I was crying so hard that it was a few seconds before I realized Marc's fingers were warmer, and they were gripping mine—not tightly, but squeezing a little.

I looked at his face and to my amazement and joy, he was looking back at me. The tears fell faster and I couldn't speak.

"Say that again." His voice was weak, but he was talking.

"Uh?"

"Say what you just said again."

"Let me get the nurse. They should know you're awake."

"No." His fingers gripped mine and I stayed where I was. "I want you to repeat what you just said."

"Okay, okay. I guess you heard me say that I am an emotional basket case, but I plan to get some help to overcome my insecurities regarding close relationships of the opposite-gender kind."

His grey eyes never left mine.

"Okay. Also...I love you."

"Do you mean it?"

"You bet I do. Can you stand it?"

"Does this mean we're getting married?"

"We have to. I told the head nurse I was your fiancée."

"I suppose you'll want a long engagement."

"How about a Labour Day wedding? That gives you six weeks to get back on your feet."

On my way out, I stopped at the nurses' station. "Marc's come out of the coma. Maybe the doctor should see him."

Rita looked up from a medical journal depicting the ghastly image of some poor soul's diseased innards. "Coma? Marc was never in a coma. Didn't anyone tell you? We sedated him, so he wouldn't move around too much right after surgery. We're moving him out of ICU to a private room this evening. He's doing extremely well."

"Good to know," I said, resisting the urge to throttle her. "He needs to be in perfect shape for our honeymoon."

CHAPTER 32

Two minutes later, I was standing under the portico of the hospital's main entrance, watching the downpour. The intense heat of the last two months had been washed away in almost an instant, and the humidity was finally raining onto the thirsty, grateful earth. The temperature had dropped at least 10 degrees. Most of the people walking by looked comfortable in rubber boots and vinyl raincoats buttoned up to their chins.

I wasn't sure what to do. My car was at Hammersleigh, and I would be soaked in seconds if I walked home. I could call and see if Conklin or Peter would come get me. I could wait until somebody like Nick or Ronnie came to visit Marc and ask him for a ride. Or I could call the town taxi. I couldn't decide.

"Lyris. How's Marc doing this morning?" The concerned faces of Patsy and Nick crowded under the portico in a flurry of umbrellas and slickers. They had matching yellow slickers, but somehow that didn't seem so weird anymore.

"He's better, lot's better." To my utter humiliation, I felt my face crumble, and I was seconds away from howling again.

Patsy took charge as usual. "Nick, honey, why don't you go on up and see Marc, while I take Lyris across the street for a bite. Here, give me your umbrella. I'll catch up with you later."

She thrust Nick's umbrella into my hand, and we bounded across the street to Ali's Pizza Emporium. I realized I was starving and ordered a medium with mushrooms and green peppers.

We sat in one of the tiny corner tables to wait for our lunch. Patsy peeled off her slicker and leaned forward. "Lyris, this may not be the best time to talk, but I'm so excited I can't wait any longer. Now that we know Marc is going to recover, maybe you can give some serious thought to my proposal. If we want to get this off the ground, we'll have to act fast."

"Speaking of proposals, I just asked Marc to marry me and he said yes. It's going to be Labour Day weekend, and you're my maid of honour—again. But this time I guess it's matron of honour."

"Oh, my God. Lyris, that's wonderful. I'm so happy for you." She made moves to leap across the table and hug me, but Ali got between us with the pizza.

"This is so exciting. You must be so happy. I'm happy."

"You already said that. You seem to be excited and happy about a lot of things right now, Patsy. After losing your job, I'm glad you found something else, but I sense you're trying to drag me into it."

I took a huge bite and waited for it.

"Okay, but promise to hear me out before going ballistic. Let me finish and then you can speak."

"I never go ballistic. Talk."

She took a deep breath. "I'll just come right out and say it, then I'll elaborate. Remember, don't get mad."

"Patsy..."

"Okay, okay. Here it is. I want to turn Hammersleigh House into an upscale convalescent estate."

I didn't say a word. I had just taken a huge bite of pizza and the cheese strings refused to be swallowed.

"You know how people are tossed out of the hospitals far too soon? Days after surgery, or an illness like pneumonia, we discharge them. Sure, there's government-funded home care and visiting nurses to change dressings and dispense medications, but there's a market for a place where people can rest and recuperate for a few weeks before they go home. A place with fine dining and beautiful surroundings."

I swallowed the lump of double cheese. "You want to turn Hammersleigh House into a *nursing home*? And you want me to be the chef?"

"No. Listen up, will you, Lyris? You promised not to talk until I was finished."

I waved at her to continue.

"You have six bedrooms on the second floor and two bathrooms. We can add four more—the bedrooms can be partitioned off to make space for ensuite bathrooms. An elevator will have to be installed—we can't expect our guests to use the stairs. We'll have to engage an architect to preserve the integrity of the house."

Architects, bathrooms, elevators? I had to stop this madness. "Patsy, you know about Uncle Patrick's will. We can't make structural changes to the house. So adding more bathrooms and installing elevators just can't happen."

"One elevator, and I've already talked to John Brixton. He was dubious at first, but when I explained my plan, he thought it quite feasible. He feels that a private convalescent estate will be a better fate for Hammersleigh than splitting it up into apartments and renting it out to yuppies."

"So John doesn't think I can handle Hammersleigh by myself? He thinks I'm going to carve the house up into apartments? I couldn't do that if I wanted to. The house has to stay true to the Victorian period, and why were you talking to my lawyer about my house anyway?"

"I'm sorry. I wanted to investigate every aspect of the plan before I brought it to the table. I called him for an appointment and made it clear that this was my own idea, and you had nothing to do with it. That way, if he refused to even consider it, then no harm was done."

"He was adamant that I couldn't make any structural changes." I could hear myself and I was whining.

"Lyris, you'll have to talk to him yourself. I think he realizes that, even if the trust pays for some things, you'll have a hard time maintaining the house on your own. John seems to have a lot of control over the trust, and if he says we can put in more bathrooms and install an elevator, then we can. We won't change the Victorian ambience in any way."

"Okay. Where will I sleep? You've changed the bedrooms on the second floor to guest rooms. If you think I'm going to sleep on the third floor, you are quite frankly nuts. And this is all hypothetical. I've agreed to nothing."

The pizza had grown gummy, but I picked up another slice anyway and took a jaw-splitting bite. I chewed it furiously. I *was* furious.

"You will be sleeping, with Marc I trust, in the current employees' quarters. There are, what, four bedrooms? And at least two bathrooms with a huge common room that can be sectioned off into kitchen and living room."

"I don't think Conklin would enjoy sharing his living accommodations with me. And what about Caroline?"

Patsy's right elbow was jammed into a pizza slice. So far, she hadn't eaten any. "This is where it gets exciting. You do know that Conklin and your Aunt Clem are moving in together?"

"Moving in together? My Aunt Clem and Conklin? No way. Where did you hear that?"

"From the horse's mouth. I had a little talk with Conklin, and he confided that he was trying to find a way to let you know he wanted to slow down, and enjoy…uh…other interests. Oh, he still wants to be part of Hammersleigh, but he wants to spend more time with his, and I quote, dear friend Clematis. He says you get so panicky when he mentions retiring that he was going to let your aunt tell you."

"Are they getting married?"

"I don't think so. If they get married, their pensions will decrease, but if they just live together, they'll have more money. I think they want to do some traveling too."

"Oh, my." I attempted to pull myself together. "Where are they planning to live? Aunt Clem sold Hollyhock Cottage to David, so that's out."

"You know that carriage house behind the pines on the west side of Hammersleigh?"

"I have a carriage house?"

"It was turned into a cottage years ago and needs updating, and that's where Conklin and Aunt Clem are going to live. Isn't that neat? They'll have their own space, but handy for us."

"I hope they have room for Luke and Florence."

"Who are Luke and Florence?"

"Never mind, I'll tell you later. Maybe. Don't distract me. So now we have six guests on the second floor, and Marc and I are in the servants' quarters. Conklin and Aunt Clem are in a carriage house I didn't know existed. I'm supposing you will sleep with Nick as usual in your own house. Do you think I'm going to run a nursing home in my spare time, alone?"

"It is *not* a nursing home. Quit calling it that. Our guests will be paying through the nose for the privilege of recovering from their surgeries and illnesses in beautiful Victorian surroundings. This is a business, a successful business."

"So in this hypothetically successful business of ours, where does the staff sleep? I'm supposing we have resident staff, other than me?"

"No problem. We'll refurbish the third floor. There's nothing wrong up there that a little decorating and another bathroom or two won't cure. I think you might want to ask Peter to start apprenticing with Conklin, before Conklin and your Aunt Clem jet off on some exotic vacation."

"I'm guessing you talked to Peter already?"

"Sort of. I knew we would need a general factotum around the place. and he's perfect. Caroline too. Of course, I don't know if she's still interested in staying, after all she's been through. I'm hoping she'll stick to her promise to attend counselling sessions, at least."

"She'll go." I was going to insist on that. "What about other staff? I refuse to clean all those toilets."

"You won't need to clean any toilets. You don't clean any now, do you? The cleaning staff paid for by the trust can do them all once a week like always, and the housekeeper, whether Caroline or someone else, can lend a hand the rest of the time. I think we'll have to hire a receptionist to handle bookings and answer the phone, but some of your staff at the Hydro Commission will be looking for work, won't they? I don't think we'll have any problems finding staff."

"Who's going to cook? And quit looking at me."

"Nobody wants you to cook, trust me. These people will be paying for professionally prepared meals, so we'll have to hire several chefs, other than Caroline. And John Brixton has heard from Marion Beadle. She's finished her little fling in the city and is coming back to Blackshore. She asked John about the possibility of working at Hammersleigh again. Isn't that lucky?"

Uncle Patrick's former housekeeper and bedmate returning to find a much younger woman installed in her old position? Yeah, that was going to work. I permitted myself an inward shudder at the very thought. I refocused on Patsy's crazy scheme.

"So now we have the house remodelled, the staff hired and guests making reservations. Who's paying for all this work to be done?"

"Conklin and your Aunt Clem are paying for the renovations to their cottage. And my severance package, and yours, will pay for the work that needs to be done at Hammersleigh. That doesn't even touch our pension buyouts, which we will reinvest in our individual locked-in retirement plans. Not to be touched until we want to start drawing pensions."

"So I'm quitting my job, just like that?"

"Think about it, Lyris. This is a chance to have an adventure. I've gone over the figures with an accountant and with John Brixton. This venture is a risk, sure, but a relatively safe one compared to other types of businesses. Take my word for it. There are lots of wealthy people who will jump at the chance to stay at Hammersleigh for a minimum of one week, to a maximum of four."

"How much are wealthy people going to pay for this privilege?"

She named a figure that left me breathless. "Do you think we'll make any money at it?"

"Oh, yeah."

"I don't know, Patsy, it seems we'll be catering to those who have tons of money. Lots of people need this service, but can't afford it. Isn't this kind of a selfish, class-conscious venture?"

"This is a *business*. Most businesses cater to those who can afford to buy the product. That's the cornerstone of our civilization. Look at spas, luxury car dealerships, fitness clubs. Wealthy people need good postsurgical and medical care too."

"Now, about this care. Who's going to change dressings and perform other distasteful jobs like that?"

"I know several nurses from the hospital who want to work part-time. We can have a nurse in residence around the clock with three rotating shifts. We won't be taking anyone in as a guest who needs anything more than three good meals a day, some gentle exercise, and perhaps a dressing changed or medication dispensed. This will *not* be a nursing home. We will require a doctor on call just in case, though, and I've already talked to Michael Grammett. He's willing to sign on with us on a fee-for-service basis."

I sat chewing the pizza, trying to process all that Patsy had just thrown at me.

"Sounds like you thought of everything, Patsy. How about insurance and liability?"

She nodded. "I've factored it in."

"So that leaves one thing. Two, I mean. What do we do, you and me?"

"Oh, sorry, I should have explained that right off. I'm the administrator. After all, it's what I know best. And you're in charge of the staff—all the staff, including coordination with the nurses and Michael."

"I don't know, Patsy. I don't think I'd be good..."

"Nonsense. You've been a supervisor at the Hydro Commission for years, and you ran the reunion like a boot camp. The parents of those juveniles you enlisted for your security and medical teams are telling everybody what a great job you did keeping their kids out of trouble. According to them, this was the first reunion in thirty years without a major drinking or drug-related situation."

She was laying it on a bit thick, but I couldn't help feeling flattered. "I haven't agreed to anything yet. I especially haven't agreed to quit my job, so you'll have to give me time to think about it."

"Of course. But don't take too long. Doesn't the buyout offer at the Commission run out at the end of the month?"

"Don't worry, I'll have a decision for you before then. I'm still not comfortable with this whole idea—what makes you think we'll get any customers?"

"Are you kidding me? Don't forget, I've been working at the hospital for years. I know there's a need for this service. And we have our first guest lined up. I ran into an elderly gentleman at the outpatient clinic the other day. He needs to have a minor operation and has decided to wait until we get up and running so he can recuperate with us. You might remember him from the reunion. He knows you, calls you Missy. He's so cute. I think his name is Herbert Pembrooke.

"Gunner. I think you're mistaken, Patsy. Gunner doesn't have the kind of money to stay a week at this hypothetical resort of ours."

"Quit calling it hypothetical. And yes he does. He has bags of money. He wants to stay for the full four weeks."

"I can hardly wait."

Then I stopped and thought about Gunner.

"I don't like that look on your face, Lyris."

"I hope you don't think I'm going to work sixteen hours a day at this job. Because I will need quite a bit of spare time."

"What for? Oh, you mean Marc. Of course you have to spend a lot of time on your relationship, the same as I do with Nick."

"Well, that's a given, but I was thinking of Gunner and all the other elderly people who will be staying at Hammersleigh. It would give me a perfect opportunity to gather material for my book."

"Oh, no. I mean, what book?"

"My book about the experiences Blackshore residents had during World War II. Both in the military and here at home. They aren't getting any younger, and if someone doesn't write down their stories now, it will be too late in a few years."

"Most veterans don't want to talk about their experiences."

"Then it will be my mission and my challenge to encourage them to do so."

"You can't annoy our guests. They will be coming to us to recuperate, but they won't stay if you harass them."

"You know how diplomatic I am. And stop whimpering. It isn't becoming to someone your age.

Both Patsy's elbows were in the pizza. She picked up one of my half-eaten slices and started chewing, her eyes never leaving my face. Webs of cheese hung from her lips, and I reached over to take the pizza away from her. I figured I had tortured her long enough, but *Begin As You Mean to Go On* was my most favourite motto of all, and I didn't want my long-term goal to come as a surprise to her.

"Give me those papers and drive me home, Patsy. I'll have an answer for you in three days, no sooner, no later."

CHAPTER 33

When I walked into his private hospital room, Marc was propped up on several flat pillows, and he was using the remote to flip through the stations on the miniscule television suspended on a hinged arm beside his bed.

Three days after his shooting and Scott's death, Marc was making amazing progress. The day before, he wanted to go home, but the doctor insisted on another few days at least, so Marc was waiting out the time.

He smiled at me as I sat in the visitor's chair. The smile was as heart-stopping as ever, maybe more so. I had come so close to losing him, and I was angry at myself for almost being too late in telling him I loved him. Gunner was right. I was a ninny.

Then I gave myself a mental slap. I was no ninny. Just an imperfect human being, a work in progress. I had made a promise over the last few days to be kinder to myself and more honest with those I loved. It was going to be difficult—while I usually didn't curb what came out of my mouth, my feelings had always been under deep cover. I was determined to change that.

"Look at this," Marc said. "Have you ever watched this talk show? The guest is this psychic, Sylvia. She's telling a woman in the audience that her dead father is still around her and looking out for her. And she told someone else he would remarry in six months to someone he hasn't met yet."

He picked up my left hand and caressed the ring finger. The finger his ring would soon encircle. To my surprise, the thought didn't make me want to yelp in terror and flee Bruce County on the first bus to Toronto.

"I guess my near death experience is making me think of the afterlife. I never knew if I believed in it before, whether we go on to something else when we die. Even though I was raised a Catholic, I have never come to terms with my own mortality. What do you think, Lyris? Do you believe there's something more after we exit these mortal bodies?"

I eyed him, trying to make up my mind. If ever there was a cue to spill my guts about the Tommy mystery, and about Leander, this was it. A couple of days ago, I would have made a joke and changed the subject. Now, unfortunately for my comfort level, I had committed myself to honesty and truth. I sighed and waded in.

"Marc, you probably don't remember what I said the other day, about what happened to Tommy?"

He shook his head and rubbed his thumb along my palm. It felt so good, but I pulled away and looked at him.

"I'm serious. I know what happened."

Marc refused to be serious. "How could you know for certain? Almost everybody concerned is dead. Don't tell me you have a pipeline to the afterlife?" At my look, he said, "Come on. I know you have something on your mind. Let's just pretend we're drunk and tell each other everything we were scared to say before. You start."

So I did. I repeated what I had shared with him when he was in a coma—pardon me, sedated—about Aunt Wisty, Uncle Thomas, Tommy, Aunt Clem, Uncle Patrick, Bruce Wingate and the whole damn thing. And when he asked me again how I knew all this, I related my dream vision on the widow's walk the Friday night of the reunion.

He looked a little uncertain at this last revelation, but nodded at me to go on. I knew he was trying his best to be supportive and open minded, but there had to be a limit to what his mind would accept—he might decide I was the Family Nut.

"How do you know this Bruce Wingate and your Uncle Patrick buried Thomas in an unmarked grave in the cemetery?"

I hesitated at that point, and was tempted to tell Marc I was just *deducing*. However, my newborn resolution of honesty won out and I confessed to my break and entry into the funeral home's records.

He winced and lay back dramatically on his pillows during this part of my narrative. "I hope I can hang onto my career long enough to lock in my pension. Are there any other crimes you want to confess to?"

"None I *want* to confess to." He groaned and I hastened to add, "Just kidding. That was the only crime I have committed." That was the truth, as far as I was aware.

"Tell me, how did you know the information on the unmarked grave would be in a metal box in a locked drawer of the desk?"

The old Lyris would have lied and said I remembered the box from the summer I spent filing in that damp basement room. The new, improved Lyris girded her figurative loins and smiled seductively to soften the blow.

It didn't do any good. Marc wasn't thrilled when I told him about Leander.

"You mean this spirit guide of yours is going to be popping in and out any time he feels like it?"

"No. Only when he has something to tell me, and sometimes when I call him, if I can figure out how. The rest of the time, you won't know he's around."

Marc didn't look reassured. "Were you by any chance talking to Leander the other day in the garden? When you had that blank look on your face."

Blank? That did it. I was going to have to convince Leander not to drop in when I was outdoors, with other people, when I was in the bathroom…" Yes, but don't worry, I promise he won't interfere with our private life."

"Well, that's a relief. I suppose we can trust this guy?"

"Ha, now you're making fun of me. At least you haven't called the orderlies from the psych ward."

I leaned over to give him a light kiss on the lips, mostly to try and distract him. It was so nice I distracted myself and forgot all about Leander myself when I finally came up for air.

"There's one thing I haven't been able to figure out, though. How did the figurine get up on the shelf behind the peacock?"

"Why don't you ask Leander?" Marc asked, glancing around the room as though that gentleman were going to appear in a flash of otherworldly light.

"It doesn't work that way. He's sarcastic and cryptic, and half the time, I don't know what he means. He seems to have a hard time answering a direct question. I'm sure the puzzle of how the figurine was hidden is far too prosaic for him to bother with anyway."

"Too bad. I thought he could help me with some of these robberies we've been having in the area, but I guess not."

"You can have your fun. I don't mind. What do you think about the figurine? How did it get up there, and who did it?"

We talked that over for a while without reaching any conclusion, although we came up with a couple of theories with nothing to back them up. Marc thought it might have been Percival V. McPherson, the police chief at the time. According to Marc, Percival, once he finally bought into the whole conspiracy—Marc's word—would have been the likely one to think of diverting attention to a thief by pretending to steal the shepherdess. When I mentioned Percival could have smuggled the figurine out in his coat and disposed of it, not leaving it in the house to be found at any moment, Marc replied rather testily that if Percival had done that, it would have been actual theft. And what was my theory if I was so smart?

"Percival was not the one who hid the figurine behind the peacock, because he was a middle-aged man. He couldn't easily access that shelf, even with a ladder. It had to be someone younger. Not Uncle Patrick. He wouldn't have left it there all these years, and I don't think he hid Tommy's body for the same reason. How could he, or anyone, live in a house with the body of a child, and a hidden figurine, which was the sole proof there was no intruder?"

"So, Watson, who was it?"

"Bruce Wingate. He was a spy about to be dropped behind enemy lines. He was used to thinking fast and taking chances. And he would be in good physical shape. He died in France shortly after, keeping the secret. All of them—Bruce, Uncle Patrick, Aunt Clem, Percival, Marcelle Lavette—covered up both deaths."

"Well, they all conspired to bury Thomas, and they took quite a chance involving the chief of police and the local undertaker. No matter how close friends they were."

"What choice did they have?" I responded. "They needed help with the burial. Afterwards, Aunt Wisty went directly to Lychwood. Aunt Clem, Uncle Patrick and Bruce Wingate went back to their war jobs. And except for Aunt Clem advising Uncle Patrick not to place a marker on Thomas' grave, I doubt they ever spoke of the affair again. Percival and Marcelle kept the secret too. It was a different world back then."

Marc was tiring. His head dropped back on the pillow, and he closed his eyes. When I started to pull my hand from his so I could leave, he gripped tighter. "You're right, Lyris. It was a different world, and we can't judge those people by today's standards. We owe them everything.

And if I had been alive and the chief of police sixty-eight years ago, I might have acted as Percival did."

"I can't blame any of them either. Even Thomas. The horrors of war defeated him physically and destroyed his reason. He thought he was saving his son by killing him. And his wife shot him to save him from the rope, even though she was convinced she sacrificed her soul by doing it."

That reminded me, I had neglected to tell Marc about the *imprint* of Thomas I had seen in the cemetery. After considering Marc's pale skin and tired eyes, I decided to wait for another day to lay that little gem on him. And lay it on him I would, in the spirit of full disclosure.

"Any questions we have will remain forever unanswered, I'm afraid," Marc said. "We'll never know any more than we do today."

Maybe not, but that didn't mean we should forget. That saying was going through my mind—those who forget the past are destined to repeat it. Somebody had to make sure that Tommy's story and so many others would never be forgotten, and that somebody seemed to be me.

It was still raining when I got into my car, more of a shower than a downpour. Water was standing in pools in the parking lot, and my feet in light sandals squished as I pulled out onto King Street. All in all, I was feeling pretty good about things and looking forward to a cup of ginseng tea and a couple of ham sandwiches.

I slammed on the brakes. A blue van behind me honked, and I avoided looking at the driver's waving fingers, or finger to be entirely accurate.

I pulled into an empty parking space and sat thinking.

I was in front of the police station, and therefore, more or less in front of Dennis's realty office. I got out of my car and walked inside. The receptionist and one or two realtors ignored me as I passed them.

Dennis was reading some papers and didn't look up until he heard the door close. When he saw me, his elbow jarred a Styrofoam cup on his desk. The coffee poured over the papers and he cursed as he jumped up and grabbed a roll of paper towel. He mopped up the mess while I watched.

Still muttering, he sat back down. There was a wary look in his eyes. "Lyris. What brings you here? I hope the Chief is continuing to recover. I heard he's out of danger."

"Marc will be fine, thank you. We're getting married on Labour Day weekend."

"Well, that's great. Are you here to invite me to the wedding?"

"No. I'm here to ask you why you were creeping around my house, and why you threw me down the stairs Saturday night."

His face expressed shock, horror and guilt.

"What are you saying, Lyris? That was Scott Fournier. Everybody knows that."

"Everybody doesn't know what I know. And Scott is dead, so he can't admit to anything or defend himself."

"I don't know how you can accuse me of such a thing."

"Cut it out, Dennis. I haven't informed Marc, and I won't if you just explain to me why you did it. Did you mean to hurt me?"

He spluttered for a while and protested that he didn't, would never, do such a thing to me.

"Do you want me to explain how I know it was you, Dennis? I didn't figure it out until just now. I thought it was Scott, too, but my subconscious must have been working on it, and now I know."

"Know what?"

"It was Scott who took those objects from the house, not to steal because I found them in the attic, but to try and discredit Caroline. He thought we would think Caroline was a thief and dismiss her, so she would have to go back to him. And he started the fire in the shed for the same reason. Pretty stupid of him, but he was desperate. I can almost understand him."

I was still leaning against the door with the knob clutched in my hand. Dennis had an unpredictable temper, and if he lunged at me, I wanted to be as close to the exit as possible.

"It was you on Saturday night. Only you ever called me a bitch. I've been called other things by other people, but only you call me a bitch."

"Is that your so-called proof?" He was sweating now and the little vein in his forehead was pulsing erratically.

"No. There was also a smell. Or rather, there wasn't a smell."

"I don't know what you mean."

"Scott wore a distinctive citrus-smelling aftershave. I noticed it when I first met him and several times in the upstairs hall, when I realized later he had been in the house. But I never noticed it the night I was thrown down the back stairs. There was no odour at all that night."

"And there was one other thing." I leaned forward and pulled up the left sleeve of his long-sleeved shirt.

A perfect oval, a perfect red impression, decorated his forearm. It could not be mistaken for anything other than what it was—a human bite mark. Thanks to two years of metal braces during my teens, I had a perfect bite.

"The price of my silence is an explanation, Dennis. I want to know why. If I leave here without knowing why, I go straight to the police station. You can come with me if you want and deny it."

He gave up. If my butt hadn't still been on fire and every other part of me didn't ache, I might have felt sorry for him. He looked beaten.

"Okay, I'll tell you. But you have to believe I didn't mean to hurt you. I was afraid you'd see me. If you charged me, my career would be over, my family would leave me for good, and I'd have to leave town."

"None of that has to happen. Although, if you don't promise to break it off with Jody, your wife will definitely throw you out, and I don't think you can afford another divorce settlement or all that child support."

He flinched. "When you wouldn't give me any money back, I had to come up with a way to raise some cash. Fast. I owe everybody in town, and the house has three mortgages."

"So you decided to rob me? What made you think you could get away with breaking into Hammersleigh House, filling your pockets, then getting out again without getting caught?"

"I got the idea when I heard about the antiques being taken from your place. There's a group of teenagers breaking into cottages in the district and I thought they had done it. I figured they wouldn't go back to the same place again to rob it, but if more stuff went missing, they would still get blamed."

"So how many times did you break in, and what did you steal?"

"Nothing. I was only in the house twice."

"Twice? And you didn't take anything either time?"

"The first time was on the Saturday of the reunion before we, you know, talked in the garden behind the house. I waited until that new girl of yours took the dog outside, and then just walked in the kitchen door. I thought I could grab a few items and hide them upstairs, then come back for them later."

"It was you on the widow's walk that afternoon. How did you know your way around Hammersleigh House well enough to find the stairs to the widow's walk?"

"You forget, Lyris, I've been a realtor for a lot of years. A floor plan doesn't exist that I can't figure out in minutes. And that includes your precious Hammersleigh House."

"How resourceful of you. So did you take some things? No, wait, you didn't have to, did you? While you were in the cupola, you found the box of items Scott had taken, hoping Caroline would be blamed."

"Right. I didn't know why they were still there, but I figured it would be safer to come back that night and take them then. And, well, you know what happened next."

"Humour me."

Dennis glanced at the closed office door, undoubtedly hoping one of his staff would come in and rescue him, then he sighed. "I just walked in the kitchen door again when everyone was watching the fire. You came in right behind me, so I had to run up that flight of stairs from the kitchen to the third floor. I waited for a while, and just when I thought it was safe to go up to the cupola and get the box, you and those damn animals came at me. If I hadn't been so startled, I never would have pushed you."

"Can you ever forgive me? Let me get this straight. You were going to steal some expensive objects from me, sell them to whom, a fence? And get enough money to pay your debts?"

"I know it was a stupid idea. But I didn't know what else to do. And it's not like I took anything in the end. I'm sorry I pushed you down the stairs and I'm glad you weren't hurt too badly. "

"It hurt plenty. But this will remain just between the two of us. I don't want Mitch knowing his father is a potential thief who assaulted his mother to save his own skin. And you hurt my cat and dog too. That was mean." Of course, I planned to tell Marc, but I hoped to convince him not to charge Dennis.

Dennis managed to look both contrite and belligerent at the same time. But I didn't give him a chance to start orating about how greedy I was to take half his money and how I didn't deserve to inherit such a wonderful house with its valuable contents. Those words had no more power to make me feel guilty.

"Well, I guess that's it, Dennis. Good luck with your financial problems. I know you aren't asking me for advice, but here's some anyway. Let Tracey help you. Tell her the truth and maybe the two of you can work it out. And if you think you can have Jody on the side, forget it. Anyway, she'll drop you as soon as she hears you're broke. See you around."

Follow my heart for career and love, but not for finances. Luke and Florence better be right about that.

CHAPTER 34

Marc and I were married in the shade garden on Saturday of the Labour Day weekend. A wet August gave way to a breathtaking September and our wedding day was sunny and warm.

The maples had not yet changed from green to crimson, and many flowers still bloomed in the gardens. I carried a bouquet of vibrant roses and their scent mingled with those of grass and pine needles. My off-white designer suit, with fitted waist and calf-length skirt, had cost me a moderate fortune in Blackshore's only bridal shop, but it was worth it. I felt beautiful. I *was* beautiful, and I have the pictures to prove it.

Marc had fully recovered and was going back to work after our honeymoon. He was even more handsome than usual in his dress uniform, and all that gold braid in the sunlight fairly dazzled the eye. I really was a pushover for a uniform.

Ronnie stood by Marc's side looking almost as splendid. He couldn't keep his eyes off Caroline, attractive and confident in a long flowered skirt and matching yellow jacket. I had firm hopes for those two, someday.

Patsy was my attendant, of course. She had insisted on wearing a burnt-orange dress and jacket to celebrate, since it was the end of summer and the beginning of the autumn season. She was a little early for the change of season, but you sure couldn't lose her in the crowd.

Our convalescent estate was scheduled to open right after Thanksgiving. I wanted to call it The Blackshore Home for the Terminally Spoiled, but Patsy insisted we stick to plain Hammersleigh House. The new bathrooms were installed and the elevator was almost completed. The contractors were putting finishing touches on my personal apartment—make that mine and Marc's. I was still having a hard time thinking of myself as part of a couple again.

We had quite a crowd that afternoon in the shade garden. Most of Marc's colleagues were there, including the scary Tammie Wilberts, still casting baleful looks my way from under her frizzy curls. But I noticed she was standing close to another stalwart officer, so close it was hard to tell where one uniform ended and the other began. From the longing looks he was giving her, I was hopeful that Tammie would soon find another target for her affections.

Marc's parents were in attendance, pleased and amiable. So were the twins, one looking cheerful enough, and the other not quite as much. Although they lived with their mother, the girls had a room in our new quarters, and I was determined to win over the reluctant twin, but that was a battle for another day.

That day was mine and Marc's. After our ritual toast, I left him talking with Ronnie and Caroline, while I wandered among our guests, champagne glass in hand—for show only. My entire extended family was in a snit since the only relatives I invited to the wedding were Mom and John Brixton, David and Denise, Mitch, and the inevitable Tiffany. Oh, and Aunt Clem. If I invited anyone else, I would have had to invite all three or four hundred of them.

Peter, dressed in a sky-blue tuxedo with ruffled collar and cuffs, drifted among the guests passing out glasses of the best bubbly the Blackshore Liquor Store had to offer. Conklin, no less resplendent in his striped trousers, black tails, rust-coloured shirt, and bow tie, followed along with trays of canapés. Aunt Clem was by his side, bright red scarves fluttering in the warm breeze and grey sequined evening dress just skimming the tops of her silver sandals. She and Conklin were leaving the next week for a Grecian cruise and would be back for the opening of our new business. I was determined to spend more time with Aunt Clem in the future to learn all she could teach me about our mutual *gift*. And I was going to find out about Camp X and her wartime adventures before the year was out.

My eyes came to rest on a bent, shrivelled man sitting on a wooden bench under the maples. His grey suit blended seamlessly with the bench, and I blinked twice to clear my eyes.

"Gunner. What are you doing here?" Maybe he was confused and thought he was already checking into Hotel Big Bucks.

"Heard you was getting married to the chief of police. Thought I'd come over and see if my new home was ready." He added, "And congratulate you, too. Congratulations."

"Thank you, Gunner. The renovations are almost completed. I hear you'll be our first guest. For four weeks." I didn't like his reference to his new home.

"That's right, Ninny. Hope things will be up to snuff. I'm paying through the nose for this and it better be worth it."

"I'm sure you'll find everything more than satisfactory."

"I need good food, and lots of it. I like to play cards too, so there better be some folks who can play with me. And I need a walk every day. You can come with me, Ninny."

"Gunner, you can call me Lyris if you'd like."

"I'll do that, Missy. Well, I'm off. Remember, my operation is the day after Thanksgiving, and I'll be here the day after that."

"Looking forward to it. Gunner, I'm planning to chronicle the personal adventures our family and other Blackshore residents experienced during World War II, and I hope I can count on you to relate your stories so future generations will understand what happened. You may not agree, but I feel it's important that we don't forget what happened during those years."

"I been thinking about that, Missy. You may be right. Maybe it's time. You'll have to convince me when I get here."

He hopped off the bench and vanished into the shrubbery.

Rasputin and Jacqueline strolled by. Jacqueline's white fur gleamed in the September sunlight and the orange sequined bows at her ears sparkled. She sat down proudly in front of me, and I told her how lovely she looked.

"And Rasputin, you look quite spiffy in your new bronze collar. Would you like an hors d'oeuvre?" The cat managed to sustain his contemptuous expression while wolfing down a cracker laden with salmon, and he even ate the bit of greenery on top. He lumbered away without a backward glance, tail swishing, and after I fed Jacqueline a tiny sandwich filled with cream cheese, she scampered after her surly friend.

"Leave the birds alone," I called after them.

It had been a long day already, after many busy weeks of preparations. What with the building renovations, plans for the wedding, leaving my job at the Hydro Commission, and hiring staff for the business, I was pooped. Both Sheila Overton and Daphne O'Rourke were joining our team, Sheila as receptionist and Daphne as kitchen help and general aide. I was hoping the leather apparel and numerous body piercings Daphne sported would speed recovery time for our guests, or at least entertain them while they were convalescing. Sheila was good with the public and had agreed to take smoke breaks outside.

We had six nurses lined up to work part-time, and young Dr. Michael promised to provide postsurgical care to our guests as required. I sighed in contentment. For once, the universe seemed to be unfolding according to my wishes.

Miss me, Lyris?

Leander. You've been gone for a long time. I hope I didn't offend you the last time we spoke. I was pretty upset.

That's okay. I understand. They've been keeping me busy here with my studies, but I wanted to wish you well.

Thanks. So, Leander, Marc knows all about you now, and he was quite understanding. I just hope you won't...won't...

Visit you at inappropriate times?

Yes. I still haven't gotten the hang of this spirit guide thing. When you contact me, how I contact you, you know?

You're doing pretty well, Lyris, for a novice. I think we can take a break from each other for a while.

That sounds good, Leander. I don't think I need a honeymoon coach unless the Bad Girl/Good Cop routine doesn't work. Any tips?

You're the one with the overactive imagination.

Can you at least tell me if my marriage to Marc will be a happy one? Will I make a success of it this time?

I'm your spirit guide, Lyris, not a Gypsy fortune teller.

His comment was followed by a strange sound, like sandpaper being rubbed on skin.

Leander, what was that noise? Are you laughing?

Sorry, it just slipped out.

Well, I'm glad you have a sense of humour. You're going to need it. And you might want to work on your people skills.

You know, Lyris, I'm proud of you. You seem to be getting the hang of our relationship. Remember, you create your own universe as you go along.

Okay, now I know that's a Winston Churchill quote. Is he there with you? Are you Winston Churchill?

I can't tell you stuff like that, Lyris.

Why not? Do you know John Lennon? Or how about Jim Morrison—you know, from The Doors? And Elvis. Have you seen him?

Better buckle up. Our journey is just beginning.

"Lyris." Marc touched my shoulder. I looked up at him and blinked. He sat down. "You have that look on your face again. Were you talking to Leander?"

"He just dropped in to congratulate us. He's gone now."

"For good?" Marc looked so hopeful, I hated to disappoint him.

"No, just for now. Is it time to go yet?"

"Yes, my darling, our single friends are gathering at the gate hoping to catch your bouquet."

Walking to our getaway car—Marc's serviceable black Explorer—I smiled to see Tammie at the front of the line. As I closed my eyes and tossed my bouquet over my head, I heard gasps and laughter. When I turned around, Tammie was clutching my roses in her fists and looking pleased. Marc helped me into the passenger's seat, and we drove through Hammersleigh's gates while our guests clapped and waved their farewells.

We had reserved a suite at a lodge just outside of Huntsville, a five-hour drive north of Blackshore. The lodge was surrounded on three sides by immense evergreens, while the fourth side faced a sparkling lake. When we stepped out of the Explorer, the sun was just sinking on the horizon, setting the water ablaze with red and gold lights. It was off-season, and we saw no other guests as we checked in and waited for our bags to be brought to our honeymoon suite.

We both collapsed on the bed and looked at each other.

"Are you nervous?" Marc asked, not looking a bit nervous himself.

"No. Although I am a bit tired. Maybe we can postpone the nuptial delights until tomorrow."

His face fell, but he took it on the chin. "Of course. I know it's been an exhausting week for you. We can wait until you're rested."

"Kidding." I snickered and slapped him on the thigh. "I just wanted to see what you'd say. I'm ready if you are."

"You'll keep me laughing, no doubt about that. Before you have your way with me, I'd better go back to the desk to get another key. I don't like having just one in case we lock ourselves out. Then I'm all yours."

As the door closed behind him, I leapt from the bed. I tore off my clothes, took a quick shower, put on a silky lavender-coloured nightie and managed to brush my teeth and run a brush through my dishevelled hair before Marc returned.

I was out of breath, but looked as seductive as possible, whatever that might be, since I wasn't any more experienced at seductive than I was at flirtatious. He pulled his gaze from me and looked around in wonder.

"How did you do all this so fast?"

I fluttered my eyelashes. "I wanted to fulfill the promise I made to you a long time ago."

"You mean, your Bad Girl/Good Cop game?"

I laughed at his eagerness. "You got it, Officer. Now, over here, we have jasmine massage oil warming over a tea light."

Other candles were placed throughout the room and when I switched off the lamp, they glowed like tiny constellations in the darkened room. I had substituted the candles for the promised twinkle lights, betting that Marc didn't know what twinkle lights were and after tonight, wouldn't care.

A peacock feather reposed on the pillow.

"What are you waiting for? Come over here and I'll show you how to play Bad Girl/Good Cop."

Sometimes I amaze myself. With six weeks to come up with a few convincing moves, I had set my legendary imagination to the task, and the rules of the game fell effortlessly into place. Our injuries had healed and we were both fit and ready. Now it was time for some human clinical trials.

The scent of exotic oil drifted over the bed and the candlelight turned our skin to amber as I moved closer to my new husband.

I whispered in his ear, "Let the game begin."

Message from the Author

Dear Reader:

I hope you have enjoyed this visit with the Pembrooke family and their friends. They were so much fun to write about, I find I can't quite let them go. So they will soon make another appearance in "Beneath the Asphalt" and other tales, as long as you like reading about them.

Blackshore is a fictional town, but Bruce County is very real. If you should find yourself driving along its tree-lined side roads or enjoying the clean, cool waters of Lake Huron which embraces its towns and villages, you may suddenly catch a movement out of the corner of your eye. Maybe you'll see a wisp of fog flit over the water or fade into the forest. No fear, you may have caught a glimpse of Leander, or even Luke and Florence. They enjoy visiting the beaches and woodlands like any other tourist. Just say hey for me.

Until next time,

Gloria

About the Author

©2011 Warner Photography Inc.

Gloria Ferris began her writing career by authoring and editing operating procedures for a nuclear power development. It was an exciting job, but opportunities for plot and character development were limited, so she turned to crime fiction and found it to be a lot more fun. *Cheat the Hangman* was shortlisted for the 2009 Crime Writers of Canada Unhanged Arthur contest.

Gloria recently moved back to her native Guelph, Ontario, after spending 20 plus years in several small towns by Lake Huron, which inspired her mysteries. The stories are written in a humorous style, but the crimes are deadly serious. A sequel to Cheat the Hangman is in the works.

http://www.gloriaferrismysteries.blogspot.com

IMAJIN BOOKS

Quality fiction beyond your wildest dreams

For your next ebook or paperback purchase, please visit:

www.imajinbooks.com

www.twitter.com/imajinbooks

Made in the USA
Charleston, SC
26 September 2011